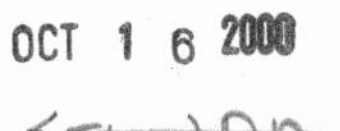

DEVIANT WAYS

DEVIANT WAYS

CHRIS MOONEY

POCKET BOOKS
New York London Toronto Sydney Singapore

W

This book is a work of fiction. Names, characters, places and incidents are products of the author's imagination or are used fictitiously. Any resemblance to actual events or locales or persons, living or dead, is entirely coincidental.

POCKET BOOKS, a division of Simon & Schuster, Inc.
1230 Avenue of the Americas, New York, NY 10020

Library of Congress Cataloging-in-Publication Data

Mooney, Chris.
Deviant ways / Chris Mooney.
p. cm.
ISBN 0-671-04059-6
1. Private investigators—Fiction. 2. Serial murders—Fiction.
3. Psychopaths—Fiction. 4. Revenge—Fiction. I. Title.

PS3563.O565 D4 2000
813'.6—dc21 00-032680

First Pocket Books hardcover printing October 2000

10 9 8 7 6 5 4 3 2 1

Designed by Diane Hobbing

Printed in the U.S.A.

RRDH/

To my parents,
Francis and Sandra Mooney

Acknowledgments

A lot of people are responsible for getting a book off and running and for supporting the writer through the rough patches, and it's important to acknowledge their hard work and efforts.

Pam Bernstein, who rescued me from obscurity and stood behind me when things looked bad, thank you for always believing. Every writer should be lucky enough to be in such capable, talented hands. And Donna Downing, who answered my endless questions with a smile, thank you for your unflagging enthusiasm.

Emily Bestler, my editor, thanks for believing and taking a chance, for your honesty, and for pushing me to make it better. I couldn't be in better hands. And to Kip Hakala for all his hard work on my behalf.

Dick Marek, the man who kept kicking me until I got it right. Working with you was a dream come true. Thanks for never once letting me off the hook.

Dr. Jack Slatoff, for his help with post–traumatic stress disorder and uncovering aspects of Jack Casey's personality, and for constantly rereading sections.

Ted Castonguay, for being there through the tough spots, your support and friendship over the years. To his lovely wife, Lynne, for your cheer and support.

Mike Hauptman, for his support and comic relief, and for being the kind of friend you always want in your corner. To his wife, Karin, and to the Cape crew: Randy and Maureen Sherman, Lenny and Marsha Lombardo, and Eric Shaunessey.

John Amirsakis, for being . . . well, Sakis.

Ron and Barbara Gondek, two people I'm proud to call friends.

Jack "Grampy" Dunnigan, for helping me with the poetry and providing some rather unique insights into life.

To the three Boston fans: Randy Scott, Neal Sonnenberg, and Mark "Elvis" Alves.

Katie, my sister, for always believing.

There's a saying that you save the best for last, and in this case it's true. I want to thank my parents, Francis and Sandra Mooney, for all their sacrifices over the years, for being the two people who helped bring me to this moment. Here, words really do fail me.

For the thing which
I greatly feared is come upon me,
and that which I was afraid of
Is come unto me.
I was not in safety, neither
had I rest, neither was I quiet;
yet trouble came.

—Job

JULY 4TH

I

LARRY ROTH COULDN'T SEE. Panic began to grip him, but then he realized what was going on and relaxed. There was no need to be alarmed. This temporary setback in sensation was one of those hallucinations conjured up by Mr. Jack Daniel's, his intimate friend, savior, prophet, and confidant for the past thirty years. True to form, his old buddy had left graveyards of dark shadows in the corners of his mind where there should have been thoughts and memories. And this time, JD had also managed to sever the connection between his brain and body. Not only couldn't he see, he couldn't move.

That would change, though. Soon, the generator would kick back on, and his body would twitch to life with a shudder of icy coldness. Control over his movements would be rationed back to him in spoonfuls of nausea, chills, and uncontrollable shaking. While his trembling hands gripped the toilet bowl in a spell of dry heaving, he would stare into the water, and suddenly, like the rows of lights being turned on one by one inside a musty gymnasium, fragmented memories and thoughts would show themselves, and he would be forced to consider his most recent actions.

Lately, the results were frightening.

He breathed through his nose, a deep, slow draw of air, and focused on that. A moment later the cobwebs cleared and he felt his skin dampen with sweat. Soon it was running down his forehead and across his scalp in long, hot beads. More breathing. It felt as if he was lying on his back, but he couldn't be sure. *Why would I be lying on my back?* he wondered. He always made a point of passing out on his side, even his stomach; he had read too many stories of people who had choked on their own vomit.

There was a strange tightness over his ears, eyes, and mouth. He thought about that for a moment.

Then, like the sun breaking through a thick layer of clouds, he saw a burnt image float up to the singed edges of his consciousness, flash, and then disappear again behind the clouds. Something to do with

(Ashley)

the club. Yes, the club. Right. It had to do with

(Ashley)

this evening's plans.

He thought about it for a moment but nothing came to him. Then he waited for the image to reappear. Waited. Waited . . . Nothing.

He didn't fight it. He had resigned himself to this condition a long time ago and knew it was best to sit tight and wait for the connections to bubble to the surface.

His throat was working now. He tried to swallow, but his mouth was as dry as newspaper. More breathing.

From his pitch-black prison he could hear the distant sound of crashing waves. The beach. He was near the beach. Okay, good. Behind it, he could hear the chatter of people talking and laughing—some close, some distant. He focused on these voices, trying to place them with faces, but they were unclear, and what he could hear didn't sound familiar. A moment later there was a booming sound, followed by a crackle and the roar of applause.

Fireworks.

Today's the Fourth of July.

Then it all came to him in a vivid rush of color and clarity. He had been in the club's dining room, looking out the large bay windows at the sunshine and reminiscing about the great nine holes he had just played when he found himself locked in the grips of one of Mr. JD's patented benders. Round after round for himself and his friends, sweet Jesus. Hours later, when the sun started to give way to the early-evening shade, he glanced haphazardly at his watch and it hit him like a punch to his gut: *he was supposed to meet Ashley at the house fifteen minutes ago.* They had plans to spend the evening on the Cranmores' boat. No wonder he had been drinking. The Cranmores walked around as if they were royalty—smug in their preppie clothing, talking about their villa in France and ski house in Vail. His wife loved them dearly.

He remembered thinking he could fudge the driving part, but on the off chance that he was pulled over, he would have to convince one of Marblehead's finest that he was clearly sober, and even if the cop did let him go (they always did), the end result would still be that he was late. Instead of sitting in the boat, sliding back into JD's patented comfort and guessing which parts of Sophia Cranmore's body had undergone plastic surgery, he would have to listen to Ash chew out his ass, and he was never in the mood for that. Once he had slapped her mouth shut for her. In turn she had removed all the booze from his hiding spots and flushed it down the toilet. She even froze his credit cards and refused to give him his allowance. Definitely best to appease her.

The cab dropped him off, he remembered that, and he clearly remembered opening his bedroom door to a strange but pleasant sight.

Ash should have been dressed in that unflattering black Calvin Klein number, sitting on the bed with her legs crossed and staring at him with eyes full of murder because once again he had come home late, sunbaked and polluted. Instead, she was dressed in a pair of old white shorts and a faded blue Nantucket T-shirt, lying facedown on their king-size bed. She appeared to be passed out. Ash was known from time to time to go on benders herself—three glasses of wine was all it took, lights out, good night, folks—but this was out of character for her.

He had walked over to the bed and started rubbing her back. She didn't wake up, didn't even move. To his surprise he felt the lonely thing between his legs spring to life. His wife, Ash, was no great lay—not like that nurse at the hospital, fire crotch, a hot little minkie with flaming red pubic hair and a *very* uninhibited appetite. But that affair had just recently ended (and rather badly), and what he was left with was Ash. So he stood in the hot bedroom, rubbing her back and getting himself worked up and ignoring that just last month when he had turned fifty-four he had discovered blood in his urine and semen.

He had started to lift up her top and then . . . and then . . . shit, he couldn't remember.

More breathing. More sweat. People outside laughing.

His body came back on. A slow but steady pounding sprang to life deep behind his temples. Next would be the tremors. If he could get to the bottle quick, he could head them off, maybe even the vomiting.

He felt the curved coolness of the headboard, then felt his head on the pillow. He was lying on his bed, had passed out in the bedroom, all of which made sense. He went to move his hands to his face when suddenly they were yanked back, and something clanked.

What the hell?

He moved his hands again, *clang-clang,* the sound of metal hitting metal; then he felt something digging into the skin around his wrists. He moved his fingers and felt the tips brush up against steel.

Handcuffs.

He was handcuffed to the bed.

His eyes flew open but he couldn't see. The tightness still pressed against his head and eyes . . . oh, God, no.

His eyes . . . they were taped shut.

This isn't some goddamn Jack Daniel's hallucination. This is really happening.

His heart pumping wildly now, he summoned all of his remaining strength to scream, but the thick strip of tape around his mouth muffled his cry. He kicked his legs and felt the rope wrapped around his ankles pull them back.

He was tied down to his bed. His eyes were taped shut and so was his mouth. *No. Oh, Christ, no . . .*

He struggled to break free, giving it everything he had. After several seconds of thrashing he felt his stomach lurch; bile, hot and sour, shot up his throat. He swallowed it back.

Deep breaths, he thought. *Take in deep breaths through the nose, that's it . . . keep breathing, it's going away.*

"Smart move, Larry," a male voice said. "I wouldn't want you to choke to death on your own vomit."

Larry Roth froze. Someone was in the bedroom with him.

"Do you know who I am?"The voice was deep, calm, and steady, unfamiliar. "Think hard. This is important."

Larry rummaged through every mental file that hadn't been washed away by the booze and came up empty.

He shook his head no. For a moment, there were only the booming sounds of the fireworks, the applause, and the distant surf. The wind blowing through the opened windows was humid and smelled of salt, sulfur, and barbecues.

"Well, that's too bad," the intruder said. "I know who you are. In fact, I know everything about you. I know the amount of money in your checking, savings, and money market accounts, what you have in your stock portfolio—I even know you just had your prostate biopsied two weeks ago. I hate to be the one to tell you, but it came back positive. You've got prostate cancer, Larry."

The words didn't register; his attention was focused inward, on remaining calm and developing a strategy. As a clinical psychiatrist, he knew the importance of staying calm and focused in emergency situations. Opportunities might present themselves, but he would be oblivious of them if he panicked.

"I even know you fuck your wife every Friday after dinner," the intruder continued. "She comes upstairs, takes off her clothes, and lies down on the bed while you get on top of her and struggle to thrill her. By the look on her face, it's the worst minute of her day. Now, that little hottie you've been porking at the hospital is another story. What she sees in you is beyond me. It must be all those zeros in your bank account."

An idea struck him. He started screaming.

"You got something you want to say?"

He nodded quickly.

His head was violently pushed back against the bed. Something sharp stung his throat. *Calm,* he screamed at himself. *For God's sake stay CALM.*

"That unpleasant instrument is a scalpel. I'll take the duct tape off your mouth, but if you scream, if you say anything to offend me or start asking me a lot of questions I don't like, I'll slit your throat. Understand?"

He nodded.

"I thought you'd agree with me."

The duct tape was ripped off his mouth, taking off skin and hair. He clamped his lips shut, wincing at the burning pain, and then quickly took in several gulps of air. He had to stay calm and think his way out of this.

"Spit it out and remember what I said."

"If you know everything about me, then you know I'm a psychiatrist." His throat and mouth felt as if they were packed full of cotton.

"You're a second-rate quack. You spend most of your time in the bottle."

"I can help you."

The intruder laughed. "What are you going to do, Larry? Take me to your hospital and stick electrodes to my nuts to shock the rage out of me?"

"No, of course not."

"Then stop trying to run a game on me, you arrogant prick."

Larry Roth swallowed. "I have money."

"I'm not interested in money."

"Everyone needs money. I can make you rich, start a new life. I can give you pills, I can give you—I can give you whatever you want." Then Larry gave in to his fear. "Please, I'll do whatever you want, please don't hurt me. Don't hurt me or my family, I'm begging you."

There was a long pause.

That's it, think about it, he thought. *Take all the time you want, please, God, please get me out of this.*

"You really want to help me?" A new tone. Hopeful.

Larry Roth felt a wave of relief wash through him. "I'll do whatever it takes."

Another pause. "You mean that?"

"God, yes."

The strip of duct tape was suddenly fastened back across his mouth. Fear blew through him in a cold chill, bone-numbing in its intensity. *Take it off!* he screamed behind the tape. *Please, for the love of God, take it off and tell me what you need. I just told you I'll do whatever it takes!*

Then he heard the sound: beep-beep-beep.

The intruder was making a call on a cellular phone.

"Hello, nine-one-one, shots have been fired at twenty-two Preston Way, the Roth home. The shooter is badly wounded and still inside the house. You better get here quick. Larry Roth is bleeding badly. I don't know if he's going to make it."

Beep, and the call was terminated.

Larry Roth lay completely frozen, listening to the sound of his rapid heartbeat.

"Now you just relax, Larry," the man said, close to him now. "You're about to make history."

II

MARBLEHEAD IS LOCATED NORTH OF BOSTON IN WHAT IS CALLED THE NORTH SHORE. The town is quiet and rather exclusive, surrounded by water and populated by historic homes, small local-owned shops, grocery stores, and restaurants. The people here, the majority of them townies, had what Jack Casey called an insular approach to living: they believed they were immune to the fragmented chaos that infected the more troubled Massachusetts cities. Predominately, they were correct. In terms of crime, not much happened here. The Fourth of July was one of the few exceptions to this rule, thanks to illegal fireworks, teenagers having all-day parties at their parents' homes, and drunk driving, so it wasn't that unusual to see an unmarked detective's car or a cruiser with its lights flashing go speeding by.

Jack Casey sped down Suffox Avenue, the street that paralleled Preston Way, where the 911 call had come from. The road curved off to the right toward the beach, and he pulled the Toyota Land Cruiser over onto a thick patch of dirt and grass, listening to the tires crunch over the gravel and sand before coming to a stop. The storm of blue-and-white cruiser lights acted like a beacon, pulling everyone up from the beach. Families, teenage couples, the elderly, and a significant number of young kids who should have been watching the upcoming fireworks were now staring at the cops moving around the beach house on the corner.

Jack tapped his fingers on the steering wheel and looked out the passenger's-side window. A long, rectangular stand of trees, a patch of grass, and a playground divided the two streets. He looked at the activity around the house through the gaps between the tree trunks. The windows facing him had drawn shades, the world behind them dark. He didn't believe the intruder was still inside the house; he doubted anyone had been shot. For one thing, nobody else had called 911.

Jack had been at the station, finishing up on a recent burglary case, when the dispatcher had come in and asked him to listen to the call. What had given him pause was the caller's tone: calm and cold, emotionally detached, and with an odd mechanical resonance he believed was caused by a voice-altering device. The intuition he had come to rely on during his days as an FBI profiler had started humming like a tuning fork.

Something was waiting for him inside the house. He was sure of it.

He got out, shut the door, and walked down the street toward the beach to get a look at the front of the house. The sprawling, two-story, oversize Cape had cedar shingles, a postage-stamp lawn around the side, and a long but narrow driveway that held three cars: a Jeep Wagoneer and two new Mercedes. The windows on the first floor were open but with shades drawn just like the others. The two windows directly above the farmer's porch were closed, but the shades were pulled *up.* The interior was dark, and none of the outside lights were turned on.

Jack navigated through the sea of bodies and cruisers and found Alex Ronayne, one of Marblehead's plainclothes detectives, leaning back against the side of a cruiser, his arms stretched over the hood like a man hanging from a crucifix, yawning.

Jack joined him. The humid air smelled of rotting seaweed and salt and was charged with the crackle of walkie-talkies and the hum of nervous activity.

"Any sign of the shooter?"

Ronayne worked the wooden matchstick in the corner of his mouth. "Not out here. Could be in the house, but I couldn't tell you for sure since you told us not to go in. So here we all are, standing around, waiting for you."

"You hear the nine-one-one call?" Jack asked.

"Sure did."

"What's your take on it?"

"A punk wanted to case a house, maybe several, to score some money to buy his dope. He's smart enough to know that the best way to do it is to create a diversion. So we're all here playing cops and robbers, like we got some sort of mass murderer running around, and this geek is probably creeping a house out on the Neck right now."

Ronayne had worked vice for several years in Boston before he was shot four times during a botched drug raid. He pulled out of the coma, lived on disability for years while moonlighting as a security guard and window installer, and when the free ride evaporated, applied for a detective's job in Marblehead.

"You may be right," Jack said.

"I know I'm right."

"But my gut tells me we've been called here for a reason," Jack said, resenting the detective's indifference.

Ronayne yawned again, opening his eyes wide, and then blinked as if waking from an unpleasant dream. "You've been here what now, three years? I've been here eight years and the most exciting thing that's happened was when I chased down a spic from Lawrence who stole Edna Burrough's vintage Mercedes."

"I remember. You pulled your gun on the kid and laughed when he wet his pants."

Ronayne's eyes filled with a dark light. "I like taking precautions. Guy like yourself, with your sort of background, should like taking precautions too."

Jack didn't bite. "I couldn't agree with you more, Ronnie."

Then Jack turned away and walked toward one of the patrolmen, a twenty-six-year-old kid named Craig Devons.

"I need your baton," Jack said.

"Sure thing."

The kid ran over to him and handed it over. Jack took it and turned to Ronayne, who was watching with utter boredom.

"Come with me," Jack said.

He walked to the house, stopped at the driveway, and waited for Ronayne to finish lumbering over. Jack pointed at the small dual lights that were mounted next to the porch door.

"You know what those are?"

"Sensor lights," Ronayne said. "So what?"

Jack tossed the baton onto the porch. It hit the wood floor in front of the door, bounced over the railing, and then landed back on the driveway, the wood making a soft, hollow sound in the hot air.

"So the lights aren't working," Ronayne said.

"Doesn't seem a little odd to you?"

"Nope."

"You notice all the shades are drawn with the exception of the two above the farmer's porch? That all lights inside are turned off?"

Ronayne placed his hands in his pockets and looked away. "Whatever you say, Jack. You're the man in charge."

"I don't think this is a prank, Ronayne. If you want to treat it as one, you have my permission to leave."

"The old man wanted you in charge of this, you're here now, it's your show. You want to relive your days as a big-time FBI profiler, be my guest, just tell me how you want to play it. I got a date tonight."

"I'm going inside and take a look around."

"You want backup?"

Jack turned away and looked toward the crowd at the beach. "No. I want to go in alone."

"Anything else?"

"Move the crowds back. They're too close. I don't want them to see anything."

"Sure. You want me to call in SWAT?"

"Can the attitude."

For the first time Ronayne smiled. He scratched his mustache, a sneer tugging at the corners of his mouth. His eyes were lit with a private joke. "You're the boss. If you need me, I'll be in the cruiser."

III

THE BACK-PORCH DOOR WAS UNLOCKED. As he eased it open, bursts of blue-and-white police lights from around the front cut a dim, flashing, diagonal blade across the beige carpet. But they only lit up a fraction of the family room. The room's blinds prevented the outside storm of lights from leaking inside the house.

A pressure-sensitive tactical light was mounted under the Beretta's long barrel. He clicked the light on and stepped inside the room, easing the screen door back. The beam moved across the wide-screen TV behind the door, the fireplace, the distressed-brown leather chair and ottoman in the corner, an antique oak sideboard with a portable stereo on it, and an oversize blue chair with a coffee table in front of it. Old country knick-knacks were on the end tables, all of them neatly arranged and in their proper place.

He walked over to a light switch and flipped one up. No lights, just as he expected.

Adjoining the family room was the kitchen. He moved the light quickly over the maple cabinets, the Corian countertops, the General Electric appliances, and then across the tile floor. He saw neatly stacked dishes on the drying rack next to the sink, and an opened bottle of Jack Daniel's. The electronic panel above the gas stove was dark; so was the built-in microwave above it.

Another light switch was on the wall adjacent to the foyer hallway. Just to be sure, he walked to it, the sound of his footsteps on the hard-wood muffled by the chatter and squawk of police radios coming from beyond the windows, and flipped up all four switches. No lights.

It wasn't a blown fuse. Had the master switch on the control panel been thrown back? If so, why?

Sweat was running down his face, and his heart seemed to be beating abnormally fast. There was a time when moving through darkness was natural to him. Back then, he had been confident. Arrogant.

But that was a lifetime ago. At least it seemed that way. He was no longer that person. He was better now. Stronger. Healthy. Despite all of that, he felt like a fish fresh out of the FBI Academy.

A floorboard depressed somewhere above him.

Jack clicked the tactical light off and moved over to the bottom of the stairs. Carefully, he moved up to the second floor. The hallway was dark. Outside he heard a patrolman yell, "Stand back, away from the house, nothing to see here, folks." Sweat kept running into his eyes and he had to blink it away. He strained to listen.

A moment later he heard, beyond the police chatter and talk, not the floorboard but a different sound, faint: *ching-ching.* Metal striking metal.

His eyes narrowed in thought.

Call for backup, the voice in his head cried out.

He considered it for a moment. Then his intuition kicked in, telling him to wait. The intruder was long gone. He was safe.

But why is the power shut off?

Ching-ching-ching.

His gun pointed up into the dark hallway, Jack clicked the tactical light back on; the wide halo showed three other doors, all closed.

"This is Detective Jack Casey of the Marblehead Police Department. Identify yourself." His voice sounded strangely foreign to him. Weak.

Ching-ching-ching. It was coming from behind the door on his right.

"Identify yourself."

Ching! Ching! Ching! And another sound: thump, like something hard and heavy was jumping up and down on the floor.

Someone was in the room. Someone was alive.

The stairs were carpeted. He moved up them carefully, his right hip sliding across the wall. He stepped onto the second floor and moved the beam of light to the bedroom door.

CHING-CHING! THUMP! CHING-CHING!

And something else: a muffled cry.

You're imagining things. You're starting to lose it.

Jack moved down the hallway. He heard the whistle and boom of fireworks outside, followed by applause.

The bedroom door was in front of him. He placed his hand on the doorknob; the muffled screams, the *ching! ching!* of the metal striking metal, and the thumping on the floor, all of it loud now, were separated from him by five inches of wood. Sweat ran out of his hair, and his eyes stung with salt; his heart was jackhammering against his ribs. More fireworks exploded in the sky like cannon fire, shaking the framed pictures on the wall next to him and vibrating through his chest. He wiped his forehead on his sleeve. His hand was still shaking.

Jesus Christ, what the hell's wrong with you?

He gripped the knob tightly to prevent it from sliding beneath his wet palm. In one swift motion, he turned the knob and threw the door open with his shoulder, the gun ready.

The king-size bed had been moved so that it faced the door. A middle-aged man, his hands above his head and spread apart and handcuffed to the headboard, lay on his back, his bare feet spread apart and tied to the knobs at the foot of the bed with the type of rope used in clotheslines. The eyes . . . the man's eyes were covered behind gray duct tape.

An old memory, long since imprisoned, broke free from its shackles and pierced him. For a moment, his vision blurred, then came back when he heard the man's sharp, muffled scream.

Jack moved toward the bed and pointed the light at the man's face. The man started thrashing.

"Hold still, I'm a cop, just hold still."

With his left hand, Jack gripped the edge of the tape that covered the eyes and peeled it back, the sweat and oil on the man's face allowing it to come off easily. The windows next to the bed overlooked the beach; fireworks burst in the sky, the glowing red and blue colors burning across the man's terrified eyes, and then fading. The room felt like a furnace, and the humid air was thick with the overpowering smells of booze and sweat.

As Jack tore the strip of tape from the man's mouth, he caught a familiar coppery smell.

"He's here, he's still in here," the man gasped. His breath was ripe with the stench of booze and bile, and his thin black hair was drenched with sweat and matted against his pale scalp.

"There's no one here."

"Goddamn it, he's in here, the son of a bitch knows my name, knows everything about me!"

"Calm down, Dr. Roth. Catch your breath."

Roth sucked in air. "Listen, he called you here. He called right here inside the bedroom and—"

"Wait, you heard him call nine-one-one?"

"That's what I'm trying to tell you. He did it right here, I heard him, the son of a bitch is—I don't know what the sick bastard's doing." Roth jerked his body. *"Jesus fucking Christ, will you untie me!"*

Jack moved the flashlight up to the cuffs fastened to Roth's hands. His fingers were swollen purple.

"The keyhole is soldered shut," Jack said. "I'll need bolt cutters to—"

All the lights in the bedroom came on.

The white explosion forced Jack's eyes shut. He turned away from the bed, his arm covering his eyes, and took two steps forward. He started blinking, the light still painful, the world slowly coming into focus. On the edge of the nightstand he could see the worn cover of a Stephen King paperback and next to it a wicker basket full of gardening magazines.

Then the man started screaming—an ungodly, inhuman sound.

Jack's attention snapped back to the bed. The man's head was off the pillows, his face a dark crimson, the veins in his neck bulging from beneath the skin like cords of blue rope. His body was straining against his restraints as if jolted by electricity; his eyes, wide and bulging, as though they were about to pop out of their sockets, locked on whatever sight lay in the hidden corner of the wide bedroom.

Jack caught sight of blood-sprayed walls. He wanted to turn around—too late—his heart ballooning with a dreadful anxiety.

The twin college-aged boys, dressed in shorts and summer T-shirts, sat on either side of their mother. All their hands were tied behind chairs with tall backs, and their feet had been stretched tight under the chair by a rope. Their throats were cut; blood blanketed their chests, dripped off their legs in gleaming wet lines and spilled onto the floor in a bright red pool. They were arranged in front of the master bathroom, tucked away from immediate view.

His eyes shifted over to the gash on the woman's throat, the way it leered at him like some sort of gruesome smile out of his past, and from deep in his mind the memory he had never been able to rinse from his blood broke free and raced toward him like a speeding train.

Amanda, his wife, is tied to the chair in front of him. Her cheeks are wet and streaked with mascara. She is no longer screaming or crying. What comes out of her throat now is a shivering plea for mercy. Amanda is begging for her life.

But it is the hope in her eyes that pierces his soul; she's still clinging to the belief that her husband, an FBI profiler who has been in desperate situations before and is right now seated directly across from her, will find a way to break free of his constraints and save her. This can't be happening, her eyes say. Isn't that right, Jack? Tell me I'm right.

"Please, Jack," she whispers. "Please . . . Please make . . . him . . . stop. Please."

He wants to say something but can't. A strip of duct tape covers his mouth. His hands are tied behind the dining-room chair, his feet tied to its legs. The drug used on him is still in his system, numbing his strength. Nothing can save her. He can't move or talk. All he can do is sit there and watch.

Miles Hamilton, the man orchestrating this nightmare, moves behind her. In one swift motion he yanks her chin back toward his stomach. His eyes are wet with a dark light, and he surveys her misery with the amusement of a child enjoying a carnival ride.

Hamilton moves the scalpel toward her throat.

Jack thrashes about in the chair and then tumbles to the floor. He can't move. This is it, a voice tells him. There's nothing you can do. It's over.

His vision fills with water. He makes one last plea to that mysterious higher power instilled in his mind from his Catholic school days.

But God doesn't exist in this room. God doesn't exist here on earth—a belief that had constantly been proven time and time again in his case files full of hurt and hell. God is not coming to save him. No one is.

Hamilton's fingers grip the scalpel, the muscles in his arm flexing as he draws it against her throat. The moment Jack fears has gelled together, and in a rush the room becomes still and alive with color and sound. He can hear Amanda's rapid breathing, her sobbing, he can smell her sweat and perfume and her fear, Jesus Christ, please help me, helpmepleasepleasePLEASE.

Hamilton licks his lips. Amanda's eyes clamp shut. She draws in a deep breath through her nose and then says with an aching anger and fear and loss the words that will forever lay claim to his soul.

"Help me, Jack . . . Do something . . . Please."

This can't be happening, this CANNOT BE—

The scalpel rips across her throat. Wet drops heated by a frightened heart splash across his face and he is drowning, unable to move, unable to help her, he is helpless, he can do nothing but lie there and watch as Hamilton throws her chair to the floor. Lying on her side, Amanda stares at him, her eyes blinking furiously, this can't be happening, Jack, please tell me this isn't happening. But it is, Amanda, oh, God, he can see her blood quickly forming a pool around her head.

Amanda opens her mouth but can't talk. She gags. Hamilton casually walks around the blood and bends down, resting his weight on the tips of his feet. With one hand, he jerks Jack's face into his. The other gloved hand dips a finger into Amanda's blood. He licks it with a moan, then quickly smears the blood and saliva across Jack's lips. Hamilton winks, stands up, and saunters out of the room laughing.

Jack flips the chair over. His back is facing her now. With maniacal strength he uses his feet to push his weight over to her, his fingers outstretched, searching. A moment later he finds her small hands. He grips them and squeezes. She squeezes back, hard. He screams out to her, his last words to his wife forever caught behind a cheap piece of two-dollar tape: Hang on, Amanda, please hang on, don't leave me, please . . .

Her grip loosens. He squeezes but she doesn't squeeze back. Her pulse is fading, he can feel its beat slowly fading beneath his thumb. Amanda is dying. His life, his world, is over.

"JACK!"

Ronayne was standing in front of him with his meaty fingers sunk deep into Jack's shoulders, violently shaking him out of his trance.

Jack pushed himself away from Ronayne's grasp. He felt light-headed. It was difficult to maintain his balance.

He grabbed the corner of the bureau, took in a deep breath, and turned around. The room was full of men staring at him. Martin Gose, Marblehead's only other detective, was standing near the doorjamb and looking at Jack as if he had just witnessed an alien step out of a UFO. The patrolmen standing in the lighted hallway had similar expressions.

Larry Roth pointed his face up to the ceiling and sobbed loudly while the patrolmen worked to free him. One of the cops, Ronnie Boyle, a young kid with a blond crew cut, looked up from the handcuffs and said, "The keyholes are soldered shut."

"Bolt cutters," Jack croaked.

Ronayne removed the matchstick from the corner of his mouth.

"Bolt cutters," Jack said again. "I have them in the back of my truck."

"Yeah, right, bolt cutters. Hey, Jack, why don't you go outside and get some fresh air, catch your breath, relax. Me and Gose will take it from here."

But Jack had already turned and was running past Ronayne. Jack pushed his way past the policemen crowding the hallway and ran down the stairs, falling at the bottom. He got himself up, the world around him still spinning, threw open the front door, and bolted out into the night air as if death itself were chasing him.

IV

JACK FLIPPED OPEN THE LAND CRUISER'S HATCHBACK SO HARD AND FAST THAT IT ALMOST SNAPPED BACK DOWN ON HIS HEAD; HE STEADIED IT, THEN PULLED AWAY THE THIN PIECE OF BLACK CARPET THAT COVERED THE SMALL TRUNK WHERE HE KEPT THE SPARE TIRE AND HIS TOOLS. His hands wouldn't stop shaking. The bolt cutters lay next to the green metal toolbox. Beads of sweat ran down his face and dripped onto the spare tire. The tools and tire seemed to be vibrating.

Psychologists call it post–traumatic stress disorder. He had experienced it only one other time, six years ago, the day of Amanda's funeral. When the afternoon had bled into evening, he had swung by the house, not knowing why; he remembered being drunk. The mailbox caught his attention. Between the copy of *Rolling Stone* and *Better Homes and Gardens* was a padded mailer with no return address. When he'd reached inside and pulled out the black-and-white autopsy picture of Amanda lying on the steel table, he was swallowed by that same consuming rush of memories he had endured just moments ago in the bedroom.

The shaking and the sweating would pass, but it could take hours. He didn't have hours. He had to push this all out of the way quickly and get back up inside the bedroom.

Breathe. Focus and breathe.

Several minutes later he opened his eyes and looked through the front window of the truck. People were staring at him. His mind no longer seemed to be in overdrive—still racing, but not out of control. He could think.

Jack wiped his forehead on his sleeve, grabbed the bolt cutter, shut the hatchback, and walked around the driver's side of the car. Ronnie Boyle, the young patrolman who had been examining the handcuffs inside the bedroom, stepped out of the edge of the woods, blue-and-white police lights flashing behind him. His face was white with shock and his eyes blinked with nervous energy as if trying to wash away the bloody sight stained behind them.

"What is it?" Jack said.

Boyle tapped his blue cap against his leg. "Detective Ronayne asked me to come out here and get the bolt cutters from you and bring them inside the house."

"I'll take care of it."

Boyle cleared his throat. "Sir, he told me to—"

"I don't care what he said, I'm in charge here. Get your ass down on the beach with the other patrolmen."

Jack's voice seemed to have all the strength and confidence of a teenager going through puberty. He looked at the beach and then back at Boyle, who was clearly uncomfortable with the situation. Jack took in a deep breath and started again.

"Ronnie, I want you to move all these people away from the house. They're too goddamn close and I want them the hell out of here, right now, understand?"

Boyle rubbed the back of his neck. Through the gaps between the tree trunks and over the blinding pulse of police lights, Jack saw Ronayne standing on the porch with one hand on the doorjamb, the screen door resting against his back, a lit cigarette hanging out at the corner of his cocksure mouth.

Ronayne blew out a long trail of smoke. "Hey, Boyle! Grab the cutters and get your ass—"

An explosion blew out all the windows on the first floor and kicked Ronayne sideways off the porch as if he had been jerked by a string. The ground shook. Jack momentarily lost his balance, reached out, and grabbed the hood, steadying himself, the sound of the explosion reverberating inside his head with a sickening, leaden thud, the final image in his mind that of Ronayne's terrified expression as he flew headfirst into the sliding glass door of the neighboring home.

Then the Roth house blew apart in a roar that shook the ground with the intensity of a major earthquake, shredding wood and all of the house's contents into pieces of debris that rocketed across the street. The Land Cruiser's windows shattered, and an invisible force slammed into Jack's body and kicked him off the ground, knocking the wind out of his lungs. He landed sideways, on his left arm, and felt the side of his head snap back against the pavement. His eyes shot wide open with the pain, and he saw Boyle's body fly over the front hood and land on his neck just inches away from him; behind Boyle, the patrol cars parked in front of the house were now bouncing across the soft ground of the woods, snapping trees and coughing up clumps of dirt and grass and rocks, while another patrol car tumbled sideways over the curb and onto the beach. Jack was still skidding across the ground, the rocks, nails, glass, and other sharp debris tearing through his pants and shirt and digging into his skin, his eyes clamping shut as a howling storm of wood and glass and sand screamed across his body.

Seconds later, his body stopped moving, but the debris was still rushing over him. Quickly moving to his side, he shielded his face with his right forearm and opened his eyes. Boyle's limp body was lying sideways on the road, only a few feet away from the Land Cruiser. Clouds of sand and white dust and wisps of smoke were blowing across the street and moving through the trees like a mist. The island of woods had caught fire, and down on the beach, he could see people screaming. But he couldn't hear them. His world had become deathly quiet, and what little sounds he could make out were muted, as if he were listening underwater. Pieces of wood, rocks, and torn tree limbs rained down around him.

Jack didn't have to look up at the sky. He knew what was about to come and knew what he had to do to survive it.

The adrenaline had already kicked in. He scrambled to his feet, ran over to Boyle, grabbed the back of his collar, and dragged him quickly across the debris to the side of the Land Cruiser. He crawled underneath the car first, and then reached out and pulled Boyle with him. Over Boyle's shoulder he saw thick concrete slabs come crashing down onto the pavement where he been standing. Canned food, pieces of tile, blown-apart concrete and brick, wood, stone, and gravel showered down over the road like hail and bounced off the car in loud pings. The Land Cruiser rocked from the showering debris, the weight of the car knocking against his left shoulder and the top of his head.

Jack couldn't hear, but he could smell fine, and what he smelled was gasoline. He didn't know where the gas was coming from, but it had to be close. He looked over to the woods. The fire was spreading quickly through the dry woods; he could feel the heat on his face. *Don't move, just wait it out, the worst is over.*

But he couldn't wait. He had to get out of there.

Something heavy slammed down on the front hood, buckling it and the sides like an accordion. The back tires jumped high in the air, and the entire weight of the car shifted. He saw the undercarriage framed for a moment against the night sky, then he reached over and grabbed Boyle's legs just as it came back down, tapping him hard against the shoulders and pinning him against the ground for a moment until the back tires jumped up again. He grabbed the back of Boyle's collar and heard the four-by-four's roof buckle. Out of nowhere the entire car came crashing down on his back. A rib cracked, possibly more; his left cheek was pressed tightly against the ground, his right sliced by a piece of metal. He wiggled his hands and feet, found that they could move, then tried to pry his head away from the vise.

He couldn't move. His head was trapped, slowly being squeezed into the ground.

One of the back tires had punctured and was leaking air in a steady hiss. He drew in a painful breath of air, gagging at the stench of the smoke. The fire was moving close, he could feel its heat against his skin. Through watering eyes he saw clothes floating in the dark air like feathers and a single line of fire inching closer to the car. He was going to burn to death. Fireworks burst in the sky in a roll of thunder and applause. He couldn't believe this was how he was going to die.

V

AROUND THE CORNER FROM THE SOURCE OF THE EXPLOSION, A VAN WAS PARKED AGAINST THE CURB OF ATLANTIC AVENUE. The windshield of the van was blown apart and the front seats and back floor were filled with shards of glass. The man in the back of the van wasn't cut. He sat in a swivel office chair on rollers.

On the card table set up in front of him was a laptop computer. Right now the screen was a sea of static. Camera four was down, no doubt destroyed by the blast. He cycled through the three remaining cameras; only one was still working.

The shot on camera three was alive with color. The Roth home was gone, and the force of the blast had destroyed the two neighboring homes; the rectangular island of trees that separated the two streets was engulfed in flames. A man was struggling to free himself from underneath a mangled four-by-four vehicle that was moments away from catching on fire.

It was a wonderful image.

The watcher pulled out his earplugs and put on his headphones. Various sounds hit him: the fire licking the woods, and the screaming; oh, the wonderful screaming. He zoomed the camera lens in on the man and hit a series of keys to record the image onto the laptop's hard drive. The man had managed to pull the upper half of his body out from underneath the mangled four-by-four and was now trying to free his legs. The fire had already engulfed the front hood and roof.

It was the cop from inside the house. Jack Casey.

The cop's face looked as if it had been scrubbed with barbed wire. A deep gash down his right cheek was bleeding profusely; his white shirt was torn and streaked with dirt and blood, and his face burned with determination and pain.

But that was not what was causing the watcher to stare. The cop's face seemed as strangely familiar as it had moments earlier when he had walked inside the bedroom to free Roth.

Jack Casey freed his legs from underneath the crushed SUV. Part of his pants had caught fire. He patted the flames down and then shifted his weight onto his knees, reached underneath, and started pulling out the partially burning body of a patrolman.

Keep your eye on Casey, the watcher thought.

He shut the laptop off, removed his headphones, and put both inside the black leather briefcase. He slid over to the side door and with his latex-gloved hands opened it just enough so he could stick his hand through. Then he removed the gloves, grabbed the briefcase, and stumbled out into the hot, muggy night.

With his tan designer shorts and green Ralph Lauren polo shirt and sports hat, he looked like a townie. He pulled his baseball cap down over his forehead and began making his way through the smoking debris littering the street. People stumbled across their front lawns, their faces pale with shock, their eyes unable to process the chaos surrounding them. The fireworks had stopped. Rescue sirens were building in the distance.

The media would be here soon, and this wonderful spectacle would be broadcast all over the TV news stations by morning.

And that was just the beginning.

By the time he was done, he would be famous. They wouldn't remember the bombs or the families. In the generations to come, they would remember *his* name, the man responsible for the destruction of the Federal Bureau of Investigation.

AUGUST

chapter 1

THE HOUSE, A VARIATION ON THE COLONIAL STYLE THAT SEEMED TO TYPIFY NEW ENGLAND, WAS LOCATED ON WHAT WAS CALLED THE NECK, A RECLUSIVE AND WEALTHY ISLAND COMMUNITY OF MILLION-DOLLAR-PLUS HOMES, AND ACCESSED ONLY BY A SMALL BRIDGE THAT CONNECTED IT TO MARBLEHEAD AND (WHEN NEEDED) TO THE REST OF THE WORLD. It was located close to the lighthouse that was a popular make-out spot with local teenagers and sectioned off by a tall iron gate. The house's massive back deck, the wood weathered gray from the salt, sun, and long winters, was large enough to hold a high school graduation and overlooked a private stretch of beach. A new black Lexus and a vintage silver Jaguar were parked out in the driveway in front of the family's two-car garage.

The house belonged to Patrick and Veronica Dolan, who had a thirteen-year-old son, Alex. All three of them, Jack knew, were dead.

The call came in to the station shortly after 12 A.M. The caller's voice was different from that on last month's 911 call, and this time the caller stated his name, Dale Porter, the Dolans' next-door neighbor. He had heard a gunshot and called the police. Dispatch called Porter's home number; no answer. Jack immediately placed a call to the Boston Bomb Squad.

At 12:35, residents were torn from their sleep by a rush of bullhorns and flashing lights. Local and state police herded the frightened families down the bridge and onto school buses that would take them to hotels in Peabody and Danvers. Less than an hour later, all of the residents of the Neck and half of Marblehead had been evacuated. Bomb techs entered the house. Arson investigators were on the horn to the ATF and the FBI's Explosives Unit. And the media was out in full force.

It was now Friday morning, a quarter to five. The sky was the color of a burnt-out lightbulb, and a cool breeze blew off the water, welcome relief from the oppressive humidity that had haunted Marblehead for the past three weeks. The power had been cut all over town; the Dolan house was dark. The news choppers were gone for the moment; the air was eerily still, filled only with the sound of the waves lapping against the shore. The place felt like a ghost town.

On the back deck Jack fidgeted with the various buckles on his padded bomb suit. He had never worn one before and was having trouble figuring out how to fasten it. Standing on the opposite side of the picnic table and leaning with his back against the balcony railing was Bob Burke, the commander of the Boston Bomb Squad, the man who for the past four hours had been inside the house with the bomb. Burke was smoking a cigar that looked like an artillery shell. His green eyes were narrow and unblinking as he watched from behind the clouds of smoke drifting up across his face.

"I told you there's no need for you to get dressed up, you're not going in there." Burke's voice was throaty, cured by tobacco and the whiskey he drank for what he called medicinal purposes. The top half of his bomb suit hung off his waist; his gray Harvard Law T-shirt was dark with sweat and stretched tightly across his barrel chest and broad shoulders. He was in his late fifties and had been working with bombs ever since completing two tours in Vietnam. Like all bomb techs, Burke had been trained by the FBI at Redstone Arsenal in Huntsville, Alabama, and it was widely acknowledged by many within the FBI's Explosives Unit that Bob Burke was one of the best in the business.

"You listening or what?"

"We've already covered this," Jack said, his attention focused on the pieces of the bomb suit that were spread across the picnic table.

"And we're about to cover it again until I get through that thick melon of yours." Burke pointed the cigar at him for emphasis. "I just told you what Semtex-H is."

"A Russian-made plastic explosive with a high shatter rate. Popular with Middle Eastern terrorists."

"Now six blocks of it are sitting in the bedroom of a residential home in Yuppietown. *Six* blocks. One can reduce a plane to fragments you can hold in your hand. I got *six*. If they go off, Marblehead's going to be relocated on the other side of the Atlantic and you'll be fish food."

"You said the bomb malfunctioned."

"No, I said I *believed* it malfunctioned and that I won't know for sure if it did until I take it apart. But I have to move it out of the house first, and there's no guarantee that it won't blow."

Burke's words hung in the still air. Jack went about attaching the breastplate. More buckles, Christ. He stopped dressing and looked over the railing. Between the pockets of fog he could see white foam along the sand and rocks.

"You took an X ray of the bomb, right?"

"We've been through this," Burke said.

"On the X ray, you find any failsafe mechanisms, like an antidisturbance switch?"

"No, but we *did* find a gravity trigger. I go to move it and in a blink we're scattered on the moon."

"But in order to activate the trigger, you have to move the bomb."

"Semtex-H is invisible on X ray. I X-ray a briefcase containing a block of that shit, it doesn't even show up as an outline. You with me so far?"

Jack knew where Burke was going. "If there was a secondary IED inside the house, you would have found it."

"That doesn't mean there isn't one in there. I didn't X-ray everything inside the house."

"There's only one bomb in there."

Burke's eyes lighted with a mix of anger and frustration. A web of deep red lines the texture of rubber ran across the left side of his face, carved through his salt-and-pepper beard like runoff beds on soil, and bled down into a thick blob of white scar tissue that covered half of his neck. The skin around his right eye looked like melted red-and-white wax, the ear practically gone.

A local mob hit man whom Burke had sent up the road for life had mailed a letter bomb to Burke during the fall of 1979. Burke had been standing behind his desk, his face turned to a subordinate, when he opened the letter. If he had been looking at it, the acid would have blinded him.

Burke removed the cigar from his mouth. "It's been a long night, my body's jacked on adrenaline and junked on a little whiskey, and when that happens, I have a habit of not making my point very clear. I apologize." He struggled above his anger to maintain calmness and clarity. "So I'll say it again, and this time I'll go extra slow. A laptop computer with six blocks of Semtex-H, probably the most lethal plastic explosive on the planet, is sitting upstairs in a bedroom behind us hooked up to the phone jack in the wall."

"The phone lines are shut down and so is the electricity."

Burke pressed on. "Right now the laptop's running on a battery. When the battery dies, it could send off enough juice to blow the explosives."

"But you don't know that for sure."

"Then there's the matter of the disc drive. Right now there's a disc stuck in there. Every once in a while, the computer starts reading it. How that fits in, Christ, I don't know. If I take it out and the computer starts looking for it, the bomb could blow. It could blow with it in there. That's the fucking problem, Jack. I just don't know. I've been doing this job for thirty-plus years now, and when I think about what's inside that bedroom, it's like someone's holding a flame under my sack. You getting the drift? Am I speaking nice and slow for you?"

Jack looked past Burke's shoulder at the sliding glass door. The killer had cut a square section of glass large enough for him to reach his hand through and unlock the door. The call came in just after twelve, and what he had done with the family took time. He had counted on the bomb wiping out the evidence. But the bomb hadn't gone off and the crime scene was intact.

"Last month this guy blew up a house and killed two officers," Jack said. "We got the media crawling all over the place, we got you and ATF agents poking around the blast site, we throw the media a report about a gas explosion and the story dies. Four weeks later and we have zero for evidence, Bob. The only thing we know is that this guy used infrared on last month's bomb. I walked into the bedroom, walked through the beam, and initiated the bomb's timer. That's all we know, correct? Or am I missing something?"

Jack looked back to Burke. Burke worked the cigar between his back molars and stared at him, his eyes as hard as green marbles. The cool air picked up and blew around them, filled with the squawk of seagulls.

"Upstairs in that bedroom is a fully constructed crime scene, complete with evidence that the bomb was supposed to erase, and you're standing here telling me to just walk away."

"I want you to think with your head and not with the hard-on you got for this guy," Burke said. "You scraped by last month. This time, you may not be so lucky."

"The fact is that he had plenty of chances to take us out and the entire goddamn town and he didn't. Why? Because he can't. The bomb malfunctioned and right now he's sitting somewhere *very* pissed off, dreaming up his next move. You and I both know this is going to happen again, and when it does, we won't be having this kind of conversation. We'll either be dead or sifting through rubble and sliding body parts into Ziplock bags with spatulas. And the whole fucking *world* will be watching. End of story."

Burke glared at him.

"Tell me I'm wrong and I'll take off this suit and walk away," Jack said.

Burke turned away and examined a thought hidden somewhere out in the morning.

"Don't let the suit give you a false sense of security," he said. "If this puppy goes off, they'll be pouring your body into the coffin."

chapter 2

THE BOMB SUIT WAS BY MED-ENG SYSTEMS, THE BEST IN THE BUSINESS, BURKE HAD SAID. It was green, thickly padded, full of straps, and it made Jack feel as if his body were insulated with car tires. The helmet and blast shield prevented Jack from hearing the sounds around him. When he passed the mirror in the downstairs hallway, he realized he looked like a cross between a green Pillsbury Doughboy and an astronaut.

Upstairs, he followed Burke down the hallway, walking beside the length of track that carried the bomb disposal robot, Johnny Fingers. Jack didn't walk so much as lumber; his movements were slow and encumbered as though he were a baby taking his first steps. His breath, hot and stale with the smell of coffee, echoed in his ears. He licked his lips, the taste of salt sharp in the pasty dryness of his mouth, while beads of sweat ran into his eyes. The only thing he could do was blink them away.

The bedroom door was already open. Over Burke's shoulder, Jack could see the window with a drawn blue denim shade, and to the right of it, at an angle in the corner, a tall pine armoire that housed a TV, VCR, and several videocassettes. When his eyes shifted back down to the hardwood floor, he saw a thin red line of blood near Burke's left boot.

The thing at the Roth house had caught him off-guard. He hadn't had a chance to prepare mentally. This time was different. This time he knew what to expect. In the hours he had spent waiting for Burke to call, he had shored up his shaky and leaking mental compartments and—*very* carefully—pieced together the mind-set from his profiling days, the one that would allow him to view objectively the gruesome sights waiting for him in the bedroom.

But he had to be careful. The mind-set would want to dive down that black hole and trade his sanity for his imagination. He couldn't afford for that to happen.

Burke walked inside the bedroom first and disappeared behind the door that swung open to the left. Jack stood back in the hallway and stared down at the blood, waiting for something to hit him, a warning tremor, a change in his heartbeat, anything. Nothing did. In fact, he felt confident, like a ship about to successfully navigate through a wild storm.

Jack placed his gloved hand on the doorway and took a step inside, careful not to disturb the blood, and then turned and met the Dolan family.

Bright red lines, crisscrossed and jagged, screamed from the walls and the ceiling. On the corner of his vision and to the left of the bed he saw the blurry, bright red figure of a small body tied to a chair, his head tilted down and looking at his father. Jack didn't have to look up to know that the boy's throat was cut. Five feet beyond the foot of the bed and wearing nothing but a pair of purple nylon running shorts was Patrick Dolan. A strip of duct tape ran across the man's mouth.

His heartbeat quickened. *Steady . . . steady . . .*

He took in a deep breath.

Start with the father.

Patrick Dolan lay on his right side in a gleaming red pool, his throat cut, his hands and feet tied behind a dining-room chair with rope and duct tape. He was tall, roughly six foot six, and had the intimidating frame of a professional bodybuilder. His hands were bloated, his fingers frozen into claws that looked as if he were trying to grab the coins, Bic pen, and driver's license that lay in the blood just inches from them. The rope had cut through the skin along Dolan's wrists and ankles as he had struggled to free himself; despair was frozen in his dead white face, and a strip of duct tape covered his mouth. Jack wondered what Dolan's last words were to his wife and son.

Patrick Dolan did not look the type to be led willingly to slaughter. With his strength, he could quickly overpower the killer—would have risked it even while staring down the barrel of a gun or with the blade of the knife pressed against his throat. He would have sacrificed his life if it meant saving his wife and son.

No marks or cuts on his arms, hands, or face indicated he had struggled with the killer. And Dolan would not have let himself be tied down to the chair, not with the lives of his wife and son hanging in the balance.

Unless he was drugged with something like chloroform.

Yes, that made sense. *But whom would you drug first?*

Starting with the child would have been risky. Even with the chloroform, the child might suddenly start awake, letting out a whimper or kicking over a nightstand, sounds that would wake the parents and summon them into his bedroom. Shooting them was out of the question. The killer needed them living. Needed them breathing with fear and terror in the role they were about to play in his healing and transformation.

The killer would start with the husband first. Sneak into the bedroom *(shoes and boots make noise. Why didn't that wake him? Or did you walk in socks or barefoot, confident that the bomb would erase your footprints from the hardwood floor?)*

and press the rag up to Dolan's face, confident that even if he woke up, the chloroform would already be in his system, disabling his strength. Then the wife and the child would be easy to subdue. Once everyone in the house was drugged, he would bring the dining-room chairs upstairs, tie his victims up, and wait for them to rise from their chemical slumber. Once that happened, the fantasy harbored in the killer's imagination would introduce itself into the bedroom and the players would act out their roles.

The sight of the boy, Alex, was more difficult to absorb.

The thirteen-year-old was tall and pencil thin for his age, with thick blond hair that hung straight down his scalp. His eyes looked confused, as if they were still searching for the reason why he was bound to his dining-room chair wearing nothing more than his cotton briefs, or why his parents, also bound, were glaring at him with faces full of terror.

During those final moments when he wet himself from the fear that had finally consumed him, Jack wondered if the boy

(not a boy, a child, you're still a child at that age no matter what they say. Not fair, remember what happened to Darren Nigro and the others?)

still clung to the belief that his father would rescue him, scoop him up in the safety of those massive arms and reassure him that it was just a nightmare, that he was a heartbeat away from waking up under the blanket of a warm sun, ready to greet another day with the boundless energy and enthusiasm that is the province of children.

Jack wanted to close the boy's eyes. Instead, he found himself staring deep inside them, thinking, the world around him melting away. Images were forming. Old voices clamored to be heard.

On the nightstand behind the boy was a stack of five-by-seven family photographs near a small white plate that contained hardened blobs of red candle wax. The top picture was a posed snapshot of the Dolan family seated on the living-room couch. The fire was blazing and the Christmas tree, decorated by an expert hand, was brightly lit. The family was dressed in jeans and wool sweaters, and their faces glowed. For some reason, the pictures seemed out of place.

Did you look at the pictures in the candlelight? he wondered. Candlelight was intimate; it would accent the fear on their faces.

A faint connection to the killer washed across his skin.

Beep.

Very faint, and coming from behind him. He strained to listen, heard it again. *Beep—beep—beep,* as strong and steady as a pulse.

Jack turned around. Burke knelt on the side of the bed. Jack noticed that the mattress had been removed; on top of the box spring was a laptop computer, one of those new wafer-thin models that weighed only a couple of pounds, its screen turned up toward the ceiling. A phone jack ran from the modem port and was still connected into the wall jack just under the queen-size oak headboard. Next to the jack was a nest of colored wires that ran like strands of spaghetti to a set of blasting caps hooked up to blocks of orange-colored explosives.

The screen was off but the laptop was beeping.

And something else, Jack noticed. On the side of the laptop, the small rectangular light on the disc drive was glowing a bright green. The computer was trying to read something from the disc.

Burke was fiddling with the wires. Jack felt the veins in his head tighten, and his scalp and spine tingled with dancing needles. Suddenly his mind was replaying that night last month when he was trapped underneath the car. If the bomb went off here—

The laptop stopped beeping. The disc-drive light went dead.

There was a pause that seemed to last for an eternity. Jack felt his body stiffen as if expecting a blow, and then it relaxed.

The house was still standing.

"The battery died," Burke said.

Jack's tension melted. His throat felt dry and tight. Slowly, he forced his mind back inside the bedroom. The key to unlocking the killer's thinking was somewhere inside this room.

You left something behind in here, something you can't afford for me to find out.

"Where's the woman?" Jack asked.

"In the next room, where the walk-in closets are. We had to remove the mattress in order to get at the bomb. I had to untie her, but she's in her original position. Looks like she was strangled."

Jack removed the bomb helmet. The air was cool and thick with a wet, salty, coppery smell.

Burke had moved up to him. He still had his helmet on, but his voice was loud and clear.

"What the *fuck* are you doing?"

"I'm getting undressed."

"We're not having this conversation."

"The bomb's dead."

"It still could blow when I go to move it. Or there could be a secondary bomb somewhere in this house. Haven't you listened to a fucking word I've said?"

"Then I'll process the crime scene now."

"There's no fucking way I'm letting a CSI unit in here."

"I'll do it myself."

"Yourself?" You have any idea how long that will take?"

"It would go quicker if I had a partner."

"Jesus Christ, I should have known you'd try and pull something like this."

"We might not get a second chance and you know it."

Burke glared at him. "Anyone tell you you're a stubborn prick?"

"I'm going to be here awhile, so why don't you leave me your cell phone number and I'll call you when I'm through."

Jack took off his glove and wiped his hand across his sweating face. A rush of ocean air blew in from the window, cooling his skin.

Burke took off his helmet. Clearly, he wasn't pleased. He stared at the bomb, his eyes focused in on a private matter. Finally, he looked up.

"We might as well start in here," Burke said. "This looks like the place where the son of a bitch got his rocks off."

chapter 3

JACK RETURNED HOME SOMETIME AFTER ONE. A CSI unit was now working over the Dolan house. Burke was on the way back to Boston with the dismantled bomb.

Jack's body was exhausted, running on the last traces of caffeine and adrenaline, his stomach growling with hunger. He wandered into his kitchen and started rifling through the refrigerator, and out of the blue and for no reason at all he saw himself opening the back door to his former home in Virginia where Amanda, dressed only in one of his dress shirts, the top four buttons seductively undone, sat on the kitchen table, her hair pulled back and fastened with an elastic band. She moved over to him and grabbed his tie. "Take me upstairs, Daddy. It's baby-making time."

A peculiar hollowness filled him. He shut the refrigerator door. The silence in the house seemed suffocating.

These moments when his mind would quickly replay distant memories had been happening more and more frequently since last month, leaving him feeling off-balance. Trying to think his way out of them was useless. In the past, he had drowned them with whiskey over ice. But in the end, drinking only forced his mind down even darker roads.

What he did instead was look around the kitchen—his new kitchen here in his new life in Marblehead. The house was falling to the ground, and he was renovating it room by room, a task that had kept his mind focused. Then he thought of Taylor Burton, his girlfriend, who was right now on a plane from Los Angeles, where she had been for two weeks.

But the past still tugged at him.

Upstairs, he dressed in a pair of running shorts and a cutoff sweatshirt, threw on his running sneakers, and did six miles through a maze of quiet, suburban streets, pumping his legs harder and harder until the images in his head burned away like film negatives held over a match.

He showered, then dressed in a fresh pair of jeans and a white oxford shirt. The clock read quarter to three. Taylor's flight was due in at five, and the plan was for him to go over there around sixish for a barbecue. That left him with three hours to kill.

He went out into his backyard. A hammock was set up in the shade between two trees. He placed a portable radio on a sawed-down tree stump, turned on the Red Sox, and settled in the hammock, the sky a bright blue with a moving blanket of thick clouds.

The image of the father, Patrick Dolan, gagged, unable to cry out to his son or wife, snaked through his thoughts. He forced it away and concentrated on the game. He saw himself at Fenway Park, watching the game from the stands, inhaling the scent of hot dogs and beer in the breeze, and hearing the soul-lifting sound of the bat connecting to the ball. Finally, his mind settled and he fell asleep.

In his dream the beach was empty of people. The abandoned landscape was familiar, and the sky, as always, was black and starless. The wind blowing off the water was cold, bone-numbing, but the water he stood in ankle-deep was as warm and inviting as a hot shower. He had a visitor.

Amanda hadn't changed much. Her eyes were round, a deep blue, her shoulder-length blond hair tied behind her head with a red rubber band. The gash in her throat had crusted into a gruesome smile, and the front of her white oxford shirt and the legs of her sun-faded jeans were caked with crimson streaks. She stood on the shore with her hands deep in her pockets.

Hi, baby. How you doing? she asks.

I'm fine.

I haven't seen you in such a long time. How long has it been, anyway? Five years?

Something like that.

You look real good. There's not a teaspoon of fat on you. You look like you could lift a car over your shoulders.

I work out a lot. Weight lifting and running. Lots of running.

You run when something's bothering you. What's going on?

I'm fine.

Then why are you standing in that water?

I don't know.

You're not back profiling, are you?

No.

She looks at him strangely.

I gave it up after . . . I'm not involved with it anymore.

You never really give it up, Case. It's always a part of you, like this place and what goes on under the water. What did you call it, sinking deeper into black?

He stares into her eyes and feels an indescribable ache throb deep inside his heart.

I miss you, Amanda.

I miss you too, sweets. It's lonely here. Just miles and miles of beach and no one to talk to. I wish Sidney was here.

Who?

Sidney, our daughter. That's the name I gave her.

Where is she? I'd like to meet her.

Amanda's face clouds.

She's down there, below the water. With the others, Amanda says, her face growing as dark as the sky above her.

She shouldn't be down there.

I know, but she won't come when I call her.

Let me go down and get—

No. You can't go down there again. Look what it did to you—what it did to us.

He looks down at the water. It is as thick and black as paint.

Promise me, Jack. Promise me you won't slip below the water.

I promise.

Will you keep your word this time?

Jack bolted awake. His body was slick with sweat and shaking with a chill. In the distance he heard his neighbor's son calling his dog to come home.

Taylor's house was cedar-shingled, with twin brick chimneys at each end, and a wide farmer's porch that stretched all the way around the front. In the back, sitting so high above the steep cliff wall that it appeared to be hovering in the sky, was the year-round sunporch and private balcony that overlooked the Atlantic. Taylor's mother had lived here alone until four years ago, when she died unexpectedly in her sleep. Taylor, hating the thought of seeing the home she had grown up in with her five sisters go to strangers, bought it from her older siblings and moved back east from Los Angeles, where she had built her reputation as a first-class photographer.

The windows were the new energy-efficient models by Anderson, the shutters had recently been painted a dark green, and last fall, Jack had transformed the third-floor attic into a sprawling office of light maple hardwood floors, a darkroom, a walkout balcony, and a handcrafted oak desk placed in front of the large bay window that overlooked the water and the sky.

The small brick driveway was lined with oak trees, two on each side. The lawn sprinklers kicked on when Jack parked the two-door Pontiac Grand Am, a rental with a dented bumper and no air-conditioning, behind a blue-gray Volvo with Massachusetts plates. He didn't recognize the car.

He got out and walked toward the front door. Taylor's neighbor was out on his deck barbecuing. His teenage sons were in the driveway, trying to skateboard up a wood ramp, their boom box blasting some godawful rap song. Jack walked up the front steps, saw that the door beyond the screen was open, and let himself in.

The foyer wall was lined with color photographs of the war-torn countries Taylor had visited. When he had met her three years ago at a Christmas charity fund-raiser at the Eastern Yacht Club, she had just finished a three-month stint in Bosnia, dodging gunfire and at one time a bomb that had killed a former childhood friend who had devoted her life to missionary work. There, she had captured the picture that would later win her acclaim: a nurse running from a shelled hospital, her outstretched arms holding a screaming baby away from the flames that engulfed the woman's body and face. Now Taylor spent her time on publicity shots. She was in demand by the movie studios, as well as by several A-list actors, directors, and musicians. Trade magazines called her the next Herb Ritts.

The air inside the house was warm and fragrant with burning wood; Ray Charles played over the ceiling speakers mounted in each of the rooms. Jack walked into the gourmet kitchen, also recently redone (which was funny, he thought, since Taylor's cooking always resembled a botched science experiment). An opened bottle of merlot sat on the island table. The balcony door was open, but he didn't see Taylor outside. He was about to run upstairs when he heard her laughter drift up from behind him.

She stepped up into the kitchen, her wide, heart-stopping smile cranked to full wattage. One hand held an empty wineglass while the other tucked a blond strand of shoulder-length hair behind her ear. She still dressed like an LA girl. A thin, white cotton sweater with a wide V-shaped neckline connected to three buttons and then spread out in an upside down V to reveal her belly button and skin so tanned and smooth it looked like cinnamon butter. Black Lycra pants snugly outlined her long legs and then split into bell-bottoms that covered the tops of black shoes.

"Well, hey there, kiddo," she said brightly.

All he could do was stare and smile back. She was five foot eleven, with a thin, muscular frame shaped by aerobics and weight training. Her blue eyes were warm and soft, and that smile always melted the day's worries from his heart. Like his wife, Taylor had an innate ability to relate to anyone and in the span of minutes make you feel you were the center of her private world.

"I haven't seen you for two weeks and you've got nothing to say?" she said.

"Why you so dressed up? We going out?"

"Actually I have a date, so I'm going to have to ask you to leave. The guy I'm seeing is one of those jealous steroid types—you know, all bod, no brains." She winked at him.

"Can I get a kiss before you go?"

She thought about it for a moment. "Well, okay. As long as it's quick."

She put the wineglass down on the island, draped her arms around his shoulders, and wrapped her fingers in the back of his hair. Her lips were warm and soft and tasted of wine. He could smell coconut shampoo in her hair and the faint hint of the perfume she always dotted behind her ears.

"God, I missed you," she said.

"When did you get back?"

"Around one. My meeting was canceled, so I took an early flight. I take it you didn't pick up your messages."

"Of course not."

"You've been busy. When the taxi pulled in, I saw school buses dropping off families in pajamas. It's all over the news, all over the radio." She pushed herself away from his chest. "Did you actually find a bomb?"

"A suspicious package. It turned out to be nothing." His forced smile felt awkward, and for a moment he thought she sensed it.

Taylor's eyes narrowed. "A drastic measure for a suspicious package."

"Just a precaution."

She searched his eyes. "I was worried sick about you. After what happened in that explosion last month—check your machine from now on, will you?"

Over her shoulders he saw the figure of a man step into the kitchen.

Jack's body tensed; Taylor felt it.

"Mike."

"Hello, Jack." Mike Abrams had a pleasant, easygoing smile. He wore a navy blue suit and a red-and-blue-striped tie.

Taylor slid her right hand down Jack's back in a gentle caress. "I was so excited to see you that I forgot to tell you Mike stopped by."

"I tried the station and they told me to come here," Mike said. "I hope I'm not intruding."

"Don't be ridiculous," Taylor said. "Jack and I were going to cook some steaks on the grill. Why don't you stay and eat with us."

Mike opened his mouth to speak but Taylor beat him to it.

"No excuses, please. It's nice to finally meet one of Jack's friends. I was beginning to think you weren't real."

Mike placed his hands in his pant pockets and smiled politely.

"I'll let you two guys catch up," Taylor said. "I have to make a phone call." She cocked a finger at Mike. "You better be here when I get back."

Jack watched her disappear up the stairs to her office.

Mike hadn't changed much physically over the past few years; he was still lean, his face was still rugged, and his short black hair, so thick and coarse it looked like melted plastic, had grayed along the temples. The tanned skin along his eyes was webbed with tiny white lines.

"You look good. I haven't seen you since . . . well, it's been awhile," Mike said. "You entering a bodybuilding contest?"

"Just working out a lot."

Mike nodded. The air was still, filled with the sound of Ray Charles's "This Little Girl of Mine."

"What about the carpentry?" Mike asked. "You still doing that?"

"Some. The house I bought needs a lot of work, and Taylor has me doing some projects. I'm enjoying it."

Jack caught the faint glint in Mike's eyes. "Taylor's a great girl."

"Yes, she is," Jack said. "I didn't realize you were in town."

"I heard about the evacuation this morning. I thought about our conversation last month about the explosion and figured I—"

"Should stop by and see how I'm doing. Mentally."

"I thought you could use a hand." Mike drummed his fingers on the counter. "You should have called me. Why didn't you?"

Jack was about to answer when he heard Taylor laughing from upstairs.

"You tell her why you're here?"

"No. I just told her I was in town, stopped by the station to get your address, and they pointed me here. She didn't press it, if that's what you're asking."

Jack nodded.

"You want to fill me in on the rest of it?" Mike asked.

"Not in here. Outside."

chapter 4

MIKE ABRAMS HAD RECEIVED A DOCTORATE IN PSYCHOLOGY WHEN HE TRAINED AT QUANTICO AS AN FBI PROFILER. Now he worked out of the Boston office as a site profiler, a position within the Investigative Support Unit made him an adviser to local New England law enforcement agencies. On several occasions Mike had been asked to join the profiling team, one of the most highly competitive and coveted opportunities within the Bureau; each time Mike had said no. The reason was always the same: he enjoyed Boston, and his wife, two junior high school girls, and baby boy were too grounded in the community. Privately, Jack suspected that the real reason had to do with Miles Hamilton.

They walked on the beach. Mike had traded in the wine for a bottle of Molson. The waves, roughed up from last night's storm, pounded against the shore. The air was cold, the sky a darkening blue dotted with seagulls.

"This is quite the view," Mike said. "We don't have this in Needham."

When did he move to Needham? Jack wondered. And then a voice replied, *This is what happens when you shut your friends out of your life.*

"Taylor," Mike said, and let out a breath. "Man, she's some kind of wonderful. She even laughed at all my jokes."

"You sure she wasn't laughing at you?"

"She's too kind for that. How long you two been going out?"

"Two years."

"Is it serious?"

Jack took in a deep breath. "We're having a good time."

"Well, she's a great girl. We should get together, the four of us. It's been what now, two years? Three?"

Jack felt his face color slightly. "It's been awhile."

"After I helped you land here, it's like you disappeared off the planet. Did I do something to offend you? Piss you off?"

"No."

Mike's eyes moved over Jack's face. "Why do I get the feeling I'm invading on personal territory here?"

"You're not."

Jack watched an overweight woman in a blue sweatsuit and holding a Walkman jog toward them, her face red from the exertion.

"It bothers you to see me," Mike said.

"Of course not."

Mike looked at him. "It's okay if it does. I'd understand."

"I don't like to conduct police business here, especially in front of Taylor. And it's been one hell of a long day."

"Well, I'm sorry for just showing up here out of the blue." Mike paused. He took a pull of his Molson, looked out at the crashing waves. "It's a serial, isn't it?"

"I don't think so. A serial that targets families is rare—almost unheard of. I only know of one such case, and the guy who did it shot everyone while they were sleeping and then had sex with the woman. Here I have a male *and* a female victim. It doesn't fit the profile."

"So there's probably a connection between the two families."

"When I removed the tape off Larry Roth's mouth, he said the killer knew him—knew everything about him."

"And he saw what happened to his wife and kids."

Jack nodded.

"What about the second family? Same setup?"

"The victim—a woman—was forced to watch. After they were dead, he strangled her." This morning Jack had seen the petechial hemorrhaging in the mucous membrane lining Veronica Dolan's inner eyelid.

"Why strangle her?"

"Because he hated her for what she did to him."

Mike's eyes narrowed. "Who's handling the autopsies?"

"I contracted a pathologist out of Boston. He's got the lab and the experience."

"How do the bombs fit?" Mike took another pull from his beer.

"To erase any evidence he might have left behind. And to gain attention."

"You're certainly keeping it quiet. On the way over, the news was saying that the town had been evacuated because of a suspicious package that turned out to be harmless."

"They say anything about the family?"

"No."

But that wouldn't last for long. What had happened to the Dolan family was probably already circulating around town. It was only a matter of time before the papers picked it up. There was no way to control it.

"If today's bomb had gone off, the press would be reexamining last month's so-called gas explosion. You read about it?"

"Two officers dead, a lot of injuries. Front-page news for one day, and then the story is swallowed up by a rock star caught jerking off a guy in a rest room. Don't you love how America works?" Mike shook his head. "You feed the press the gas-explosion angle?"

"We had to feed them something. If they found out it was a bomb and that the killer called us, we'd be dealing with copycats. We're not equipped for that."

"But you know you can't keep the truth hidden much longer."

"I know," Jack said, and felt a heaviness boom inside his chest. "You hear my name mentioned at all?"

"No."

"Good. I want to keep my name out of the papers."

"Yes. Yes, you have to do that," Mike said, and shot him a look. "How's Burke working out?"

"He's bright, knows his stuff. Up-front, no bullshit. I appreciate the referral."

"Tell me about the bomb."

"A laptop hooked up to six blocks of Semtex-H. One phone call and Marblehead Neck would be on the ocean floor."

Mike stopped walking. He looked as if he had swallowed a shard of glass. "Semtex-H is a Russian explosive."

"I know. This afternoon I called Mark Graysmith at the Explosives Unit. He's going to see if he can track it down. That stuff doesn't show up in residential homes."

Then the thought that had been lying dormant inside Jack all day resurfaced and stroked him like an obscene hand. He looked out at the water and watched the waves break.

"What is it?" Mike asked.

"This bomb malfunctioned. Today I got to see how it was constructed, and now I have a full crime scene to work with. But this guy's going to pull out all the stops the next time. He wants the whole world watching."

"And he'll target you and Burke."

The thought had already occurred to Jack. Hearing Mike say it out loud only reinforced it.

Jack kneaded the knots in the back of his neck and let out a long, tired breath.

"Besides Burke, who else you got working with you?" Mike asked.

"State police and ATF. And now Graysmith. He owes me a few favors."

"I'm more concerned about the homegrown talent."

"It's a small town. The Roth explosion killed two officers, and what's left over are rookies."

"So you're planning on shouldering this one by yourself."

"This falls under your job description. You have access to resources I don't. You up to this?"

"I'll help you any way I can, you know that. Why didn't you call me?"

"Because until today, I didn't know what I was up against."

Mike nodded, tapped his beer bottle against his leg. "You given any thought to calling Alan?"

Alan was Alan Lynch, the director of the Investigative Support Unit, and Jack's former boss. The name was a lesion.

"Why the fuck would I call him?"

"He might send a profiler down here, maybe even a team who could—"

"I don't need Alan to help me profile. Besides, he won't be interested in a case where the only place he's going to see his name in print is in the local paper next to supermarket coupons. The guy's a media whore and a first-class prick and you know it."

"Why did I have a feeling you'd say that?"

"You telling me I'm wrong?"

Mike reached into his back pocket and came up with a folded sheet of paper. Jack took it, holding it tightly in both hands so it wouldn't blow away. There was a name and an address, no phone.

"Malcolm Fletcher," Jack said.

"He's a retired profiler."

Jack heard a sound like a Popsicle stick snapping in the back of his head. A rush of hot red color flooded his eyes.

"He was there when Behavioral Sciences first started. He's got quite an impressive record. Caught twenty-three serials," Mike said. "Like yourself, he has a one hundred percent capture rate. I couldn't find any specifics on his cases. He's been retired for twenty years now, but I was able to track down his address off a recent motor-vehicle-accident report. No phone though."

"Is this your way of saying I'm not up to the job?"

Mike's gaze didn't waver. "When you walked into that house last month and saw what happened to this guy Roth and his family, what was your reaction?"

"I was surprised."

"And that's all?"

"Jesus Christ."

"Come on, Jack. Just answer the question. I'm not here to judge you."

"I was a little shaken."

"Shaken. That's it?"

"That's right."

"What about today?"

"Today went fine."

"You having bad dreams again?"

"You shrinks amaze me. Someone takes a shit and you guys want to write a textbook on it."

"I'm not trying to run you through psychoanalysis. Look, your department can afford to bring on some consultants. Why not bring in another guy to help? What do you have to lose?"

"I'm not going to have a relapse, if that's what this is about." Jack folded the paper up in his fist.

Mike stared at him a moment. "You remember Dale Gavins?"

"What about him?"

"He took a two-year hiatus after working those child murders in Syracuse. Therapy, medication, everything's fine, let's go back to profiling. Eight months ago he kissed his wife and baby daughter good-bye and drove to work, only he stopped at a rest room. When the gas station attendant unlocked the door, he found Dale slumped to the floor with a knife in his hands. The coroner said Gavins was watching himself in the mirror when he slit his throat."

"So what are you saying? That if I don't follow your instructions, I'll end up killing myself?"

Mike moved in closer. "It's been what, six years, seven, since you profiled?"

"What's your point?"

"You spent a lot of time burying that part of your life. You try to unlock that part of your imagination and you'll wind up back in that world full of hurt. It took you a long time to rebuild yourself, Jack. You try to slip back down and regain that way of thinking, you could relapse, that's a fact. If that happens, you may not be able to come up for air."

"Gavins was delusional and an alcoholic with a history of violence."

Mike's face pinched with a dark thought. "You had problems with alcohol."

Jack felt his face flush. "Not like that."

An unspoken image passed between them.

"This conversation's over, Mike."

"That's it, end of discussion?"

"Thanks for the psych evaluation. Mail the bill to my house."

Mike's face reddened. "Taylor's something real special. I just hope I'm not standing with my arm around her at your funeral, but, hey, what the fuck do I know?"

Jack watched Mike walk back up the beach to the house. He turned the beer bottle upside down, a long trail of gold liquid blowing in a spray behind him, an unrelieved anger twisting his face.

chapter 5

MIKE TOLD TAYLOR HE HAD AN EMERGENCY AT HOME AND HAD TO DECLINE THE DINNER INVITATION. By the time Jack reached the house, Mike was gone.

The grill was set up on the wide balcony off the living room. Jack flipped the steaks over with metal tongs, and a cloud of cooked-meat smoke blew up across his face. Taylor had turned off Ray Charles and switched over to the local radio station, WBCN; U2's "Mysterious Ways" played over the balcony speakers. Taylor was inside, in the living room, lighting pillar candles on the coffee table. The fire behind her lit up the ceiling and walls with dancing flame and accentuated the curves of her body, the smooth, sharp edges of her face.

Watching her, Jack thought he was living someone else's charmed life.

What should have been on his mind was their night ahead; instead, the projector inside his head had started replaying an incident that had occurred a week after he had buried his wife.

With his house now a part of a homicide investigation, and with his own family dead, he had stayed in the spare bedroom of Mike's house in Arlington, Virginia. The majority of his time was spent in bars with tall, soothing glasses of Jim Beam over ice.

But the liquor also kicked open locked attic doors, exposing dark thoughts and unleashing a rage that could not be doused. That rage had always been with him, it seemed, burning in his veins like acid, only lately it was demanding certain forms of expression. He saw it staring back at him in the mirror—and so had the other bar patrons, friends and fellow agents who had stopped by wanting to console him. They had seen it in his eyes and decided it was best to keep their distance.

One night, for a reason he still couldn't explain, he drove drunk from a bar to his house and wandered through the dark rooms until he stumbled his way upstairs. A horizontal sliver of light showed at the bottom of the closed bedroom door; a shadow moved inside the room.

The photographer did not look up from his camera when Jack opened the door; he clicked away at the bloodstained chairs and rope, at the dried pool on the tan carpet, at the spray of lines and clots that looked like angry slashes of black paint on the walls. Jack's heart squeezed with a painful tightness. This wasn't true, he thought. This was just another alcohol-induced nightmare, and if he took several deep breaths, it would go away.

The photographer, tall and grossly overweight, with a black goatee and a face slick with oil, looked up from his camera, his eyes growing wide in recognition, and then he turned the camera around and started taking pictures of Jack, the clicking sound of the shutter as rapid as machine-gun fire.

It took four neighbors to pull Jack off. When they did, he realized he was on his front lawn. The photographer was lying on his back on the grass, his nose broken, his face a dark purple while his opened mouth made wet, choking sounds. Alicia Claybrook, his next-door neighbor who worked as a nurse, the woman who had seen Hamilton leave the house, was kneeling next to the photographer's head and working furiously to clear the man's tongue from his throat. Mike Abrams was there too, standing by the curb at his car with the cell phone pressed against his ear, his face pale as he surveyed the street full of witnesses.

Later Jack pretended that the photographer, who worked for a well-known newspaper tabloid, had deserved it. But he knew the photographer had simply paid for what had happened to Amanda, his failure to protect her, the steady supply of guilt and the long-held images that he had tried, unsuccessfully, to rinse from his blood.

That incident marked the beginning of a downward spiral of alcohol abuse and rage. The Bureau was forced to let him go: that's it, thanks for all your help.

Mike Abrams had got him into treatment. Mike Abrams, his friend, had stepped in and saved him from drowning.

When Jack was working as a carpenter in Vail, Colorado, Mike had stepped in again and—despite Jack's protests—landed him the detective's position here in Marblehead. After that, though, Jack had seen less and less of Mike. Weeks stretched into months. Into three years.

The truth was he liked Mike. He just didn't like what was reflected back in Mike's eyes.

Now Mike had come back here after all this time wanting to help, and what did he do? Turn him away.

Taylor walked to the railing next to the grill.

"You okay?"

"Fine," he said, and blinked.

"You look like you're trying to swallow a mouthful of tacks."

"I'm operating on about two hours of sleep. I'll get my second wind as soon as we eat."

"Too bad Mike had to go. I was looking forward to spending some time with him."

Jack turned over the steaks. The warm breeze blew Taylor's blond hair over her face. She grabbed a strand with one hand, flipped it back over her ears. " 'Fess up. What's eating at you?"

"Just some old stuff. Nothing important."

"Talk to me about it."

"It's nothing, honest. Did I hear the phone ring?"

Taylor nodded. "That was Rachel. You remember my niece, right? The four-year-old with the dog that acts as her bodyguard?"

"Mr. Ruffles." Mr. Ruffles was the name given to a thick and muscular, hundred-pound boxer-and-pit-bull mutt. The name came from the dog's wrinkled face; Rachel thought it looked like a Ruffles potato chip. No one knew where the *Mr.* came from.

"Well, she and Mr. Ruffles will be spending the next three weeks with us. I'm picking her up tomorrow at Logan. She's very excited. In fact she said, 'Is Uncle Jack going to be there?' "

"I'm not her uncle," Jack said a little too sharply. *You're angry. Don't let it get away from you,* a voice warned him.

"Take it as a compliment."

"I do. It's—" *Tell her, for once be honest.* "I'm tired, that's all. Don't mind me."

Her eyes continued to move across his face, as if his real thoughts had suddenly become exposed.

"Tell me about Mike," she said.

"What do you want to know?"

"How long have you known him?"

"A long time."

"You met in the FBI?"

Jack nodded and looked around for his beer.

"Mike told me he's a site profiler."

"That's right." Jack's beer was resting on the balcony floor near the grill. Beer didn't turn on him the way whiskey did. He reached down and grabbed the bottle.

"But he's not an actual profiler like you were."

"Right." Jack drank some of his beer, his second since Mike left. A voice said, *You better ease back on the throttle. It may not turn on you, but it won't keep you from dreaming.*

"He screens local cases," Jack said. "He helps the cops out and passes the more interesting ones on to Quantico."

"Why didn't he get into the profiling?"

"Don't know. You ask him?"

"No."

Jack looked down at the steaks, examining them with the tongs. "How long was he here?"

"About an hour."

"What did you two talk about?"

"All of your dark secrets."

He looked up with a smile. "Seriously, what did you two talk about?"

"Nothing much. He was interested in the pictures I took in Sarajevo. Jack, we've been going out for two years now and this is the first I've seen him. Why is that?"

"Mike's a busy guy."

"But not too busy to drive all the way to Marblehead out of the blue and drop in on the girlfriend of his best friend who he hasn't seen for at least two years?"

Jack came up with something quick. "He went to the station to drop off some equipment. They pointed him here."

"Why didn't he leave the stuff at the station? Why didn't he call you and meet you there?"

"Don't know. You're not upset that he came here, are you?"

"Of course not. Why are you avoiding the questions?"

"What questions?"

"The ones about your life before Marblehead. We get on this track and you always clench up."

There was no anger in her voice, just a gentle concern. This conversation was not a new one.

Jack grabbed a steak and placed it steaming on the white plate set up on the counter attached to the grill.

"What is it? You afraid that I won't understand?" she asked. "That I'll love you less?"

He felt a quickening in his pulse, a tightness wash across his skin. "Of course not."

"Good, because I won't."

He started slicing through the meat.

"Jack."

"Yeah."

"Look at me."

He did, through the waves of smoke blowing up from the grill.

"I won't love you any less. No matter how bad it was, no matter how bad it gets." She had told him that before.

"I know." He could see the questions lined up like dominoes behind her eyes.

Jack placed the knife and fork on the plate, grabbed his beer, and straightened. The sun was sinking on the ocean's horizon like a molten ball, the sky above the color of plum and full of thick, moving clouds, their bellies glowing a bright red in the sunset. A magnificent summer evening, he thought. The mood seemed so right, so perfect; he found words actually building on the back of his throat. What made it seem so tempting was that the woman standing before him had, unlike his wife, traveled to the dark corners of the globe and borne witness to evil.

But questions unleash more questions, a voice warned. Maybe not tonight, but over time he would be forced to explain his thinking and the rationale behind certain actions that was at times difficult to justify even to himself. No matter how expertly he painted the pictures, she would form her own judgments. Things between them would change. Maybe not for the worse, but they would definitely change. They had a good thing going, something strong, maybe even permanent. Why risk soiling it with discussions of a past life that he would rather forget?

And there was something else: despite her intelligence, her background, her gentleness, warmth, and empathy, and the nightmarish stories she had willingly shared with him, Taylor was not a profiler. She couldn't understand some of the things he

(wanted, be honest)

was forced to do.

Taylor's eyes were free of judgment, her expression gentle. He felt an aching need to touch and hold her.

He hooked two fingers under her elastic waistband, feeling the smooth coolness of her skin, and pulled her gently toward him. She resisted it at first and then gave in, placing her hands on his chest as he wrapped his arms around her waist.

"Someday you're going to have to open up and share."

"Taylor, it's a beautiful night and I haven't seen you for two weeks. I don't want to talk about my past or Mike or anything else. I just want to be with you."

She tapped his heart with her hand. "When are you going to let me in?"

"You're already in."

He moved his mouth to her ear. Her body relaxed a little.

"I missed you something awful," he whispered.

She pressed closer to him, wrapped her arms around his waist. "You did?"

"I felt like I was drowning."

Slowly, her hands moved up his back. She stopped and squeezed him close to her. She felt soft and delicate in his arms. She moved her chin onto his shoulder. He could hear her breath against his ear.

"I love you, Jack. No matter what happens, I'll always love you."

Behind the music he heard the phone ringing.

"That's probably my sister calling with Rachel's flight information. Hold that thought," she said, and kissed him.

Jack watched her walk through the shadows in the living room. The projector in his mind began to play again. This time he managed to shut it off. He was moments away from being enveloped in the warmth of skin and whispers of

(Amanda)

a beautiful woman who had helped heal him.

He was a new man now. He had transformed his body, had patched the cracks in his mind, and was living in a new town and sharing his life with a new woman. He looked and felt different. There was no need to brood on the past.

Taylor walked back on the deck, the cordless phone extended in her hand. "It's for you."

"Who is it?"

"Someone from the station. He says it's important."

It was probably the police chief. The media was all over the station, and Jack had called him earlier and asked him to handle the press conference, telling him what to say. Not that the chief needed much coaching. The man had worked homicide in Chicago and then in Boston before moving on to the more administrative tasks. Jack had asked him to check in.

He took the phone from her. "Keep an eye on the steaks. I'll be back in a minute."

He walked inside the living room. "Casey."

"Jack Casey, the FBI profiler? My God, I can't believe it's really you."

It wasn't the chief. He didn't recognize the voice.

"Who is this?"

"Did you like what I did to the Dolans?"

chapter 6

THE VOICE WAS LOW AND BREATHY AND CAUGHT DEEP BACK IN THE THROAT, LIKE THE VOICE OF A MAN RIDING THE AFTERGLOW OF A PROFOUND ORGASM. It didn't sound like the first voice recorded on the 911 call, it didn't sound disguised at all.

"It's so good to finally talk to you, Jack. Do you mind if I call you Jack? I feel this . . . connection, I guess you could call it."

"Who's this?"

"You know who this is."

"You could be a reporter."

"Now's not the time to be coy. You and I have so much to discuss. So much to share. You look different from your old pictures. More muscular now. Lots of sharp edges and creases. You look like a new man, but I guess that's the point, isn't it?"

Jack looked out at Taylor. She was on the balcony, leaning over the plate and examining the steaks with the knife and fork. Then she placed one back on the grill. She would be back inside any minute now.

"I watched you out at the house today. You seemed much calmer this time. Not like last month when you bolted. This guy you got working with you, Bob Burke, I hear he's the best in the business."

How does he know about Burke? Jack hadn't read anything in the papers.

"What did Bobby have to say about me?"

"Mostly he called you an asshole," Jack said.

The man laughed, a low, rumbling sound. "I'm glad to see your sense of humor's survived. I was wondering if you had become one of those pathetic souls who spend their days carrying around their guilt like a cross. This new life must be agreeing with you. I wonder if your new gal pal has something to do with it."

"You called me. What do you want?"

"To share. You and I have a lot in common."

"Like what?"

"We both know what it's like to have the things we love destroyed by madmen. To be . . . powerless . . . drowning."

Jack saw the opening and dived ahead. "How did Larry Roth hurt you?"

"It's too soon for that."

"Then let's talk about Veronica."

Silence.

"You called me. You said you wanted to talk and share. You have me on the phone. I'm listening."

Jack's eyes whisked over the phone on the wall in the kitchen. It had a built-in answering machine and a memo button for recording messages and conversations.

"By the way, great job last month," the voice said. "Blaming the explosion on a faulty gas line was brilliant. Imagine what would have happened if the people of Marblehead found out how the Roths really died, or that three blocks of composition C-4 was the cause of the explosion."

Jack moved to the kitchen. Taylor was still out on the balcony.

"You remember that serial you caught back in '84, the plumber, the guy who was hacking up those hookers in cheap motel rooms with an ax, what's-his-name there?"

"I don't remember," Jack said as he walked quickly across the tile.

"Of course you do. Keating, that's it. Ray Keating. You nicknamed him the Michigan Mangler. Accurate, given what he did to those girls, but that stuff about reciting passages from Revelation as he hacked them into sausages—please, it's been done in every horror movie."

Jack pressed the Memo/2-way button on the wall unit. The tape clicked and started recording. He slid the volume down so Taylor wouldn't hear.

"Ray Keating didn't have any style. It's his own fault he faded from public memory. But your friend Miles Hamilton, the 'All-American Psycho'—now *that's* a name. Plain and simple and remains forever in the head. He's been in the insane asylum for seven years now and people *still* talk about him. How is Miles doing?"

In his mind Jack saw Miles Hamilton lying back in a bed, reading and watching TV, content with his thoughts. Jack felt a spike of rage and had to quickly push it away.

"I wouldn't know," he said.

"You haven't visited him?"

"No."

"Did you come up with his nickname before or after he butchered your wife?"

"The press called him that."

"Yes, that would make sense, wouldn't it? They need to pander to kindergarten mentality. It's a sad state of affairs, Jack. People living their trailer-park existence at the altar of Jerry Springer and Rickie Lake, drinking their cheap beer and eating their fast food and knocking up teenage girls. The white-trash audience is a tough one to capture, but I'm confident in my abilities."

Jack moved onto the other side of the living room. The fireplace was dancing with flames that lit up the ceiling and carpet.

"I've been giving a lot of thought to my name," the voice said. "Let me run this by you, tell me what you think: the Sandman. The monster who murders families in their sleep. How's that sound?"

"I think it's an inappropriate name for someone whose actions are clearly misunderstood."

"That's something out of a freshman psychology class. You're more imaginative than that. Or did all that time spent in Colorado bury the old Jack Casey and his deviant ways of thinking?"

Jack looked up from the fire.

"And the house you bought, it's falling to the ground. But I know why you bought it, Jack. You need to keep your hands occupied. It's the only way to keep you from remembering past sins."

The phone felt loose and wet in Jack's hands. "I'm afraid you lost me."

"No, I didn't. I've hit a nerve. Beneath that good-looking exterior is a mind and heart that is as dark and turbulent as the river Styx. How familiar are you with Greek mythology?"

"Thetis dipped Achilles in the river to make him invulnerable."

"Very good. In addition to the water's magical properties, it was also used by the gods for pronouncing oaths. You and I need to take an oath, Jack. It's the only way to keep Taylor safe."

The sliding glass door slammed shut behind him; Jack jumped slightly at the sound. Taylor hustled through the living room with the plate of steaks. She winked at him, disappeared around the corner, and then headed into the kitchen.

"Promise me you'll drop this case. Become a full-time carpenter and spend all your time popping Taylor's muffin, I don't care, but you need to take your final bow and exit. We both know you're not up to this. Those mental scars are already tearing."

Jack watched Taylor pour another glass of wine near the sink. He walked out onto the balcony and leaned his back against the railing so he could watch her. "Let's get back to you. Tell me about Larry Roth."

"I've seen Taylor around town. Stood behind her at CVS today when she was picking up her birth-control pills. Her beauty is blinding, isn't it? All those hard muscles, that flawless face, and the smile that can heal the wounds in your heart—Amanda just doesn't stack up. I wonder what you would do if you had to choose between them. Don't tell me, Jack. I already know the answer."

"Taylor's a friend of mine and has nothing to do with why you're calling me. So why don't we get to it? What do you want? What do you need?"

"She's more than a friend, Jack. I saw the way you looked at her when she walked onto that plane for LA. You need her. Without her I'm quite confident you'd drown."

That was two weeks ago, he thought, his body growing still. *How long has he been following me? And how the hell does he know all these details about my past?*

"If I step aside, other people will continue to look for you. They won't stop."

"They can't search for me from their coffins, can they?"

"Why spare me?"

"Because you've had enough hurt for one lifetime. But if you keep going, I'll make sure you spend the rest of your waking days knowing you could have spared her if only you had stepped aside. I understand you're having a visitor."

"What are you talking about?"

"Taylor's niece, Rachel. I hear she and her dog are flying in from Wisconsin tomorrow."

How does he know?

The Sandman answered the question for him. "You really shouldn't talk on cordless phones. They're so easy to pick up. If you're thinking of telling Taylor about this conversation, don't. If you tell her, I'll kill her. If the little girl is sent back home, I'll kill them all. And don't think of putting bodyguards on them, either. If I even *think* she's being protected, if I even *think* she knows she's in danger, I'll kill them all and leave you to live with that guilt all over again. And don't think I won't find out, Jack, because I know *everything.*"

Larry Roth's voice came back to Jack: *The son of a bitch knows my name, knows everything about me.*

"Why are you warning me?"

"Because you're already dead, Jack. Taylor interrupted your plans to bleed into nothingness. She's the only thing that breathes life into your pathetic, hollow shell of an existence. Remember what I said, Jack, or I'll make sure that incident with your wife looks like a trip to Disney World."

The line went dead.

Jack pulled the phone away from his ear and stared at it as if it were about to speak to him. Then he placed it on a small, circular table next to the grill and watched it for a moment, half-expecting it to ring. Taylor was in the kitchen, rifling through silverware as she sang along with the radio. The images were no longer playing in his mind, but that old fear was back and gripping his heart.

The call didn't surprise him. The Dolan home was standing; right now, it was being pored over by a CSI unit in search of evidence, and the killer—the Sandman—knew that and was afraid. That he had called and tried to intimidate Jack was expected behavior.

What threw him off was the mention of his time spent in Colorado. He was working as a carpenter in Vail when Hamilton's trial started. The crew he worked with was careful not to leave newspapers around or talk about it, and he never followed the progress of the trial on TV. No reporters came to Vail to ask him why he wasn't at the trial because they didn't know where he was. What had actually been printed in the papers? he wondered. How much did the public know about him?

Taylor's hand touched his shoulder. "Whatcha thinking about, kiddo?"

"Nothing much. Just enjoying the sunset."

"Everything okay?"

"Sure."

Jack reached up and grabbed her hand; but he didn't turn around right away. Taylor was a pro at detecting worry. He blinked the frantic energy out of his eyes before he looked at her with a smile.

Her eyes moved over his face and then narrowed.

"Hungry?" she asked with a sly grin.

"Yeah. Really hungry."

He undid the buttons on her sweater and then slid his palms up her stomach to her breasts. The clasp of her bra was in the front. He undid it and moved his hands up over her shoulders and down her arms. The wind blew her hair over her face. Her eyes were still and unblinking, looking deep into his.

The sweater and bra came off and blew across the balcony floor to the corner. Her eyes never left his face, even when he stepped back and drank in the sight of her body. Her breasts were firm, her nipples erect from the cold air, the stomach muscles flexing as she took in small, excited breaths.

He placed his hands on the elastic waistband of her pants and panties and knelt down in front of her like a man before an altar. She placed both hands on the back of his head and looked down at him with a tender confidence and approval. He slid the pants and panties down and saw her step out of her shoes. He leaned his forehead into her stomach and closed his eyes, and she grabbed the back of his head with one hand. The touch of her skin against his was like a rush of water across parched lips. The citrus-scented perfume that she had dabbed on her wrists mixed with the salt air . . . it was like coming home to something familiar. Something warm and safe.

Her hands moved away from his head and pulled up his shirt. He stood up and his clothes came off in a rush. She wrapped her arms around his neck and he picked her up and carried her back to the side of the house near the screen door. She took him in her hand and placed him inside her, the moan escaping her lips loud against his ears. With her back pressed against the house, she hooked her feet around the small of his back and pushed him deeper inside her. All of his fears, the weight of the days and the images from inside the bedroom, melted away in a flood of kisses and sweat and whispers. He saw himself diving down a deep cone of white water to a place where there were no screams and no hurt. Here, in this haven between skin and skin, there was only comfort that numbed the pain twisting inside his heart.

A moment later he felt a hot pressure build and burst forth. When he stopped trembling, he pulled her close to him and sat down on the deck. Taylor kissed his forehead and cheek, her breath still hot against his ear. He moved the hair away from her shoulder and kissed the salty dampness along her neck and shoulder. He didn't want to let her go.

Through the strands of her hair blowing across his vision, he saw the crumpled piece of paper Mike had given him sticking out of his jeans pocket, like a fist that raps on a front door in that deep part of the night to deliver unbearable news.

chapter 7

ALAN LYNCH, THE DIRECTOR OF THE INVESTIGATIVE SUPPORT UNIT, THE BRANCH OF THE FBI THAT DEALS WITH SERIAL MURDER, SAT IN THE BACKSEAT OF THE TAXI RACING DOWN THE TWISTING STREETS OF LA JOLLA. It was not even 5 A.M. and all the houses—modern, multimillion-dollar structures of stone and slanted glass—were quiet and dark under a sky the color of lavender.

The call had come at six last night in the middle of his first sit-down family dinner in over three weeks. Paul DeWitt, the thirty-three-year-old MIT graduate and network-security administrator for the FBI's computer complex located in the top-secret facility in Harrison County, West Virginia, had told him what he had uncovered during a routine audit log of the documentation system. The news was not good.

Dr. David Gardner was a psychiatrist who worked for the Behavioral Modification Program, or BMP, a highly classified research program maintained and operated by the FBI. Gardner had apparently entered the FBI research building, also in La Jolla, and using a specialized laptop computer had logged on to the system's patient database on June 3, 4, and 5—Friday through Sunday. Each time the doctor had spent well over five hours on the system—an abnormality since the audit log showed he usually logged on to the patient database once a week.

But that wasn't the reason for the call. Gardner was required to post vacation time on the system. The doctor was taking four weeks' vacation—all of June and the first week of July, the log said—and when he came back, he was supposed to log back on to the system.

Weeks had passed with no word from Dr. Gardner.

A check of the local obituaries revealed that Gardner had not died. Calls were placed to Gardner's house, his private office, and to his cellular and beeper numbers. All calls went unanswered. When two agents drove out to his house, they found a tidy home recently cleaned. The refrigerator was empty of all perishable foods, but the freezer was well stocked. No missing person's report had been filed with the police department.

After he finished talking with DeWitt, Alan placed a call to Henry Munn, the head of the BMP's Emergency Response Team, and asked him to investigate. Matters regarding patient problems and ensuring the research program's secrecy were Munn's field of expertise.

Neither of them had ever encountered a missing *doctor* before. A missing patient who had for some reason gone off the deep end, yes, but a doctor—that was a new one.

The taxi took a right. Through the front window Alan saw a gathering of federal cars parked in the driveway and along the street in front of a towering structure of white stone and mirrored glass that had all the warmth of a mental institution. He knocked on the partition and pointed, paid, and got out.

The strong morning breeze blew his tie over his shoulder. He flattened it back across the slight paunch of his stomach, moved one hand across his bald head, and pushed his green-tinted aviator sunglasses back up his nose. His heart was racing; that worried him. He had suffered his first heart attack a decade ago at the age of forty-two. Six years later, the second one necessitated quadruple-bypass surgery. Now the first forty minutes of each day were spent chugging on a treadmill. After that came the pills, vitamins, chicken, fish, and an endless stream of fruit and vegetables. In spite of what his wife and the nutritionist called clean living, he still sneaked away to the local McDonald's for a couple of Big Macs every once in a while (but never when his wife or kids were around), and he refused to give up his scotch or Cuban cigars.

He entered a wide, airy foyer of gray marble floor and framed pictures that looked as if they had been painted by the hand of an angry child. A small team of agents were inside dusting for prints. He moved past them without a word and turned down a corridor that deposited him in a large, well-appointed kitchen. More agents were milling about, going through drawers and examining documents. Alan removed his glasses, tucked them in the breast pocket of his Calvin Klein suit, and through the gaps between the pots and pans hanging from a rack caught a glimpse of Henry Munn looking down at a series of papers.

Munn had the solid build of a football player and always wore clothes that seemed too small for him. With his blond crew cut, his tree-trunk arms, and barrel chest, he looked more like a middle-aged bouncer at a Florida nightclub than the head of the program's ERT.

"I take it you didn't grab any shut-eye," Munn said, not looking up. His voice was dry with fatigue and gruff from years of chain-smoking. Dark circles were puffed under both eyes. "There's coffee on the counter, mocha blast, mocha jump, tastes like mocha crap to me, so help yourself."

Alan cut right to it. "You find Gardner?"

"Not yet."

"But you have an idea where he is, right?"

Munn scratched the corner of his lip with his thumb. His face was perfectly composed, his eyes tiny green slits that as usual depicted no anxiety, interest, or excitement. "When did you talk to DeWitt last?"

"Last night," Alan said.

"DeWitt's pretty sure that Gardner did a little more than examine some patient files, like maybe he got at some of the other more classified information on the computer database. The CIA stuff, the Pentagon weapons-research program. Schematics mostly."

"That's impossible. Gardner doesn't have clearance. There's the random password generator, for one. And even if he got past that, there's no way in hell he could get past all the biometric security measures we have in place."

"DeWitt seems confident that's what went down."

"It doesn't make any sense. Why would Gardner be interested in military weapons?"

"Not Gardner—the guy *posing* as Gardner."

Alan felt a sharp tightness in his chest. He swallowed, moved in closer. He could smell Munn's cologne and talcum mixed with the stench of nicotine. Munn's face was deadpan.

"You're telling me a stranger got on and— No, that's impossible. The network security we have in place would prevent that. Even if someone knew Gardner's passwords, he couldn't get past the retina scan. That's foolproof."

"That's why it wasn't an outside hack."

"It's an inside job?"

"Here's the skinny. This audit program that DeWitt coded, it not only tracks the amount of time each shrink is on the system, it tracks the typing speeds of each user. For the past nine years Gardner, who's sixty-one, types something like eight words a minute—hunt and peck, right? Those three days, Gardner was typing *ninety-six* words a minute. As for the network security, the passwords, the retina scan, the random keycard generator, it all checks out. So we know Gardner was in the room on the laptop—"

"While someone else was working the keyboard."

"Right. So it has to be someone who not only has access to Gardner's office but was in there with him."

An unpleasant thought bubbled up. "Like a patient," Alan said.

"It's the only scenario that makes sense."

The entire room drained of color and sound.

Munn took in a deep breath and then continued, "Patient is in there with the doc, keeps him there in order to pass the retina scan. The patient gets on to the system, downloads the information—"

"Downloads. Those laptops don't have disc drives."

"Right, but if someone were knowledgeable in computers, they could open up the laptop, rework the wiring, and hook up an external disc drive, like one of those Jazz drives, and do downloads. Or he could send the files via the Internet to some secure location."

"If he rerouted the files over the Internet, it would have left a trace."

"Right, and DeWitt couldn't find it. Was this guy smart enough to wipe the trace out? DeWitt thinks so. The good news is that if the intruder tries to log on to the system again, we'll be able to track him down in a matter of seconds."

"But he hasn't logged back on during the past two months."

"Not necessarily true. DeWitt thinks he may have left some sort of coding, a virus maybe, or what he called a trapdoor program. This trapdoor would allow him to sneak past the security and log back on to the system without anyone knowing. DeWitt's looking into it."

"So we have no idea to what extent the patient database is contaminated."

Munn nodded. "Right now DeWitt and his team are going through the entire system to figure out what's missing, what's been contaminated, if any other classified systems have been compromised. . . . It's going to take awhile, Alan."

Alan felt like an amateur boxer who had barely survived one round with a pro. His body ached, his equilibrium was off, and his head was buzzing with a faint but familiar pressure.

"Tell me more about the downloads." That frightened Alan more than anything else.

"We'll have a better idea once we find the laptop. If it's been tampered with, then we'll know for sure."

"The laptop's not here?"

"No. It might be at Gardner's private practice. I got guys there right now tearing up his office."

Again Alan felt his world go out of focus. If Munn's scenario was correct—and Alan had every reason to believe it was—then it was highly probable that a patient was out there with documented evidence linking the FBI to a classified government research program.

A sickening flash of what was to come hit him: waking up one morning and seeing the program as front-page news, in-depth reporting on CNN . . . Christ, Jesus H. fucking Christ.

"We have to find him," Alan said, nauseous. He took in a deep breath. "We have any idea where he is?"

"No missing report has been filed. He's old and lives alone. And I just started sorting through his financial stuff." Munn waved to the papers spread out before him. "There is one interesting item. On June seventh, he cleaned out his savings account to the tune of one point six million. It was a wire transfer."

"To where?"

"A bank in the Cayman Islands. We're tracking it down. My guess is that the Cayman account's cleaned out. As for Gardner himself, my gut tells me he's fish chum."

Alan stared at Munn. They were looking at the possibility of a national scandal, and Munn was treating it with the energy given to a bowl of cornflakes. But this was Munn's approach to everything, and it reminded Alan of that Christmas party three years ago when Munn's wife, Anne—now his ex-wife—told her husband they were to be grandparents. Munn's face never registered any excitement. When a colleague asked if Henry was happy, jokingly prodding him if in fact he ever got excited about anything, Munn's wife said with a mean-spirited laugh that Henry had the same expression when they had sex, and the only way she knew he was done was when he stopped moving.

The cellular phone on the island counter rang. As Munn reached for it, Alan grabbed his wrist and leaned closer. "We could be sitting on top of the nation's worst scandal, one that could bring down the FBI. You *do* realize that."

"Of course I do."

"I need answers, Henry, and I need them fast."

Alan released his grip and walked away, an icy vapor filling his heart.

chapter 8

MUNN'S WORDS RANG INSIDE ALAN'S HEAD LIKE A FIRE ALARM. All he could see was a patient handing over a stack of computer discs to an investigative reporter. Such as Tom Preston from the *New York Times.* If that Pulitzer Prize–winning prick got ahold of a story like this . . .

Stop it. This is getting you nowhere.

Of course it wasn't. He tried to refocus, but the image of waking up and seeing the program exposed kept playing over and over inside his head. His throat felt as if it were being squeezed by a pair of invisible hands.

He realized he was walking over the papers on the floor of a high-ceilinged study. Three agents were inside it. One was examining manila folders in a cabinet while another rummaged through the drawers of a massive mahogany desk. The third agent, the one he had seen moments earlier examining the books, was now sifting through the contents of a wall safe. They all seemed to glance up at him at once; then they caught the look on his face and turned their energy back to their work.

A stone balcony was attached to the study. The glass door leading out to the balcony was open. He walked outside and shut the door behind him. The air was still cool, and slivers of yellow light burned across the tops of the surrounding homes.

You better get ahold of yourself, Alan, before you have heart-attack number three. You collapse here, you'll have to run the investigation from your hospital bed. You want that to happen?

No. No, of course not. He needed to think. And he couldn't think clearly if he was angry.

Solve the problem.

Right. Solve the problem. He was a pro at getting himself out of situations. His whole life—hell, his entire career—had been based on his ability to maneuver his way through obstacles.

Pacing, Alan started to regulate his breathing. He focused his attention on the waves breaking in the not-so-far distance. Moments later, his heartbeat under control, he was back inside his head, reviewing the problem.

The Behavioral Modification Program was his brainchild. The idea had come to him back when the department had just formed a small unit called Behavioral Sciences, his staff of four agents traveling across the country to interview all the serial killers in captivity.

They all came from broken homes, he had discovered. The father was almost always nonexistent, his role nothing more than the accidental sperm donor, and if he was the type to linger, the love for his son was usually expressed through beatings, psychological degradation, and more often than not sexual abuse. The mother usually did nothing to stop it. Like the father, she was absent most of the time, often a drunk or a prostitute, and if she did work, it was always in some sort of menial capacity. Meals came in shrink-wrapped containers along with cans of soda.

Soon, the years of psychological pain formed a complicated fantasy that promised relief in the blood and screams of a victim, usually a woman. Later her mutilated body would be tossed aside like an empty food container.

For a while afterward, the killer would reenter society, acting normal, feeling a renewed sense of self and confidence in his future. Then the pain would force him back down into depression and despair, and he would revert to the rush of innocent blood washed across his skin.

Once the killing started, there was no chance at rehabilitation. The FBI profilers who would later work their cases were nothing more than cleanup men. This approach to solving violent crime was reactive, not proactive.

The Behavioral Modification Program changed all that.

Mental health care professionals associated with the program found children from their dealings with DSS and private practice. The program removed these violent children from their trailer-park existence and provided them with a new life in a stable foster home with loving parents; educational opportunities all the way up to college, even graduate school; private therapy with psychologists; psychiatric reviews and access to cutting-edge medication. Later came job and housing opportunities and the chance to become a productive member of society—the whole package made possible by a joint effort between the FBI and the federal government.

Were there problems? Of course. Naturally some children were tougher to rehabilitate. Their stints in juvenile prisons, psychiatric hospitals, the unknown level of sexual and physical abuse they had suffered during their formative years, sometimes left psychological scars unreachable by intensive therapy—mental wounds that ran so deep that not even medication could heal them. And then there were those rare biological misfits who for reasons unknown had been hardwired for violence back in the womb. No amount of emotional stability, no therapy or combination of medicines, could successfully erase the dark needs from their blood. For lack of a better definition, they were evil.

Yes, there were problems; they were to be expected. But there were *successes.* Not only did the program heal lives, it *saved* the lives of possible future victims.

But the public cares little about success stories. Show them statistics and case studies, give them testimonies of men who had transformed themselves into well-educated, well-adjusted adults, and what does it do? It *yawns.* The public wants to know about the failures, the more titillating the better. God knows there had been failures. During the program's infancy, there had been a few outright disasters, but they had been fixed, cleaned up, and forgotten. The failures didn't matter, especially when you stacked them against all the lives saved.

But not with the public. Throw them one bad apple with the label "patient from top-secret government program" and suddenly it's all over the TV and the papers, and soon you have the nation talking conspiracy theories. Why? Because the public was dumb. They listened more to tabloid shows, to Oliver Stone conspiracy movies, and the events portrayed in TV shows than they did the truth. A sad state of affairs, but undeniably true.

And don't forget the Internet. If Munn's patient scenario is true and the patient decides to unleash downloaded documents, the whole world will know in a matter of seconds.

Alan heard the sound of loafers behind him. "What is it, Henry?" he asked without turning around.

Munn came up and stood next to him, placed both hands on the railing, and looked out at the water, a wooden coffee stirrer working in his jaw. He squinted in the early-morning sunshine.

"Gardner booked a one-way plane ticket to Russia on June tenth. Paid for it with his American Express. According to the flight records, he was on board."

The rage that had consumed Alan just moments earlier had suddenly evaporated. He was composed now. Focused. "So we're supposed to believe Gardner accessed the BMP database, downloaded patient files, top-secret government documents, then fled the country to sell it to the Soviets?"

"That's what this yahoo wants us to believe. The Soviet angle's not good. They're not a global player anymore. Maybe the Chinese, but not the Soviets."

"Christ."

"Maybe this scenario would make sense if it weren't for some major inconsistencies in Gardner's investment portfolio. The guy only cashed in his savings. With his IRA accounts and stocks he's worth over eight and a half mil, and that's not including this house or those shitty paintings he's got hanging all over the walls."

So if he really did sell out, it makes sense to cash everything. If you're going to be on the run, you'll need every goddamn cent. It doesn't make sense to leave that kind of money behind.

"Besides, the guy's got no reason to sell out," Munn said. "Even if it was Gardner who got on to the classified systems, there ain't a country in the world that's going to give him big bucks all in one lump sum."

"And he wouldn't use his American Express card to book a getaway flight."

"Or book it in his name. Not only that, he left his passport here. It was in the wall safe." Munn rubbed the corner of his lip with his thumb. "Someone's trying to make us look the other way."

Alan sighed. "Seems so."

"One more thing. My guys just got through searching Gardner's private practice. They didn't find the laptop, and it's not here in the house. There's only one other place to look."

Munn was referring to the FBI's classified-research building in La Jolla.

"My guys are fifteen minutes away from it," Munn said. "You want me to send them over there?"

"The place is tighter than a flea's ass. You need keycards and access codes—and there's the thermal-imaging recognition system. It's a goddamn vault. I'll have to figure out a way to get you in there without alerting the higher-ups."

Munn turned away from the ocean. "You tell Paris what's going on?" Paris was the director of the FBI.

Alan looked up at him. "What the fuck do you think?"

Munn nodded, his face expressionless. "You think that's wise? He's got access to services we don't."

"Paris is looking for an excuse to fire me. Besides, we tell him this, he'll fuck it up. The guy needs directions on how to jerk off."

No laugh from Munn, just that deadpan expression. "We'll find this one, Alan. We always do."

Alan didn't say anything. A bead of sweat ran down his forehead; he saw it splash on his palm. Something told him this time was going to be different.

chapter 9

KODADJO, MAINE, WAS THE PERFECT PLACE TO GO IF YOU WANTED TO DROP OFF THE PLANET. The town was located at the state's northern tip, not far from the Canadian border, and was not so much a town as deep woods with addresses identifiable through handwritten names on wood planks nailed to the trees. The houses were set back far from the road, some of them miles apart from each other, all of them a lifetime away from any trace of civilization. The farther he drove down the winding roads, the more he felt as if he were traveling back through time.

It was a strange place for an FBI profiler responsible for solving twenty-three serial-murder investigations to make his home.

Malcolm Fletcher's house was, like the others, set back from the road and had a driveway of packed dirt and a lawn of weeds and brown pine needles. But the plot itself had been cleared of trees, and a two-story, brown structure with a new coat of paint sat under a wide oval patch of blue sky. The partially stained deck looked new and stretched across the front of the house. All of the windows were open. Classical music—Tchaikovsky, Jack recognized—played in the morning air.

He walked up the driveway, noting a brand-new silver Ford F-250 pickup in the garage. He walked up to the porch; the door behind the screen was open. Inside he could see a small kitchen that extended into a living room with an L-shaped couch, bookcases built into the wall, and a nineteen-inch TV tuned to a news program. Good, he thought with a sense of relief. The man was home.

Jack rang the doorbell. Waited. Rang it again. Then he tried knocking and calling out Fletcher's name. Nothing.

Maybe he's stepped out. But where? The closest neighbor was six miles away. *He's got to be around,* Jack thought. *Maybe he went for a jog.* Jack didn't think the people here were big on personal fitness, but the idea was possible. Whatever the reason, he had only one choice.

He would have to wait.

It was shortly after 8 A.M., and the air was already thick with humidity. Sweat ran down Jack's forehead and back, and his jeans and T-shirt were already damp. He placed an expandable file folder on the unstained deck floor and sat against the railing. Woods surrounded him. Between the gaps in the soft, classical music, he could hear bugs whining in the distance.

He had gone something like thirty-six hours without sleep; his eyes felt as if sand were trapped behind the lids, and a dull throb was building steadily in his temples. His body was running on a high-speed buzz of too much caffeine, his thoughts scattered like cars fishtailing over patches of ice. Right now he felt a detached distance from his surroundings, as if this place were nothing more than a manufactured dream. There was no way he could drive home without pulling over to the side of the road and taking a nap.

What made him come had more to do with his conversation with Mike than the Sandman himself. Fact: the Marblehead force had never encountered anything like this (*And neither have I,* Jack had admitted privately), and the state police, while helpful, lacked the necessary experience to see this through, which meant that he had to shoulder the entire investigation. Fact: he was dealing with a clever, organized psychopath whose life's purpose was fueled by a rage that he had been building for years. Right now the Sandman was amused. Corner him, and the son of a bitch could plant a bomb at the station or under Jack's car—there was no way to predict when it would happen, but it was definitely coming. On some level he could deal with it, but when he thought about Taylor . . . it was as if he were suffocating.

There was also another truth, one that was easier to admit on the long ride up here. His imagination and its . . . projection, you could call it, could no longer be trusted. It had betrayed him years ago and cost him his wife's life. Unlock it from its prison, let it roam unleashed inside his head, and yes, it would tell him things about the Sandman, but it would also resurrect dangerous images and feelings. Privately, he could admit it might destroy him.

Fact: Mike was right. He couldn't handle this one alone.

But if you don't get this guy Fletcher on board, then you may have to.

"He ain't in dare," a voice said.

Jack opened his eyes. Standing in the shade of the driveway was a painfully thin boy of maybe sixteen. His cutoff dungaree shorts hung loosely off his hips, and his tight gray T-shirt had rotted into cheesecloth. The black high-top sneakers, mended with strips of black electrician's tape, were missing their laces. The boy was covered head to toe with streaks of dirt.

"You mean Malcolm Fletcher?" Jack said. "This is his home, right?"

The boy blinked rapidly, his eyes dancing with a manic energy and staring off at images only he could see. "I just done told you he's not in dare. You got . . . You must got shit in your ears."

"Do you know where he is?"

"Out *here.*" The boy made sweeping gestures with both arms.

"Where?"

"You best not skunk around here."

Jack opened his mouth, the words already formed on his tongue, and then shut it. There was no point in asking the boy questions. He was operating on burnt fuses.

Jack looked around the woods and wiped the beads of sweat from his face. All he could see were tall pine trees and dirt. Where was Fletcher? Or was he inside the house, unable to hear the knocking on the door? In college Jack had a roommate who could sleep through fire alarms. If Fletcher was one of those people, he wouldn't hear the doorbell or knocking, especially above the music.

Jack reached for his file folder, stood back up, opened the screen door, and stepped inside. He didn't feel right doing it, but the long ride here, the exhaustion, and the anxiety that was welling inside his heart made it seem justified.

He put the file folder on the kitchen table, walked to the foot of the stairs, and looked up. The bathroom door was wide open and filled with shade; so were the two doors on each side. No lights were on, but the music was clearly coming from one of the upstairs rooms.

"Mr. Fletcher, are you there?"

Jack waited. Outside, over the music, he could hear the boy's sneakers digging into the gravel.

"Mr. Fletcher?"

He walked back through the living room, past the TV and L-shaped couch, to the grouping of windows that overlooked the deck and the seemingly infinite expanse of woods. The living room was a fifteen-by-fifteen square that was clean and neat and devoid of the knickknacks, letters, magazines, and personal items that would hint at the personality of the owner. The only clues came from the laptop computer that rested on top of a low maple coffee table and the bookcases that filled the wall behind the TV. Mostly computer and electrical textbooks and manuals filled the shelves, but there were several hardcover titles in German, French, and Latin. He recognized one, *Le Morte d'Arthur,* its cover a lime green, the title along the spine embossed in gold lettering that had flecked in several places. He picked it up and thumbed through it. The pages were yellowed and watermarked. The words were in French.

A former profiler who caught an unheard-of number of serials and can read foreign languages is up here in the middle of nowhere, living in a shack with a computer but no phone. What's wrong with this picture?

The music shut off.

"A burglar who can read. My, isn't that refreshing," a voice behind him said.

Jack wheeled. A man was standing by the kitchen table, his left hand clasped on top of the file folder, the other hidden behind his back.

"Are you Malcolm Fletcher?"

The man smiled. "Were you expecting someone else?"

chapter 10

MALCOLM FLETCHER WAS WELL OVER SIX FEET TALL; HIS HEAD WAS JUST INCHES FROM THE CEILING. The skin of his lightly tanned face was stretched tight across the bone and free of wrinkles and lines, making it impossible to guess his age, and his thick arms were long and corded with blue ropes of veins. His chest and shoulders looked as if they had been pumped full of hardened concrete. He wore black pants, black utility boots, and a black pocket T-shirt stretched so tight it looked to be about to tear.

But it was the man's eyes that held your attention. The pupils and irises had formed into pitch-black pools the size of a quarter; they stared at Jack, the gaze intense and calculating, like a man who had sighted an intruder in his home and was deciding what act would cleanse the violation from his blood.

"*Le Morte d'Arthur.* Interesting that you would have picked that particular title." His voice was smooth, almost hypnotic. There was also a faint hint of an accent, maybe English, but Jack couldn't be sure. "Have you read it?"

"Years ago, back in college."

"Give me your impression."

"Unfortunately, I don't remember much of it."

"The work explores the rise and fall of a powerful kingdom. The forces that create it are also responsible for its destruction."

"I'll have to reread it sometime." Jack put the book back. "Mr. Fletcher, my name is—"

"Jack Casey."

Hearing his name cut through his tired haze; his mouth opened in surprise, his eyes blinking several times before they narrowed.

Fletcher came three steps closer. His movements seemed calculated, like a scorpion closing in on its prey. A sneer tugged at the corner of his mouth.

The hand behind his back came up swiftly. Held between the long fingers was a thin black wallet containing a police shield and Jack's identification.

"You were in my *car.*"

"More specifically, your glove compartment." Fletcher's eyebrows danced twice, his eyes wide and still and locked on Jack's.

Why did he search my car? Jack's curiosity outweighed his sense of violation. "What were you doing in my car?"

"Research. It's not every day I come home to find someone sneaking around my home."

"I wasn't sneaking."

"What would you call it then? Breaking and entering?" The tone was polite, almost playful.

"I rang the doorbell twice. I heard the music and thought you might not have heard me—"

"So you decided to let yourself in and inspect my belongings." Fletcher smiled.

Jack took in a long, deep breath. He thought about the long ride home and couldn't bear the idea of leaving here empty-handed.

"Let's start over," he said with a tired smile. "My name's Jack Casey. I'm a detective from Massachusetts. I drove up here so I could talk to you about a case I'm working on, hoping I could hire you on as a consultant."

"Drove up here from"—Fletcher looked at the ID—"Marblehead, Massachusetts."

"Yes, that's right."

"On the North Shore."

"You've been there?"

Fletcher grinned pleasantly. "Lots of designer clothing and kisses at the country club. Has Muffs tired of the new Lexus? Oh, dear, Chandler has to choose between Harvard and Yale. What in the world will he do?"

"Something like that. How long were you in town?"

"I wasn't." Fletcher lowered the wallet and folded it over one finger. "The gun in your hip holster, what is it? Nine-millimeter what?"

"Beretta, ninety-two F."

"French model, twenty-shot clip."

"That's right."

"Rather grand for a small town. The salary must be nice. I don't know many homegrown dicks who can afford antique Porsche cars."

"It's a friend's." When Jack had told Taylor he had to drive to Maine, she had forbidden him to take the rental. When her new Ford Expedition wouldn't start, she handed him the keys to her vintage '62 Porsche 356. Her little silver bullet, Taylor called it.

"Tell me, Detective Casey, do your fellow officers carry members of the nine-millimeter family?"

"No. Most of them carry thirty-eights."

"And yet you insist on being different."

Jack was about to speak when he heard screaming. He broke away from Fletcher's intense gaze and, through the grouping of windows above the kitchen table, saw the boy roaming out near the deck, his face bright red, locked in a heated argument with his invisible tormentors.

Fletcher didn't turn around once. "Did you meet Charlie?"

"Who?"

"Charlie, the boy standing outside my house. Did you talk with him?"

"Briefly."

"How would you describe his dementia praecox?"

"His what?"

"His mental condition."

Jack stared at him.

"Are you stumped, Detective Casey, or are you still racking your brain for an answer?"

"Paranoid schizophrenia."

"Yes. The incongruous mood swings and monosyllabic speech patterns were the telltale signs when he turned fifteen four years ago. Did you get a good look at his face? It's twisted, like a Goya etching."

Jack decided to pursue it, to get a feel for Fletcher's own abilities. "What have his parents done about it?"

"They blame his fitful episodes on puberty. They think his hallucinations and voices are all part of Charlie expressing his frustration. If they weren't three generations in the woods, they would realize biology is the culprit. I wouldn't be surprised if a CAT scan revealed lesions on the cingulate cortex. Such are the benefits of inbreeding."

"You've had medical training."

"No. I just know where to look."

"Why haven't you helped him? A man with your intelligence would know where to get him treatment."

"What would you suggest?"

"Medication."

"Such as?"

Jack thought about it for a moment. "Clozaril."

"Charlie's already showing signs of akenetic mutism. The dopamine roller coaster he's locked on is leading him towards suicide or catatonia. Treatment with Clozaril would lift the fog, but where would that leave him? Reality isn't as forgiving as the voices he hears. He's better off lost in the comforts of his own delusions. He knows that monochromatic landscape well."

"That's an interesting opinion."

"Who gave you my name?"

"A criminal-profiling coordinator from the FBI's Boston office."

"The Federal Bureau of Investigation isn't in the business of farming out information. You'll have to do better than that if you want my help."

"Mike Abrams."

"I don't know him."

"He's the one who gave me your name. He discovered your name on some old case files. I understand you solved twenty-three serial-murder investigations. That's quite an impressive accomplishment."

Charlie stopped screaming. Jack shifted his eyes to the window and saw the boy, his face a dark red and spittle flying from his mouth, beating a tree as if it were about to cause him grave injury.

"This case I'm working on, the killer ties a person up to a bed and then forces him to watch the other family members being butchered. Then the killer calls nine-one-one and disguises his voice with a voice-altering device and plants a bomb inside each house. Last month he killed two Marblehead cops with a bomb made out of C-4."

Fletcher listened, his eyes absolutely still, his face devoid of emotion, as if he measured each word against an already prescribed action.

"I would have called, but we couldn't locate a phone number," Jack said.

"I don't own one."

"But you own a computer."

"You must be at your wit's end to drive all the way up here." Fletcher's head tilted to the side as if a thought had threaded its way deep inside. His eyes were like two black holes that sucked the dim sunlight out of the small room. "You strike me as a man with imagination."

"I'd like to talk with you about this case. Could I have a moment of your time?"

Fletcher didn't answer, just stared with that dead, unnerving gaze. Jack stared back at him, gripped with the strange feeling that the man was inside the dark corridors of his mind, trying to take a personal inventory of his hidden wounds, fears, secrets, and desires.

Then, as if he had discovered something amusing, Fletcher grinned and tossed the wallet badge over to Jack.

"Have a seat, Detective Casey. I have the strangest feeling that this will be interesting."

chapter 11

JACK SAT IN FRONT OF THE GROUPING OF WINDOWS. He unwrapped the elastic band from the file folder, flipped open the top, and started removing the contents, arranging them in front of Fletcher like an exhibit. The morning sun had broken over the tops of the trees; soft yellow blades of light poured over the back of Jack's neck and splashed onto the table.

"What has VICAP told you?" Fletcher asked. He sat with both elbows propped up on the table, his chin resting on his thumbs and his fingers interlocked. His eyes never blinked.

"I haven't consulted the database."

"Why not?"

"I don't place much faith in computers." Jack looked away. He placed next to Fletcher's elbow the Olympus tape recorder containing his conversation with the Sandman.

"That's surprising. Usually your generation abandons original thought at the altar of technology. Do you know how many cases VICAP has solved?"

Jack leaned back in his chair. "Zero."

"Not very impressive for a multimillion-dollar system."

Specs of dust as bright as diamonds danced in the blade of light washing over Fletcher's face. Even in the sunlight, his eyes were black and luminous.

Jack cupped his fingers around the stack of the Dolan family snapshots he had found on the nightstand. Fletcher's eyes didn't move down to the pictures; they stared straight ahead, as lifeless and still as marbles.

"This is the second family, the Dolans," Jack said. "Fortunately, the bomb didn't go off so we were able to process the crime scene. These were next to the bed. I believe the Sandman went through them and left—"

"The *Sandman.*" Fletcher laughed, a deep, throaty sound that was neither pleasing nor inviting. "Did you come up with that ridiculous name?"

"No. It's what the killer calls himself. I talked to him last night. I have a tape of the conversation." Jack moved his hand to the tape recorder.

"Did you play the tape for your peers?"

"No."

"Hmmm." Fletcher's eyes narrowed. "Do you have a girlfriend, Detective Casey?"

Jack tried to follow Fletcher's train of thought. "A girlfriend?"

"Yes. A girlfriend—or boyfriend. Someone you fuck on an exclusive basis."

"I'm involved with a woman. Why?"

"You were at this woman's house when he called."

Jack felt a chill of surprise. "Yes. How did you know?"

"He'd want to call you where you felt safe—to demonstrate that he is in control and you are not. He threatened to harm her if you didn't back away, didn't he?"

"Your insight is impressive."

"But that's not why you're here, is it?" Fletcher grinned.

Jack tapped the top picture: Veronica Dolan standing in the waters of some tropical island, wearing a red bikini that complimented her full body. Her hands were cupped under her young son's armpits; Alex Dolan's face was alight with laughter, his mother's smile full of warmth.

Jack had specifically chosen this picture because it had triggered an emotional reaction in him. Now he was hoping that the sight of her and her son, or maybe the beauty of her body or smile, would cause Fletcher to look through the others and awaken some sort of emotional need or memory.

But Fletcher wouldn't look down. Jack picked up the picture and held it directly below the man's line of vision.

"This is Veronica Dolan, the one tied to the bed and forced to watch her family die."

Fletcher was still staring at him. Jack waited. He could hear the boy's rantings in the not-so-far distance.

"Aren't you going to look at it?"

"What you want is for me to look at them in the hope of procuring some sort of emotional response. Boring. Very cliché."

"I thought you might see something in these pictures that I didn't."

"A man with your background should have a more polished approach."

Jack returned the picture to the stack. He folded his hands on the table and waited.

"How did she die?"

"She was strangled," Jack said.

"And the one from last month?"

"The bomb killed him."

"Him. Ah. A male *and* female victim. Atypical. What about the other family members? What happened to them?"

"They were tied to chairs and arranged around the bed. Their throats were slashed."

"Single or multiple cuts?"

"Single, as far as I can tell."

"And the tool used?"

"I don't know. Their bodies were destroyed by the blast." What little they had found had washed up on the shore and was useless.

"Use your imagination."

"It would be something intimidating, like a hunting knife with a long, wide blade."

"Why not a knife from the house?"

"That would suggest he isn't prepared, that he isn't in control. He's rehearsed this moment thousands of times in his head. Everything's been thought out."

"Why does he tie them to the bed?"

"Humiliation. Fear. Hopelessness." Jack cleared the images that flashed in his eyes. "It's the ultimate form of punishment."

"Did I hit a nerve, Detective Casey?"

"Why do you think he tied them to the bed?"

"For the same reasons you just mentioned. The first one, what was his occupation?"

"A psychiatrist for Bridgewater State Hospital for the Criminally Insane. We're going through his patient records, seeing if there's a connection there."

"And the woman?"

"As far as I can tell, a housewife. We're still digging."

"What about the bombs?"

"The first one was made with C-4. The triggering mechanism was an infrared beam placed across the door. When I opened it, the bomb's timer was initiated. That's all we know."

"And the second bomb malfunctioned."

"That's right."

"How was it constructed?"

"A laptop computer hooked up to the phone line. One phone call would have set off the six blocks of Semtex-H. Fortunately it malfunctioned and we were able to process the crime scene."

"An improvised explosive device detonated by a phone call," Fletcher said. "Very sophisticated. Are you familiar with Semtex-H?"

"It's a Russian-made terrorist explosive."

"Who told you this?"

"The bomb expert I have working on the case."

"Is the Bureau involved?"

"I've contacted the Explosives Unit. They're running the bomb fragments through their Rapid Start system to—"

"What do you think the Bureau's bomb expert will say regarding the excessive amounts of explosives at the crime scene?"

"I haven't talked to them about it yet."

"Then enthrall me with your analysis."

"I believe the extra blocks are an insurance policy. He doesn't want us to find any evidence. And I think he has a grudge against the police."

"Because he calls nine-one-one?"

"That and because he waits until we arrive to initiate the bomb."

"Bombs gain attention. Not the best method to use to keep your activities quiet."

"I think he wants the attention."

"Why?"

"He's killing these victims out of revenge. My feeling is that he wants the media to focus in on him so he can expose how these people hurt him."

Fletcher collapsed his hands on the table and leaned forward. "Usually small-town dicks are barren of original thought—but not you, Detective Casey. *You* are decidedly *different.*"

Fletcher smiled politely. Jack waited for him to elaborate. When he didn't, Jack said, "I'm not sure what you're getting at."

"You show traces of imagination. You can think. Yet you drove all the way up here to find a man you've never even met. You break into this house—"

"I didn't break into your house."

"—and here you are, asking me for my assistance when you're perfectly capable of catching this man yourself. Such an action would normally smack of desperation, but you're not desperate, are you? No, Detective Casey, you are here for a different reason altogether."

"I told you I want to hire you as a consultant. I can use a man with your knowledge and expertise."

"It's more than that. Some scars, Detective Casey, are more transparent than others."

Fletcher's eyes were hot and seemed to be drilling past Jack's guarded gaze and staring at the back of his skull. In his mind Jack heard doors shut and lock, felt walls go up. *First the Sandman, and now this guy. Am I that transparent?*

A phone rang.

"Maybe this will give me the answer I'm looking for," Fletcher said.

Fletcher reached behind him and placed on the table a Samsung cellular phone. At least that's what it looked like. He pressed a button and the cell phone flipped open like a briefcase. From where Jack was sitting, he could see part of a screen and a small keyboard. The phone was actually a small computer.

Fletcher was reading the words on the screen. His right hand slid away from the table.

"Special Agent Jack Casey." Fletcher looked up, a grin tugging at the corner of his mouth, his eyes wide and perfectly still. "You're a *profiler.*"

"Was. I left the Bureau years ago."

Fletcher's eyes were now threaded with a liquid light. "Why are you here, Detective Casey?"

"I told you, to hire you as a consultant."

Fletcher's right hand came up lightning quick, and the next thing Jack felt was the barrel of a gun pressed firmly against the center of his forehead. It was a nine-millimeter Glock.

"No sudden movements please. It's too hot to clean up." Fletcher's tone was still polite and calm.

"Whatever you say," Jack said, the words coming out more angry than afraid.

"Now reach in and grab your gun."

Jack slid his hand over the gun, his thumb clicking off the safety. *Play it cool,* a voice said. *Just play it cool and get the fuck out of here.*

"That's it, put it on the table, keep your hands there. Very good. Now, who else is here with you?"

"I'm here alone."

"I don't believe you."

"Tough shit."

Fletcher cocked the trigger. Jack's heartbeat quickened.

You're deep in the sticks, nobody knows you're here, and this maniac has a gun cocked and pointed at your head. For chrissakes, don't challenge him, just do what he says.

"I told you, I'm here alone. If you don't believe me, call the Marblehead police station. They know I'm here. Ask them to describe me. I'll give you the number."

Fletcher's eyes seemed to be focused inward; Jack couldn't tell for sure. But for a brief moment he thought he saw something spark in those wide, black pools: amusement.

"Make the phone call," Jack said. "You don't want to make a mistake here."

Jack watched Fletcher's index finger slide up and down the trigger. His heart leapt.

"You're trapped in the role of a proselyte," Fletcher said. "Still looking for that one act of conversion that will heal those wounds."

"Look, I don't know what you're talking about, but you—"

"Try reading Camus's *The Myth of Sisyphus.* You'll find the similarities striking."

Jack opened his mouth to speak again; Fletcher pressed a finger to his lips and silenced him.

"It's time for you to take your exit."

chapter 12

THE FEDERAL FACILITY IN LA JOLLA IS A SIX-FLOOR BUILDING MADE OF MIRRORED GLASS, GIVING IT THE MODERN, FUTURISTIC LOOK USUALLY ASSOCIATED WITH LOS ANGELES. It was tucked at the end of a solitary road, several miles from downtown. An attached cafeteria sat on the edge of a cliff and overlooked the weathered cliffs and the Pacific. A set of concrete stairs led down from the restricted parking lot for the two-hundred-plus employees who worked here, but only a handful were actually associated with the Behavioral Modification Program; the rest were employed by companies that were working on federally funded projects, the majority of them classified.

Alan wasn't kidding when he described the building as a vault. The second Munn walked off the elevator, he was standing in a box lit up by a single canister light. In front of him was a thick steel door that was well over seven feet high and a paperback-book-sized unit that contained a keypad and a slot to insert the keycard. He slid his card inside and entered the eight-digit universal access code that would allow him entry to every room inside the building by disabling the thermal-imaging sensors that measured each person's heat signature and compared it to the one on file. He opened the door and then walked down a long corridor, wondering what kind of research projects warranted such sophisticated security measures.

He began negotiating the maze of narrow hallways and doors that required the keycard and access code. All the corridors were windowless and smelled of recycled air and carpet cleaner. Men and women, armed with briefcases, cell phones, pagers, their building ID badges, and keycards wrapped around their neck or clipped to their belt, whisked past him, their focus locked on the mounting concerns of their day. *You probably have to enter a special code to go to the bathroom,* he thought. *One to flush and the other one to allow you access to the toilet paper.*

Munn navigated his way through the fourth floor. He would search the doctor's office; Paul DeWitt was up on the sixth, heading to the Operations room, where the building's main computer and security systems were located. Each employee was assigned his own access code, which was logged on to the database. Paul wanted to see if the doctor had traveled to any of the restricted areas inside this facility.

Munn should have been focusing on the job. A lot was riding on this, he knew, but he was thinking of all of the sprawling mansions he had seen on the way here. His wife, Annie (*No, your ex-wife,* that pesky voice reminded him again), now lived in a similar home in Palm Beach, Florida, shacked up with a guy who had owned a software company that had been bought out by Microsoft for some obscene amount of money. She had been having an affair with the guy, Dale Pinkle (Munn still couldn't get over that name), for something like five years; the minute the geek cashed in for the big score she jumped ship for the flamboyant lifestyle. That was eight months ago. Packed up her valuables and took a first-class ride down to Florida—no warning, no note or phone call; she had simply disappeared. The private investigators he hired found her two months later. Annie wasn't coming home. That was all she said. After twenty-one years of marriage, he thought he deserved an explanation, something more than "not coming home."

The corridor ended and his attention shifted back to his job. Munn grabbed the sheet from his suit pocket and checked his map. This was the last of the series of hallways; here were three numbered doors, all on the right. Gardner's, number 496, was the last one.

Munn walked up to the door, slid the card into the slot, and entered the universal access code Alan had given him. The light turned red: access denied. That wasn't right. The universal access code was supposed to open every door inside the building.

On the last sheet was Gardner's access code. He slid the card back into the slot and gave Gardner's a try.

The light turned green and the lock clicked open.

"We're in business," he said aloud, and pushed open the door with his shoulder.

The light switch was on the wall directly by the door. He flipped it up, and halogen floor lamps lit up the far right wall. He entered a sitting room, the heavy door clicking shut behind him.

Six blue plastic chairs were arranged around a low glass coffee table holding magazines at least two years out-of-date. Framed Ansel Adam prints hung on the pale walls. A closed-circuit security camera was mounted over the door leading into the doctor's office.

He placed his forensic kit on the floor and then reached into his pocket for his latex gloves. Given the posh digs the guy lived in, he would have thought Gardner would have invested a few bucks in some colorful prints or, at the very least, some current magazine subscriptions. But the cheapness didn't surprise him. The rich ones spent lavishly on their own needs, but when it came to their employees, they were penny-tight and consumed with a yard-sale mentality. As a group, he found the rich boring and couldn't for the life of him understand why Annie would have fallen for one.

Annie is gone, Annie isn't coming home, get over it and get to work.

He picked up his kit, walked over to the final door, and slid his card inside the security unit mounted into the wall. Again he used Gardner's access code. Again the light turned green and the door clicked open.

He flipped on the lights. Whereas the waiting room was drab and functional, the doctor's office looked as if it had been decorated by Martha Stewart herself. The mahogany desk was as wide and long as a pool table. In the far left corner, behind the deep burgundy leather couch and chair, stood two dark credenzas containing Oriental vases and figurines. A private bathroom was on the left, directly behind the door. No keycard unit there.

The blinds across the floor-to-ceiling window were drawn shut. He walked across the Oriental carpet and used the string levers to pull them back. Bright sunlight exploded inside the room. From this high up, he could see more of the weathered cliffs and the waves crashing against them in white bursts of spray. He'd busted his ass his entire life in the gray-walled dungeon of Quantico, saving lives, and would never be offered such an office—or such a grand lifestyle. Annie, a housewife her whole life, was now fucking a geek who gave her a view like this every day. Funny how life turns around and rewards you for all your hard work.

You're doing it again, Henry.

He shook the thought away before it consumed him. He had a job to do.

According to Alan, for the past nine months the building's cleaning crew had come in once a week, on Saturdays, and emptied the trash, scrubbed the bathrooms, vacuumed the carpets, done a little dusting, maybe even cleaned the windows—all of which meant that evidence, mainly fingerprints, would be gone. He had expected that.

What he hadn't expected was how tidy the doctor's desk was. The blotter looked brand-new, and so did the neatly arranged white legal pads. A pen-and-pencil holder, a tape recorder, and a silver stapler were arranged perfectly next to the Tiffany lamp. It looked like an ad out of an office catalog. He pulled out the bottom desk drawer and saw that the hanging file folders were empty. The drawer above it was full of memo pads, boxes of pens, and a phone book, all neatly arranged.

He had seen Gardner's other office, the one at his private practice. That desk looked as if it had been organized by a cyclone. Post-it notes and scraps of paper were stuck between the pages of a thick personal organizer and to a calendar bloated with times, dates, and people's names. There were reams of therapy notes on yellow legal pads, all of them scattered, all of them written in Gardner's illegible scrawl. The metal, stackable bin in the corner was stuffed with folders, psychiatric journals, prescription pads, napkins, and so much crap that it looked like a trash bin.

Gardner may have been a millionaire shrink with a proper mansion, the closets full of top-of-the-line designer clothing, but in his business life, the man was an unorganized pig.

A cleaning lady wouldn't tidy up his desk—especially the drawers. Someone else was responsible for the neatness here.

Which means that when the patient was on the system, he found out the FBI was involved, and he knew that sooner or later we would come looking for him. So he cleaned up the office to wipe away his tracks.

Only it didn't work like that. You walk into a room, sit down, and touch things, no matter how carefully you cleaned up, you *were* going to leave trace evidence behind. With all the modern advances in forensics, it was borderline impossible not to find something.

Munn placed his kit on a chair seat, ready to get to work, when his eye caught something odd. On top of the chair were tiny white specks that looked like paint chips. He pressed his gloved finger on one and examined it in the sunlight.

The speck was roughly half the size of a pencil eraser. It wasn't a paint chip. On the other side were tiny threads, like cardboard fibers. Where had it come from?

He looked at the ceiling. A drop-in, composed of long, white, rectangular tiles. Had the speck come from there? Maybe maintenance people had been in here, working on the wiring in the ceiling. All that shifting of ceiling tiles, the place would be loaded with dust and these specs.

Munn sighed and looked around the room. Finally, his eyes drifted back up to the ceiling. The white spec seemed as good a place as any to start.

To get to the ceiling he would have to stand on the desk. The problem was that his knees had taken a beating during his high school football days, and now at the age of fifty, arthritis had successfully eaten away most of the cartilage; it took him almost a full minute of grunting to get up on the desk. Finally, he straightened, touched the tile with the tips of his fingers, and pushed it up and over the metal gridwork that held it in place.

White specks floated down on his arms like snow.

He reached inside his jacket and retrieved a small penlight. His face was flushed with exertion, his forehead damp—all from just climbing up on the desk and standing up. *This is how I'm going to spend the next phase of my life,* he thought grimly. He stood on his toes, his eyes barely making it over the top of the tile. Gently, he brought the penlight up. The thin, narrow beam washed across the rafters, and the wires that held metal gridwork to the beams and the heating vents. Between one of the vents and a diagonal sliver of metal he saw a small rectangular screen.

Gardner's laptop.

No. That can't be right. Maybe I'm looking at part of the building's computer system. This whole place is computer-operated.

The problem was that he could barely see above the tile. Munn forced himself up higher, his calves already straining from his weight: *Come on, Henry, just a little more.* Moving the penlight slightly, he saw the miniature video-camera device attached to the side of the computer—the retina-scanning device. Right next to it was the small keycard device where the doctor slipped his passcard to activate the laptop.

It was Gardner's laptop computer all right.

But why the hell is it up here?

That, of course, was the magic question.

His calves were burning, his muscles turning to jelly. Munn moved the penlight away, about to give his legs a rest, when he caught the blip of something flashing in the center of the black computer screen.

No. No, that's wrong, he thought. *There's nothing on the screen. Gardner's been missing for nine months now, there's no way the batteries would operate that long.*

Unless the laptop was being powered another way. The building's power supply? Had to be. That was the only goddamn thing that made sense.

But why is Gardner's laptop hooked up to the building's electricity? And what the hell is it doing up here?

Any thoughts he had disappeared when his eyes caught the tiny, blinking letters in the middle of the screen—no, wait, just wait a goddamn minute, they were numbers. He moved the light up at a different angle: 9:50. At first he thought it was the laptop's clock. That idea washed away when the numbers went from 9:50 to 9:49, then 9:48, 9:47, 9:46.

It wasn't a clock at all.

It was a countdown.

That rational part of his mind kicked in and started searching for an explanation. With growing fear, he looked around the ceiling tiles and rafters. He didn't have to look far.

A multicolored nest of wires lay at the base of the laptop and snaked across the tiles like a massive spiderweb. With the light he followed the wires until they ended on a brown-wrapped brick stamped in black: C-4.

Munn's eyes widened.

He was staring at a bomb.

chapter 13

THE OBVIOUS THING TO DO WAS TO PANIC—AND WITH THE BOMB THIS CLOSE, WITH DOZENS OF BLOCKS OF C-4 SPREAD ALL OVER THE CEILING, HE WAS DEFINITELY STARTING TO PANIC. He could feel it welling up inside him, choking off his ability to breathe and turning his knees weak. He put the emergency brake on the panic and started to think. When he was younger, Munn had learned the importance of thought over feeling; thinking solved problems; panic or anger only clouded your judgment and ability to navigate your way out of situations.

If the bomber was smart enough to hide a laptop computer up here for three months and avoid triggering it until the right access code was entered, then the possibility of built-in fail-safe mechanisms to prevent tampering was high. Munn had no knowledge of even basic bomb construction, let alone microcircuitry, so trying to disarm it before it blew was not an option.

Problem: You're four floors up in a building housing two-hundred-plus people, staring at a sophisticated IED that is loaded with enough plastic explosives to wipe out a small town. How are you going to get everyone out, and once you do, how are you going to get them away from the building?

Solution: a fire alarm.

And the alarm better disengage all of these goddamn keycard devices. Otherwise, we'll all be trapped inside here.

His eyes registered the clock one last time—8:28 left and counting—and recorded it. He looked around the office. There was no fire alarm, but sprinklers were mounted on the ceiling.

His dollar-basement necktie was made of rayon. Rayon didn't burn, it melted. He needed something that would burn and smoke. He padded down his pant pockets and felt it. Reaching in, he grabbed the cotton handkerchief

(hurry, Henry, goddamnit, hurry!)

and wrapped it around the sprinkler. Then he fished inside his pant pockets for his Zippo lighter, found it, and then held the flame on a corner of the handkerchief. A bright orange tongue started snaking through the cotton in small clouds of black and gray smoke. Tossing the lighter, he jumped down, daggers of pain exploding behind both knees, and reached for the phone on the corner of the desk, planning to call DeWitt.

There was no dial tone.

He hit the receiver and tried again. Nothing.

The fire alarm sounded and the sprinklers kicked on. Sprays of water showered the room. He raced for the office door, the water cold on his face, and yanked at it. The door was locked. *That can't be right,* he thought. There was no keycard device inside here; the door should open. He tried it again, but the son of a bitch wouldn't *open.*

The laptop's controlling this, has to be, it must be linked into the building's security system because the door only opened when I entered Gardner's access code, which must have activated the bomb, and now the fucking laptop has locked the door on me. HOW THE FUCK CAN THIS BE HAPPENING?

Panic began to eat its way through his composure; he swallowed it back. *Think. You're four floors up and you have to find a way out. THINK.*

The sound of the fire alarm drilled into his head. He turned away from the door and faced the room. Through the water, he saw the weathered cliffs outside the window.

Before the thought could complete itself, his right hand had removed his Glock from its holster. He stumbled through the cones of water, pointed the gun at the window, and started firing.

The roar was deafening. The first shot pierced the thick pane of glass in a spiderweb of cracks, but the window didn't shatter. Munn kept firing in a tight pattern. Then the hammer snapped dry and he felt his body sag in defeat. The window was peppered with holes but it remained intact.

Inserting another clip wasn't going to do it. Tossing the gun to the floor, he ran behind the desk, picked up the office chair by the seat and arms, took three steps forward, and with all of his weight and strength slammed the wheels into the window. The glass splintered some more but didn't break. Munn kept slamming the chair into the window, his face red with exertion. In the back of his mind he heard the sound of a clock ticking down.

"Come on you son of a bitch, COME ON!"

Suddenly the chair broke through the window and went sailing out of his hands in a shower of shards and a mist of water. Below him, dimly, he heard a scream.

The jagged hole was waist high and had the look of an open-mouthed shark. He kicked away the shards until there was enough room for him to move through. With one hand on the inside section of glass he forced his way through the opening, razor-sharp teeth biting through his clothes and digging into the skin on his shoulders, arms, and knees.

Munn wiped the water from his eyes. Four floors up, Jesus H. Christ, it seemed as if he were about to jump off the roof of a skyscraper. Below him was the chair and the shards of glass that sparkled like diamonds in sunlight. A steady line of people were moving out the front door—*they probably think this is a freakin' fire drill,* he thought—but a small crowd, off to the side of the others and closer to the sidewalk, were dividing their attention between the chair and the man waving to them from a shattered window on the fourth floor.

Munn cupped his hand over his mouth. *"GET AWAY! THERE'S A BOMB UP HERE GET AWAY!"*

That was all it took. People started scrambling in all directions. Munn looked up and saw the parking lot. Saw his rental car not far away at all, felt the keys digging into the skin of his thigh. To get to it, he would have to jump. He looked down at the ground.

You can't do it. The fall will kill you.

Time check, Henry. You got five minutes left and only one way down. You want to take a vote or do you want to get the fuck out of here?

With a small prayer, he let go of his grip on the inside of the window and pushed himself forward.

The ground came up in a rush. He mentally cushioned both his mind and body for the impact, firmly believing that he could survive. *Focus, think positive . . .* He hit the pavement with all of his weight, and the confidence that had been building burst like a balloon. He fell backward, his head slamming against the pavement.

His knees, Jesus H. fucking Christ, the roaring pain was worse than that day in Vietnam when he had stepped on a Bouncing Betty. His eyes wouldn't open, but his ears were working fine, and they were taking in everything: the screaming, the cars doors slamming shut, engines racing, and tires peeling against the ground.

Get up, goddamnit, get your ass UP!

Munn turned to his side and howled. Both knees felt as if they had been ripped off, and he was distinctly aware of a throbbing, wet wound on his right leg. He had to wait for the pain to subside. He couldn't move. Didn't *want* to.

A voice came roaring over the pain: *You got your ass up in Nam and managed to move, you can certainly do it now. Stop being a goddamn pussy and move, damn it, MOVE!*

He forced his eyes open and rolled onto his left side. Then he saw it: a spike of bone was sticking out from just under his right knee, which was hanging off to the side in a spray of blood. His other knee, he noticed, looked fine.

Goddamnit, you know what plastic explosives can do. Is that how you want to die? Torn apart and buried alive under a pile of rubble? Want to sit here when your car is just up those stairs?

The determination that had saved his ass in Vietnam was suddenly back, bringing along with it a new adrenaline rush that seemed to ease back the throttle on the pain. He rolled up onto his good knee and managed to force himself up. He stumbled over to the stairs.

Boy, you're almost out of time, you got maybe five minutes, and unless you want to be buried alive, you better haul ass and get up those stairs, move it, boy, PLENTY OF TIME, PLENTY OF TIME, SO MOVE IT MOVE IT MOVE IT!

Focus on the car.

That's what did it. The car was his way out of here. He had the keys and all he had to do was get inside and drive the fuck away. He kept hobbling forward, his arms windmilling like some sort of maniac, his breath coming in such hard, labored bursts that he wondered if his heart was going to quit.

Munn didn't know how he made it up the stairs without fainting or how he suddenly managed to jog across the lot with his right leg flapping uselessly beneath him. It didn't matter because there was the gray Buick right in front of him. But no sign of DeWitt. He fished the keys out of his pocket and prayed that the kid had the smarts to bolt.

He unlocked the door and threw himself behind the wheel. With his shaking hands he picked up his fractured right leg and draped it halfway over the passenger's side, the pain jolting through him so sharply that he felt as if his eyes were going to pop from their sockets. He would have to use his left leg to work the pedals.

Time's run out, a strange, eerily calm voice said.

"Fuck you."

He started the car, threw it into reverse, and punched the gas. The car lurched backward and came to a sudden, jolting stop when the back bumper slammed into a parked car. He jerked violently in his seat, throwing himself forward and slamming the gear into drive. With his good foot he slammed on the gas and went screaming through the lot.

The scene was like a demolition derby—cars slamming into each other, sometimes hitting people, everyone fighting to get first to the narrow opening that led to the main street and safety. But the lot's entrance/exit lane was a three-car pileup. Not that it mattered. Cars swerved past the pileup, bounced up over the curb, and fishtailed across the wet grass popping with lawn sprinklers.

He checked his mental clock.

Time's run out, the strange, calm voice said again, and this time Henry listened to it.

Don't you DARE give up, you chickenshit coward, you're almost there.

You still have a shot at catching the son of a bitch.

He didn't know how the idea came to him. His cell phone was on the seat next to him, and with his right hand he powered it on and quickly dialed with his thumb.

His own recorded greeting started playing. It was hard to hear his voice over the car crashes, but when the beep came, he yelled into the phone:

"Bomb was a laptop computer in ceiling hooked into building's security system, activated by Gardner's access code, C-4, on a timer in Gardner's office—"

An explosion roared through the air and shook the car. His eyes automatically jerked to the rearview mirror. Shredded furniture and plaster and glass from Gardner's office were flying through the air. The building, however, was still standing. *The building's still standing and the car is moving, I'm in one piece, thank you, God, thank you, O sweet Jesus.*

The second explosion ripped through the morning sky with such fury that his eardrums burst. Still looking in the rearview mirror, he saw the entire building blow apart, the sound roaring through his chest and numbing his heart, and the next sensation he had was of the car being tossed off the ground as if kicked by an angry god. Shards of glass filled his mouth and eyes, and the last memory Henry Munn had before he lost consciousness was of Annie on their wedding day, beautiful Annie smiling as she looked into his eyes and vowed to share in his life forever.

chapter 14

AT THE SAME TIME HENRY MUNN LOST CONSCIOUSNESS, JACK WAS STANDING ON THE SIDEWALK IN THE HOT SUNSHINE ON ATLANTIC AVENUE, LOOKING DOWN PRESTON WAY TO WHERE THE ROTH HOME HAD ONCE STOOD. The mangled cars from that night had been moved away; the remaining debris had been bulldozed into a neat ten-foot mountain that ran up from the sidewalk like a wall, hiding the decimated shells of blasted homes from view—all except one.

The two-story, white Cape on the corner of Atlantic and Preston was still standing—barely. Something large, probably a car, had plowed through the front door, taking down walls and furniture until finally coming to a stop between the living room and the kitchen. An elderly woman in a housedress, her doughy legs thick with varicose veins, her flabby arms pink with sunburn, trotted across the hills of rubble in a pair of sandals near the collapsed porch. Clasped in her arthritic hand were two silver-framed wedding pictures.

Normally Jack would have offered her some assistance. But he felt out of sorts, his equilibrium was off, and the world around him felt distant and somehow separated. The reason, he knew, had to do with the feeling that had gripped him moments ago at the station.

He had been standing inside his air-conditioned office staring at eight-by-ten color photographs of the blast site mounted on the display board when a voice from his profiling days tried to speak to him for the first time in over six years. He didn't hear the actual words, just jumbled parts. He waited for the voice to speak to him again, to offer up an image, something, but nothing came.

He was left with the feeling that he had overlooked some vital piece of information out at the Roth home. He couldn't explain where the feeling came from, just that it was there. So he had decided to drive out to the house and maybe find something that would resurrect the profiling voice from its grave.

"Hey, Jack."

He turned to his left and saw Barry Lentz, a twenty-eight-year-old patrolman, walking up Atlantic, a plastic tumbler cupped in one meaty hand. Lentz was tall, with strawberry-blond buzz-cut hair, and his freckled arms and face were bright red with sunburn. Last year he had married his high school sweetheart, who was, as Amanda had been, a kindergarten teacher. They had a two-month-old baby girl. Jack knew that Barry had recently applied to the Treasury. He wanted to be a Secret Service agent.

"What brings you out here?" Lentz asked.

"Just looking around," Jack said. "Everything all right?"

Lentz cocked one squinting eye down Preston. "You run into that guy yet?"

"What guy?"

"Reggie Kinter. Big fat guy, bald, wearing baggy jeans and a white polo shirt?"

"No. Who is he?"

"Reporter for the *Herald.* He was here rummaging around the Roth site, taking pictures."

"That all he was doing?"

"He saw me, came up with a smart-ass look on his face. Asked me why I was guarding the site of a gas explosion."

Jack believed the Sandman might come back to the Roth site to relive the event—the safer alternative to the Dolan home and gravesites, which were being watched around the clock. He had assigned Lentz and another patrolman, Jeff Clark, to be on the lookout for a white male between the ages of twenty-seven and thirty-five who might be taking a sudden interest in the blast site or start talking to the police—a favorite tactic employed by Ted Bundy. But the Sandman wasn't a serial killer—not in the true sense of the word—and would probably not behave like one.

"I told him I wasn't guarding anything, that I was down here patrolling the beach 'cause we've been having a lot of problems with some punks from Lynn," Lentz said. "Kinter smiles and then asks me about my thoughts on the Sandman. The monster that murders families in their sleep."

Surprise bloomed on Jack's face before he had a chance to stop it. "The Sandman? He used that word?"

"Yeah. It's the first time I heard it. That what you named this guy?"

"No." Jack had told no one at the station about the name.

Which meant the Sandman must have contacted Kinter directly. *Shit.*

Jack's mind flashed forward. Once the story broke, the town would be covered with reporters and photographers; then there would be the crank calls, all of which would have to be investigated. Every strange noise someone heard in the middle of the night would be the Sandman trying to sneak into the house. And there would be the fake bomb threats, of course. Christ, he could see how the whole mess was going to play out.

"I say something wrong?" Lentz asked.

"No. No, you didn't. This guy Kinter, he ask you anything else?"

"Yeah. He wanted to know why the Dolan bomb malfunctioned."

Wonderful. "What did you tell him?"

"That I didn't have a clue to what he was talking about. Then he . . ." Lentz drifted off, looked to the ground.

"Then he what?"

"He started in with questions about your FBI days. Stuff about Hamilton and"—Lentz made a clearing sound in his throat, then looked back up—"what happened to, you know . . ."

"What happened to my wife."

Lentz didn't say anything. Jack just nodded.

"Okay. Anything else?" Jack said, growing impatient. He wanted to get away from Barry, get down to the debris.

"Kinter had some questions on those serial cases you worked on, started talking about a guy—shit, what was his name? A guy from upstate Vermont who was kidnapping little boys and putting them in cages—"

"Charles Yerkies." Jack felt his heart quicken.

"Right, that's him."

"What did he want to know about Yerkies?"

"I don't know because I didn't give him the chance to ask. I told him that you were a good detective, that Marblehead was lucky to have you, and that any questions about your personal and professional life were none of my business. That's when he gets this shit-eating grin on his face and says, 'Tell Casey that it would be in his best interest to call me.' "

Jack looked down the street at the rubble. Then his eyes shifted over to the crowds of people packed on the beach. He knew where all this was leading and didn't want to think about it.

"Why all the questions about you?"

"The stuff about my wife, the cases I worked on, it's all a matter of public record. He was fishing."

"The killer's feeding him information, isn't he? So he can cast the spotlight on himself and what he's doing here."

Not bad, Barry, Jack thought.

"This guy, the Sandman . . . you got any thoughts on him yet?" Lentz asked.

It was the question everyone at the station was asking him, and each time it grated on his nerves like an iron claw scraping across a chalkboard. It wasn't the question that bothered him; it was that look of uneasy curiosity in their eyes, as if he possessed some sort of sinister black magic that allowed him access to a dark river of thoughts that normal men didn't have.

"I'm still working on it," Jack said. "Do me a favor. See that woman over there in front of her house? Go give her a hand. She looks like she's going to pass out."

"Sure, no problem. Oh, hey, I meant to tell you. I got in."

"That's great, Barry. Congratulations." Jack shook his hand.

"I owe part of it to you. If you hadn't've put me in touch with the right people, helped me get the right recommendations and all that, I wouldn't be on my way."

"You got in on your own merit, Barry. I had nothing to do with it."

"Well, I want to thank you. Hey, maybe this weekend, why don't you come over to the house, let me and Patty cook you dinner? Our way of saying thanks."

Jack thought about watching Barry and his wife, Patty, playing with their infant daughter and felt a painful squeeze in his heart.

"This weekend might not be too good."

"Okay. Check your calendar and get back to me. We'd love to have you over. Oh, and bring your girlfriend too. We promise not to grill her on all those famous people she knows."

Jack watched as Barry ran to help the woman. That was the luxury of being in your twenties. Always eager, always willing to do or say anything to secure your place in this world.

Jack walked toward the beach. The hot air was swollen with the thumping of dance music, the pounding of the surf, the cries of seagulls, chatter and laughter and screams and inaudible bits of conversation. Jack's eyes settled on a middle-aged father who was letting his three young boys bury him in the sand and suddenly felt like a foreigner in a distant land.

On Jack's left was the island of trees. The grass had been scorched black and the trees looked like burnt matchsticks. He shifted his focus to the wall of debris erected where the Roth home had once stood. In the past, touching personal items, such as the victim's clothing, the murder weapon, sometimes even the victims themselves, would trigger his imagination; then he would let it run loose, and after a period of time, he would sink deeper into black until his sense of self completely disappeared, giving way to the cold profiling voice that would instruct him where to look and how to think

(and feel)

At least that was the way it had worked over six years ago. Back then his habits were different. He would lock himself in a hotel room, alone with his thoughts and the bloody photographs pinned to the wall, and through immersion he would be able to understand the killer's thoughts and emotional state. Now, he wasn't sure if he could pull it off.

After the death of his wife, when he was spiraling down into a pit of rage and despair, Mike Abrams had made arrangements for him to spend time at Ocean Point, a private mental hospital in New Canaan, Connecticut. During his six-month stay, he had rebuilt his mental foundation through a psychotherapeutic regimen of medications and intensive therapy. The nightmares he had hunted for a living, the mental photo album of the victims, their voices and screams—all of it, he had discovered, had taken root in his mind like poisoned tentacles. *And that rage, Jack. Let's not forget the rage,* a voice reminded him. He had spent six months removing the psychological tumors from his waking mind. All that time and now they didn't visit him in his sleep anymore. Did he really want to risk bringing them back?

The problem wasn't retrieving his imagination. With enough coaxing, it would come out on its own. The problem was that his imagination was a double-edged sword. Yes, it would tell him things about the Sandman, but it would also unlock the mental ward of nightmares and voices from past cases, the feelings attached to them, and the dark, turbulent emotions that had almost buried him.

Amanda's voice from the dream came back to him: *You promised me, Jack, remember? You promised me you'd keep your word this time.*

He stared at the mound of rubble. In his mind he saw Alex Dolan strapped to the chair in his pair of urine-soaked cotton briefs. He saw the faceless victims of family number three, who were days, maybe even hours away from being butchered.

I don't have a choice, Amanda. I'm sorry.

Jack walked to the rubble and started sifting through it.

Before the area was bulldozed, he had examined it with Burke, who had found part of an infrared sensor, the kind used in home security systems. The Roths didn't own a security system, nor did the majority of people who lived on the street. When Burke examined the fragment with a mass spectrometer, he found the residue fingerprint for C-4.

That was the only bomb fragment they had found. The majority of evidence was resting somewhere on the ocean floor. During the weeks following the blast, no evidence or body parts had washed up onshore.

So Jack was surprised to see a six-inch piece of nylon rope peeking out from behind a blasted chunk of plaster. He picked it up, saw a bloodstain on the end, and started massaging it between his fingers. He recalled the images from that night and focused on them.

Sometime later, he didn't know when, the heat on his back, the hot wind, the sweat running down his forehead, the noises from the beach, the normalcy of everything surrounding him—all faded away. It was like comfortably sinking down through a warm skin of black water.

The grouping of rational voices that safeguarded his sanity warned him to stop, pleaded with him, and for a brief moment, he felt a part of himself about to reach up and rise back to the surface; then he thought about Taylor, who had breathed life back onto his fragmented shell of an existence, her smile and body and her healing warmth for the moment safe—*but for how long?*—and surrendered to the force pulling him deeper into black, all of it as easy and gentle and natural as breathing.

The night inside the Roth home: *I'm walking down the hallway. Beyond the bedroom door I can hear Larry Roth struggling. I grip the doorknob and turn it, feeling how cool it is in my hand, and then I rush into the bedroom. Snapshots of the room. Memory fragments: how hot and wet the air is, the sweat, I draw a breath and I can smell the copper. And the windows, I notice. The windows are open. Fireworks burst outside, glowing beads and lines of green and blue and red and orange popping across the dark sky, colors washing over Larry Roth's frightened face.*

Watching.

Then the Sandman's voice from the other night: *I watched you out at the house today.*

Jack could recall the Sandman's exact words. Fortunately, Jack had made a copy of the conversation before driving up to Maine, where he had been forced to leave his tape recorder, as well as the file folder and his gun.

Something else the Sandman said. About running out of the Roth house . . .

You seemed calm this time. Not like last month when you bolted.

How did you know I bolted out of the house? You were there that night, watching, weren't you? Of course you were. You wanted to be close to it all—that's the only way to feel, isn't it? But where did you watch from? The beach? There you could blend in with the crowds and watch the chaos. But it put you dangerously close to the bomb. You wouldn't risk that, not with your plans for the Dolan family only a few weeks away.

Watching . . .

Close?

You could watch from a boat. A boat would be safe. You could watch all the chaos you created through binoculars—or better yet, night-vision goggles. No, not night vision. The fireworks would disrupt night vision, they would prevent you from seeing everything clearly. So would the police lights.

But watching through binoculars, that would be impersonal, wouldn't it? No sounds. No textures. No way to connect. *You'd been planning this moment for years and you needed to be there, to* connect, *and that, along with remaining safe, is your priority. You needed to see everything but from WHERE DID YOU WATCH?*

A new image forced its way through: the bedroom lights, the cog shoved in the turning wheels of his imagination. The bedroom lights were turned on at just the right moment. True, he had later learned that the street was experiencing brownouts that night just as Ronayne had stated, but Jack still believed the Sandman had turned on the lights. *Maybe when I opened the door and tripped the infrared beam and activated the bomb's timer, I also did something to the lights. Were the lights on a timer? If they were, how would you do that?*

Then he remembered something about the bedroom in connection with the rest of the house. The windows on the first floor were open but the shades were drawn; the bedroom windows were shut but the shades were *up. Yes. Larry Roth was shouting. Granted, his mouth was taped shut, but people were out on the beach, and if the bedroom windows were open, you ran the risk of having someone hear him and possibly ruining your plan.* That night the fireworks lit up the room, the colors glowing across Roth's wide, frightened eyes. *Did you leave the shades up on purpose?*

Of course he did.

Why?

To see you.

A faint connection washed across Jack's scalp like a tingle of static electricity.

To see me, you would need light inside the bedroom. That's why you left the shades up, didn't you? You needed the fireworks to illuminate the room so you could watch me. But from where? Not from a boat or from the beach. You wouldn't be able to see me from there.

Infrared beams. A laptop computer designed to allow you to detonate the bomb by a phone call. It's all safe, all of it orchestrated by remote control. And why did the lights come on just moments after I removed the tape from Roth's mouth? That wasn't a coincidence at all. That was planned, wasn't it?

The thought swam away from him. Jack didn't chase after it, just waited. A moment later, it came back and gripped him like a lost friend, and that flat, cold voice spoke to him for the first time in seven years: *Not where did he watch but* HOW? HOW *did he see you inside the bedroom?* HOW *did he see you run out of the house?*

Recognition jolted through him as if he had touched an exposed wire.

"You son of a bitch," Jack said, and squeezed the rope in his palms. The sheer brilliance of it. The simplicity.

"Surveillance cameras, that's how. You were watching me the entire time."

chapter 15

THE CALL CAME IN WHEN TOM DAVIS WAS IN THE MIDDLE OF HELPING HIS ELEVEN-YEAR-OLD SON PACK HIS CLOTHES AND MEDICINE FOR HIS TWO-WEEK STAY AT A MARINE BIOLOGY CAMP IN BAR HARBOR, MAINE. Davis, special agent in charge of the FBI's San Diego field office, took the call in his office. He had been stationed here for over twelve years and, thanks to his wife's love of jewelry, was *very* familiar with La Jolla; but he had never heard of a federally owned building in one of the wealthiest, most exclusive sections of San Diego.

He lived just outside of Ocean Beach, so the ride should have been reasonably quick. But not less than ten minutes into the trip the traffic came to an abrupt halt. People stood outside their cars, staring in amazement at the thick cone of gray smoke swirling up in the perfect blue sky from somewhere downtown. He hit the siren and made a good distance before he suddenly had to pull over. The roads leading into La Jolla were packed with mounds of rubble. Car windows had been blown out—so had the windows on all the surrounding homes and businesses. Twists of thick smoke rose into the sky, and clouds of dust snaked like a fog through the streets and houses. The destruction spread for miles.

Several hours later, his clothes reeking of sweat and smoke and stained with blood, he was resting on his knees on what looked to be part of a desk in the parking lot across from the building. The explosion had thrown the cars in all directions; they sat overturned and on top of each other, on their sides and hoods, covered in smoking debris. Some bodies were still inside them.

An overturned gray Buick Century was the subject of his attention. Blood dripped down on the roof from the driver's seat, soft and steady, the sound barely audible over the rescue sirens and the thump of news choppers. Bloody handprints were smeared along the steering wheel and dashboard. The majority of prints were on the cell phone.

Davis caught the stench of burnt flesh. His stomach lurched.

"Christ, I can never get used to that smell," said a voice behind him.

Davis stood and brushed the concrete dust and fine splinters of glass from his pant legs. It was Bret Laffy, the agent who had discovered the body inside the Buick. Laffy ran his fingers through his hair and pushed the sunglasses back up his nose. Like everyone else, he looked like someone who had stumbled away from a train wreck.

Davis squinted. "You got a shit-eating grin on your face."

"Because I got something good—*real* good. You remember that guy we found there in that Buick, the one with the latex-gloved hands? We just IDed him. His name is Henry Munn. He's one of us."

"Out of the San Diego office?"

"No, he lives in Virginia. Here's where it gets interesting." Laffy pulled a slip of paper from his shirt pocket and read the text. "This guy Munn, he called his home phone number at ten forty-five and left this message on his machine: 'Bomb was a laptop computer in ceiling hooked into building's security system, activated by Gardner's access code, C-4, on a timer in Gardner's office.' " Laffy looked up. "The explosions cut him off."

"Explosions?"

"That's right, two explosions. When you listen to the tape, you'll hear one, like a cannon shot, and the next one took down the whole building." Laffy made a sweeping motion with his hand. "And to cause all this, we're talking about a shitload of C-4."

"What I want to know is how someone got C-4 inside one of our own buildings."

"That's the million-dollar question. We're trying to get a building layout and a list of who worked here. It's going to take awhile, you know how it is." Laffy blew out a long stream of air. "Laptop computer hooked up to the building's security system, activated by an access code . . . pretty sophisticated stuff."

"Might be an inside job. We have any idea who this guy Gardner is?"

"Not yet. Once we get the list of people who worked here, I'm sure Gardner's name will be there. As for what this place is, the word I keep hearing is *research*. I know they hold conferences here—it had quite the layout—but as to what the actual research is, we're still digging."

Davis nodded. There was something else, an anxiety that he couldn't explain or shake. He was gripped with the distinct feeling that he wasn't supposed to be here—that nobody was. *You're being paranoid,* a voice told him. Maybe. But when you worked with the FBI and saw all the shit that went down, paranoia became a job requirement.

"We know Munn's status yet?" Davis wanted to get to the hospital and speak to him. This guy Munn was their only lifeline to what had happened here.

"I have someone at Scripps right now—that kid Maples, the guy with the purple blotch on his left cheek? He'll call us when they wheel Munn out of the OR."

In the distance, the sound of aggravated voices grew into shouts. On one of the debris-covered roads, standing like protesters in front of the two ambulances, a mob of reporters, photographers, and TV cameramen were blocking the ATF and FBI agents and the San Diego police who were trying to get a woman with a missing leg on a stretcher to an ambulance. The media swarmed all over her, their cameras pointed down at her wounds, their microphones shoved near her face to record her screams. *We've made advances in medicine and technology, but our taste for blood hasn't diminished one damn bit,* Davis thought. Scenes like this made him wonder about the direction and fate of humanity.

"It's a fucking zoo," Laffy said. "And it's only going to get worse."

Over Laffy's shoulder Davis saw an agent trying to make his way over the rubble. The agent had a Ziploc freezer bag grasped firmly in his hand. A purple-colored mark was on his cheek.

"Shit."

"What is it?" Laffy asked.

The agent Maples, his face red from exertion, reached Davis and handed him the bag.

"Sir, John Doe expired an hour ago," Maples said. "These are his personal belongings. His name was—"

"Henry Munn," Davis said, and felt his heart sink. Not only had one of their own died, the only link to what had happened here had died along with him. Back to square one.

Next came an agent wearing a windbreaker stamped FBI on the back. He had a square jaw and a shaved head. "Sir, Director Paris is on the phone and wants to talk to you right away. We have a secure line set up in the trailer. Follow me."

As Davis walked, he sifted through the bag. There was Munn's wallet, which contained nothing interesting, his photo ID card and badge, and some folded sheets of paper spotted with circles of drying blood.

The first piece of paper was a floor-by-floor layout of the building. A trail from the elevator to office number 496 had been highlighted in green—Gardner's office, no doubt. There were several technical notes on the building's state-of-the-art security system and the codes needed to bypass it. But that was not what caused Davis to stop walking.

On the second page was a yellow Post-it note, the words handwritten clearly in blue ink: "Find out where patient traveled those last three days and call me immediately. We have to clean up this thing quickly and quietly." The word *quietly* had been underlined three times.

The top of the Post-it note was preprinted in black with a name: Alan Lynch.

The director of the Investigative Support Unit.

Was Munn a profiler? And if he was, what was he doing here poking around an office in a federal research building? And how did this guy Gardner fit into all this?

Davis saw the trailer. Perfect questions to pose to FBI director Harrison Paris.

chapter 16

THE WIRELESS SURVEILLANCE CAMERA HAD BEEN CAMOUFLAGED WITH A BIRD'S NEST AND SCREWED INTO THE END OF A LONG BRANCH OF A HUNDRED-YEAR-OLD MAPLE TREE ON THE CORNER OF THE ISLAND NEAR THE STREET—AFFORDING A PERFECT VIEW OF THE ROTH HOME. Now the camera was partially dismantled, its gutted contents spread over the top of a folded red wool blanket on the trunk of the Porsche.

Jack used a Phillip's screwdriver to move aside a thick grouping of multicolored wires inside the camera. Even here in the shade, the gusts of wind blowing up from the ocean felt like a steam bath.

"You see it?" Jack asked.

Mike Abrams leaned his face down to the camera, his eyes narrowing in concentration and thought. He wore pleated brown pants and a crisp white dress shirt that had sweat pockets under the arms and down the back. Standing this close, Jack could smell his cologne and the hint of the spearmint mint he was working on the back of his molars.

"It looks like an LED screen of a pager," Mike said.

"It *is* a pager. And to answer your next question, I think it was installed in there as a power-saving device. Even with backup batteries, these wireless cameras have a limited supply of power—nine hours max. The pager allowed our friend to turn the power on and off remotely."

Mike's eyes roved over the gutted insides. "It looks like he really revamped this thing. What's its range?"

"Three hundred feet, max—and that's under optimal conditions. No wind, no electromagnetic interference."

Mike cocked his head. "Three hundred *feet,* Christ, that's not that far."

"My guess is that he was probably parked somewhere on Atlantic Avenue. He'd have to be sitting somewhere safe, like inside the back of a van. That way he could watch the action without drawing attention to himself. When the house exploded, away from the van's windows, he would be protected from the debris and the glass."

Mike looked back at the camera. "With this type of equipment, he probably recorded the explosion."

Jack nodded. "A guy like this, obsessed with control and consumed with revenge fantasies, he'd want to keep something of significance to allow him to relive the event. There's no better way than with your own homemade videotape."

Jack tossed the screwdriver on the blanket. His shirt was torn in several places, and his four ribs, the ones he had broken last month, were throbbing painfully—the result of his partial fall from the tree. He had had to climb the tree himself, of course, too anxious to wait for the fire department and not wanting to cause a scene. So he had just snaked out at the end of the long, thick branch, had removed the bird's nest, when he lost his balance and fell. *Lucky you managed to grab ahold of another branch and break your fall; otherwise, you would have broken your neck and they'd be carting your ass out on a stretcher.*

"I sent the fire department over to the Dolan home, told them what to look for," Jack said. "They found two of the same surveillance cameras, both of them camouflaged like this one. I got patrolmen there right now guarding them. I'm going to swing by and pick them up and go see Burke. The cameras are expensive. I'll run a trace on the serial numbers." But Jack didn't expect to gain much from this angle. The Sandman could have walked in and paid cash, could have purchased them over the Internet with a phony credit card—however he did it, he no doubt took extensive measures to hide his identity.

"And you believe our guy planted cameras inside the Roth bedroom?"

"That's the only way he could have known when to turn on the lights. I'm willing to bet he did the same thing inside the Dolan bedroom."

"But you didn't find any cameras."

"We weren't looking. Not that we would find them. I'm talking about pinhole cameras. You can mount them in electrical outlets, a radio—even a TV. You've seen it done." Jack looked at the surveillance camera. "It's the perfect setup. He breaks in once and sets up the cameras. Then he watches the family, follows their patterns, and starts planning. He watches them fall asleep and moves in."

"Which means he watched you and Burke work the crime scene. Then watched the CSI unit work over the crime scene. If he was smart enough to plant pinhole cameras, he probably planted some microphones."

The thought had occurred to Jack. He sighed with defeat. "Not only did he watch us, he heard us. Right now, the son of a bitch knows everything we do."

Mike blew out a long stream of air. "Pretty fucking clever."

"To find the cameras, we'll need sweepers." Specialized sweeping equipment used by the FBI to check for listening devices would pick up the camera's frequency—if the cameras were still turned on. "Can you rustle up some bug hunters?"

"I'll make the call," Mike said. "What about the autopsy report? Any luck there?"

"Wilson found what looks like a partial thumbprint on Veronica Dolan's forehead, but not enough for a match. You know the shelf life of a latent on human skin."

"What method did he use?"

"Cyanoacrylate fuming followed by dusting with luminescent magnetic powder. No prints."

"Well, at least he's using the current methods. If this guy has priors, all we need is a full latent and I think we'll have a name and a face. What about the rest of the autopsy report?"

"They were all drugged with chloroform. Veronica Dolan died from strangulation. While he was doing it, he bashed her head against the oak headboard."

"Nice."

"That's it. The Sandman may have a problem with rage, but he's very clever and very thorough."

"The Sandman? That's what you're calling him?"

"A nickname that's being passed around the station," Jack lied. He hadn't told Mike about the Sandman's call. Jack wanted to, but he had to protect Taylor. Keeping her safe was his top priority.

Mike was focused on a thought. "Jack, there's a product manufactured at the University of Texas called benzoninhydrin. It's specifically designed to lift prints from the skin. They've had excellent results with it."

"I'll call Wilson. Oh, one interesting and maybe promising item. I talked to Mark Graysmith in the Explosives Unit."

"Graysmith—that's the guy you saved from that serial bomber. A dentist, if I remember correctly."

"Right, that's him. Burke sent him all the items from the Roth blast and the Dolan bomb. In the blast residue he found a polymer with what appears to be a serial number: A-TX-88-92. Graysmith thinks it might be a tagging agent. There's been talk for years about developing tagging agents in explosives. The idea is that when a bomb goes off, the investigator will find the tagging agent, which will lead him back to the explosive's last known point of origin. Burke found a similar tagging agent in the Semtex-H. The explosives came from the same place."

"Our first solid lead."

"Hopefully it will open up some other doors, because right now, we got squat."

Jack folded the ends of the blanket around the camera, carried it to the passenger's side of the Porsche, and placed it on the seat. He could feel Mike's steady gaze.

"Go ahead and ask me," Jack said.

"You get in touch with Fletcher?"

"What do you think?"

Mike squinted. "I think you're a stubborn son of a bitch who has a problem accepting help from your friends."

"Well, here's a news flash for you." Jack filled Mike in on his trip to Maine.

A moment later, Mike took in a draw of air. He widened his eyes, blew out the air. "That's . . . that's quite a story. You call the town sheriff?"

"Right after I got out of there. Said he'd look into it, call me back. I talked to him this morning. Fletcher's house was cleaned out. The computer, books, my files and my gun—all gone and no sign of Fletcher. The sheriff told me that the name on the house deed is listed as Francis Harvey and that it was purchased in cash six years ago."

"But I found him through the DMV. If this guy's hiding, why is he using his real name?"

"I don't know." *But I know it has something to do with my former employer,* Jack added privately. "How long will it take you to scrounge up the sweepers?"

"It shouldn't take long." Mike looked at his watch. "It's past noon. Want to meet at the Dolan house around three?"

"Sounds good."

"Jack, has the Sandman contacted you yet?"

Again Jack fought back the urge to tell his friend the truth. "No, he hasn't."

Mike stood in the shade, his gaze as penetrating as a laser beam.

He knows I'm lying. Jack kept his face neutral.

"But you know at some point he will," Mike said.

"I've considered the possibility."

"Then you've also considered the possibility that he'll threaten you with the loss of something important."

"Like what?"

"Taylor."

Jack removed any meaning from his eyes. "And how would he know about Taylor?"

"The guy knew everything about Larry Roth. It makes sense he would want to know everything about the investigator running the case. When he finds out you're also a former profiler . . . Jack, I've been giving this some thought. Why don't we put some protection on Taylor, just in case. I can call in a few favors, have some guys watch her, she won't know a thing, I promise."

The Sandman's words came back to Jack in a vivid rush: *If you put bodyguards on her, I'll kill her. And don't plan on sharing our conversation with her, either. If I even* think *she knows she's in danger, I'll kill her.*

Jack didn't believe it was an empty threat. But that didn't mean he was going to sit back and keep Taylor in the dark.

After dinner the evening the Sandman had called, they had walked along the beach. He told her the truth about the bombs and how the two families had died. Then he asked her and Rachel to stick close to the house for a few days—strictly a precaution, nothing to worry about. Taylor, knowing the details of what had happened to his wife, had agreed.

Taylor may not have known about the Sandman's threat, but she was being protected. A few well-placed phone calls had led Jack to a former Secret Service agent named Ronnie Tedesco, who owned and operated a private security firm out of Boston. Right now, Ronnie and his team, made up of former agents from the Secret Service, CIA, and FBI, were watching Taylor's every movement and keeping an eye out for a white male who might be taking a sudden interest in Taylor or her house. The federal agents Mike would want to use would be clumsy at best. If the Sandman intercepted a conversation over a cell phone discussing security for Taylor and her niece, the Sandman would kill them. The former Secret Service agents knew how to play it.

Jack looked at his friend. *You have to tell Mike something.* "Taylor's safe. Her niece is here. They're staying at the house, spending some quality time together. They're safe."

"Jack—"

"She's safe, Mike. Trust me."

Mike placed his hands in his pant pockets and started jingling his change—a sure sign he was measuring just how far he should venture into personal territory. Jack expected something about Amanda, some past mistake that Mike would reshape and expertly apply like pressure on an old wound.

Instead, Mike said, "Just give it some thought."

Jack nodded. "See you at three."

Mike started walking up Preston toward Atlantic, where his Volvo was parked. Jack fished his keys out of his jeans pocket and heard the beep of a pager. He opened the car door, got himself settled behind the wheel, and picked up his beeper. Nothing. He tossed it back on the seat and started the car. Mike was standing in the middle of the street, patting down his pockets.

Jack pulled up next to him. "Need to use my phone?"

"No. I was looking for that tin of mints I'm addicted to."

"Did you just get paged?"

"No. Why?"

Panic gripped him. *No. It can't be.*

"What's wrong?" Mike asked, moving toward him now.

Jack turned to the passenger's seat, unfolded the blanket, grabbed the camera, and pulled aside the nest of wires. Through the sunshine pouring in through the front and side windows, he saw on the LED screen the black digital number: 35.

34.

33.

Mike leaned in the window, his face full of alarm. "What is it?"

"The Sandman just turned this thing into a bomb."

chapter 17

FOR A MOMENT ALL JACK COULD DO WAS SIT THERE, FROZEN IN PLACE WITH HIS EYES LOCKED ON THE PAGER'S SMALL RECTANGULAR SCREEN. Then the number clicked from 30 to 29 and his mind snapped back on in a rush of adrenaline, sending his heart soaring high in his chest. Light-headed, he looked out the front window, looked out the sides and back, frantically searching for some place, *something,* that would absorb the blast. Quick, time's running out and you're holding a bomb. Think, Jesus fucking Christ, think *QUICK.*

Mike came up with the answer:

"The ocean. Throw it in the water." Mike turned and sprinted down the pavement, his right hand reaching for his shoulder holster.

Jack threw the gearshift into reverse, slammed on the gas. In a squeal of tires, the Porsche raced down the street toward the beach. *Too many people packed on the sand,* he thought. *No way I can drive down to the water without running someone over.*

He was going to have to run the bomb down there by himself.

Jack slammed on the brakes; the car skidded and stopped halfway on the sand, a group of nearby people screaming at him. Grabbing the bomb, he leapt out of the car. Mike whisked past him and stopped on the sand, the Glock already pointed up to the sky. He fired off two successive rounds that roared through the air like cannon shots.

"FBI, clear the beach. There's a bomb, clear the beach!"

Two more rounds. The immediate crowd of people were already running, but down on the distant shore laughter and play and idle conversation were in full swing.

Four more shots. *"There's a bomb, clear the beach, CLEAR THE BEACH!"*

That did it. As Jack raced toward the water, one hand clutching the bomb to his chest, the other arm stretched out defensively, pandemonium broke out. Parents scooped their children into their arms and ran in all directions, confused, not sure where to go, bodies slamming into each other, everyone trampling over blankets and toys and chairs, tripping and screaming.

The crowd finally broke; there was the shore, free of people, and Jack was running full force into the water. Knee-high now, the screams behind him still loud and piercing over the hot wind and the breaking waves, his movements slowing from the water. Waves broke and slammed into him. More than once he almost tripped and tumbled forward.

Don't trip, Jesus Christ, you trip and it's over.

Twenty seconds, his mind screamed. *You got less than twenty seconds, you're not going to make it.*

He's watching you. He was watching you the entire time, he was listening to you and Mike a few minutes ago, and he's watching you now.

Taylor, what if she's in danger—

No, she's safe.

Jack stopped, got his footing, and wound up and with all of his strength and energy and anger tossed the camera into the air. He turned and ran full force back to the shore where Mike was now standing.

Mike, his chest heaving, followed the camera's trajectory. Then he moved into the water, grabbed Jack by the arm, and helped pull him out.

An explosion. The ground shook. Jack lost his balance and fell face first, taking Mike down with him. Behind them a spray of water shot into the air, as if a depth charge had gone off. Jack rolled on his side and, over Mike's shoulder, saw the cone of water shower back down like a curtain of rain.

The beach was quiet, still. Mike crawled up over to him and gripped him under the arm, helping him up. "You okay?" Mike asked, out of breath, his words shaking from the adrenaline rush.

Jack nodded and wiped the sand out of his eyes.

A cell phone rang. It was his. He had been carrying it inside his shirt pocket; now it had fallen at his feet.

He bent down to pick it up. He didn't have to guess who it was.

"Excellent job, Jack," the Sandman said. "Throwing the bomb in the water—absolutely *brilliant.* Even *I* didn't think of that one."

Jack was having difficulty standing. Everything around him seemed to be vibrating and slightly out of focus and he couldn't catch his breath. Blinking rapidly, he looked around the beach. People were lined along the street and crowded by a wall at each end of the beach.

"I see you've resurrected the old way of thinking from its grave," the Sandman said. "It was easy, wasn't it? So *effortless.* Do you know why?"

Jack walked up the sand to the street, his eyes sweeping the mob for a white male on a cellular phone. *He's got to be close. He'd want to watch.*

"It was so easy because it's a part of you. It's as natural as your breathing."

All phone calls to Jack's cell phone, his offices at the station and at home, and Taylor's phones could be traced. Jack checked his watch. *Keep him on the phone.*

"Look at all these people staring at you, Jack. How do you think they would react if they were to discover that dark nest of thoughts and cravings you keep hidden? Do you think their small-town mentality could absorb the truth of *what you really are?*"

The words had a cold precision, a certainty that caused Jack to stop walking.

"And what about Taylor? How do you think she'll look at you once she discovers that the man she lets slide between her legs is really a mental deviant?"

Where's he going with this? Jack tried to think through the words, couldn't, and continued scanning the stares aimed at him.

"Did you know your friend Mike Abrams thinks of you as some sort of sick, tormented creature? Abrams and his wife went out to eat Friday night and *you* were the subject of conversation. His wife, Michelle, she's absolutely *terrified* of you—she never left you alone with the kids, did she?—and Mike doesn't think you're up to the job. Kept using the word *relapse.*"

Jack shifted his eyes to Mike, who was standing only a few feet away, hunched forward with his hands on his knees and breathing hard.

Who is it? Mike mouthed.

"I'm disappointed to see you've decided to play the game, but I'm not surprised," the Sandman said. "You know why, Jack? Because you can't help yourself. You're *drawn* to it. What alarms me is that I warned you about Taylor. I repeatedly told you that if you persisted, I would destroy the one thing that breathes life into your cracked shell of an existence. And look what you're doing right now. What does that say about your mental condition?"

Taylor was safe, Jack reminded himself. She was home today, at the beach with her niece, both of them guarded and safe.

What if she's in danger—

NO.

Jack looked at his watch. Almost there.

Keep him talking.

"You could have killed me a moment ago. Why the timer?"

"Peeling back the layers is a far more rewarding exercise," the Sandman said. "And so we begin: Turn to your right. From where you're standing, you should be able to see Marblehead Neck."

Jack's body stiffened. *He's here on the beach.* But where? All he could see were sunglasses and puzzled expressions. No cell phone. *Where the hell are you?*

Mike jogged up next to him. Jack covered the mouthpiece with his hand and whispered to Mike, "He's here on the beach on a phone, watching us." Mike ran up the sand to the crowd of people at the street.

"Abrams is running in the wrong direction," the Sandman said. "Now look out at the Neck."

Jack pushed his way through the crowd of people to get to the street. Frightened stares were pointed at him.

"You think I'm sitting in your car? You think you're going to find me standing on the beach? You're not up to this, Jack. You should have listened to me."

Checking his watch again. *Just a few more seconds, come on, goddamnit. Come on.* "I'm not playing your game."

"My game? This isn't *my* game, Jack. Don't turn this around on *me.* I didn't send you up into that tree. I didn't send those officers over to the Dolan home and ask them to guard the two surveillance cameras you found. That was *your* doing."

The meaning suddenly hit Jack. An icy fear twisted up through his stomach and closed around his throat. *Those two cameras are bombs, just like the one I just threw in the water. They're probably set up the same way this one was so all he has to do is call the pager and—*

The Neck's less than five minutes away, you got a chance, but you're going to have to buy some time, and the only way to do that is to keep him talking.

The Porsche was running. He got inside and threw the car into gear.

"You should see them, Jack, the four of them standing around the cruiser, talking about their new brides, their infant kids—they're all so young. You should see Barry Lentz. Right now he's showing a picture of his two-month-old girl, Alexandra. Too bad he doesn't know he's standing right next to two bombs packed with blocks of C-4."

A sickening pressure ballooned inside Jack's chest. He pulled out onto Atlantic and sped down between two lanes of traffic. Cars pulled over to a screeching halt. Horns blared.

"This is between you and me," Jack said. "Keep them out of it."

"This is about you, Jack. Your failure to keep your word. I told you to back off and you didn't. Their blood will be on your hands, not mine."

Jack could feel the words lodged in his throat, wanting to escape. *Don't beg. That's what he wants.*

"They have nothing to do with this and you know it. You want to direct your anger, direct it at me."

"You can't save them, Jack."

The right turn that would lead him to the Neck was a few seconds away.

"You've sentenced these kids to death. They'll never hear your apologies. You'll have to save them for their widows."

"Please, I'm begging you," Jack said, the words coming out tight. "Spare them and I give you my word that I'll step away from the investigation."

"You had your chance. But I don't blame you, Jack. You and I burn with the same cravings. It's in our blood."

"Listen to me—"

"Time to get back in touch with those dark feelings, Jack. Time for your walls to come down."

"DON'T—"

An explosion suddenly burst against his ears. His body jerked as if hit. The phone dropped onto the passenger's seat and tumbled onto the floor. From the phone's speaker he heard the officers screaming. *Hang on, please, God, just let them hang on, don't let them die.*

Then came the Sandman's voice in a mock wail of remorse: "Their arms, Jack, and their faces . . . they're bleeding to death. . . . Their poor wives, their children, dear God, Jack, *what have you done?"*

chapter 18

WHEN RONNIE TEDESCO HEARD THAT BOOMING SOUND RIP THROUGH THE AIR THE FIRST TIME—IT WAS AN EXPLOSION, NOT SOME KID PLAYING WITH FIREWORKS—INSTINCT MADE HIM WANT TO REACH OUT AND GRAB THE WOMAN AND THE FOUR-YEAR-OLD GIRL WHO WERE LESS THAN THREE FEET AWAY FROM HIM AND BRING THEM UP INTO THE HOUSE. They shouldn't have been out here anyway. It was too dangerous.

But he couldn't move them inside, nor could he tell them where to go. Jack Casey's instructions had been specific: under no circumstances was Taylor Burton to know she was being guarded. Ronnie, a former Secret Service agent who had worked body detail for two presidents, had told Casey that this Mickey Mouse covert approach to protection was bullshit. Casey didn't want to hear it.

So now Ronnie was back standing knee-high in the water on a private section of beach separated from the public by a row of boulders. Only a few people were out here, most of them elderly. They had all been minding their own business when the dual explosions bolted them off their chairs and blankets. Now they were huddled together and staring through the haze of humidity toward the area everyone was calling the Neck. Behind his pair of mirrored Oakley sunglasses, Ronnie looked for any signs of a white male in his late twenties to early thirties (Casey's lame profiling description; it matched every goddamn WASP in this town, for chrissakes). He had already surveyed the area with binoculars; all clear. On the periphery of his vision he saw the little girl, Rachel, approach her aunt.

"What was that noise?" Rachel asked, wading into the water. She was dressed in a one-piece bathing suit with silver fish on it, and she wore a kiddy Red Sox baseball hat that matched her aunt's.

"I don't know," Taylor said.

"Auntie, it was really *loud.*"

"Yes. Yes, it was." Taylor's voice sounded far away and troubled.

"Is someone screaming?"

The beeper Ronnie had tucked in his pant pocket vibrated.

Ronnie looked at a tall, angular man in baggy tan shorts and white T-shirt, Paul Sherman, who was literally standing next to Taylor; so were the two other guys Ronnie had posted on beach detail. Guns were tucked inside the waistbands of their baggy shorts, but guns were useless here. When the guy Casey was calling the Sandman made a run at the woman, his weapon would be a bomb detonated by remote control. Because of the tremendous amount of mail she received, a mail bomb would be the easiest way to kill her. Given the current bullshit setup, Ronnie knew there was no way he could protect her from it.

Ronnie's blanket and beach chair were set up close to Taylor and the little girl. The dog, the one they called Mr. Ruffles, was sleeping inside the house.

Ronnie sat down, pulled the phone out from the cooler, and dialed. After a slight pause as the encryption technology engaged, the number started to ring. The man on the other end, Paul Grexley, a former CIA operative who now performed the company's surveillance work, told Ronnie about the Sandman's call. Grex had managed to lock onto the cellular phone signal but couldn't trace it. As he'd listened to the phone conversation between Casey and the Sandman, he'd watched with surprise as the signal bounced from Marblehead to Swampscott to Lynn and then to Peabody. To do that, the Sandman had to have the kind of sophisticated equipment normally employed by the CIA and the FBI. As Ronnie listened, his eyes locked on Taylor and the girl, his beeper vibrated two more times. The number was the same. He knew who it was.

Ronnie hung up and dialed the second number.

"Where is she?" Casey asked, his voice full of panic.

"You're on a secured line, I hope. You got that scrambling device on, like we talked about?"

"I'm using your phone, I'm in the car, now tell me where she is."

"Standing in the water with her niece, roughly forty feet away from me."

"You're not close enough."

"I have my four best guys next to her. She's layered. She's fine." *For the moment,* Ronnie added privately.

"He might be there. He's close by, he watched me on the beach."

"The only white males within an earshot are my men." Ronnie let a few seconds pass. Then he asked the question to which he already knew the answer: "I just heard an explosion—two of them. What happened?"

There was a pause.

Ronnie said, "I can hear screaming. It's faint, but I can hear it. So can Taylor and her niece. What's going on, Jack?"

Casey didn't answer. Ronnie knew what had caused the screaming and knew that Casey was afraid right now. Good. Ronnie wanted to feed his employer's fear. It was the only way to get the pigheaded son of a bitch to listen to reason.

"There was an accident." Casey's voice was tight.

"Another bomb?"

A long pause. "Yes."

"Last month and now this. Casey, you're a lucky man."

"He called me."

"I know all about it. My guy couldn't trace the signal. Son of a bitch has state-of-the-art stuff and is smart on top of it. Guy's making me real nervous, Jack. *Real* nervous."

Silence on the other end. *You beginning to see the light yet?*

Ronnie said, "Common sense tells me that if you corner a rabid animal, that animal is going to come out fighting. Finding the cameras, you pissed him off. He's going to make a run at you—or her. Right now, I got her layered, but there's too many ways for him to slip through. We need to tell her what's going on, Jack, and we need to get her—"

"We've already went over this at your office."

"And we're about to go over it again because the current setup is bullshit and you know it."

Ronnie looked out at the water. Taylor Burton wore a black bikini that accented her perfect breasts. *If she were mine, I'd have her locked in a house and surrounded by a SWAT team twenty-four/seven. Jesus fucking Christ, Casey, what is it going to take to wake you UP?*

"When Hinckley made his move on Reagan, the only reason the president survived was because I had him surrounded by bodies," Ronnie said. "He was completely layered. Now if Hinckley could penetrate a wall of Secret Service agents, what makes you think this wacko who just tried to blow you up can't get to your girlfriend?"

"If the Sandman finds out she's being guarded—if the son of a bitch even *thinks* she's being protected—he'll kill her. You heard the tape."

"I think it's bullshit. The guy's playing with your emotions."

"I'm not going to take that chance."

"I don't blame you, but you still need to tell her."

"He's into high-tech surveillance. He could be listening to you right now."

"You're on a STU-III phone with digital encryption, there's no fucking way he can break it. Look, bottom line, she's in the line of fire. I have contacts in Witness Protection. We'll tuck her and the little girl away until this mess blows over."

"But you can't guarantee her safety."

"I can guarantee that if we stay with the current setup, she'll be dead. All it takes is one good shot." Ronnie didn't like his next choice of words. It was a low blow, but he had to say them. "After what happened to your wife, I would think you'd want to take a more realistic approach."

There was a long pause. *Good,* Ronnie thought. *Maybe Casey was finally thinking.*

"Redirect Taylor's mail to your office," Casey said. "Have your guys fluoroscope everything."

The guys Ronnie had posted at the end of the street posing as Bell Atlantic telephone technicians were making note of the FedEx and UPS trucks constantly pulling up to her house.

"How are you going to explain this sudden lack of mail?"

"I want you to sweep her house for bugs," Jack said. "I want the house locked tight; set it up with state-of-the-art countersurveillance equipment, I don't care how much it costs. I don't want the son of a bitch to be able to see or hear a thing, got it?"

"Not a problem."

"You have to do this discreetly. You have to assume he's watching her, watching the house, watching me."

"To do it right, to do it discreetly, that will take time. I say we move them out tonight."

"Not yet."

"Goddamnit, you need to tell her—"

"After the house is locked tight. Then I'll tell her what's going on and we'll move her, but I'm not going to risk it, not with the Sandman watching, so we're doing it my way." Casey hung up.

Ronnie pulled the phone away from his ear. This conversation cemented his feeling that Jack Casey's head wasn't screwed on right. You hunt nightmares for a living, and then you're forced to sit there and watch while your wife is carved up like a Sunday roast by the nation's prime-time nightmare, there was no fucking way you could spend the rest of your waking days without struggling against an undertow of dark thoughts wanting to drag you under. No fucking way.

chapter 19

JACK HAD PARKED THE CAR FACING NORTH SO HE DIDN'T HAVE TO LOOK AT THE DRIVEWAY, WHERE THE WORST OF IT WAS. The windows were rolled up, the motor running. Jack was working a rag over his bloodstained hands. He had tried to keep Roger Delaney's heart beating before the ambulance arrived, but the blood loss had been too severe. Over the loud, steady whoosh of the air-conditioning, he could hear the blare of the car and house alarms.

Jack dialed Taylor's number again, hoping she might have gone back to the house. He needed to hear her voice. Just a quick hello and that awful, sinking feeling inside his chest would stop, he was sure of it. When the machine picked up, he didn't leave a message. She was all right, he reminded himself.

For now, a voice told him.

With some minor adjustments, the Sandman had turned a wireless surveillance camera into a bomb. When he made a run at Taylor—he could be doing it right now, Jack didn't know—how would he do it? A mail bomb seemed the most likely scenario. Or maybe he had something else planned, something more

(fun)

memorable. It was impossible to predict the Sandman's next move because of his ingenuity. He had a lot of choices, a lot of time to think and prepare.

Ronnie's right. The current security setup is bullshit and you know it. Given today's events, you have to tell Taylor the truth.

Fine. But where could he tell her? Jack knew he was being watched—maybe even right now. The Sandman had stated he had overheard Mike talking with his wife at a restaurant. Jack couldn't risk telling Taylor in a public place. What if the Sandman was listening? What then? The only countersurveillance security currently installed was here in the car. Ronnie had given him a device the size of a hockey puck; mounted on the rear window, it prevented eavesdropping. But that didn't mean the Sandman couldn't follow them. If he saw them talking, saw Taylor's face change when she was hit with the knowledge—no, it was too risky. The only safe place was Taylor's house. It was familiar, private. Once Ronnie had swept the house for bugs (highly unlikely, but Jack wasn't about to take chances) and installed the countersurveillance equipment, the Sandman wouldn't be able to see or hear anything. Jack would tell Taylor, then pack up her and Rachel that same night and get them the fuck out of here.

A knock on the driver's window startled him. Mike Abrams, his clothes splattered with blood, motioned him out.

Jack stepped into the thick, wet heat. Now he could hear the ambulance sirens and the cries of a woman from up the road, the EMTs shouting orders. The blood-covered body of Jeremy Gates, a twenty-six-year-old patrolman and newlywed, lay on a stretcher and was being quickly ushered inside an ambulance.

"The staties are on their way," Mike said. "So are Burke and ATF."

"What about the media?"

"They're out. We got them cornered off. They know about the bomb."

Wonderful. "How's Harmon?" Mark Harmon was the patrolman Mike had been helping.

"He didn't make it, Jack. I'm sorry."

In the driveway was the shell of a Marblehead police cruiser. The dual explosions had ignited its gas tank. The fire department had put out the flames that had spread over the lawn and along the side of the house. Now what remained of the cruiser sat hissing in the sunlight. On the front lawn, Patrolman Barry Lentz's body was covered by a tarp.

That hollow feeling inside Jack's chest felt like acid eating its way through his body. This was his own doing. He had created this moment.

Mike stepped in front of his line of vision.

"Don't do this."

"Do what?"

"Blame yourself. This isn't your fault."

"I shouldn't have sent them over here. I should have called Burke and let him handle it."

"How the hell were you supposed to know that the son of a bitch could turn a fucking surveillance camera into a bomb?"

"I *should* have known. All the signs were there, and finding the camera . . . It was too fucking easy. I fell right into it."

"There's no way you could have predicted it. It's not like he called and warned you."

A strong breeze picked up. On the front lawn the tarp blew partway off and Jack could see Lentz's remaining good eye staring up at him. *The Sandman warned you and you decided to play along,* the eye said. *Tell Mike the truth. You owe me and my daughter and wife that much, don't you?*

"Who were you on the phone with?" Mike asked.

"No one."

"I saw you pick up that phone five times."

"I was trying to call Taylor."

"Jack, it's time we put people on her—experienced people. No more dicking around. I'm going to make the call."

Jack didn't say anything. The sun was unbearably hot, the air still reeking from the scorched patrol car. He wiped at his face. The explosions had blown out windows of the nearby homes and cars.

"Jack, you hear what I said?"

Tell him. "Get in the car."

They got inside. Mike was staring at him curiously.

"Putting people on Taylor—it's already taken care of."

Mike's eyes lit up with surprise. "Who?"

"Guy named Ronnie Tedesco. He's ex–Secret Service, did body detail for two presidents and now has his own private security company in Cambridge. He's got a whole team covering her."

"When did you do this?"

"The night you came by Taylor's house."

"What prompted you?"

Jack had a copy of his conversation with the Sandman. He reached into the glove compartment, removed a cassette, and inserted it into the tape deck. Mike listened. Jack watched an ambulance race by.

"How's Taylor handling this?" Mike asked.

"She doesn't know all the details yet."

"What *does* she know?"

"She knows to stick close to the house. Not to let Rachel out of her sight for any reason."

"Does she know about Tedesco?"

"No."

"You have to tell her."

"I have to play this carefully. I don't know if the Sandman is watching us, watching her—he could even be listening."

"I doubt that."

"But what if he is? You think I should take that chance?"

Mike didn't say anything.

"If he finds out she's being guarded, if he even thinks she knows, he promised to kill Taylor and her niece," Jack said. "It isn't an idle threat. He's been dreaming of this moment a long time."

"Then why didn't he kill you today? He had the perfect opportunity."

"Because he's having too much fun. Right now I'm not a threat. When I am, he'll take me out of the way."

Mike thought about it, sighed. "I don't like her not knowing. She's a sitting duck and so is Rachel."

Jack told him of his plan of telling Taylor at her house.

"When?" Mike asked.

"Ronnie's going to sweep her house for bugs, plant some countersurveillance measures—but that's going to take some time. We have to do it discreetly in case the Sandman's watching."

"I don't like this, Jack. Not one fucking bit."

"I agree, but what are my options?"

"You really think this guy's watching?"

"Friday night, did you and Michelle go out to eat?"

"Yeah, why?"

"The Sandman was there."

Mike worked through several thoughts. "How would he know about me? That Michelle and I were going out to dinner?"

"I don't know, but he was close enough to hear you and Michelle talking."

Mike's eyes became veiled. Guarded. "What did he say?"

"He didn't mention anything specific."

"Did he threaten—"

"No, he didn't, but to play it safe, I think you should make some arrangements. Put some people on her, your kids, maybe even get them out of the state until this blows over. She has relatives in Colorado, right?"

"Denver." Mike's voice sounded far away, his attention focused on his own private flurry of fear. "I'm going to give her a call."

"You have to assume he's listening and watching us all the time." Jack handed Mike his cell phone. "This is encrypted. Call her from the car. I'll have Ronnie send you a phone."

Jack got out of the car, shut the door, and then watched Mike call his wife. He thought about Mike's solid marriage, his four kids and the life they had built together, and then slammed the door shut on all of it, as if his friend's happiness and solidity in life were the destructive, vile, and violent tendencies of a delusional alcoholic.

Stop the pity party, Jack. The Sandman warned you and you ignored it. You decided to roll the dice and lost, so deal with it.

Jack looked back to the tarp. An EMT had weighted the corners down with rocks. A moment later the strong breeze picked up again and Jack saw Barry's bloody hand.

Something in the back of his mind twitched. An image, maybe even a thought; he wasn't sure, but it had the distinctive, comfortable feeling of something familiar. A moment later, it came to him.

The night manager of a twenty-dollar-a-night motel is throwing up outside room number 306. Cars and trucks race across the highway. The lighting inside the room is poor, but he can make out the cracked TV, the water-damaged paneling, and the stained yellow-and-brown carpeting. The mirror on the wall behind the TV is sprinkled with blood and skin that has snaked down toward the bureau; the scene investigator has used a dark wool blanket to cover the female's body, but the hand is visible and is reaching out as if trying to touch her lover. The splayed fingers drip blood onto the floor like a leaky faucet, the hand just inches away from the nightstand that contains a Bible opened up to Revelation.

The figure under the blanket is a girl named Virginia Mathers, a sixteen-year-old runaway turned prostitute, the latest victim in Ray Keating's holy war.

A fragment from Friday's conversation came into the picture, something the Sandman had said: *Ray Keating. You nicknamed him the Michigan Mangler. Accurate given what he did to those women, but that stuff about reciting passages from Revelation as he hacked them into sausages—it's been done in every horror movie.*

Ray Keating murdered eighteen prostitutes over two years. A divorced, unemployed plumber, he had left several seemingly innocuous pieces of evidence that had made him easy to track down. Keating didn't even show surprise at being caught. ("It's just God's way," Keating said in his soft, Southern drawl. "He told me the devil was coming and what I had to do to prepare.")

In the basement of Keating's run-down house were four wooden crosses made out of two-by-sixes, cut in different lengths to match the sizes of his ex-wife and three teenage sons. Keating had purchased railroad spikes and leather straps that he had used to secure their hands and feet against the wood, and he had written each of their names at the top in his own blood. "That's the only proper way to offer up my sons to Jesus," Keating told Jack in a later interview. "That's the way he told me to present my sacrifice for the gifts he has bestowed upon me."

Why did you mention Keating?

Fact: the dismemberment of prostitutes, no matter how grisly, was not in the eyes of the Michigan media front-page news. Keating's capture was relegated to two columns on a back page. There had been no national coverage—not even a blip.

So why mention him? Why tell me he recited passages from Revelation?

Jack knew about Revelation only because Keating had told him. It hadn't come out during the trial.

But the Sandman knew.

How would you know? And why would you—

Jack ran back to his car, his world going in and out of focus, his legs so weak he nearly collapsed.

Mike had already rolled down the window. "What's wrong?"

"You call your sweepers yet?"

"Why? What's going on?"

"Have them meet me at twenty-six Main Dunstable. The son of a bitch was in my house."

chapter 20

THE NINETEEN-INCH TV IN THE CORNER OF THE OFFICE WAS PLAYING WITHOUT SOUND. Alan had muted the volume on purpose; he didn't want to hear what the CNN correspondent was saying. The images on the screen were bad enough.

The reporter disappeared; on the screen now was a shaky aerial shot from a news helicopter. The entire research building had been reduced to rubble. From the blast site gray and white funnels of smoke moved up into the sky like a twister. The destruction spread for *miles.*

Alan pointed the remote at the TV and clicked through the channels. EMTs trying to resuscitate the dead; firemen and federal agents tossing bodies on stretchers; others rushing to hands reaching from the mounds of debris; more and more images playing on and on over every fucking channel like some never-ending parade of the macabre, Jesus *fucking Christ.*

It had to be a patient. *Had* to be. It was the only scenario that made sense. First Gardner was missing, most likely dead. Then there was the matter of the last three days Gardner was on the system: DeWitt's team of programmers and network administrators had discovered a backdoor program that bypassed all of the system's network security, allowing entry on the system and full access to virtually every aspect of the Behavioral Modification Program's vast patient database. DeWitt's team was still sorting through the mess, but they had uncovered one disturbing item: "Gardner" had tried searching the database for information regarding Graves Rehabilitation—a now defunct group home for children once based in Massachusetts. Alan was all too familiar with the atrocities at Graves. *That goddamn place is like herpes; it keeps coming back.*

Fortunately, the files on Graves were either confiscated and destroyed or had been destroyed by the fire. The electrical fire that had burned the place to the ground was the best thing that could ever have happened. If a patient was responsible for this, what was his connection to Graves? What was he looking for?

Alan looked back at the TV. *Why did you bomb the building? Why didn't you just erase your name from the patient files and take Gardner's money and go live on some exotic Caribbean island?* Every time he examined the questions, he always came back with the same answer. The patient wanted to expose the program. *You don't know that,* a voice countered. But what if it was true? What if the patient did in fact download files—or had information on Graves? What then?

Alan closed his eyes, not wanting to think anymore. A dull sensation was slowly spreading across his forehead, the beginning stages of a migraine. Within the next few hours, any sound would be spiked with pain; even the dullest light would be like a needle jammed into his brain. He hadn't had one in years, but experience told him this one was going to be a *pisser.*

The neurologist had given him sample packets of medication, he remembered. He rummaged through the junk in his desk drawers and finally found one. His secretary opened the door without knocking.

It's Munn, he thought with a ray of hope. *She finally got Munn on the phone.*

"Director, line two," she said.

An uneasy feeling twisted inside his chest. He took in a deep breath, wiped his face one last time, and then picked up the phone.

"You on a secure line?" Director Harrison Paris asked.

"Go ahead."

"When were you planning on telling me that we had a runaway patient?"

Alan was too drained to argue. There was no use in asking how Paris had found out, or how much he knew. So Alan told Paris everything he knew about Gardner.

"Gardner's office was the last one to be searched," Alan concluded. "I'm waiting for Munn to call me back. Once I found out what was going on, I was going to give you my full report."

"Munn's not going to be calling you, Alan. He died on the operating table two hours ago."

Alan didn't say anything, just sat there with the phone pressed against his ear, the TV spitting out images. "How?"

"He was driving away from the building when it blew."

"What about DeWitt?"

"Buried in the rubble would be my guess. Alan, Munn saw the bomb. He called his answering machine and left a message: 'Bomb was a laptop computer in ceiling hooked into building's security system, activated by Gardner's access code, C-4, on a timer in Gardner's office.' Then the explosion cut him off."

Alan straightened in his chair, took in a slow draw of air. He had given Munn only two codes: a universal code, which would open any door inside the building, and Gardner's private access code. The universal code should have opened the door to Gardner's office. *So why did you use Gardner's access code, Henry?*

No one knew about Gardner's private access code except the doctor himself and the FBI. Gardner, fearing for his life those final three days, probably gave it to the patient, who then turned around and designed a bomb that would respond only to the doctor's code—the perfect way to alert the patient to the FBI's involvement in Gardner's "disappearance." Bombing a federal building guaranteed instant global media; right now the son of a bitch was watching the events unfold, plotting his next move. And what would that be? Exposing the program, of course. Alan pinched his temples and swallowed, his throat dry and tight.

"Right now we got the media pursuing the terrorist angle, and that's what we're going to keep feeding them," Paris said. "The San Diego field office is being flooded with calls from terrorist organizations who want to claim responsibility. We've had to evacuate the majority of our federal buildings—we'll keep their focus on that and tie the bombing to some militia group out in the Midwest."

"Who we got working the blast site?"

"Mark Graysmith from the Explosives Unit. He worked Pan Am and Oklahoma. Thanks to Graysmith, we know exactly where the bomber is."

Alan stood up, hope bursting in his chest, his eyes glued to the TV. "Where?"

"The San Diego bomber—our patient—has moved to the East Coast, to Marblehead, Massachusetts. Two dead families and one bombing."

"How did you find out—"

"The second bomb didn't go off. The detective sent it to Graysmith, who discovered a tagging agent in the explosives. The same tagging agent was discovered in the blast residue from our research building.

"Tomorrow morning, SIOC, eleven o'clock sharp. You a religious man, Alan?"

"When I need to be."

"Then you might want to call in for any overdue favors from the man upstairs. We're going to need a miracle."

chapter 21

MIKE ABRAMS SAT UNDER THE SHADE OF A TREE IN JACK'S BACKYARD. On the periphery of his vision he could see Jack pacing across the grass. A lawn mower hummed in the distance.

It would be best, Mike knew, to get Jack to open up. But Jack didn't operate that way. Even after he calmed down, there was still no guarantee he would talk. Jack detested talking about himself in any capacity. His true thoughts and feelings were constantly hidden behind a protective wall; when he did finally talk, his words were carefully crafted to prevent anyone from getting a glimpse into his feelings. The only person who had been allowed inside his secret world was his wife, Amanda.

Moving through life in this manner was limiting and, as far as Mike was concerned, a cheat since you were denying yourself a connection with anyone on a meaningful level. People were like this to varying degrees; you always wrestled with your past. But Jack's reticence *was* pathological.

"How much longer is this going to take?"

Mike looked up. Jack was standing ten feet away from him, looking up at the bedroom window.

"I don't know," Mike said.

"They're tearing the bedroom up. What the fuck are they looking for?"

"I don't know," Mike said again. But that wasn't what was really bothering Jack. It was pointless to ask. So Mike waited. The answer came ten minutes later.

"The box is gone," Jack said.

"What box?"

Jack didn't answer. Mike waited. To his right, behind the chain-link fence, he could see a young boy next door tossing a tennis ball to a small black puppy. He watched the boy for several minutes until Jack spoke again.

"It was in the attic. The son of a bitch stole it."

"What was in this box?"

"My wedding album, the photographs, the death certificate. Her pillowcase, it still smells like her . . ." Jack's words seized up.

Mike waited for Jack to elaborate. You didn't force things out of him.

You might hit him with facts to get through his stubbornness and his sometimes linear approach to problem solving, but you always had to wait for him to come to you.

"There was a journal," Jack said.

A journal? Mike thought, surprised. "How long have you been keeping a journal?"

"I'm not keeping one."

"You've lost me."

Jack turned and faced him. "The journal's from Ocean Point."

Mike was glad he had his sunglasses on; otherwise, Jack would have caught the fear and amazement that sparked in his eyes.

"This journal," Mike said. "The psychiatrists made you keep one as part of your therapy?"

Jack nodded. He looked away, his eyes blinking rapidly, like a man trying to absorb a horrible, life-altering piece of news.

"What was in it?"

Jack looked sick. "Everything."

Mike knew about Jack's history—was well aware of several intimate details that had been kept from the public.

Mike looked out to the road, thinking about the journal. All those private thoughts now in the hands of a psychopath. If the Sandman decided to release parts to the media . . .

It was like walking through an icy patch of air. Mike shivered. Suddenly, he didn't want to think anymore.

The back screen door slammed shut against its frame like a gunshot. Agent Roger Simpson, a tall man with a blond crew cut, bolted down the steps and stormed across the lawn.

"Sorry to interrupt," he told Jack, "but there's something you need to see."

chapter 22

AMANDA IS SMILING IN THE SUNSET.

She stands on the pulpit, her hands on the railings, her small, red-painted toes gripping the netting as the bow of the sailboat dips into the water and comes rising back up to the sky. The tails of her pin-striped shirt are tied around her waist, the shirt puffed out from the wind blowing past. Amanda's face, the color of cinnamon, is smooth and radiant in the sunset, her blue eyes as bright and clear as the water rushing underneath them. She is hugging a future bursting with promise and expectation.

Amanda is twenty-two, and this trip to St. Martin is their first together. They are in love.

Amanda picks up her bottle of Amstel, takes a long pull, and winks at him. Van Morrison's "She's an Angel" plays from the stereo boom box tied against the mast.

Despite the clarity of the moment, the rightness of it, he still feels nervous. His heart is pumping with such force that he feels light-headed, and his stomach is climbing, as if he's about to jump out of an airplane.

"Amanda."

She looks down at him, at his face first and then at the box in his hand. Her face grows still. For a split second, he fears the worst: that she is desperately searching for an excuse to say no, they are too young or she isn't ready or she wants to have some freedom after college, you know, taste the world and all, I'm sorry, Jack, so sorry.

Then her eyes well with tears, and her mouth parts into that wide smile that melts away those deep pockets of doubt and fear from his heart. And in the way that only she has, she reaches for him as if he were a lost child, brings him close to her, and hugs him. He can feel the warmth of her skin through his T-shirt, can smell the salt in her damp hair, her perfume. She presses her face against his chest. Amanda's words drift softly across the wind: "Until the stars fall from the sky, Jack. Always."

But memory is cruel. The window slammed shut on Jack's pleasant thoughts, and he was back inside the sweltering bedroom, alone, the only sound the murmured conversations of the agents in nearby rooms. The photograph of Amanda had been tacked on the wall; it had originally been stored in the box in the attic, the one the Sandman now had in his possession.

"Jack?"

Simpson, the agent who had retrieved him from the backyard, was standing right behind him. His smile was pleasant but guarded. "When was the last time you were in here?"

Jack had to think about it.

"Friday. Late afternoon." His voice sounded foreign to him. He cleared his throat. "I came in here to change and went over to my girlfriend's house. Why?"

"So you haven't slept here?"

"No."

Jack watched as another agent walked inside the bedroom and moved to the window near the bed. The agent draped a piece of thick black cloth over the entire window and started stapling it in place.

"What's going on?"

"It's better if I show you," Simpson said. "Bear with me just one moment."

From his pocket Simpson pulled out a similar piece of black cloth and moved over to the adjoining window. Jack watched both men. *Why the hell are they covering the windows?* He looked away, back to the picture of Amanda, trying to piece it together.

Mike Abrams came into the bedroom. "The bug hunters are downstairs setting up. They'll start on the first floor."

"How long is it going to take?"

"It shouldn't take long." Mike's eyes searched Jack's face. "What's wrong?"

I just want you to get everyone the fuck out of here, that's all. Jack gestured toward Simpson, who had just finished stapling up the remaining cloth. "You know what this is all about?"

Mike shook his head. A moment later the stapling stopped. The bedroom was charcoal gray and unbearably hot. Outside, Jack could hear the neighbor boy's giggling mixed with the barking of the puppy.

"If you came in here at night and turned on the lights, you would have seen it," Simpson said. He was standing next to one of two nightstands, each containing a lamp. "That's how he probably wanted it to play out. The only reason I know about it was that one of the guys noticed the lightbulbs."

Before Jack could ask the question, Simpson nodded to an agent near the door, who clicked on the light switch.

The Sandman had replaced the original lightbulbs with one of those fluorescent purple bulbs found in college dorm rooms and seedy night-clubs. The bedsheets, the shirts, the cracked white paint flaking off the walls, and their teeth and eyes all glowed a brilliant white.

Simpson's gaze drifted up to the ceiling.

Jack looked up with him at glowing yellow words that had been neatly printed and arranged so that if he was lying in bed, he would have been able to see them clearly.

The invisible worm
That flies in the night,
In the howling storm,
Has found out thy bed
Of crimson joy,
And his dark secret love
Does thy life destroy.

"You recognize it?" Simpson asked.

Jack answered the question in his head. *It's a poem by William Blake called "The Sick Rose." Miles Hamilton had someone write it on the back of my wife's autopsy picture and had it placed inside my mailbox the day I came back from her funeral.*

Mike walked up next to Jack. "This mean anything to you?"

Jack kept his eyes on the ceiling. "It's about evil."

chapter 23

THE IMAGES ON THE LAPTOP'S ACTIVE MATRIX COLOR SCREEN WERE VIVID, BUT THEY WERE NOT IN REAL TIME AND THUS HAD A JERKY QUALITY TO THEM; THE SURVEILLANCE CAMERA PLANTED INSIDE THE BEDROOM WAS FEEDING THE IMAGES THROUGH A PHONE LINE INTO A SERVER. The server captured the video images, storing them on the massive hard drive, and then shot them through the air to the cell phone attached to the laptop balanced on the Sandman's knees. There was roughly a minute delay between what was actually going on inside Jack Casey's bedroom and what was being displayed on the laptop's screen.

On the screen now Jack ripped the cloth from the window, flooding the bedroom with sunlight. A pause as more images were fed into the laptop, and then the Sandman watched Jack standing there making fists by his sides. The agents in the room were staring at him. Bodies stiff, they stood absolutely still, keeping their expressions free of emotion. They didn't want to provoke the animal a breath away from them.

Click-click-click and the Sandman zoomed in on Jack's face. Almost a minute later, Jack's eyes were staring into his own.

The Sandman wished he could be there. Watching a man's fear burrow deep into his soul was an experience best savored in person.

Jack's friend Abrams whispered something into Jack's ear so softly the Sandman, wearing headphones, couldn't hear what he was saying. Abrams had that almighty look on his face that shrinks always had—come to me, I know all the answers, let me help you. The truth was that they didn't know shit about human experience. The management of pain could not be learned from textbooks. You had to live with it, learn to inhabit the same space like some sort of forced marriage in order to understand, and if you were open and willing, over time the pain would show you the way to transform yourself.

Jack's eyes narrowed. A peculiar light came back into them; white-hot sparks ignited by an inner heat. *What's going on in that deviant mind of yours?*

Smiling, the Sandman pulled the camera back. *Come on, Jack. Do something pretty for the camera.*

Jack's eyes looked toward the hallway for a brief moment and then looked back to the camera. Something in his face had changed.

The Sandman cycled back through the image. There. Jack's eyes had locked on someone or something in the hallway. There was no way to see who or what had become the focus of Jack's attention; the camera planted inside the bedroom could only zoom; it couldn't sweep. But the change in Jack's face was clear.

He knows. He knows he's being watched.

It was impossible for the FBI to trace his phone calls, but the video signal could be traced through the phone line. If they did, if that was what was occurring right now, the agents would trace the signal back to the server. The Sandman wasn't worried. He smiled. If their trace was successful, they would find the house and, inside, the server and computer equipment. He hoped they did. If they tried to tamper with the computer, the hidden bomb would explode.

The feds must have discovered the video signal and passed the information on to Jack, told him to do something to keep my attention occupied. Clever, Jack, but you still have so much to learn.

The Sandman clicked furiously over the keyboard. Screens closing, he finally entered in the code to initiate the server's security, which activated the bomb. He typed in the commands to shut down the server. Kept waiting . . . The modem link disconnected. On the screen Jack's face froze into thousands of color pixels and then turned to black.

Sorry, Jack, you just weren't quick enough.

This time, a voice added.

A faint nervousness tugged at him, as if Jack Casey had just walked by him. Jack's thinking wasn't as rusty as originally thought. He had discovered the wireless surveillance camera this afternoon—amazing, really. Jack's dark intellect—the one that had solved every serial-murder investigation he had worked on—had risen from its forced hibernation and was now fully awake, instructing Jack where to look.

The Sandman knew he had been lucky. And despite Jack's recent brush with death, the man would not stop looking. In fact today's bloodshed had only fueled Jack's determination. The Sandman smiled. He knew a thing or two about such matters.

The Sandman looked up from the laptop. On the TV in the airport bar, the San Diego bombing was the lead story. He had designed the bomb to go off only when the doctor's code was entered (which, along with information about explosives and other interesting items, was stored on the building's main computer). Now it was official: the FBI had discovered Gardner's disappearance.

He wasn't worried about the feds discovering his real identity. All traces had been erased from the BMP database. And there was no evidence left in Gardner's home or office. As for Gardner, the good doctor was fish food, his body weighted down on the ocean floor somewhere in the Pacific.

The FBI was looking into the matter—had maybe even discovered that a patient from their top-secret Behavioral Modification Program had accessed their system and downloaded some *nasty* files. The scandal of the century, if the information ever became public.

And it would.

But first, he had to deal with the other families. Then he would summon the FBI here, kill them, and finally expose them.

The events in Marblehead were not global news. The Roth bombing was a blip in the Boston papers, and the Dolan bomb had failed. He had to grab the nation's attention away from San Diego and get it to look here. To do that, he would have to do something memorable. That would be easy. He already had something special in mind for the third family.

The Sandman packed the laptop and attached cell phone into a leather briefcase. *What about Casey?* that nagging voice asked, the one that had helped guide him here to the East. *You have to do something about him.*

Killing him was too easy. Besides, it was more fun watching Jack suffer.

He may be suffering, but he's smart. He's dangerous. Kill him.

No. Too soon for that. Better to watch Jack stumble.

The Sandman thought about the stolen box stocked full of Jack's razor-sharp memories—and that journal . . . he whistled. It was like having a blueprint through every dark corridor in Jack's head. The Sandman thought about a recent idea he had for Jack—a revelation, actually. He thought about it some more . . . Yes. It was perfect.

The Sandman smiled. It was going to be fun watching Casey drown.

The Porsche's air-conditioning was running at full blast. Jack had been sitting behind the wheel for five minutes and couldn't stop sweating.

The black Sony alarm clock in his hands was a popular model; Jack had purchased one several months ago. Problem was that he didn't buy one with a surveillance camera and microphone. The agent, Simpson, had discovered the clock. The wire should have run into an electrical outlet. Instead it ran into the telephone jack of a laptop computer, placed underneath the bed; another wire ran from the laptop to the telephone jack in the wall. The Sandman had managed to disconnect before the agents could trace it.

Got to sweep Taylor's house. Got to get her and Rachel the fuck out of here.

He put the clock down on the seat and picked up the cell phone to call Tedesco, the reason Jack had come out here. He had hit the speed dial for Ronnie's number when he caught a whiff of Calvin Klein's Eternity. Amanda's perfume. She always dabbed it behind her ears and wrists. Back home in Virginia, when he slid into bed, he could smell traces of it mixed with baby powder on the pillowcases and sheets.

You've got to get ahold of yourself, he thought, listening to the number as it started to dial. He took in another sharp breath of cool air and caught it again, very faint, and this time he didn't question it, he just let his mind slide back to that warm memory of that perfect day on Cape Cod. Amanda's parents owned a summer home in the village of Pocasset, right on Barlow's Landing Beach, and the year after they were married, they took a month off and spent it with her parents. He had been sitting at a redwood picnic table, drinking a Budweiser and playing backgammon with his father-in-law, when he looked up and saw her outside. He watched her arrange fresh-cut flowers in a crystal bowl on the table beneath the tall maple. He loved the way her body moved, the way her hair fell over her face, her constant smile. He could watch her for hours.

Later that night, they snuck out of the house and went down to the beach and stripped. He lay on his back in the wet sand as Amanda straddled him, the moonlight accentuating the perfect shape of her breasts, her nipples hard, her brown skin glowing. She rocked her hips back and forth slowly, in full control of her body, and with the wind whipping her hair across her face she placed two fingers in his mouth. He could still taste the cilantro herb and red onions she had used in making the mango salsa for the salmon, and when she leaned forward and pressed her chest against his, the cool water broke across her back and washed over their hot skin, and as they came together, a first, he looked up in the night sky bursting with stars and a full moon and felt an overwhelming sense of solidity, of complete wholeness, as if the woman shaking in his arms and whispering "I love you" against his ear had been specifically designed to be the caretaker of his soul.

"Hello?"

Jack blinked and was back inside the car. The memory was gone, but the feelings were still there, warm and sharp.

"Jack? You there?"

"Yeah. Yeah, Ronnie, I'm here, I just spaced it for a second. I got something for you." Jack looked up and in the rearview mirror caught the flash of something white in the back. He turned his head and stared.

"Jack?"

He had to clear his throat to get the words out. "Let me call you back."

A white pillowcase spotted with thin lines and dots of brown lay on the backseat. The brown spots were blood. The pillowcase had belonged to Amanda. It had been stored inside the box, the one the Sandman had in his possession. Had he placed it in here back at the beach, or when they were all in the house?

He retrieved it from the backseat and held it like a delicate flower. He closed his eyes, pressed it against his head, and inhaled the perfume and scent of her, the only living memory of hers left.

Amanda, why did you have to leave me?

"God I miss you."

A moment later the phone rang.

He took in a deep breath to clear his voice and then said, "Sorry about that."

"Drowning yet, Jack?" the Sandman asked.

He's watching you RIGHT NOW.

Jack threw open the car door and with the pillowcase in hand stormed down the front lawn to the middle of the street. Like a drunk seeing hallucinations, he turned his head every which way, his eyes frantically searching cars and houses. *Where are you hiding you son of a bitch, where the FUCK ARE YOU HIDING?*

His neighbor saw Jack Casey's expression, then saw the spotted pillowcase, and without a word gently placed his hand on his son's head and ushered him and the puppy back inside a house that was safe and untainted by an unspeakable grief.

chapter 24

IN THE DREAM THE MIDNIGHT AIR IS BREATHLESS WITH HEAT AND HUMIDITY SO THICK IT'S LIKE STEAM HISSING FROM A RADIATOR. The woods boil with insects, and a full moon glows in the pitch-black sky, illuminating the branches and leaves like an iridescent silver blanket. Sweat rolls down his face like tears; mosquitoes buzz past his ears, and the woods throb with crickets. Behind the barn door he can hear the screams of a boy.

His gun is drawn. Slowly, he pushes the door open, praying that the madman cannot hear him. There is no light inside, but the moonlight cuts through the narrow opening like a silver wedge, and he can see gas cans, stacks of lumber, and part of an old, rusty lawn mower. The floor is covered with junk, mostly newspapers, old magazines, and rotting food. He steps inside, careful of the pressure he applies to the floorboards. No sound. He is relieved.

He closes the door softly and his world turns black. The air is fetid with hay, mold, and disuse, and beneath it all, the sharp, sour smell rising up from his own armpits.

From somewhere below him the boy screams again, and there is another sound, a whir of a motor. The motor noise stops and the boy lets out an agonizing scream so sharp that it rattles the floorboards and squeezes his heart. The urge to run climbs inside him and he pushes it back. He is here alone, without backup, and has to work slowly. If he trips on the junk covering the floor, if his footsteps are too heavy and the old floorboards creak, the man downstairs, Charles Yerkies, may decide to hide and wait for him—or he may take it out on the boy he is torturing.

He risks the tactical light on the Beretta; a thin beam cuts through the humid darkness. He watches the floor as he moves.

After what seems like a lifetime, he finds a ladder leading down. The boy is no longer screaming; he is begging, crying out for his mother—soul-piercing sobs that ignite Jack's rage. A pale light bleeds through the downstairs rooms, and on the wooden floor where the ladder ends he can see shadows moving behind what looks like bars. He can hear crying. Whimpering. Metal clanging, *ching-ching-ching!* Screaming.

But not from just one voice. From several. Charles Yerkies has more than one boy down there.

He tucks the gun in his waistband and carefully descends the ladder. Charles Yerkies yells at the top of his lungs, *"I said be still, goddamn you."* Slapping. The boy cries. The slapping stops. The whirring sound—it's a drill, he's sure of it—starts, and when the boy screams again, it pierces his soul like a needle.

The door on his left is open. He brings his gun out and clicks back the hammer. He moves to the door. He backs against it and in one swift motion turns the corner and moves inside.

The boys, ages twelve to fifteen, are in dog crates that are lined up against the concrete wall and floor. Their clothes are bloody and fetid, their faces white with shock. One is curled up in a ball in the corner of his cage; the other two are gripping the bars with their hands and screaming. One small hand has managed to push its way through the space between the bars, his three remaining fingers furiously trying to pull free the padlock. The boy in the last cage, the farthest one, is trying to break down his cage like some sort of rabid animal. His face is frozen in absolute terror as he stares into the next room.

It is not the sight of their blood that sends Jack's mind reeling; it's the wild look in their eyes, the abandonment, the terror—eyes that no longer belong to children. He stands there for a moment, unable to move. His mind tumbles back to Darren Nigro, the eight-year-old boy who a week ago had somehow escaped from this very place and was found by a hiker. He sees Darren Nigro huddled in his hospital bed, a white sheet and a blanket wrapped around his body, shaking despite the medication, two pillows propped against him like a shield. His mother gently pulls the pillows away and then reaches out and touches her son.

The sheet and blanket are thrown back with a high-pitched wail that cools the blood and chills the bone. An eight-year-old boy is now standing up on his bed, ripping the IV away from his arm, his face dark crimson and his eyes charged with terror and rage, his teeth bared like an animal's. He looks down at his mother, spittle flying from his mouth, and he is making an inhuman sound.

Not fair, not fair, what are you going to do?

The sound of the motor brings him back inside this room of dog cages, of mangled hands and scarred limbs thrashing against bars, and the screaming, the inhuman screaming of the boy in the next room. He feels the heaviness of the gun in his hand and flashes forward to the civilized route Charles Yerkies's life is about to follow. Charles Yerkies, the monster responsible for the destruction of over two dozen teenage boys, will stand trial. After that comes life in a hospital for the criminally insane or a life term on death row, it doesn't matter. What he gets is a bed, meals, hot showers, time to dream and read and think. What is waiting for the boys and their families is an endless road loaded with misery and rage. They will never awaken from their real-life nightmares; all the boys will have to do is look down at their scarred and mangled bodies and they will remember, they will remember, they will remember.

On a corner workbench on the opposite wall are tools. In his mind a picture forms. In the daylight, such an idea would repel him, but down here, in the bowels of the earth where terror breathes, he embraces the thought and the sweet release it promises. Quickly he reholsters the gun and picks up the hammer, the weight of it comforting in his hand. A mirror is hung on the wall. He catches his reflection. He doesn't recognize the man staring back at him and doesn't care. He turns the corner and moves inside the room, the hammer raised high above his head.

Charles Yerkies is not there; neither is the boy. Standing in the clean concrete room is a girl no older than five. She is barefoot and wears a powder blue sundress; her baby-fine blond hair is pulled back tight over her skull and fastened with a red elastic. Her attention is focused on the rag she is working methodically over her tiny hands.

The hammer sinks to his side. She looks up at him. Her eyes are full of warmth and joy.

Hi, there! she says brightly, as if he were a long-lost friend.

Hello, he says, confused. He looks back over his shoulder. The dog crates are still there but the boys inside them are gone. He is still holding the hammer. The rooms throb with silence.

It's so good to finally see you, she says.

Who are you?

You don't recognize me?

No.

I know you. You're Jack Casey.

How do you know my name?

Oh, I've been shown some pictures, heard some . . . stories.

Her squeaky, childish voice is playful and radiant, but there is an edge to the words, a confident authority, as if she is in possession of an indisputable knowledge that is centuries old.

Who are you? he asks again.

I have your eyes.

Sidney?

Hello, Daddy. It's so nice to finally meet you.

Then he notices that the rag is smeared with blood.

What happened to your hands? Did you cut yourself?

She giggles.

No, Daddy. I didn't cut myself at all.

Then what happened?

She continues to look up at him with her bright smile, her warm, round eyes, casually working the rag between her fingers as if the blood were nothing more than fruit punch.

I was in here playing with your friend Charlie Yerkies.

He's not my friend.

Charlie showed me what he did to those little boys—Terence and Bobby and Greg, the ones you saw in the dog cages. And I know about the ones buried in the backyard. Those little boys are still crying from the ground. I've heard them, Daddy. It's awful. Why won't they stop crying?

Where is he?

Oh, he's around somewhere. She giggles again. Then she glances at the hammer, looks back up at him with a knowing smile. *I don't blame you for what you did to Charlie, and you shouldn't blame yourself. That's the nice thing about this place. There's no blame, no boundaries . . . well, I don't have to explain this to you. You know what goes on down here . . . at least you should.*

Take my hand.

Where are we going?

I'm taking you out of here.

I like it down here. It's fun and I'm learning so much—especially about you.

You're not my daughter.

She stares at him in shock. Her eyes pucker. Tears well along the rims.

I was kicking inside Mommy's womb when Miles slit her throat. I can't imagine what you went through, having to watch that, but see, I was still alive *when they zipped the plastic bag over Mommy and carried her out of the house. I was* suffocating *in there. I was kicking and screaming for them to let me out,* but no one listened. *Why didn't they listen?*

I don't know.

Couldn't you hear me calling out for you?

No. I'm sorry.

I wished you delivered Miles down here. I could show him a trick or two. She winks.

I'm leaving.

You never really left, Daddy.

Good-bye.

You're not going anywhere, Daddy. Here, take my hand. I'll show you where it is.

She lifts a tiny, blood-smeared hand into the air. He takes it. She leads him to a door that opens into a dark tunnel. There are no lights or sounds, nothing to see, the only sensation he has that of the smallness of her hand wrapped inside his.

She stops. Beams of moonlight pour through rock-size holes in the stained-glass window. It's a depiction of Jesus on the cross. Across from it is a closed steel door, the kind used to house the criminally insane.

She jumps up and down. *Pick me up, Daddy, pick me up!*

He lifts her into the air and cradles her rump between his biceps and forearm. With just the touch of her skin against his, her innocent smiles and giggles, he is no longer a glued-together fragment of a man. He is holding the event—the life—that should have belonged to him. In that brief magical space he feels complete.

She kisses his ear, a wet, smacking sound. Then she pushes the door open.

Moonlight floods the Dolan bedroom. Veronica, Patrick, and Alex are here, tied to their chairs, their mouths gagged, struggling to break free of their constraints. The Sandman walks among them, but it is impossible to see his face. No matter where he moves, his head is covered by a black fog. But not the scalpel; the tip of the blade glitters in the moonlight like a diamond.

The Sandman moves quickly behind Alex. Veronica sobs for mercy. The father, Patrick, is thrashing about in his chair, his words stifled behind the tape across his mouth. Alex doesn't know what to do. He sits there naked except for a pair of white cotton briefs, his thin body rigid with terror.

Stop, he says, and takes a step forward.

They can't hear or see you, Daddy.

The Sandman peels back the tape from the boy's mouth. Alex is crying. He doesn't want to die and begs his mother and father to help him.

There's nothing you can do to stop it, Daddy.

I have to try.

He walks forward. She splays her small hand over the frantic beating of his heart.

You can't save them, Daddy, just like you couldn't save those boys in the cages. There was nothing anyone could do. It was too late then and it's too late now.

The Sandman places a hand under Alex's chin and then yanks his head back, exposing his throat. Alex Dolan wets himself.

You're watching the wrong person, Daddy. Why do you always let your feelings get in the way? You should be thinking. Paying attention to your instincts. We've been trying to show you things for days now.

He looks at Veronica, but knows he should be watching the father. Patrick is the key. Patrick is why he is here.

Patrick has fallen to the floor; he lies sideways, the chair scraping against the hardwood, his muscles engorged with blood, the road map of thick veins on his massive arms and tree-stump neck bulging out of the skin.

Veronica screams one last time. A spray of blood splatters across her face and chest.

Patrick has suddenly stopped struggling; his muscles sag in defeat and his eyes are now focused inward on a faint thread of hope. Blood is pouring over his son's twitching legs, his small body convulsing. As Patrick watches, his fingers are reaching across the hardwood floor, feeling the change, the license, and the pen that have spilled from his running shorts. The smell of fresh slaughter is pungent.

His daughter inhales deeply.

God, it really fills the sinuses, doesn't it? she croaks. *It must bring back a flood of memories.*

His eyes water from the stench. He gags. Outside the window, fireworks burst and pop like machine-gun fire.

Come on, you love it. What you did to Uncle Charlie inside that barn—we all felt what was really beating inside your heart. Pretend all you want but the heart never lies.

She moves her mouth against his ear. He can hear a snarl building in the back of her throat, can feel her hot breath against his cheek.

You can't hide your nature from us. We've traveled with you. We know what you really are.

He looks up. His daughter's eyes look reptilian; the pupils glow a liquid black.

Birth and death, it all begins in the same place, Jack, it all begins in blood, his daughter says, and brings up her hand—it's a claw—and the last thing he sees is the scalpel right before it rips across his throat.

chapter 25

JACK BOLTED AWAKE. The dark room was spinning. He grabbed his throat, found that it was not bleeding, it was just a dream, just a dream, and with his free hand he frantically reached for Taylor, an apology already rising in his throat: Yes, Taylor, I'm fine, everything's fine, just a bad dream.

All he felt was a bare mattress, no sheets. Taylor wasn't here. This wasn't her room. He looked around. He was inside the Dolan bedroom.

It all came back to him, or at least most of it. He had been lying next to Taylor and trying to fall asleep. A thought gnawed at the edge of his consciousness. Something to do with how the Dolan family was arranged. Not before—the aftermath. When it wouldn't come to him, he drove over here and wandered through the rooms trying the coax the feeling into a word or sound or image—into something tangible.

But he couldn't remember how he ended up falling asleep. He sat there on the mattress propped up on one hand, trying to remember and couldn't.

Not good, Jack. Not good at all.

He had to get to the phone.

His mind still fresh with dreams, he slid off the bed and stumbled downstairs.

The living-room windows were open and the shades were up. That thick, stale smell of disuse, like a gymnasium closed for the summer, was gone now. He navigated his way to the coffee table. His cell phone was right next to his badge and replacement gun, a .38. He always removed them when revisiting a crime scene. Wearing them prevented him from connecting to the threads of the madness that had roared through the rooms.

His heart was still pounding hard inside his chest when he dialed Mike's number. The glowing hands on his diver's watch read 2:33 A.M.

"Mike, this is Jack."

"Jack . . . It doesn't sound like you."

"Is Alex Ninan still in Special Photo?"

"Ninan . . . Ninan, yeah, I think so, last time I heard." Mike took in a deep draw of air. "Are you all right? Your voice, it's . . . Where are you?"

"That morning, there was a Bic pen lying in the blood. Patrick Dolan wrote something on his hand."

"I read Wilson's autopsy report. I didn't see anything about writing on a hand."

"There was no writing. The pen was out of ink. The writing's etched in his skin."

"Wilson was thorough. He would have picked it up."

"Wilson *was* very thorough, but to see the writing, he'd need to look at it under an alternative light source. Ninan's lab is the only place in the world set up to do it."

"Christ. You'll have to exhume Dolan's body."

"Call Ninan, tell him what we got. I'll talk to you in a few hours."

Jack placed the phone on the windowsill. Exhaustion was working its way back into his system. His body wanted to shut down—but not his imagination. His imagination never tired, and right now it was roaring, like a bear caught inside a camper.

He rested his forearms on the windowsill and closed his eyes. In the past, he had rinsed imagination away by thinking of Amanda. He was able to slide under the comforter on a chilly winter evening and press his body against hers, moving his face to the back of her neck and inhaling the smell of powder on her clean skin, and his imagination would lie still.

But Amanda was dead. Now he focused on Taylor. Focused on the way her naked body, tanned and hard, looked that Friday night out on the deck. On the way he felt when she placed him inside her. Sex, the perfect antidote for death. Sex was like a fire hose washing away fear and loss and regret.

Black images from the dream kept tugging at him, calling him back. He threw his energy into Taylor. Taylor, Taylor, Taylor. Focused on her face. He was vaguely aware of the crickets' rhythmic chirping music, the way the wind picked up and shook the branches. A floorboard depressed behind him.

His eyes flew open and he wheeled around. A shadow walked into the moonlight pouring in from the two windows on his left.

Jack had to struggle to free the word from his throat. *"You."*

Malcolm Fletcher's face glowed in the silver blades of moonlight, his strange black eyes sparkling like polished onyx.

"Congratulations, Detective Casey. I see the old ways of thinking have returned."

chapter 26

MALCOLM FLETCHER SEEMED PERFECTLY AT EASE, AS IF SNEAKING AROUND A STRANGE HOME IN THE DEEP OF THE NIGHT WERE AN EVERYDAY EXPERIENCE. He was dressed in the same outfit he wore in Maine: black pants and a black T-shirt, and his hair was combed back across his scalp.

"You don't look happy to see me, Detective Casey."

"I'm waiting for the part where you pull a gun on me."

"Don't tell me you're still sore about that. Here, catch." Fletcher tossed an object toward him.

Jack caught it. It was his Beretta.

"I also have your case files."

"And you decided to drive all the way down from Maine and give them to me," Jack said flatly. "How kind of you."

Fletcher grinned.

"You could have dropped them by the station. Why three in the morning?"

"I like making a grand entrance."

"The same could be said of your exits. I understand you're no longer a resident of Maine."

"I'm flattered you checked up on me. With whom did you speak?"

"Sheriff Peterson."

Fletcher laughed. "I wouldn't place much stock in what he says. The man needs a map to find his zipper."

"Actually, he was quite informative, Fletcher. Or do you prefer Francis Harvey?"

"Francis Harvey is an alias."

Fletcher's candor ignited his curiosity. "Why would you need an alias?"

"Oscar Wilde said consistency is the last refuge of the unimaginative. You're quite an interesting person when you slip out of your purgatorial fog."

Mentally drained and physically exhausted from the day's events, the idea of trying to battle wits with Fletcher wasn't appealing. But Jack's curiosity as to why the man was standing here was overwhelming.

"It's odd that a man of your talents would seek refuge here in a town whose collective intellectual abilities are limited to the four walls of their existence," Fletcher said.

"I always wanted to live near the ocean."

"It's more than that. The people here remind me of veal—trapped and in the dark. Can you imagine their reaction if they find out the truth of what's happening around them? You'd have to throw Prozac in the town's water supply."

"How long have you been in town?"

"Long enough to recognize the impatience. Reporters stumbling about here and the Roth home asking questions about a serial killer called the Sandman, ATF agents examining the blast site. Your town's illusion of safety is about to be shattered. Guess who they'll anoint to reclaim it?"

"Where are you staying?"

"The Washborne Inn."

That surprised him. The Washborne Inn was Marblehead's premier bed-and-breakfast. A weekend stay cost a paycheck for most average people. It was an odd choice for a man who lived in upstate Maine in Spartan surroundings.

"The owners, Mr. and Mrs. Jacobs, are wonderful people, so eager to please. Are you still eager, Detective Casey?"

"I'm still conducting the investigation, if that's what you mean."

"Conducting—interesting choice of words. What you should be doing is *thinking.* The writing on Patrick Dolan's hand was obvious. You should have discovered that days ago. And this."

Fletcher opened his hand. Dangling from the wire pinched between his fingers was a small, round orb of glass attached to a circuit board.

"A pinhole camera," Jack said.

"Yes. One of several I found in the master bedroom."

And from my home, Jack added privately. The FBI technicians had found two dozen of them carefully placed in each of the rooms of the house. They too had been removed.

"Your friend was watching the families. And you."

Jack nodded.

Fletcher tossed the camera idly on a couch. "You don't seem surprised."

"We found those cameras all over the house."

"But you didn't expect to find them in *your* house, did you?"

Jack's eyes widened. "How did you know?"

"Did he steal anything personal?"

Jack kept his voice neutral. "He took some items."

"But he left something behind to tip you off, didn't he? Tell me, when you saw the picture of your dead wife hung on a bedroom wall and the Blake poem written on the ceiling, did you break into a verse of 'Unchained Melody'?"

"You son of a bitch. You were in my *house."*

"Someone has to protect you."

"Protect me? Protect me from what?"

"The Sandman. Throwing the camera into the water was clever. What would you have done if you had placed it in the trunk of your car?"

"You were at the beach? How long have you been following me?"

"You don't have to tread these dark waters alone."

"I asked you for help and you pressed a gun to my head, remember?"

"I didn't know the nature of your true intentions."

"And now you do? Somehow I doubt your sincerity."

"Without my help, everything you love, the shell of a life you've built here, and those craftily constructed illusions you maintain about yourself will all be destroyed. Or have you simply resigned yourself to the idea of once again packing up and trying on another life in another new town?"

"I have people working with me, some of the best—"

"What you're all doing is playing catch-up. I've seen your efforts. A high school freshman trying to unclasp a bra has a more polished approach."

"Why are you hiding from the feds?"

"Not from the FBI."

"Then from who?"

"From the same forces that want to destroy you."

Jack waited for Fletcher to elaborate. The hot room throbbed with the sound of crickets.

"Tell me something useful," Jack said.

Fletcher didn't say anything, just stared with his wide, fathomless eyes.

A moment later Fletcher walked away. Jack saw the man's shadow pause near the back door.

"Look into San Diego," Fletcher said.

"San Diego's a big city. How about narrowing it down?"

"Amanda was such a beautiful woman, one of those rare creatures that inhabits the body and soul. This new one you're using to cauterize your regret, what will you do if something happens to her? Where will you go this time to retrieve your sanity? Who will you use to patch those hollow pockets in your soul?"

Somewhere in the darkness a door opened and shut. Jack stood in the muggy darkness, once again alone.

chapter 27

ALAN STOPPED OUTSIDE THE DOOR MARKED RESTRICTED ACCESS AND QUICKLY ENTERED THE ACCESS CODE. The four cups of coffee he had chugged since seven this morning burned in his stomach like lead. He turned the lock and entered the world of the FBI's Strategic Operations Center.

SIOC was a suite of four windowless rooms divided by thick panes of glass. Alan walked to the farthest room on the left, the command room, where the director was leaning back in his chair, his attention focused on a red-covered booklet spread across his lap. Mounted high on a wall shelf behind him were five TVs, each muted and tuned to different news stations playing the same event: the San Diego bombing.

Director Harrison Paris did not look up when the door opened. As always the man looked like a new doll freshly unwrapped from a box. His tailor-made beige suit, white dress shirt, and conservative blue tie were crisp, not a wrinkle or stitch out of place. His gray hair was parted razor sharp on the right, and his salt-and-pepper mustache was neatly trimmed. His polished black wing tips reflected the brightness of the overhead lighting.

Alan took the chair to the left of Paris, dumped the files on the table, and crossed his legs. Paris continued reading.

"A man calls nine-one-one requesting emergency service for a family who's been shot," Paris said, not looking up. "The first time, the police rush inside the house. They find a man tied up to a bed, alive, the man's wife and kids slaughtered. Ten minutes later, a bomb hooked up to C-4 explodes."

Alan propped an elbow up on the table, cupped his forehead in his hand, and closed his eyes as Paris continued.

"The second family was slaughtered the same way. This time the police were prepared. They called in the bomb squad. The bomb commander found a laptop computer hooked up to the phone line. One call and the six blocks of Semtex-H would have relocated the town to the moon. Fortunately for us, the bomb didn't go off."

Through his tired haze, Alan remembered Munn's last words spoken into his answering machine: *Bomb was a laptop computer in ceiling hooked into building's security system, activated by Gardner's access code, C-4, on a timer in Gardner's office.* Same bomb design, same elements.

"The laptop computer taken from the house is the same make and model as the one used to blow up our research building," Paris said. "Not only that, the laptop computers belonged to us. They were stored inside the building."

Christ. Alan opened his eyes, leaned back in his chair. "How did he gain access? Do we know?"

"That, of course, is the magic question."

"We have any idea what else he took?"

"Guess where the C-4 and Semtex came from?"

Alan leaned forward in his chair. "What were explosives doing there?"

"We were working with a company who was developing a tagging agent for plastic explosives. The idea is that when a bomb goes off, these tagging agents would be visible and we would be able to trace the explosives back to their owner. That's how Mark Graysmith made the connection."

"Who else knows?"

"Graysmith's asking everyone about the tagging agents—wants to know about the building, what went on there, but he keeps running into walls. I have people there to prevent him from . . . Something wrong, Alan?"

"Do you know Mark?"

"No."

"I do. He worked with us on a serial-bomber case."

"What's your point?"

"He's one persistent son of a bitch—they call him the junkyard dog. Once he sinks his teeth into something, he doesn't let go."

"I wouldn't worry. He's about to be removed from the case."

"That doesn't mean he won't stop looking."

"Are you telling me how to do my job?"

"All I'm saying is be careful. Mark is very intelligent."

"I was head of the CIA for eight years, Alan, I know how to run a covert operation."

Alan didn't want to get into it. Paris had his own way of doing things and rarely listened to the opinion of his peers.

"I understand you found a"—Paris glanced at his notes—"Trojan-horse program that allows the patient to bypass the computer security and log back on to the system."

"That's right. It's been there for some time now. If he tries to get onto the system again, we'll be alerted. If he stays on long enough, we'll be able to trace him."

"What was he looking for?"

"He seemed to be very interested in information regarding Graves."

"Graves?"

"Graves Rehabilitation. It was a group home for children based out of Harvard, Massachusetts. They . . . we had some problems there."

"What sort of problems?"

Alan took in a deep breath. "Teenage boys, the majority of them psychotic and unresponsive to normal methods of therapy, were sent to Graves—the worst of the worst, you could say. Normally we involve patients in clinical testing for new medications, but at Graves . . . the doctors were receiving big payoffs from major drug companies to sign up patients for clinical testing. The doctors changed patients' diagnostic criteria and placed them in drug studies in which the patients didn't belong. The doctors also fixed the patient records. You know what Pall-Richardson is?"

"A big drug company."

"A multibillion-dollar drug company. They had a new antipsychotic drug called Diaplex, so they tested it out at Graves. The majority of the patients had no business being in the drug study. They all experienced catatonia and memory loss. Those were the lucky ones. Others had brain hemorrhages. Several committed suicide. It . . . it was a disaster."

"And these records were stored on the system."

"God no. This was before we moved everything to the database. When we found out what was going on at Graves, we moved in and started confiscating records. Fortunately for us, the place burned down. Electrical fire. We destroyed all the evidence. There's nothing on the system on Graves. *Nothing.*"

"Then what was the patient looking for?"

"I don't know." *But I'd be willing to bet it has something to do with Graves,* Alan added privately. "We have any idea why he's killing families in Marblehead?"

The director's luminous eyes were threaded with anger and something else. Fear, Alan realized. *Paris is afraid.*

Paris folded the booklet on his lap and tossed it like a Frisbee. It skidded across the table and slid right into Alan's hand.

"Your runaway patient has written a goddamn press kit on his activities in Marblehead, complete with full-color pictures. The son of a bitch has even given himself a name: the Sandman."

Alan felt sweat break out along his hairline.

"One of my sources at the *New York Times* intercepted this and forwarded it to me." Paris pointed at it with his pen. "Go ahead and look it over. I think it will outline our position *very* clearly."

Alan opened the booklet. In his mind the sky grew dark and cold.

Page one: a handwritten letter that had been scanned into a computer, then laser-printed. The Sandman was claiming responsibility for the death of the Roth and Dolan families. He stated in precise detail how they were killed and announced his intention to kill a third family sometime during the next two weeks. He would, he promised, continue his killing until the FBI delivered him to his grave.

Alan stared at the letters *FBI.* The surrounding text blurred away. His heart started racing faster. He flipped to the pictures. Snapshots of the families bound to the chairs and beds, struggling. Up-close color pictures of them with their throats cut and covered with blood.

"Lucky we intercepted this," Alan said.

Paris leaned forward. "That booklet you're holding was mailed to every major newspaper and news outlet across the country," he said evenly. "That sleazy prick Barry Silvera over at *Hard Copy* received one this morning. Not only has he sent a crew to Marblehead to investigate, a group of his fucking parasites were camped out at my house, wanting to know if there's any connection between this and the San Diego bombing. *American Journal, A Current Affair*—they're *crawling* all over Marblehead with the legitimate press. And the goddamn Internet is already buzzing with conspiracy theories."

Alan felt his stomach lurch. It was suddenly becoming very clear what was going on.

"The son of a bitch is going to expose us," Paris said. "Expose the program and the business on Graves—if he has any evidence on that."

"I doubt he has anything on Graves. The market for information on Graves is scarce."

"Then he must have evidence on the program. You said he downloaded files."

"I said it's a possibility. There's no mention of the BMP or Graves in here."

"Well, the son of a bitch is there for a reason, Alan, and I want to know what it is."

"You have any information on the two dead families?"

"We're gathering that right now."

Alan nodded. He looked over at the phone in the corner, the one that was hot-lined directly to the White House. "I assume the president is up-to-date on the recent turn of events."

"He's been apprised of the situation."

Which was political speak for, yes, the president is well aware of the problem and, yes, he's figuring out a way to cover his ass.

And so was Paris. That was why Alan had been summoned here. *Paris wants to find out how much I know so he and the president can form a strategy to protect themselves.*

Alan suppressed a sneer. If Paris and his boss actually believed they were going to use him as their sacrificial lamb, they were in for one *hell* of a surprise. *You're not the only one who's taken precautions, Harry. You don't think I prepared for a moment like this?* Alan had the evidence to bring all the major players down.

Paris reached inside his jacket pocket and produced an envelope. Again, he tossed it across the table. It contained a first-class plane ticket to Boston.

"You'll be staying at the Four Seasons," Paris said. "There's no place for you to stay in Marblehead without sticking out. In Boston, you'll blend in with the other suits and ties. Nobody will even suspect you're a federal agent, let alone head of the FBI's profiling unit.

"The suite is equipped with computer, fax, and phone, all of them secured, all of them wired into our computers. You'll have twenty-four-hour access to anything you need. Victor is there right now making sure everything's in place."

"Victor who?"

"Victor Dragos. He's had experience with these matters."

"What sort of matters?"

"Cleanup."

Victor was an assassin.

"If you're using him, why do you need me?" Alan asked.

"I want you to talk to the chief investigator running the show. Offer him our help, access to our labs, whatever he wants, but you are to remain behind the scenes. The media will be out in full force, and we can't let them know we're in town."

"There's no guarantee this detective will want our help."

"That, my friend, is the one bright spot in this mess." For the first time Paris smiled. "Take a look at the last divider."

Alan saw a grainy color picture taken from what must have been a surveillance camera: a man trying to free himself from the mangled wreck of what appeared to be an SUV.

"Jesus Christ," he whispered. "That's Jack Casey."

"Yes. Imagine. One of your own profilers has ended up running the Sandman investigation. What a stroke of luck."

Accompanying the picture was a brief history of Jack as an FBI profiler. Alan skimmed through it quickly. Then he saw the name Charles Yerkies and his reading slowed.

"How involved was Casey in the program?" Paris asked.

"Jack was strictly a profiler, nothing more."

"What's this business about Yerkies?"

Alan ignored the question and tossed the booklet back on the table. "Let Victor talk to him."

"Victor's skills aren't in verbal persuasion. You know Casey. You were his superior for several years. You know what buttons to press, how to get him to do what you want."

"That doesn't mean he's going to listen to me. Jack has his own way of doing things. He doesn't flow well with the tide of bureaucracy—never did. You have me talk to him, he'll turn me away, guaranteed."

"Casey desperately needs you and your services. He's calling in favors left and right with the lab, and he's using one of the site profilers from the Boston office, a guy named Mike Abrams. If the next family's killed in the next few days, you'll be there with the best equipment and Casey will jump on you."

"It's a mistake."

"Work the same magic brand of bullshit you float around here and everything will be fine. Just keep your face out of the limelight. I know it's hard for you, but I think you'll find a way to do it."

Paris stood up.

"You're jeopardizing the success of this operation," Alan said.

"Casey's the one who caught Hamilton after all those years when none of your other people could, right?"

"So?"

"So Casey will catch this one. When he does, we'll be ready. The Sandman's not going to live to tell his story."

"And if Casey doesn't want our help?"

"Either way, Victor's already punched his express ticket to meet his wife."

chapter 28

THE CALL CAME DURING BARRY LENTZ'S FUNERAL, THREE DAYS AFTER THE BOMBING AT THE DOLAN HOUSE. Jack was standing next to Taylor, both of them away from the crowd of a hundred-plus mourners who had gathered at Pine Grove Cemetery in Lynn, the place where Barry was born and raised.

Jack's pager vibrated. The number wasn't one he recognized, but he had an idea who was calling.

Jack placed one hand on the small of Taylor's back and felt her flinch, as if his touch were somehow lewd. He whispered, "I have to make an important phone call. I'll be right back."

She nodded, her eyes focused on the baby girl Patricia Lentz cradled in her arms.

He walked toward the road lined with the cars. It was 10:30 A.M. on Saturday, and the day was as hot and uncomfortable as the two before. Taylor's Porsche was parked under the shade of a maple tree.

Jack retrieved the cell phone Ronnie Tedesco had given him. He dialed the number from the pager and had to wait a few seconds for the encryption software to kick in.

"Jack?" It was Mark Graysmith, head of the FBI Lab's Explosives Unit, who was now on the West Coast working on the San Diego bombing.

"Yeah, Mark, it's me."

"This line you on secure?"

"Go ahead."

"Look, I might have to hang up on you. I decked out on them. They probably got a search team looking for me right now."

Decked out on them? "Where are you?"

"Playing hide-and-seek. You been following the news?"

Jack had. Yesterday morning, just hours after Fletcher's nighttime visit, Jack had learned of the bombing of a federally owned building in La Jolla. Sometime during yesterday's chaos, he had left a message for Mark Graysmith to call him.

"You remember the laptop computer used in the Dolan bomb?" Mark said.

"What about it?"

"After Burke went through it, he sent it to me. Very sophisticated stuff, Jack, we're talking the next generation of bomb-making. I fed it through the Rapid Start system and came up blank. It was the computer's serial number that gave it away."

"You tracked it down?"

"Sure did. Guess what building it came from?"

A door blew open, letting in light and air. The laptop was federal property. Six weeks had passed since the Roth explosion, and Jack had found nothing, but now he had a lead, a solid fucking lead, something to work with, thank you, sweet Jesus, *thank you*.

"This is where it gets screwy," Graysmith said. "Two days ago, this suit-and-tie prick from headquarters, a dumbo named Paul Dinkens, comes charging into my trailer like a fucking tornado. I'm at the card table examining fragments when Dinkens starts in with the grilling—no introduction, no small talk, nothing but questions he needs answered right now 'cause the director's on the line. Dinkens's sweating like he's got malaria. All of a sudden the guy grabs his stomach like he's about to barf and makes a beeline straight for the commode. So while the guy's in the shitter moaning with the Hershey's squirts, I take the liberty of going through the folder he so carelessly left behind on the table. That's when I come across an inventory sheet."

Jack felt his heart quicken with excitement. He was about to ask his next question when Graysmith broke in.

"Last week, you remember when I called you about the Semtex, I said that I found these microscopic polymers embedded inside the plastique, the one with the letters and numbers?"

"You thought it might be a tagging agent or serial number."

"That's *exactly* what they are. I flip through the stack of pages and guess what I find listed."

"The Semtex." Jack said. Another lead. *Keep them coming, Mark.*

"That *and* the C-4 used to blow up that house last month. They're listed right there on the sheet with those serial numbers. All the explosives, all the materials used in the bombs from your two houses *and* the materials used in the San Diego bombing, came from *inside this building.* The media keeps playing up the terrorist angle, blaming it on some Midwest terrorist organization called the Watchdogs—someone's feeding them shit and they're licking it right up. Jack, this isn't the work of a terrorist. You got the bomber running around in your backyard."

Jack remembered Fletcher's words: *Look into San Diego.*

How did Fletcher know? Was the Sandman a former federal agent? Did Fletcher know who he was?

Only one person has the answers you need, and he's shacked up at a bed-and-breakfast in Marblehead . . . for the moment.

"Mark, can you fax me a copy of this list?"

"Story number two. While Dinkens was in the can, I took the liberty of confiscating this list and locked it up in my safe. After lunch, I came back with these possible bomb fragments I wanted to check against the list. I open up the safe and it's gone."

"Gone?"

"The thing was locked when I left, and I'm the only one who knows the combination. Someone cracked the safe and took it. It's gone."

"You confront Dinkens?"

"He's disappeared. Nobody down here knows who he is and headquarters can't track him down. It gets even weirder still. You know a profiler named Henry Munn?"

"No. Why?"

"Munn was inside the building before it blew. He was driving away when the second blast turned him into pulped fruit. Get this: before the bomb went off, he called his home machine and left a message: 'Bomb was a laptop computer in ceiling hooked into building's security system, activated by Gardner's access code, C-4, on a timer in Gardner's office.' A laptop computer, Jack. Same thing your guy is using."

Another connection to San Diego. Jack's mind raced.

"I talked to the SAC here, guy named Tom Davis out of the San Diego office," Mark said. "We got eyewitness accounts of two separate blasts, and we got people saying they saw some guy jump from a fourth-floor window. Taking down an entire building with C-4—you have any idea how much explosives we're talking about? Add in the microcircuitry and the remote-controlled detonation—this is the next generation of bomb-making, Jack, the worst of the worst. You got no control."

Which is the same thing Burke had said.

"Tell me about this guy Gardner."

"Don't know a thing about him," Mark said. "Nobody down here does."

"That's impossible."

"If someone does, they ain't talking. That's the fucking problem, Jack. Gardner, this building—*nobody* is talking. We know it was used for seminars, we know research went on there—stuff on nonlethal weapons, things like that. But no one knows specifics. The more questions I ask, the more blank stares I get. It's like I'm on another planet."

"What about Munn? You call Alan Lynch about him?"

"Lynch is gone. You'll love this: guess where your best friend is going."

"Here." Why was Alan coming here? How did he find out about Marblehead? Three days ago, the story of the bombs and how the families had really died had broken the day after the bombing on the beach; the whole town was buzzing with news of the Sandman. Had the story gone national already?

"How much did you tell Lynch?"

Graysmith snorted. "Lynch? I wouldn't give that pompous asshole a weather report."

"So you haven't talked with him."

"I haven't, but someone has. Look, the only person I have talked to is Director Paris, who's extremely vague on the subject. I got fucking suits from HQ crawling all over me with their clipboards, I got evidence disappearing on me—"

"What evidence?"

"The bomb fragments I sent back to the lab. Nobody can find them. Now I find out there was basically a bomb-making facility on the fourth floor of a federally owned research building that nobody knows a thing about or wants to talk about, and to top it all off, my key people are being reassigned. The SAC, Davis, the guy I just told you about? The director bounced him."

As Jack opened his mouth to speak, he heard on the other end what sounded like fists banging against the doors.

"Christ, they found me. Look, Jack, I don't know what the hell is going on, but they're pulling out all the stops on this one. You remember my crappy penmanship, right?"

"Yeah."

"If I find anything, I'll mail it to you."

"Mark, listen—"

"Watch your back."

Then he was gone.

Jack felt hyperkinetic, as if he had just stepped off a two-hundred-mile-an-hour roller coaster.

He tossed the phone on the passenger's seat and looked out the window. People were throwing carnations and roses onto Barry's coffin.

Mark had been working on a serial-bomber case in Missouri when the profiling unit had been called in. The bomber tried to kill him twice: once with a pipe bomb attached to his car, which malfunctioned; the second with a mail bomb sent to his home, which agents intercepted.

When Jack caught the bomber—a disgruntled dentist of all things who had lost his kids in his divorce and had decided to wage a personal war against everyone in the legal system—they found in his basement a batch of homemade C-4 and the outline for a plan to attach a bomb to the steps leading into the bus that Mark's twin, first-grade boys rode to school.

Mark Graysmith had a mind that could strip apart and analyze debris-blasted items, and an encyclopedic knowledge of bomb-making. He could recall seemingly innocuous objects used in past bombs and connect them to a recent case. He abhorred bureaucracy and never stopped working on a case until it was solved. More importantly, he had a nose for bullshit.

What Mark Graysmith had just clearly described was a cover-up, and the forces behind it were now on their way to Marblehead with Alan Lynch, his old boss, the media whore, leading the way.

chapter 29

JACK TOLD TAYLOR HE DIDN'T WANT TO GO TO THE WAKE AT THE LENTZES' HOME. Taylor persisted in that gentle way of hers. The house was right around the corner, she said, they could stop by for a few minutes, it was the right thing to do, Jack, her husband *died*. Jack told Taylor that he had some urgent business to take care of, which was true; Mike had paged him ten minutes after he had hung up with Graysmith, and Jack hadn't had a chance to call him back. Also he wanted to visit Fletcher and present him with Graysmith's news on San Diego.

But there was a more pressing reason, one that was expanding inside his chest like a cold ball of air: it was time to move Taylor and Rachel out of Marblehead.

Jack told her he wanted to talk to her alone. Fine, she said, let's go grab some lunch at the club, sit out by the water, and try to salvage the day. He wanted to talk to her at the house; last night Ronnie had finished his sweep of Taylor's house—no listening devices. Ronnie had also installed the countersurveillance measures to prevent electronic eavesdropping. At the house, Jack could talk to her without the threat of the Sandman listening—or watching.

They rode home in the Porsche listening to the radio. Jack didn't talk. He tried to use that time to figure out how he would tell her everything, but his mind kept turning with images from the funeral. When Taylor pulled into her driveway, he marched upstairs without a word and stood in the shower with his head under water as hot as he could stand it. It eased the tension out of his body, but it did nothing for the images behind his eyes. All he could see was Barry's baby girl, Alexandra, tugging at her mother's hair. Envying her for that. Thinking, *At least you have your daughter. At least you can look into her eyes and see your husband.* Then his guilt. The truth was that Patricia Lentz would still have her husband if he had called Burke to remove the surveillance cameras—not twenty-something rookies. Not newlyweds with infant children.

He had widowed them. He had taken their fathers away.

He grabbed the glass of Crown Royal from its corner and swallowed, his third, in one gulp.

Remember what happened the last time you hit the bottle like this? You want me to replay those results?

But he rarely listened to his own counsel. He turned the shower off, toweled off, and then walked into the coolness of Taylor's bedroom where he put on a fresh pair of jeans and a gray T-shirt. He was feeding the gun holster through his belt when Taylor came in. She had changed into tan shorts and a white T-shirt.

"Feel better?" she asked.

"A little. Where's Rachel?"

"Still down at Billings's." Jay Billings, a sixty-two-year-old retired schoolteacher and widow who babysat Rachel some afternoons, was watching Rachel and the dog. So were Ronnie Tedesco's men.

Tell her, a voice said.

He was about to initiate the conversation when her eyes shifted over to the glass in his hand. "You're hitting the bottle pretty hard."

"I always drink after funerals. Bad habit."

Jack could see the words in her eyes even before she gently said them: "You've been drinking a lot lately."

"I'm having trouble sleeping."

"Then take the afternoon off."

"I can't. I have to go visit someone."

"Who?"

"A former profiler."

"He's in town?"

Jack nodded. He grabbed his watch from the bed and fastened it to his wrist.

"Can't it wait?" she asked. It didn't sound like a question.

"No."

"I think your mental health is more important, Jack."

My mental health. What did she mean by that?

"You haven't slept in weeks," she said. "You toss and turn, you're sneaking out of bed in the middle of the night, you're running on coffee, and now you're starting with the booze."

"I'm not drinking that much."

Not true.

"Yes, you are," she said with some force. "The day the bomb killed those patrolmen, you finished off a bottle of Crown Royal."

He couldn't argue that; it was true.

"I'll ease up, I promise." He offered up a reassuring smile.

Taylor wasn't finished. "And you're . . . you're withdrawing. I don't know how else to describe it." There was no reproach in her voice, just gentle concern. "It's about . . . it's about how the families died, isn't it?"

"No."

"Why haven't you talked about it?"

"There's nothing to talk about."

"You're hunting a serial killer who's also a bomber and you're telling me there's nothing to talk about?"

"He's not a serial."

"That's not what the news reports are saying."

"They're full of shit, as always. You of all people should know that."

"Then what's bothering you? Was it this morning's *Herald?"*

"I didn't read it."

Then he saw the tightness in her eyes and the way her body stiffened as if expecting a blow, felt that cold withdrawal from her that he had sensed earlier at the funeral. It was as if she was, what, *afraid* of him?

"What is it, Taylor?"

"There was a side article . . . it talked about your profiling career."

Jack felt his pulse quicken. "What sort of article?"

"It's not important. What is—"

"No, I want to know what it said. You brought it up."

Stop it, a voice warned. But he didn't want to stop. He wanted to give in to his anger right now, give in to the release it offered.

Taylor's face colored.

"What did it say, Taylor?"

She wouldn't look directly at him. She cleared her throat and said, "That you were fired from the FBI because of what you . . . that what you did to Charles Yerkies wasn't self-defense."

He stared at her, his heartbeat building inside his chest. White worms of light burned across his vision, faded, burned again. His body grew cold and still. The Sandman was behind this. *That goddamn journal.*

"I wasn't fired, I resigned," he said flatly. The distinction seemed important.

"What happened?"

He picked up the towel from the bed and wiped his face. Despite the cool air, he was sweating.

"Taylor, I don't want to talk about it now. Look, I have to tell—"

"That's the problem, Jack. You never want to talk. *Never.* Look at it from my point of view. I wake up and over my cereal read about my boyfriend's past life. Then I watch it on the news. It's playing out around me and I don't have the slightest idea as to what's really going on. I was hoping you'd bring it up, but you didn't."

"Where's the paper?"

"I threw it out."

"Where?"

"I don't know. Jack, the paper's not important. What it said, what they're saying on the news—"

"What are they saying on the news?"

"It doesn't matter. That's not what I care about."

"Then why the hell did you bring it— Look, I need to tell you—"

"The point is that I have to learn about my boyfriend's past from the goddamn media. Why? Because he won't talk to me about it and I just can't understand why."

The conversation was slipping away from him. He looked out the window and saw two little boys playing kickball on her neighbor's lawn.

"What is it about me, Jack?"

The booze invited all of the pent-up anger to the surface. Jack took in a deep breath to keep it down.

"What is it about me that prevents you from opening up?"

"It's not you."

"You think I can't handle it? Is that it? After everything I saw in Northern Ireland? In Sarajevo?"

The words were already formed. *Don't do it,* a voice warned, but the words were already there. He turned back to her.

"Charles Yerkies was a serial killer from upstate Vermont who kidnapped boys and had sex with them in his barn and then tortured and murdered them. Three boys were stuffed inside dog cages when I got in there—one of them was missing the fingers from his entire hand, and another one had been lobotomized with a drill."

Taylor's face went white, but that didn't stop him.

"You want to hear more? You want me to get into the real specifics, the stuff the paper won't print, about what I saw on the videotapes? You want a blow-by-blow description of how this sick fuck was working over a fourteen-year-old when I got in there, or how the others were forced to watch?"

"N-no, I don't," she said, frightened.

Stop it.

"You sure now? I can take you through every detail. That the kind of intimacy-building exercise you're looking for?"

"Goddamnit, Jack, that's not my point and you know it."

"Then what is it? Why are you deciding right now to hit me with this bullshit?"

She slammed her fist against the doorjamb. *"It's you, Jack! The goddamn problem is you!"*

His anger suddenly evaporated. Her words stung in the silence of the bedroom.

"You don't allow *anyone* in! No one! You're like this goddamn impenetrable wall that no one can get through. I try and try to get in there, and the closest I can get to you, the real you—whoever *that* is—is when we make love. Well, you know what, Jack? Fucking isn't brave. It's *hormonal.*"

"That's a rotten thing to say."

"So's having to watch the news to learn that your boyfriend spent time—" She stopped.

"Spent time in a what?"

"Never mind. Look, it's—"

"Tell me, Taylor. Tell me right now."

She looked down at the floor, her tongue working over her back molars. Several seconds passed. She didn't look at him when she spoke.

"It said you spent time at a place called Ocean Point."

A sick feeling ran up his stomach and exploded through his head.

"It's a mental . . . Why were you there?" He could hear the traces of compassion in her hard tone.

"What else did the article say about Ocean Point?"

"That you were committed—"

"I wasn't committed. It was voluntary."

"So it's true. You did spend time there."

This wasn't supposed to be happening. He had left all of this ugliness behind during his stint at Ocean Point. He had done his time, had moved here to Marblehead and started something new, something fresh and untainted, and—listen to this—had even managed to assemble a workable shell of a life with someone new. Now the whole fucking package was starting to crack and leak, and why? Because he had decided to interfere with the private agenda of a psychopath.

"Jack?"

The muscles along his jawline twitched. What he wanted to do more than anything was to get the fuck out of the room and into the air so he could *breathe.*

"Jack," she said again, and took a step closer.

He stared at the shadows on the wall. Every muscle in his body felt tight.

"Jack?"

"What?"

"Do you trust me?"

"You know I do."

"Then why don't you show it? Why can't you share that part of your life—*any* part of your past life—with me?"

He exhaled slowly. "It's . . . complicated."

"I know you're private, Jack, and I've always respected that, but please, for the love of God, please just let me in, just a little." Her voice broke and he looked back at her. Tears stood along the rims of her eyes. "I've been waiting all this time for you to let me feel that I'm a part of your life and you never let me in . . . why, Jack? Why won't you let me in . . . just a little?"

He had never seen her cry before, and the sight of it alarmed him.

"Jack, say something. Please. I feel like I'm drowning."

He knew he had to somehow deal with this moment. Behind his own fear was the overwhelming need to let it out and finally unburden himself.

But Taylor wasn't a profiler. There was no way she could understand each case file of misery and hurt, the endless stream of victims who sat in a jury box in your mind day after day, demanding answers and robbing you of small chunks of your soul, like parasites that feed on connective tissue. How could she understand waking up one day and staring back at the reflection in the mirror and no longer recognizing what was staring back at you—or liking it?

No matter what he told Taylor regarding Charles Yerkies, the truth was that Taylor would form her own judgments and come to her own conclusions, maybe not now, but over time. It was unavoidable. It was human nature.

"Say something, Jack. Please."

He could feel self-destructive tides moving in him, could feel himself giving in to them, in to the rage. Then the fresh images from today's funeral came back to him, and so did Ronnie Tedesco's words, and the rage went away, leaving him standing there, exhausted.

He walked over to the window. Hidden underneath the shade in the top right-hand corner of the window was a round black device the size of a half-dollar. He looked back to her.

"Taylor." His voice was slightly hoarse and lacking strength. "Taylor, I want to move you and Rachel away for a while."

"Move us?" She blinked the lingering tears away and looked at him, confused. "Why? What's going on?"

"You and Rachel are in danger."

Alarm spread across her face. "What are you talking about?"

"The Sandman may hurt you or Rachel. I need to move you until this thing is solved."

"How can you be so sure this . . . person will go after me or Rachel?"

"He told me he would."

"And you believe him?"

"Yes."

Silence. She stood there and studied him, her eyes still.

"He's after you, isn't he?"

Jack didn't say anything.

"Goddamnit, don't lie to me."

"He won't kill me—not physically, anyway."

"What—I don't understand."

The room suddenly seemed robbed of oxygen, and for a moment he couldn't breathe.

"It's why Hamilton let me live." The words came out detached, as if someone else were speaking them. "Having me live with the memory of watching Amanda die, knowing that I couldn't save her, Hamilton knew it was worse than killing me." Jack took a deep breath to steady his voice, then added, "He was right."

"And you believe the Sandman will try the same thing."

"The day of the bombing—the one that killed Lentz and the others—the Sandman had an opportunity to kill me and didn't. He let me live and killed the others instead. For fun."

Taylor started to say something and stopped. She just stared at him, her face blank with shock, her mouth slightly parted. Her body was still.

"I have people watching you who—"

"Watching me?"

"Experienced people. They've been watching you and Rachel. They're watching Rachel right now, in fact."

"How long has this been going on?"

"Since you came back from LA."

"That was weeks ago. Why didn't you tell me, Jack?"

"If I did, the Sandman promised to kill you. And Rachel."

She pressed her fingers against her temple. Her face was blank, all of her attention focused inward on the horrible images parading inside her head. "Christ," she mumbled under her breath. "Jesus Christ."

"You and Rachel are safe. The bodyguards are down there now, watching her. Nothing can happen."

"If he promised to kill me and . . . Why are you telling me now?"

"Because it's safe to talk in here now." Jack pointed to the window. "There's a device behind the shade—it's a jamming device. It prevents anyone from listening to us talk—or watching."

"Are you trying to tell me the Sandman's been *watching* me?"

"I'm saying it's a possibility. He watched the two families. He planted cameras inside the houses."

"Did you find any in here?"

"No."

"So these people have been through my house."

"And your car. There're devices installed in there. And they installed encryption units to your phones."

"I can't . . . This is so—I have to tell my sister."

"You can call her once you're moved. I don't want to take any chances. And I want you and Rachel to stay inside the house until it's time to leave."

His new pager, the one provided by Tedesco, went off; the shrill beep seemed abnormally loud and caused him to jump slightly. He picked the pager up from the bed and read the number.

"I have to take this call."

Taylor nodded. "I'm going to get Rachel."

"Taylor, I'm—"

But Taylor had already turned and walked out the door. Jack opened his mouth to call after her, but couldn't form the bruised apology lodged inside his throat.

Alex Ninan, the head of the FBI's Special Photo division, came on the phone.

"You were right about the hand, Jack. The ballpoint tip etched the words pretty deep in his skin."

Jack had the phone wedged between his ear and shoulder so he could write. "What did it say?"

"Gabriel LaRouche," Ninan said, then spelled it for him. "Name mean anything to you?"

"No." But Jack knew it would mean something to Malcolm Fletcher, and Jack wanted to be there, looking deep into the man's fathomless black eyes when he said the name.

chapter 30

MALCOLM FLETCHER WAS STAYING ON THE THIRD FLOOR IN THE PRESIDENTIAL SUITE. The room's name wasn't given for its opulence but for the fact that three presidents had stayed there. In the photographs lining the wall, Clinton, Reagan, and Bush all walked on the grounds with the owner, David Jacobs, the pudgy man in Tommy Hilfiger clothing Jack had met downstairs.

He knocked on the door.

"Come in, Detective Casey."

The sliding glass door leading out to the deck was open. Malcolm Fletcher sat with his back to Jack in a chair, reading. His right arm hung over the armrest, the tips of his long fingers cupping the ridge of a wineglass that dangled inches from the whitewashed balcony floor. Steepled between his long, narrow fingers was an opened book.

Jack moved to the railing directly across from Fletcher. It was close to seven o'clock, and the sun was setting along the ocean, the sky a brilliant hue of red. Fletcher had traded his Maine wardrobe for a pair of black dress pants and an expensive, form-fitting black T-shirt that accented the thickness of his biceps. With his black hair slicked back, and with the wineglass and book, he looked like some sort of exotic, middle-aged model.

"Why so dressed up?" Jack asked. "You going out?"

"Like you, I want so *desperately* to blend in. There's a wonderful bottle of cabernet sauvignon on the table you just passed. I can have Mr. Jacobs bring up another glass if you wish."

"Thank you, no."

"Your loss."

Jack slid his hand along the dampness of the whitewashed railing. "How did you know it was me at the door?"

"Urgency. You're the only man I know who feels *urgent.*" Fletcher snapped a page back with his thumb. " 'A heap of broken images where the sun beats, and the dead tree gives no shelter, the cricket no relief.' What about you, Detective Casey? Have you found relief?"

"I take it you've read the *Boston Herald."*

"And seen the news. My, my, Detective Casey. I never realized the extent of your deviant ways."

The Sandman's words came back to him: *Look at all these people staring at you, Jack. How do you think they would react if they were to discover that dark nest of thoughts and cravings you keep hidden? Do you think their small-town mentality could absorb the truth of what you really are?* That goddamn journal.

Jack pushed the words away. "I looked into San Diego."

"And what did your research turn up, Jack? May I call you Jack? Thanks to the papers, I feel I know you so well."

"Of course. The laptop computer used for the Dolan bomb came from inside the bombed San Diego building. So did the explosives."

Fletcher didn't seem surprised; he continued to read.

"This building . . . nobody seems to know anything specific about it," Jack went on. "They call it a research building, but there's no mention of what exactly the research was. I never heard of the place, and neither had several agents working the blast site."

"You're not supposed to know about it."

"Why?"

With a snap of the wrist Fletcher moved the book away from his face. His eyes were absolutely still and focused as he drank his wine. In the fading sunlight, they had an electric glare, like a man a thread away from committing a violent act.

"It seems the Sandman is privy to your thoughts."

Jack didn't say anything.

Fletcher's eyes studied Jack's face. "What are you hiding, Detective?"

"I'm not hiding anything."

"What was your reaction to the paper's revelations regarding your friend Charles Yerkies?"

"I didn't read it."

"You should follow the news. I have a feeling you're about to become a star attraction."

"Let's talk about San Diego."

"If you tell me why the Sandman is privy to your private thoughts."

"It doesn't matter. Look, what's important right now—"

"It matters to me."

Fletcher waited patiently, his strange black eyes still and unblinking. Jack took in a deep breath, looked in the distance at the waves crashing against the shore. What had happened that night inside the barn—he had told no one. Now it was about to have a national audience. Not only was Taylor looking at him differently, soon everyone in Marblehead would be casting uncomfortable stares. *And when that happens, where will you go?*

"There was a journal in my house."

"And the two of you had a reading group?"

"Not exactly. He stole it."

Fletcher grinned. "I bet it's a real page-turner."

Jack leaned the small of his back against the railing and gripped the wood with both hands.

"You don't strike me as the literary type. This journal must be from your stay at Ocean Point."

"You read about it in the papers," Jack said flatly, and then thought about his recent conversation with Taylor.

"They didn't mention the place by name."

"Then how did you—"

"We live in the information age. Personal privacy is gone. Bits of your life are stored in databases all over the country. Medical information is always the easiest to extract. Did you commit yourself, or was it a melodramatic effort orchestrated by our former employer?"

"I'm more interested in discussing your need to be involved with this case—and about San Diego."

"You came to me looking for a consultant. I'm here. Do you want my help?"

"Maybe."

"Why the hesitation?"

"I'm not sure your intentions are good."

Fletcher laughed. "Your coyness smacks of misology. Sinking back down to that dark place within yourself, the one that you tried so desperately to suffocate during your stint at Ocean Point, won't be as easy as you think. Those scabs in your imagination are throbbing, aren't they? Peel them back and you risk infection. If that happens, will you turn to your Prozac?"

Jack's face washed tight, his eyes flying open.

"How did I know? Your medical records were very informative. Are you medicated now?"

"No."

"Are you sure? From what I've seen, you've become a bore."

Jack felt his anger come back to life. His skin felt hot. He didn't want to talk about the past. "I want to talk about the Sandman's connection to San Diego."

"What you want is to avoid the inevitable. 'I remember the very things I do not wish to; I cannot forget the things I wish to forget.' "

"Goodbye, Fletcher."

"Did you find writing on the hand?"

"We did."

"A name?"

"Yes."

"Was it Gabriel?"

Jack straightened, his skin tingling. *He knows the Sandman.*

Fletcher's strange black eyes stared back at him. Darkness within darkness. "The last name is LaRouche, if memory serves."

"How do you know him?"

Fletcher sipped his wine. "Trust is vital to any working relationship, wouldn't you agree?"

"What's your point?"

"According to the media, you're a mental deviant."

"You don't strike me as a man who listens to reporters."

"Quite right. I'm more interested in examining the scars myself. The question is, are you?"

Jack looked out to his right at the series of homes that stretched across the bay. He saw the third family that visited him each night in his dreams—they were days, maybe even hours, away from dying. He saw Taylor with tomorrow's paper in her hands reading a startling and more disturbing revelation, the image she held of him slowly changing into a picture of a man she no longer recognized or loved.

He shifted his attention back to Fletcher, who was gazing at him impassively. Behind those eyes was the key to finding the Sandman and saving

(*yourself*)

the next family.

"Family number three awaits your answer," Fletcher said.

"What do you want to know?"

chapter 31

"CHARLES YERKIES," FLETCHER SAID. He examined his wineglass as if a thought or truth were lurking somewhere in the purple liquid. "A high school dropout born and raised in the woods of upstate Vermont, a borderline illiterate who spent his formative years in trailer parks being raised by a mother with a fondness for cheap whiskey and violent men."

The sound of waves pounding against the shore filled the cool, salty air. The sky had turned a light gray, and the temperature had dipped sharply. A storm was coming.

"Odd that the Sandman would throw such a loser to the media. Why not go with Miles Hamilton? He certainly has more sex appeal than an out-of-work auto mechanic with a penchant for dismembering little boys."

"I don't know."

"I think you do. And I think if I wait long enough, I'll be reading about it in the papers along with the rest of New England. Your girlfriend casting uncomfortable glances at you yet?"

Fletcher's stare felt like spiders crawling around the back of Jack's skull.

"There was a boy who escaped from Yerkies's barn," Fletcher continued. "An eight-year-old named Darren Nigro. A hiker was out in the woods about fifteen miles from Yerkies's property when he discovered the boy huddled and wearing nothing but a pair of blood-soaked cotton briefs with pictures of Superman stitched into the waistband."

Jack took in a deep breath. "That's right."

"I understand Chucky did quite a number on him. Used a drill on various parts of his body—even clipped off three of his fingers. With the severity of the wounds, it's surprising that the boy didn't bleed to death in the woods."

"Yerkies cauterized the wounds with a blowtorch," Jack said.

"How did you know it was a blowtorch?"

"Because Yerkies videotaped his . . . sessions with them."

"Ah. And let me guess: he kept these sadomasochistic documentaries near the bed, possibly on a shelf in the headboard. Cleaned the boys' clothes, ironed them, and hung them all up on nice hangers in his closet."

Fletcher's insight was remarkable. "How did you know?" Jack asked.

"The vagaries of sadomasochist fantasies, especially those involving children, are as predictable as the seasons. Did you talk to the boy?"

"I tried to."

"Was he responsive?"

"Not verbally."

"Catalepsy?"

"Somewhat. He was responsive when his mother touched him."

"What happened?"

"He screamed." Jack immediately felt the memory of that day in the hospital—as bright and vivid as it was nine years ago—pierce him.

"Did you pull the mother out into the hallway and give her the name of a good psychiatrist?"

"No."

"Why not? Certainly a *civilized* person such as yourself would have made such a recommendation."

"I knew that no amount of therapy, no pill in the world or love from his family or friends, would ever erase what he had endured inside that barn. All he would have to do is look down at his missing fingers or his scars . . ."

"And that was the moment you decided you were going to hunt down the man who tortured these boys and kill him."

"No."

"But you were thinking about it. That could be the only logical reason why you chose to enter that barn by yourself."

"I didn't say that."

"Charles Yerkies was a full-time, professional loser, a flower stem of a man who was afraid of his own shadow. When you walked into that barn, he didn't attack you. There was no struggle. He saw you with your gun and then cowered and begged for mercy."

Jack couldn't look away from the hypnotic black eyes boring down on him like a shotgun.

"You found three boys locked in dog crates, and they were screaming, weren't they? Screaming because Chucky was in the next room with the fourth boy. You walked into that room and saw the boys and heard the fourth one screaming, you saw Darren Nigro lying in his hospital bed with his missing fingers, not really a boy anymore, not even human, and then *you* decided there would be no courtroom trial, that *you* were going to dispense justice right then and there. So you put the gun away and picked up the hammer. A gun wouldn't satiate that appetite for retribution, would it? You need hands and imagination for that."

The truth Jack had kept buried for so long simply drifted off his tongue:

"Yes. I killed him."

"How did it feel?"

Jack looked down at the people walking over the small, narrow streets of Old Town. Not a care in the world.

"The cruelest lies are often told in silence."

"He got what he deserved," Jack said.

"So why the moral melodrama? Are you religious?"

"I was raised a Catholic."

"You might as well say you were brainwashed." Fletcher laughed quietly. "You should visit the Siberian Tiger Park in China. Twelve dollars buys you a rabbit to sacrifice to the tigers. One hundred and twenty buys you a pig. I witnessed a young Chinese couple buy the even pricier Black Angus calf for their two children. After several minutes of running, the calf was cornered and the tigers ripped it apart. The seven-year-old girl was taking pictures and her four-year-old brother was clapping. What does that tell you?"

"I hope some of us are more evolved than that."

"Yes, I forget how *evolved* we've become as a society. A sixteen-year-old boy from Wyoming was bludgeoned to death by his friends because they found out he was a homosexual. Christian protesters in front of the funeral home had signs that said 'God Burns Queers in Hell' and 'AIDS Kills Faggots Dead.' Animals kill to eat. We kill for fun and profit. We kill out of imagination and fear and want and need and use religion and psychological angst to label our actions." Fletcher laughed. "It all springs from the same well. And why shouldn't it? We are, after all, created in His *divine* image."

"Deliberate, premeditated—"

"A gunman walks into a church and kills fourteen teenagers with an assault rifle. One girl is wounded. She's crawling to the door, crying out for help, when the gunman sees her, places the gun to her head, and asks if she believes in Jesus. When she says yes, he smiles and blows her head off. Why didn't God save her, Detective Casey? Where was God when those boys were being tortured in Yerkies's basement? When Darren Nigro watched his fingers being clipped off? Why doesn't God answer the prayers of an eight-year-old boy screaming out in pain? Let me spare you the mystery. *God* doesn't exist here on earth. People die in plane crashes, entire generations are wiped out from ethnic cleansing, and children are massacred and worked over with drills and put in dog crates because *God doesn't care.*"

"It still doesn't make it—"

"How would Darren Nigro find justice? What would it take to stop the worm of memory from twisting inside his mind?"

"I wouldn't know. He hung himself."

"Did you ever hear from him?"

"Once. About two and a half years later while I was at Ocean Point."

"You talked to him?"

"No. He sent me a card. It was forwarded to me by a friend."

"What did the card say?"

"There was a news clipping of Yerkies inside."

"What did it *say?*"

"It said, 'Thank you.' "

"So what continues to haunt you?"

"Why is the Sandman in Marblehead?"

Fletcher took a sip of his wine and let his eyes drift out to the water. "Have any interesting thoughts on Larry Roth and Veronica Dolan?"

"Roth worked for the Graves Rehabilitation Center for Young Adults in Harvard, Massachusetts. Veronica Dolan worked there for one year as a psychiatric nurse."

"And all this time I thought they were star-crossed lovers," Fletcher said. "How did you find out?"

"Tax records." Mike had called him this afternoon with the news. "We know Graves was a privately owned group home and hospital, and that it burned down nearly twenty-three years ago—they suspected arson but couldn't prove it. That's about it. Information on Graves is scarce."

"It's supposed to be."

"Why?"

"It's true Graves Rehabilitation was a haven for wayward children—malcontents ranging from ages six to sixteen, all of them from abusive homes, budding psychotics and the lot. All of them from poor economic backgrounds with little or no future—what our highly *evolved* society labels disposable. Throwaways, if you will. Because Graves was privately owned, they had more liberties than their sister state-run organizations and indulged in some rather unconventional methods of therapy. Our friend Gabriel was a patient there, under the care of Dr. Roth. Have you ever seen a ten-year-old strapped down to a bed and administered electroshock therapy? Or injected with high doses of lithium carbonate?"

"You saw this happening?"

"That and other things. Essentially Graves was nothing more than a testing facility for new psychiatric medications—the majority of them highly experimental. The only way to test the effectiveness of these advanced medicines was to administer it on subjects who exhibited the specific mental disorder the medication was supposed to cure. There were quite a lot of side effects and many overdoses. In one study, boys from ten to eighteen were injected with an antipsychotic medicine that was still in its infancy. The medicine caused internal hemorrhaging. Sixteen dead, and two dozen more with severe neurological impairments—the whole affair cleaned up with paperwork and signatures. The pharmaceutical company went back to the drawing board and resumed new tests six months later."

The world felt as if it had suddenly stopped moving. "That's . . . This is—"

"Unbelievable? Ridiculous? In the 1930s, the psychiatrist Auguste Forel convinced Swiss officials of the need to adopt a racial hygiene law. Over sixty thousand women were sterilized. Hitler later adopted the same law, and we know what happened there. Remember the syphilis scandal in the South where they left unsuspecting black males to die of the disease? Want more? The British government coordinated efforts to ship orphan children to the Catholic monasteries of Australia. It seems the Brits didn't want to pay for those members of society who were going to be a financial drain, and the Aussies were looking to increase their white population. The trade-off? Decades of slave labor. Sexual abuse. Beatings. Death. All a part of our evolution, all a part of God's divine plan."

"What does this psychiatric-care facility have to do with the profiling unit?"

"Several members from Graves's board of directors—politicians and researchers who knew how to summon research grants with a long string of zeros—were supportive of the FBI's early efforts in organizing a criminal profiling unit. Psychiatrists associated with the profiling unit came across these potential killers, removed them from their no-future lifestyles, and shuffled them through various psychiatric units. True, the majority of boys were given education, therapy, and access to resources unobtainable in their former existence. The more difficult ones like Gabby were shipped off to Graves for more aggressive means of rehabilitation—all made possible with your tax dollars."

Jack took a moment to digest this.

"You shouldn't look so shocked," Fletcher said. "It's no accident that the profiling unit was named Behavioral Sciences. That's where their interest lies—*behavioral sciences.* The profiling unit is secondary."

"You haven't explained your involvement with Graves."

"I wasn't involved, I stumbled onto it by accident. Our mutual friend and former employer, Alan Lynch, was often careless with his phone calls and paperwork. I decided to lead my own independent investigation. While posing as a psychiatrist from Alan's *laudable* program, I ran into our friend Gabriel. It was rather difficult not to take notice of him. He overpowered one nurse and tied her to the bed. When they broke down the door, they found Gabby on top of her, strangling her with his hands. Another nurse found a remote-controlled explosive device tucked away in the ventilation grate in his room—a rather sophisticated one, given the fact that Gabby was only thirteen. It seems he wasn't content with his role as human lab rat." Fletcher sipped his wine. "Maybe all that shock therapy with Dr. Roth got him in touch with his rage."

"So you met him."

"Oh, yes. Gabby and I had become very familiar with each other. During several therapy sessions, he confided to me his dream of tying Dr. Roth to a bed and forcing him to watch as his wife's throat was cut. Gabby also wanted to blow up Graves."

"And when I came to visit you in Maine, you saw the name Roth in the case file and you knew."

"Bravo, Detective Casey. You connected all the dots by yourself."

"If you saw all this, why didn't you expose them?"

"I was collecting evidence when my presence was discovered. Records and surveillance tapes on Graves and two other testing facilities—the casualties ran into the *thousands*—were confiscated from my storage unit. It seems a doctor inquired about me, and Alan was alerted. He wasn't pleased with my project and decided to thank me by posting three agents inside my home." In the dimming light Fletcher's eyes seemed darker. "Fortunately, I was ready for them."

"And then you went into hiding."

"Just as you're hiding in Marblehead."

"I'm not hiding. I like the ocean."

" 'And this is why I sojourn here, alone and palely loitering.' Amanda wanted to live here, didn't she?"

It was as if Jack's thoughts were written on a blackboard behind his head. He felt something deep inside his heart tear.

"She wanted you to give up life as a profiler, come here, and raise a family under the guise of *normalcy,*" Fletcher said.

"The year before she died, we spent Memorial Day weekend here. Her college roommate lived in the next town over, in Swampscott."

"Of course. That can be the only *rational* explanation as to why an intelligent person would willingly condemn himself to a town that thrives on shallowness and rote. You're here as a peace offering to your guilt. So. Why didn't you make the move then?"

"I was too absorbed in my work."

"Maybe you liked the taste Yerkies left in your mouth."

"The Hamilton case came along. Nobody was making any progress with it so I decided to take it on."

"Why?"

"Arrogance, mostly. I was on fire. The profilers assigned to the Hamilton case kept coming up dry."

"Only you underestimated Miles Hamilton's abilities."

Jack didn't blink, didn't look away. "Yes."

"How did you catch him?"

"A twenty-year-old woman—a daughter of a senator—was found mutilated in her parents' Washington home. Her body parts were displayed in various rooms—a signature from the other crimes. I found a wine cork under the bed. It was odd, since the senator didn't keep booze inside the house. And the girl was allergic to alcohol.

"I found out that the wine was rare—it came from an exclusive winery in Europe. The Hamilton estate in North Carolina bought several cases each year.

"I went to his house to talk to him. A dinner party was going on. I asked him some questions about the woman. As expected, he knew her—they traveled in the same social circles. He was very polished, very polite. As luck would have it, he took me to the wine cellar so we could talk in private. I saw the wine. My expression changed, I'm sure—I remember being surprised."

"And he knew."

"I don't know. I've analyzed that night thousands of times and I can't come up with an answer."

"Did you arrest him that night?"

"No. I thanked him and left."

"Did you obtain a warrant?"

A pause, then Jack said, "No."

"Of course not. No need to drag bureaucracy into your private agenda."

"I wanted to gather more evidence. Hamilton's estate was vast. Very rich, very powerful—and he had a prestigious law firm at his disposal. If I had brought him in that night, he would have made bail, and with the little evidence we had, if it went to trial, Hamilton would win."

"There's no need to pretend with me. I know what's moving beneath the skin. The question is, do you?"

"I should have obtained a warrant. If only I had," Jack said, and his throat seized up.

"If you had only got the warrant instead of thinking about how you were going to trap him and dispense justice . . ."

"Amanda would still be alive."

For a moment there was only the sound of the wind, the smell of the sea.

"And so you've moved here and sentenced yourself to this walking purgatory, performing small acts of grace in the never-ending quest to silence the guilt that feeds on your soul. It borders on Jansenism. *Very* boring. I thought you had more imagination."

But Jack barely heard the words. For a moment he was imprisoned by memory: Amanda tied to her chair, that look in her eyes. *Help me, Jack . . . Please, help me.* Then the scalpel slit her throat and she was bleeding to death, the baby dying, his world gone, forever. *If only I had*—Jack blinked the images away.

"Memory, Detective Casey, is one of God's many acts of cruelty. No real hideaways in the mind to neatly tuck away all those nasty thoughts and regrets and feelings—no place to *bury* anything."

"You haven't explained the Sandman's connection to San Diego."

"After Graves burned down, the patients were shuffled around to other psychiatric facilities, ones that had vested interests with the FBI. Patients like our friend Gabriel became part of the Behavioral Modification Program."

"I've never heard of it."

"You're not supposed to. Only a select membership know of its existence. The program is a case study in rehabilitation—the brainchild of our former boss. Alan's theory is that if you remove a child from his miserable surroundings and place him in a stable family setting with emotional guidance, direction, and educational opportunities, you'll produce a fully functioning member of society. Doesn't it sound grand?"

In that moment Jack felt the week's events come together.

"The Sandman knows about the FBI's connection to this program, doesn't he? He knew the San Diego building was owned by the feds. He bombed it to grab their attention—to grab the nation's attention—and now he's waiting for them to come here. He's feeding information to the media because he wants to expose the program. Wants to expose what happened at Graves."

"But first he'll want to kill the families. He'll want them to pay before he exposes the program. Gabby has been dreaming of this moment for a long time. What fuels him is his fear of not being remembered—of not having the public know what happened to him and the others at Graves. He wants a place in the history books."

"The FBI is already on their way," Jack said, and filled Fletcher in on his conversation with Mark Graysmith.

"So Alan is coming here," Fletcher said. "My, won't *that* be fun."

"What made you decide to risk coming out of hiding?"

"It's not every day one can bear witness to the fall of a great empire."

"It's more than that."

"I'm here to make sure Gabby lives to tell his story."

"We have to warn the families. Do you remember any names? Anything?"

"My files were confiscated by our friend Alan. I remembered Dr. Roth and Dolan, and the names of two other doctors who died of natural causes some time ago."

Jack's beeper went off. He unclipped it from his belt, looked at the screen, and frowned. He didn't recognize the number. He patted his pocket for his cell phone, then remembered he'd left it in the car.

"There's a phone in the living room," Fletcher said.

Jack took a step toward the sliding glass door, then stopped.

"You were the one who set fire to Graves, not LaRouche. You couldn't expose what happened there so you burned the place down."

Fletcher finished his wine. His unblinking eyes were remote as they stared out at the sea. "I believe it was Plutarch who said, 'Death plucks my ear and says, "Live, for I am coming." ' If you cherish the memory of your wife, you owe her at least that."

The cordless phone was in the bookshelf next to the fire. Jack dialed the number from his beeper.

"Duffy," a voice said.

Jack didn't recognize the name. "This is Detective Jack Casey from Marblehead. Did you just—"

"Beeped you, yes, I did. I'm chief of detectives here in Newton, and I think I'm going to need your help. I think you should listen to this nine-one-one call that just came in."

chapter 32

THE CITY OF NEWTON, THE PLACE TO LIVE IF YOU WANTED TO SHOW OFF YOUR MONEY AND STATUS, WAS LOCATED SOUTH OF MARBLEHEAD, AN HOUR'S DRIVE UNDER THE BEST CIRCUMSTANCES. The way to Parish Road reminded Jack of a nightmare handpicked from a disaster movie in which the end of the world was just moments away. Terrified families ran out of their homes to the rows of school buses jammed between a scattering of police cruisers. Local cops and staties yelled at the small congestion of commuter traffic to pull over and let the buses through. Orange roadblocks lined the roads; behind them were cruisers parked at angles to stop any commuters who had decided to try to make a run home down a side street.

With a plastic bubble mounted on the dashboard, its red light revolving slowly, Jack pulled Fletcher's truck out of the stop-dead traffic and with his hand planted on the horn drove up the sidewalk. A small platoon of blue uniforms ran toward him, shouting over bullhorns to stop and pull over.

Jack flipped open his shield and slowed. A portly cop came up to the driver's window. He didn't even look at the shield.

"Casey, right? I recognize your face from the papers."

"I'm looking for Detective Bill—"

"Right, right, he's on Parish. Take this left here, go straight down. The amusement park will be on your right, you can't miss it."

The cop moved the roadblocks. Jack drove down the sidewalk, across lawns and driveways of upscale homes, and then bounced back onto the road and took the left hard. *Good,* he thought as he looked at the darkened homes. *They've shut off the power.* For a while there was only the sound of the Porsche's engine.

"Pull over here," Fletcher said.

It was the first time he had spoken since leaving the Washborne Inn; his attention had been focused on his computer. During the forty-minute drive, he had calmly typed on the laptop, his eyes never lifting to see the truck riding dangerously close to the guardrail or wondering why they had suddenly swerved and skidded.

Jack pulled over to the curb.

"Guess who's watching?" Fletcher said. Glowing snakes of white, red, and blue lines washed over his face; his eyes were wide with pleasure.

"Wireless cams?"

"The area's flooded with microwave. No doubt we'll find them in the trees. Gabriel is too confident to change his style."

On the laptop's screen was some sort of program that seemed to be measuring frequencies. A thick rubber antenna sprouted from its side; below it was a long, rectangular, black box—a sophisticated scanner.

"Can you lock onto the video signal?" Jack asked.

"Do you honestly believe you'll find Gabby sitting in a van on a side street?"

"What do you suggest we do besides you sitting here and entertaining me with your wit?"

"This round, the stakes are much higher. No doubt he's devised safeguards to protect himself from being discovered. So have I."

On the floor was Fletcher's black briefcase. He reached inside and came up with a beeper.

"You're going to page him," Jack said.

"High-energy radio frequency, or HERF." On the pager's LED screen was a small black bar. "At its current setting this pager will emit electromagnetic interference with my laptop and your cellular phone. If I increase it, I could destroy all of the circuitry inside this car. Once I locate a camera, all I need to do is place this pager next to it and at its current setting all our friend Gabby will see is static."

"And what if that prompts him to blow the bomb?"

"The wireless cameras he's using are subject to interference. With all the activity, he'll think it's normal. Besides, he's far too enraptured with the scenery to think otherwise." Fletcher handed Jack the pager. "As for the pinhole cameras inside the house, you'll have to increase the frequency level. Just touch the button and he won't see a thing. Don't go into the house without it."

Jack clipped it to his belt and opened the truck door.

"In the meantime I'd suggest finding a way to disguise yourself," Fletcher said. "I'd hate to be the one consoling your girlfriend at your funeral."

"Take care of the cameras. I'll talk to Duffy."

"Please do. And keep your eye out for the members of our federal family. I have the strangest feeling they're going to crash tonight's party."

• • •

A small fleet of cruisers was parked on Parish. To Jack's immediate left were three fire trucks parked against the curb and in front of them, parked at odd angles, five ambulances. Firemen and EMTs were out pacing the street. A fireman was leaning against the side of a truck, taking a private inventory of the activity. Jack jogged over to him and the fireman turned around. He had a pug face and his short brown hair stood up like needles on his scalp.

"You're that detective from Marblehead," he said. "The one that's all over the news."

Jack nodded. "Bill Duffy called me. You know where he is?"

"Standing right there in front of that Colonial on the right—number one twenty-two, the one with the farmer's porch. He's the guy in the blue PEBBLE BEACH golf shirt."

"I need to borrow your jacket and hat."

The fireman's eyes narrowed. "Please tell me you're not thinking of going in that house."

"No, I just need to look like a fireman."

The man's face clouded with confusion, then he shrugged it off. "You want to look the part, you're going to need the whole outfit. Hold on."

The fireman disappeared to the rear of the fire engine and returned a moment later with an armful of clothing. Jack slid into thick, suspendered pants and boots, put on a heavy jacket and a helmet that shadowed his face.

Blue uniforms and plainclothesmen moved in the narrow spaces between the cruisers, talking on walkie-talkies or on the mike to dispatch. It was the look in each of their eyes that caught Jack's attention: they were petrified.

The Colonial was set back from the road and shaded by the thick branches of sugar maples. The rooms beyond the windows were dark and still, the front door ajar. Bill Duffy stood in the middle of the front lawn. He was pencil thin and wore a pair of razor-creased, tan khakis and a baggy golf shirt with the words PEBBLE BEACH stitched into the cloth above the breastbone. Jack placed him somewhere in his late fifties.

Jack moved across the lawn, staring at the house. How much plastic explosive was in there? And how was this bomb constructed? The stakes this round were much higher, he knew. His mind flashed back to the night at the Roth house, and his nerves started to hum like a tuning fork. Thunder rumbled in the distance.

"Christ, just what we need now, a fucking rainstorm," one detective said.

Duffy looked up to the blackening sky and popped a fresh cigarette in his mouth. "I think I hear a helicopter."

"The media's already gotten wind of this, I'm sure," another detective said, and sighed. "This is going to be one fucking long night."

Jack came up behind Duffy, grabbed his arm, and leaned into Duffy's ear. "We're being watched and recorded. Let's take a walk."

Duffy casually lit his cigarette. His face registered no fear or apprehension; his hazel eyes were as unreadable as stone.

They started walking back toward the fire trucks. The air seemed charged with an electrical current; everywhere officers were scrambling. *That should keep the Sandman occupied,* Jack thought, pulling his fireman's helmet farther down his forehead. He looked at the ground as he talked.

"What's the status?"

"We're in the process of evacuating all the homes within a mile radius." Duffy's voice was gruff. "As for the house, the power's shut off and so are the phones, just like you asked. Family's name is Beaumont, they have an eleven-year-old kid named Eric. I didn't feel good about shutting off the phones. . . . You're sure they're dead?"

"I can't be sure. Why?"

"Since I last talked to you, I've gotten six phone calls from a man claiming to be Roger Beaumont. Says he's tied up to a chair in the bedroom and managed to get out his cell phone. Says the killer shot him in both kneecaps and he can't move and is screaming why the fuck won't we come in there and save him and his wife, who's handcuffed to the bed and bleeding to death. I could hear a woman crying in the background. You should hear the tape."

"He uses a voice-altering device. Both calls to our station were different. The second time, he pretended to be a neighbor of the Dolans', saying there was a gunshot. He wants you to go running in there to activate the bomb."

"The first family, the Roths, that guy was alive when you went in there, right?"

Jack stopped walking. He looked over his shoulder at the house. Could the Sandman have left a survivor, someone wounded and dying to summon the police inside? A new scenario—and entirely possible. The thought made him shudder.

"Roger Beaumont, he give you his cell phone number?"

"Yeah. And we called him back on it, and sure enough, he was screaming out in pain. Then his cell phone battery died."

"Supposedly."

"The calls . . . they were pretty convincing."

I'm sure they were. "Are any of the second-floor windows open?"

"No, they're all shut, and the shades are drawn. We haven't heard anyone screaming or crying out for help."

"The family's dead."

"But you don't know that for sure."

"I'm sure of one thing: we rush inside that house, not knowing how this bomb's constructed or where it is, we'll blow the house and probably take the entire street along with it. The first bomb used infrared beams. I walked across one and started the timer. The second one was to be detonated by a phone call. Who the hell knows what he's got in store for us this round." Carefully shielding his face, Jack looked around the street. "Where's Burke?"

"Haven't the foggiest. And we've been keeping an eye out for him."

Shit. When Jack had gotten off the phone with Duffy, he had immediately called Burke's office. The secretary said he was on a job in Dorchester; someone had found a pipe bomb in an apartment mailbox. His pager and cellular phone were turned off, but she promised to have somebody personally deliver the message.

"What about the FBI? Guy named Alan Lynch. You see him?"

"No," Duffy said. "You expecting the feds?"

"They might be on their way here. If they show up, I want to keep them out of this."

Duffy walked on, saying nothing.

"You have a problem with that?" Jack asked.

Duffy flicked his cigarette into the wind and rubbed his chin. "Look, I got to be up-front with you. I'm standing here, knowing there's a bomb inside the house, possibly even a survivor barely hanging on to his life—I don't know what to do. On top of that, I have all these people with wives and kids, and they're all looking to me to make a decision, and all I can think about is a goddamn bomb that's sitting inside the house loaded with C-4 or Semtex. I've been through two tours in Nam, worked as a cop in Roxbury, and been shot at more times than I care to remember. I'm not afraid of dying. What I *am* afraid of is spending the rest of my waking days wrestling with the decision that cost the lives of dozens of people. Take a look around you. I'm surrounded by kids."

"What are you asking me?"

Duffy took one last drag on his cigarette, flicked the butt into the wind.

"Run the show," he said in a long stream of smoke. He reached for the pack of Marlboros inside his shirt pocket. "I can't be calling the shots on this one. I'm out of my league here. I'll do whatever you want, but you have to be the man."

Jack was about to say something when he noticed Duffy's eyes narrow and lock on something in the crowd behind him. Jack turned around, careful to keep his face from being seen. An overweight man in cream khakis and a blue shirt and tie was pushing his way through. The man's face was white and dripping with sweat, his eyes charged with fear. He ran breathlessly over to Duffy.

"What is it, Frank?"

"It's the kid, Eric Beaumont. Duff, the kid says he's calling from inside the house."

chapter 33

THE CIGARETTE IN THE CORNER OF DUFFY'S MOUTH BLEW AWAY. "That can't be right," he said. "He can't be calling from inside the house. The goddamn phone lines are shut *down.*"

"Duff, the kid's on a cell phone, he's talking and he's scared out of his mind," the cop said.

"His father's phone? The battery went dead. He told me—"

"But we don't know if it was really the father, right?"

Duffy and the cop looked to Jack, who was staring at the house, thinking, *It's a trap. The Sandman can manipulate the tone and pitch of his voice. Maybe he's impersonating a child this time. He tried impersonating Roger Beaumont and nobody moved. Now he's impersonating a child, he wants to get us inside the house.*

Why? Why would he do that?

Jack didn't know. Why not blow the bomb right now? Why the need to get everyone inside?

What if it isn't a trap? What if there really is *a survivor and this boy is really inside the house? If the Sandman's placed cameras, he could be watching and listening right—*

Jack grabbed the cop by the arm. *"Terminate that call right now."*

"You want me to *hang up* on the kid?"

"Cell calls are easy to monitor. All you need is a cheap scanner." Jack turned to Duffy. "If there really is someone in there and the Sandman's listening in and finds out—"

"He'll blow the bomb, Jesus H. Christ, Frank, terminate that call *right now.* Then we have to get all these cruisers off this street."

"No, keep the cruisers where they are," Jack said. "Let's get everyone out of here, but do it casually. If the Sandman sees everyone running, he'll know we're onto him and detonate the bomb.

"Duffy, get me the kid's cell phone number and meet me at my truck, a silver Ford parked around the corner. My cell phone is equipped with encryption technology so the Sandman won't be able to hear my voice. Tell the kid we'll call him back and we'll navigate him out of the house."

Jack had to fight the urge to run. He lumbered down the street in the heavy fireman's gear, pushing his way through frightened stares. All he could see was the image of a small boy wandering through darkened rooms in search of his parents—wandering toward the bomb. *If this one's detonated by infrared like the Roths' and the kid stumbles across the beam—*

He pushed it all away. Had to. Had to focus on talking to a terrorized boy and getting him safely out of the house.

Tick, tick, tick, how are you going to save this one? Tick, tick, tick . . .

He threw open the truck's door, took off his helmet, and with shaking hands grabbed the cell phone. Officers were moving off Parish; once they turned the corner, they broke into a run and stampeded past the truck in a blur. Still no sign of Burke. And where was Fletcher?

Duffy joined him a moment later, wedged himself into the seat, and handed him a slip of paper with the number on it. "This phone number is different than the father gave me. You really think this kid's the real deal?"

"We're about to find out." Jack placed the cell phone into the bracket. The scrambling unit attached to the back window was on. He hit the speakerphone and started dialing.

"I think it's best if you talk to him. You have a better handle on the nightmare in there than I do."

Jack nodded. He finished dialing the number and was ready to hit the SEND button when he stopped.

"You know, Duffy, if the bomb goes off and we're sitting here—"

"I know the score, so let's get to it."

Jack hit SEND.

"Hello?" The eleven-year-old voice was small and frightened. Very young. And it didn't sound disguised.

"Eric Beaumont?"

"Yes."

"Eric, I'm sorry we had to hang up on you like that, but we needed to change phones. Are you hurt?"

"What?"

"Are you hurt? Are you cut or bleeding? Can you move?"

"I can't hear you that good. You're all staticky."

Jack could hear the boy fine. The signal strength of the phone was at its highest setting. Then why . . .

Fletcher's beeper.

Quickly Jack unclipped it from his belt and fiddled with the two buttons until the black bar disappeared. He tossed the pager on the backseat next to a Coleman flashlight.

"Eric, can you hear me better now?"

"Yes."

"Eric, how old are you?"

"Eleven."

"Okay, good. Eric, the first thing I need you to do is to tell me where you are."

"Upstairs."

"Where upstairs?"

"In the hallway. Near my mom's bedroom."

Jack's stomach tightened. He exchanged a nervous glance with Duffy, who shifted uncomfortably in his seat.

"Eric," Jack said calmly, "you have to stay away from the bedroom."

"But my mom and dad are up here. I want to make sure they're okay. I heard them . . . I heard them screaming."

"Are you walking right now?"

"Yes." The voice was about to break.

"Stop walking."

"Why aren't the lights working? I keep flipping up the lights and they won't turn on."

"Eric, stop walking right now."

A pause, then, "Okay." Nervous.

"Did you stop walking?"

"Why can't I go in the bedroom?"

"There's something in there that might hurt you." Jack wanted to avoid the word *bomb.* "It's like an electrical surge. If you go inside the bedroom, you could get hurt. It could knock you unconscious."

"Do you think that's what happened to my mom and dad?" Eric's voice was suddenly bright with hope.

Jack closed his eyes. "Yes."

"Can you help them? Help my mom and dad?"

"I can help them but I need you to help me first. I need you to listen to me. Can you do that?"

"Yes."

"Okay, good. Now this is what I need you to do. I want you to go downstairs and meet me at the back door—"

"No."

"What's wrong?"

"I'm not gonna go downstairs."

"Why not?"

The sound of small, sharp intakes of breath—a child struggling to fight his fear. Jack wondered again if it was the Sandman. No. No, the boy sounded too real.

"What's wrong, Eric?"

"He's d-down there."

"Who?"

"The bad man."

There was no way the Sandman was inside the house; but how was Jack supposed to impose logic on a child's imagination?

"Eric, I can promise you that nobody is in your house." Then a voice broke in and added, *Not physically, but the Sandman is in there watching the boy.*

Then why are you waiting to blow the bomb?

Where's Fletcher?

Trap?

No, not a trap, the boy is in that house and he's alive.

But you can't be sure, can you?

Eric said, "But I *heard* him. When I was in the closet, I *heard* him run down the stairs and start yelling and throwing things."

The question crept up on Jack. He knew he might never have the opportunity to ask it again.

"Did he know you were downstairs?"

"I don't know. I was hiding."

"Did he call you by name?"

"No." More rapid breathing. "I'm scared." Eric started to cry. "Please help me. Please, someone, please help me, I'm scared."

"You're a very brave boy, Eric. Even brave people get scared sometimes." The words sounded cheap and phony and Jack knew it.

"Do you ever get scared?"

"All the time. Eric, I'm going to help you, but I need you to be brave for me one more time. Can you be brave for me one more time?"

"I'm not going downstairs. He's waiting for me."

Duffy shifted in his seat, looking as if he wanted to crawl out of his skin.

"Eric, there's no one in the house," Jack said. "You need to believe me. I wouldn't lie to you."

"Then why aren't you in here? Why's everyone waiting outside and why did everyone start running away from the house? I saw them through the window. They know he's in here and they're scared—*that's* why they won't come in here, *that's* why they ran away."

You're losing him. Switch his focus.

"I'll tell you what. I'm driving a silver truck. How about I pull up to the house, come in there, and pick you up? How's that sound?"

Silence. Duffy was staring at Jack.

"Eric?"

The silence lingered. Outside, thunder ripped across the black sky.

"Eric?"

"Mom . . . My mom's lying on the bed."

The words spiked Jack's heart. "Eric, you have to stay out of the bedroom."

"My mom's . . . she's hurt. My mom's hurt and I have to help her."

"Eric, listen to me, you have to stay out of the bedroom. I'm going to come in there and get you, but you have to sit still for a few seconds. . . . Eric? . . . Eric, are you listening to me?"

"My dad's . . ." The boy's cries had become full-blown hysterical sobs. "My dad's . . . Daddy . . . bleeding . . . *he's bleeding all over the floor."*

Jack felt his control floating away like a balloon rising into the sky.

It's a trap, it has to be, the Sandman wouldn't leave a survivor.

AND WHAT IF IT ISN'T?

"What's . . . wrong with *you?"* Eric was hyperventilating, the shock of whatever he was seeing overtaking him.

"Eric, listen to—"

"You're supposed to help us!"

"Eric—"

"My mom and dad are really hurt and you won't come in and help us. YOU'RE SUPPOSED TO HELP US!"

Eric's phone clanked against the floor; words seized up in Jack's throat.

Jack heard the sound of small footsteps running across a hard floor, the sound of Eric Beaumont's sobbing drifting away.

"ERIC, PICK UP THE PHONE!"

From the bedroom, muffled, came the blood-chilling screams of a little boy.

"Jesus Christ," Duffy said.

Jack looked toward the house. Washing across his vision were—

Amanda's eyes, wet and running black with mascara, watching the scalpel come into sight and then following it as it travels down past her chin and disappears somewhere close to her throat. Her eyes dart back up and lock on his, her pale face is terrified and bloodless, and Jack feels the stitches of his sanity rip apart a seam at a time and opens the floodgates of despair and horror and terror just as Amanda whimpers, "The baby, Jack, don't let him hurt the baby. . . . Do something, Jack. Please."

Eric Beaumont stands alone in the middle of the blood-soaked bedroom that reeks of slaughter and he's screaming.

The car keys were dangling from the ignition.

Infrared, if there's an infrared beam across the door like the Roths' and the boy walked across it, then we have time—ten minutes. That's about how much time I was inside the Roth house.

The boy was screaming.

The boy was still alive.

Help me, Jack . . . do something . . . please.

Jack threw the truck in gear.

chapter 34

THE OPENING BETWEEN THE FIRE TRUCKS AND THE AMBULANCES WAS TOO NARROW, JACK THOUGHT, BUT HE RACED BETWEEN THEM ANYWAY. The street was packed with cruisers, which only left one route: the sidewalk. He hit the curb and bounced up, and a moment later he was racing toward the house with half the truck on the sidewalk, the other on the lawns.

"Grab that flashlight from the backseat," Jack yelled.

Duffy twisted to retrieve a compact Coleman flashlight with a rubber grip and handed it to him. Jack tucked the flashlight in the front of his jeans.

"When you get the kid, go out the back door and run straight across the yard until you hit the next street," Duffy said, his voice steady. "I'll be waiting for you on the other side. There's a street that cuts straight to the highway. How much time you think you got?"

"Ten minutes, max." *You hope,* a voice added. *You don't even know if the bomb's on a timer. For all you know the thing could blow in the next minute.*

Turn around, save yourself.

The truck bounced down the slope and started racing across the lawn toward the Beaumont home.

"Get ready." Jack shifted into neutral, threw the truck door open, and jumped out.

The lawn was soft, but the tumble wasn't. He got up, the truck sliding past him, and ran to the porch. Behind him he heard the engine climb as Duffy jammed the car into gear and hit the gas. It tore down the sidewalk and disappeared.

Jack threw the front door open with his shoulder. Pulsating cruiser lights illuminated the rooms in blue and white flashes, like some nightmarish disco. He took the flashlight from his jeans and turned it on. With one hand on the banister he raced up the stairs, the fireman's clothing weighing him down, the flashlight pointed into the dark, the sound of his heavy footsteps loud and urgent.

The beam of light reflected off the glass front of a black-and-white seascape on the wall and slid up across the ceiling. He climbed the remaining steps, the ring of light washing across six pine doors, all closed. He reached the top of the steps and stopped.

The stairs continued upward to a third floor.

Shit. Which floor is he on?

"Eric?" he yelled. "Where are you?"

He stood in the dark, listening for sounds over the blood pounding past his ears. He breathed rapidly, his chest hot and wet beneath the fireman's jacket.

"Eric?"

There was no answer.

Then he remembered unclipping the beeper from his belt and tossing it on the backseat. *Don't go into the house without it,* Fletcher had told him.

Jack's eyes moved across the ceiling and walls. If pinhole cameras were mounted in this hallway, that meant the Sandman was watching him right now, had just heard his voice.

Jack scrambled down the hallway, kicking open doors and sweeping the flashlight through two bedrooms, a linen closet, a bathroom, a second-floor laundry, until he reached the last door at the end of the hallway, threw it open, and stepped quickly inside a spacious bedroom. He made out a neatly made bed, light tan carpet, contemporary blond oak furniture.

No sign of the boy.

You're running out of time.

The fear cranked up another notch. Jack ran full force down the hallway

(get out of here, you still have a chance, get out of here now)

and started moving up the stairs to the third floor.

The four doors facing him were all shut; the hallway was long like the one below and stretched into a pocket of darkness. He moved swiftly, the flashlight pointed straight ahead, washing over white walls. Down the last stretch of hallway now, the flashlight searching . . . searching . . .

A cell phone was in front of a slightly opened door, its green light blinking steadily like a heartbeat. A cold stillness gripped him, his breath catching in his throat. He brought the flashlight up, opened the door, and splashed light over the walls and a headboard splattered with blood.

The world screamed at him in red-smeared snapshots: a woman with auburn hair lying on her back, her wrists handcuffed to the headboard, an eight-ball hemorrhage with a quarter-sized hole in the center of her forehead, barefoot in jeans and a black T-shirt, the skin along her pale face and arms peppered with blood. A male body dressed in a navy blue suit lying facedown on the blood-soaked carpet between the bathroom and the foot of the bed; on the far wall an opened door that revealed another hallway and a set of stairs leading down.

No sign of Eric.

Jack walked around to the other side of the bed. The bloody, small footprints led across the carpet to the headboard and stopped next to the nightstand.

Jack hit the floor and slid the beam of light under the bed.

Eric Beaumont lay on his side in the fetal position, his knees tucked to his chest. His blue jeans, high-top sneakers, and white oxford shirt were stained with blood, his mother's blood. His eyes were still and vacant.

He came here, thinking she was alive, praying that he could save her.

The boy's body twitched.

He's in shock.

Jack gripped Eric's arm; the boy didn't register his touch. As Jack slid the curled-up body from under the bed, the boy's small muscles were as rigid as wood beneath his hand. He had moved him less than a foot when he saw the horizontal line of a laptop computer screen. He yanked the boy toward him, saw nine bricks stamped C-4 behind the laptop. White numbers flashed in the center of the black screen:

29.

28.

Jesus Christ, GET MOVING!

Jack dropped the flashlight, pulled the boy out, stood, and in one sweeping motion, lifted the boy up with both hands. Eric's limbs were frozen. Jack tried to straighten him out, but it was as if the boy's body were carved out of stone; he wouldn't unbend. Jack pressed him hard against his chest, feeling the boy's frantic heart beating against his own.

He moved out the door in front of him, the one that would hopefully lead him out to the backyard. He took two and three steps at a time, focusing on getting down them without tripping. The second floor. Now the first. He was in a kitchen. There was a door and it led out to a deck.

Jack ran for it, his blood-slicked boots making squeaking sounds across the tile. With the boy cradled in his left arm, he had to bend down and reach out for the doorknob with his right. It was slippery in his hand.

HURRY!

He wiped his hand on his jeans, clasped the knob again, and this time it turned. The door opened to a porch that stretched across the back of the house. He kicked the screen door open and ran. The night air smelled of ozone and his sweat. A gust of wind blew over him, then died down.

The backyard was lit up by squares of blue and white light. He started to run across it.

Fifteen seconds, that's how much time you have left, you're not going to make it.

Holding the boy, weighted down by the fireman's clothing, and with a good stretch of backyard still left to run, Jack knew he wasn't going to make it to the truck.

Frantically he looked around the backyard, like a drowning man trying to save himself.

A tool shed was off to his left. In front of it was an in-ground swimming pool shadowed by tall maples. A concrete divider bracketed the shallow end from the deeper.

Jump in the deep end and stay underwater and the blast will blow right over you.

Jack yelled at the top of his lungs, *"Duffy, get out of here. I got the boy, we'll be in the pool!"*

He lumbered across the grass, gathering his remaining fragments of strength, and forced his body through the shrubs surrounding the pool.

Ten seconds left.

The deep end was ten yards away. He hugged the boy tightly against his chest, gulped air until he thought his lungs would burst, then jumped feetfirst into the pool.

Cold water flew up his legs and chest and enveloped his head; then he was sinking down past a column of silver bubbles that whisked past his face.

Seven seconds.

When his feet hit the bottom, he pushed himself against the side of the pool, sat down, and moved the boy between his knees and chest. He pried the small mouth open, clamped his mouth down, blew a breath of air into Eric's lungs.

Four seconds.

Jack released his mouth and clamped Eric's lips shut. The boy's eyes were wide and still, lifeless, locked on some point in space. Jack wondered if the boy had heard his shouts, if Eric had sensed Jack's fear and knew that they were now sitting below the water of the pool.

Three seconds.

Hold on, Eric. Just hold on and we'll both get through this.

Jack's heart was bursting in his chest, his lungs aching for air. He leaned back against the side of the pool and looked up at the skin of water dancing just a few feet above him. The black sky cracked with veins of silver and purple lightning, the countdown almost over, his body tensing as it waited for the new night sky that would scream and burn.

chapter 35

BOB BURKE RESCUED HIM FROM THE POOL.

Unable to hold his breath any longer, Jack had risen to the surface with the boy, then felt a pair of hands grab him under his arms and pull them both up onto the concrete. A Dodge van was parked in the backyard near the edge of the pool, its engine running. Burke helped them inside the back of the van and then drove them up the road to where Duffy and an ambulance were waiting.

The Beaumont home was still standing.

Two hours later and his clothes still damp, Jack was back inside the pitch-black bedroom with the two bodies. The windows behind him, the ones facing the street, were shut; the room was close with the smell of blood. Per Burke's instructions, all of the cruisers had been moved to opposite ends of the long street. With their revolving blue and white lights turned off, Parish Road was dark. Bill Duffy was out there somewhere on the phone with the mayor of Newton.

Burke placed a Maglite flashlight on the end of the nightstand. In the halo of light, resting next to the woman's bloodstained feet, was the laptop computer that Jack had seen under the bed. Wires ran from the laptop to nine blocks of C-4. The power was still on, its timer frozen at zero.

Nine blocks, Jack thought, and felt the hairs on the back of his neck rise. *If it had gone off . . .*

"Why isn't it disconnected?" Jack asked. It was safe to talk. Both he and Burke were wearing Fletcher's specialized pagers; at their current setting, all the Sandman could see and hear was static.

"I wanted you to take a look at something. Figured if I didn't, you might pull one of your temper tantrums like you did that morning at the Dolan house." Burke had an unlit cigar clamped between his molars. He was wearing grease-stained jeans and an old, faded white T-shirt with a green Molson bottle on the back.

Burke took a silver spray can from the bed, grabbed the flashlight, and walked around slick pools of blood to the half-opened door that Jack had first slid through in search of Eric. Burke depressed the spray can's nozzle.

Bright red beams glowed and then disappeared.

"Infrared," Jack said. "Same as the first one."

"There's roughly two dozen of them in here. Four pairs on each of the doors, the rest are mounted all over the room. You walk across a beam, it sends a signal to a small box that transmits a signal to the laptop to start the countdown." Burke picked up the flashlight and ran the light over to the corners in the walls where the devices were mounted. "No way you could've walked in here and not hit one."

"Why didn't it go off?"

"Short circuit. I saw it on the X ray. Nice and neat." Burke grew pensive. In the odd play of light, his scars seemed more pronounced. "The son of a bitch thinks I don't know a setup when I see one."

"What do you mean?" Jack asked, alarmed.

"The laptop and C-4—it's a decoy." Burke tossed the can inside a duffel bag on the floor. "There's a second bomb in here."

"Where?"

"Right behind you." Burke moved his flashlight down to a brown leather briefcase with gold combination locks. It was standing upright, directly behind the door so that the slightest push would have knocked it over.

"The placement of it was odd, so I had the bomb robot take an X ray for the hell of it." Burke pulled the door away and squatted down, pointing with his cigar to the bottom left part of the briefcase. "Sitting right there is a cellular phone. It's powered on, and so's the beeper next to it. There're wires running between the beeper and the phone. As for the explosives, there's no outline or shadow on the X ray."

"Semtex."

"It's the only explosive impervious to X ray." Burke moved the light up to the latches. "Under the combination locks and hinges are antidisturbance switches. I try to pop open the locks, boom. He also placed them along the creases where the briefcase opens, so I can't drill or saw into it. You know what a mercury switch is?"

Jack shook his head but had a feeling where Burke was about to lead him.

"A mercury switch senses a change in position. If, for example, you pushed open the door when you rushed in here, the briefcase would have tipped over and I'd be scraping fillets of your body parts into plastic sandwich bags with a spatula. Semtex *and* nine blocks of C-4—shit, you might as well rename this neighborhood Beirut."

Jack now knew why Burke had first maneuvered him carefully through the bedroom, why he had shut the windows. If a strong wind had blown through here . . . Jack stared at the briefcase and heard a high-pitched whining sound in his head. His mind quickly fast-forwarded through dozens of nightmarish scenarios and suddenly he felt light-headed.

"So you're telling me the bomb's active," Jack said, his voice tight.

"You got it."

A thought occurred to Jack. He removed Fletcher's pager and held it in his palm. "This operates on a high-energy radio frequency. Right now, it's on a midsetting—simple interference. If I jacked it up to its highest setting and placed it right next to the briefcase, it should fry all of the bomb's circuitry."

"And it might trigger the bomb. I'm sure our buddy has built in *numerous* fail-safe mechanisms. You want to be the one to try it, because I sure as hell don't."

"What about having the robot do it?"

"The robot doesn't have fingers, it has claws. Once the robot carried it in here, he couldn't manually turn up the frequency. If I jack the frequency to its highest setting and then have the robot bring the beeper in here, the HERF will cook the robot. The other thing is that there's a lot of sensors inside the briefcase—a lot of shit I can't figure out. If the HERF disrupts them . . ." Burke looked at Jack. "This thing is set to blow."

Jack stared at the bomb, his skin tingling. Burke rubbed the back of his head and neck. The scars along his face and neck looked like globs of white rubber.

"I can't figure out the design, how all the fucking pieces fit together. Inside the briefcase is a cell phone and beeper. The Sandman could call the beeper right now and blow the bomb. Or maybe he calls the cell phone. Or maybe he calls the beeper first and that activates the bomb—maybe he already did that before I got inside here." Burke's eyes were weighted with anger and fear when he looked up. "I don't have a fucking clue, Jack. The son of a bitch covered *all* his options this time around. The only reason I'm here is to clean up his fucking mess."

Jack clipped his beeper back on his belt and looked around the bedroom. If the Sandman was close by and was trying to watch what was going on inside the bedroom, he was seeing and hearing nothing but static. He had to be impatient. *You could blow the bomb right now and take out all the key players. What are you waiting for?* Was the thrill of watching what he really wanted? Or had he found out that a boy was rescued from the house, a boy who might possibly have seen him killing his parents and be able to describe his face or something even more useful, something that could allow the police to locate him instantly? Was the Sandman on his way to try to bomb Newton-Wellesley Hospital, confident that the bomb would blow and having decided not to stick around?

Too many questions. Answer one and a dozen more sprang up.

Jack looked at the man's body slumped on the floor. His back was riddled with bullets, and there was a single shot to the back of the head. The woman's feet were tied to the bed; she too had been shot.

Why did the boy survive?

"I think I can move it out of here," Burke said.

Jack jerked his head to him. "You just said—"

"I said that a mercury switch senses a change in *position.* If the robot comes in here and moves the briefcase straight up, the bomb is still in its original position, only higher up off the ground."

"What about the stairs?"

"That's the tricky part. They're at an angle. I have an idea—it's a long shot, but it's the only chance we got."

Jack looked back to the bodies. His imagination was already awake, whispering to him. Something was in here. He could *feel* it. All he had to do was spend a little time with the dead and they would speak to him, his imagination revealing the things inside here he couldn't see.

"How long is it going to take you to set up?"

"An hour."

"I need some time alone in here. Me and someone else."

"That guy Fletcher?"

Jack nodded, vaguely aware of Burke and his words. "Half an hour, max."

"Take your time. For all I know, we'll all be dead in fifteen minutes."

chapter 36

FLETCHER PLACED THE FLASHLIGHT ON THE NIGHTSTAND NEXT TO HIS LAPTOP, THEN WORKED HIS WAY THROUGH THE DARKNESS OF THE BLOOD-SMEARED BEDROOM. Drawers and closets were opened and searched with great care; jewelry, photographs, and objects from bureau tops and nightstands were picked up, caressed, and studied with the authority and precision of a man who could extract larger truths about the people who owned them. Bloodstain patterns and the bodies were studied with the type of uplifting, emotional intensity given to rare paintings.

Jack's attention was on the woman. She had been shot in the center of her forehead; dura mater mixed with skin and bone and blood was splattered against the headboard and fanned up the white walls in red coils. In the semidark stillness he stared at the hopeless look frozen on the woman's face. In his mind he saw flashes: the gun pressed to her head as her lips mumbled a final prayer beneath a thick strand of duct tape; her son coming inside and seeing her body; the boy under the bed, silent screams rattling though his mind like electrical charges.

Rage was slowly gaining momentum inside him. Rage at what had happened here inside the bedroom, at what had happened to his wife—rage at what an eleven-year-old would be facing when he woke from his psychological coma.

And Jack could feel the madman's rage, could taste it gathering on the back of his throat.

Fletcher drew in a deep breath. "Nothing quite like the smell of slaughter to awaken the senses." He was standing at the foot of the bed and calmly looking at Jack.

Jack glanced up to the ceiling.

"Don't worry. Our friend can't hear you."

"Is he watching us right now?"

"He's trying. My guess is that he's feeling frustrated."

"Burke told me you found four surveillance cameras."

"Yes. Two pairs, each pointed at the opposite ends of the street." Fletcher looked down at his laptop. "The cameras still haven't turned on yet. He knows the storm will wreak havoc with his surveillance. My guess is that he's decided to conserve his power and wait for it to pass. After that, I'm confident the fireworks will begin."

"You recognize her?" Jack asked, nodding to the dead woman.

"No. As I stated earlier, Graves was a large facility."

Fletcher walked around the bed to the other side where Jack was standing. Fletcher faced him, his black eyes shining with a liquid light.

"What will it be, Detective? Shall we whip out your evidence Baggies and start the tedious process of collecting, or are we going to get down to the business of *thinking?*"

"The Sandman was interrupted."

"Yes. The crime scene reeks of incompleteness. Who do you think the unfortunate man slumped on the floor is?"

"Her ex-husband."

"How can you tell?"

"His driver's license has a different address."

"But that's not what led you to that conclusion."

"It's clear she lives alone."

Fletcher's eyes sparkled. "I see you found the Jelly Candy Cock in the nightstand drawer."

"There's no male objects, no ties, socks, cologne—nothing to suggest that a man shared this room with her. The Sandman knew that. He wasn't expecting them. Her ex-husband and her son interrupted his plans."

"Maybe he called them over here. Our friend has an affinity for theater."

"No. He was expecting to be alone." Jack pointed to the bathroom. "The Sandman was waiting in there when the husband came into the bedroom. He came up from behind him and shot him once in the back of the head. The woman was alive when it happened."

"How can you tell?"

"The blood-spray patterns are present only on the right side of her face. She saw the Sandman emerge from the shadows, saw the gun pointed at the back of her husband's head, and jerked her head to her left to avoid watching. The exiting wound sprayed her face with his blood."

"Odd that the boy would have stayed inside the house if he heard shots."

"The Sandman used a silencer. The contact wound on her forehead has powder burns. The boy probably heard strange sounds—the thud of his father's body hitting the floor, maybe—and for whatever reason decided to hide."

"Why the excessive shots in the back?"

"Rage for being interrupted."

"And how are you managing *your* rage?"

"I'm fine."

"No, you're not. You're standing here thinking about what happened to the boy, desperately trying to fend off your rage. *Embrace* your imagination. *Embrace* your rage—embrace the *taste* of it and maybe the next time you close your eyes you'll find that blessed silence you so desperately crave."

A vein of lightning flashed outside; sliver flashes illuminated the dark splatter of the bedroom. From beyond the closed windows, Jack heard car doors slamming. Fletcher was looking out the windows facing the street.

"So begins the march of the hollow men."

Jack followed his gaze. Two black vans were parked across the street. The driver's side window of the first was rolled down.

Jack cracked the window open and heard a voice say, "—can't go in there, I'm sorry."

"Get him, *right now,*" a familiar voice replied.

"Leave it to Alan to crash a perfectly good party," Fletcher said.

The bomb tech turned and mumbled something to someone over his shoulder. A moment later, Jack heard the front door open and shut.

"We have to get him out of here," Jack said. "If those cameras turn on and the Sandman sees him, he'll blow the house."

"When the cameras do turn on, all our friend will see is what I'll allow him to see," Fletcher said. "While you were playing hide-and-seek in the pool, I took the liberty of placing the proper equipment to secure our privacy. Still, you might as well head Alan off. We wouldn't want to make our archangel *anxious.*"

"I'll take care of Alan. Where will you be?"

The tip of Fletcher's tongue slid across the edges of his bottom lip like a snake.

"Why, watching, of course."

chapter 37

MALCOLM FLETCHER LISTENED TO JACK'S FOOTSTEPS GOING DOWN THE STAIRS, THEN TURNED HIS ATTENTION BACK TO THE WINDOW.

Below, the front door clicked shut. He looked down. Alan Lynch was less than fifty feet away.

So close, Fletcher thought.

Old memories marched through his mind with order and precision. He ruminated over them the way an entomologist might consider the insect that had stung him.

He wondered if Alan still thought of him—and what Alan's reaction would be when he discovered that the man who had tried to expose the FBI's dealings at Graves, the man he had tried to hunt down and kill, knew the identity of the Sandman, a former Graves patient.

Fletcher turned away from the window. Gabby would first go after the boy in the hospital. A bomb in the lobby, perhaps. After that, the next family would die. Fletcher was certain they would die within the next few days. More national attention—exactly what Gabby wanted.

But first Alan. Something to keep Alan and his brood occupied while Jack tracked down the Sandman.

Fletcher looked around the bedroom. His eyes settled on the woman on the bed. A small clear patch of skin was on her left cheekbone.

An interesting thought presented itself.

With his left hand, he cupped the top of her head, holding it still as he pressed his right thumb firmly on the skin. Then he gently guided her head back to its resting position and, laptop in hand, walked out of the bedroom.

A full latent print on the woman's cheek. A child with a brush and fluorescent powder could pick that up.

Malcolm Fletcher smiled. Such a lovely way to announce his resurrection to Alan.

chapter 38

ALAN LYNCH HAD HIS BACK TOWARD HIM, SO JACK GOT A CHANCE TO ABSORB THE SIGHT OF HIS FORMER BOSS WITHOUT BEING SEEN. Alan had changed little over the years. He had that same round belly, and his face was still dark and thin, almost gaunt. Even more noticeable was his look of studied casualness: no suit jacket, the top two buttons undone on the slightly disheveled shirt, the tie hanging loosely around the neck, the shirtsleeves rolled up to the elbows—portrait of a man ready to get the job done. The cameras always loved it.

Alan stood next to a tall man with blond hair. They were both hunched forward and huddled close so they could talk without being overheard.

Jack walked up to them. Alan caught sight of him over his shoulder.

"Jack," Alan said, surprised. "That you? Christ. I almost didn't recognize you with all those muscles. What are you doing, bench-pressing the entire gym?"

Alan laughed at his own joke. So did the tall man.

Alan said, "Victor, meet Jack Casey, one of the best and brightest from my pack."

Victor extended his hand with an easygoing smile. Jack shook it, surprised by the man's strength.

"Nice to meet you," Victor said, then turned back to Alan. "I'm going to make that call now. Excuse me, gentlemen."

"You a profiler?" Jack asked.

"Lab rat," Victor said.

"Which section?"

"Fingerprints."

"Victor's one of our best fingerprint experts," Alan said. "Probably *the* best."

"Hey, how's Paul Woodman doing?" Jack asked Victor. "That snowmobiling accident really screwed up his back."

"He's taking it day by day, just like the rest of us."

"Tell him I said hello."

"I will."

Only you'll have to go to Clearwater, Florida. That's where he retired to two years ago, Jack thought. *Keep your eye on this one.*

He watched Victor disappear behind a black van. A door slid open and shut. Then there was only the sound of the wind.

"You look good, Jack," Alan said. "Healthy and strong. I'm glad to see the Northeast has agreed with you—although I have to admit I was surprised to find you back in the game." Alan's practiced tone was full of concern. "Last I heard you were in Colorado doing carpentry. Why'd you give it up?"

Jack wanted to unsheathe the knowledge Fletcher had given him like a dagger and sink it deep into Alan's bureaucratic heart. Instead, he said, "Why are you here?"

"You just met a fingerprint expert, and you just watched him walk back to one of *two* vans loaded with the latest technology and the brightest minds in the field, *and* we're standing less than fifty feet away from a major crime scene of a serial killer who has the potential to become the nation's new number one nightmare." Alan's tone was polite and friendly. "Why do you *think* I'm here?"

"I don't recall placing a call to ISU."

"You were in contact with some people at our lab. I was there on another case and overheard your name. I saw what you were up against, looked into a few things, and here I am. I was at the hotel when the story broke on the news, so—"

"ISU gave up the traveling road. You're strictly consulting now."

"That's right."

"So you just decided to pack everyone and travel here without notice, all out of the goodness of your heart."

"You're saying I need an invitation to help out an old friend?"

"I'm not your friend and you have no jurisdiction here. Pack up your stuff and leave."

Alan's expression didn't waver. "You don't have any jurisdiction here either."

"You're right. Go talk to the chief investigator, Bill Duffy. He'll tell you the same thing. Good-bye, Alan."

Jack turned and walked away. Behind him, Alan said, "Wait a minute. Just wait one goddamn minute."

Alan cupped Jack's biceps and moved in front of him. "Stop being a goddamn stubborn son of a bitch for just one minute, will you?"

Jack stared into his eyes, the anger building. *Careful . . .*

Alan put his hands in his pockets, his face haggard. He took a moment as he struggled with his next choice of works.

"Seven years ago . . . I did wrong by you," Alan said. "After Yerkies, I let you take on the Hamilton case. I didn't know just how deep your . . . problems ran. I knew full well you weren't in the best shape psychologically, and I still let you take on the case anyway. Why? Because you were the best profiler I had, and I knew you would catch him. And you did. Still, it was a mistake.

"What was happening to you . . . Back then, we weren't correctly trained to see the warning signs. That's all changed now. Today we've got policies in place—rigorous psychological screenings, all profiling done in teams, we offer counseling, time off, you name it, it's there to prevent anyone from having a meltdown or worse."

Jack barely listened. He was watching Duffy, who was talking to a plainclothes detective standing next to an unmarked car.

"Hey, Jack, you hearing me? I'm trying to tell you something important and you're ignoring me."

Jack locked his eyes on Alan's face.

"What happened to Amanda . . ." Alan stopped and took in a deep breath. "It's my fault, Jack. I blame myself for what happened to her. And you. I should have put the brakes on. I should have taken you off the case. But that's the problem with hindsight. It always points out what you *should* have done."

Hearing Amanda's name caused Jack's anger to boil over. He made fists at his sides; in his mind he saw himself reaching out for Alan and beating the living shit out of him. *You lying, cheating fuck . . .*

Don't, Jack. Don't give in to it.

Lynch cleared his throat. "I've been carrying this guilt for too long. All this time . . . It's been eating me up. It gave me my second heart attack, for chrissakes."

"Yes, I remember you were so racked with guilt you deep-sixed me two weeks after I buried my wife. Then again, you always were a classy guy."

"Hey, let's get something clear: *I* didn't want to fire you. The decision to cut you loose was made by my bosses, and when I say cut, I mean *everything:* back pay, your retirement account, your medical. Who the hell you think fought for you? Who do you think picked up your six-month hospital tab that ran into the *thousands?* Not your medical plan."

"Anything to help you sleep better through the night."

Alan's face tightened, relaxed. "Let's face some hard facts. I didn't try to kill a tabloid photographer with my bare hands. When he decided to sue, he didn't go after you, Jack, he went after us, and guess who coughed up the money? Guess who got him to settle out of court and kept your name out of the papers? You're lucky you didn't go down for attempted murder. And as for your other *extracurricular* activities—hey, I'm not judging you for it, but the people that count did. They started asking some questions, did a little digging, and didn't like what they found. I protected you as long as I could."

Jack was amazed at how smoothly Alan lied. Amazed but not surprised. Deception came naturally to him.

Jack knew he should have turned and walked away; Lynch had no jurisdiction here, and this conversation was pointless. But what kept Jack here was that he knew Alan's real agenda.

Careful, a voice that sounded like Fletcher's warned.

"Look, I'm here to help. I *want* to help," Alan said. "You're already using our resources—we're practically working together. Now how can I help you?"

Jack stared at him for a moment, then said, "You got a point, Alan."

"Good. Where do you want to start?"

"Tomorrow morning I'll hold a press conference and announce to everyone that the FBI is here to help out. I'll introduce you and you can share your thoughts on the Sandman."

Jack caught it, that faint drain of color in Alan's face, the quick tightening of the eyes as the truth speared him. Then it was gone, quickly covered up by Alan's well-practiced stony exterior.

"All those cameras there, the whole world watching—why, you'd be in your glory, Alan."

"You don't want to provoke this guy. And I think you should be careful of the media."

"Why's that?"

"They seem to know a few things about your past," Alan said evenly. "I don't think you want the rest of it to become public knowledge, do you?"

"That a threat?"

"I deal in reality. And the reality is that you don't want me fielding questions. It's best I stay behind the scenes on this one."

"One thing before you go. If you feel the need again to use my wife's death to get me to play your game, call your HMO and make sure your premium's paid up because the next sensation you're going to have is waking up in a hospital room. You hear me, you fucking prick?"

"It's nice to see you've changed," Alan said, and turned away.

Bill Duffy walked up to Jack, an unlit cigarette stuck to the corner of his mouth.

"What the hell did you say to that guy? He looks like his nuts just got squeezed in a vise."

chapter 39

THE BACK OF THE VAN HOUSED A SURVEILLANCE STATION, TWO FAX MACHINES, PHONES EQUIPPED WITH THE LATEST IN ENCRYPTION TECHNOLOGY, AND TWO COMPUTERS WITH SECURED LINKS TO THE FBI LAB. Victor Dragos, a phone pressed against his ear, sat in the two-seater black leather chair located behind the driver's seat. The pale gray light glowing from the computer screens cast his face and the objects in the van in shadows.

Alan slid the door shut and took the seat across from Dragos. Outside, bomb technicians lumbered their way up the porch steps.

With his neatly combed baby-fine hair, his contagious laugh, and athletic build, Dragos looked the part of the all-star athlete from a small Midwestern high school. He hung up the phone.

"The benzoninhydrin arrived," he said. "The pathologist Casey's using, Wilson, his lab is all set and ready to go. Why the long face, Al?"

"Casey's not on board."

Dragos frowned. "He's been using the FBI lab, calling in favors, consulting Mike Abrams, and we show up here with two vans full of the same equipment and minds he wants access to and suddenly he doesn't want your help? What am I missing here?"

"Jack and I have a past. I told you that and I told Paris that, and both of you told me not to worry. Not only are we not wanted here, we try to take over the investigation, he'll go to the press."

Dragos's cold blue eyes narrowed. "He said that?"

"That's right."

Dragos played with two marble balls he brought from his pocket. As he rubbed them together, they made a faint, chiming sound. "Casey had two conversations today. The first was with someone from the FBI lab. I don't know who, but we're looking into that. The second was with Mark Graysmith. We don't know what Casey said there, since Casey's cell phone uses encryption technology."

"I thought you were monitoring his phone calls."

"Bugging Casey's house and his office at the station were no-brainers. The problem is the girlfriend's house, where Casey spends almost all of his time. He's hired an ex–Secret Service guy by the name of Ronnie Tedesco to watch his girlfriend's house—we got no way of getting inside there without Tedesco or one of his goons nailing us. That and the fact that the house phones and Casey's cell phone have also been encrypted. We can tail him, but as of right now I have no way of finding out what he's saying."

"You told me Graysmith's trailer was bugged."

"Apparently the man is a quick study."

"What do you mean?"

"When he called Casey, he used a white-noise device so we couldn't hear what he said. We found it in his trailer an hour ago."

Alan didn't like this. First Graysmith had discovered the inventory list, and had no doubt passed on that information to Jack, who had just told him to fuck off—just as Alan had predicted. His control over the situation and its players was slipping through his hands. They had to regain control—and quick.

"Any way Casey would know about the program?" Dragos asked.

"No. What are you going to do about Graysmith?"

Dragos grinned. "Mark Graysmith won't be bothering us anymore."

"I hope you made it look like an accident."

"I put him on a flight out of San Diego." Dragos laughed quietly. "You thought I killed him?"

"Graysmith won't stop looking. And Jack . . . we need to be careful. If he goes to the press and the Sandman finds out we're here . . ."

"The Sandman has been calling Jack, playing this creepy game of cat and mouse. My money's on Casey. One way or another, Casey will draw the Sandman out, and when he does, we'll take out the Sandman quick and quiet." Dragos knocked on the wall behind him, where the driver was sitting. "Let's get out of here, Paul."

"We're leaving?"

"We're not wanted here, so we might as well split. I'll drop you off at Wilson's lab."

"And where are you going to be?"

"I'll stick around and take in the sights. I have a feeling something big is going to happen."

The van started and moved forward. Dragos placed the balls back in his pocket.

"Casey's hiding something. One way or another, I'll find out what it is."

chapter 40

THE INSIDE OF BURKE'S VAN LOOKED LIKE A MAKESHIFT FLEA-MARKET BOOTH FEATURING ELECTRONIC GADGETS. Tall metal tool chests were stacked against the long wall of Peg-Board containing extension cords, rope, wires, and an array of plastic boxes with dozens of trays holding screws and nails. Two metal buffet tables were set up against the long side of the van, and between them, sitting low to the metal floor on an old office chair mended with strips of duct tape, was Bob Burke.

He was staring at the bomb control unit, a large metal box containing a black-and-white screen, joystick, keyboard, and a pair of Yamaha speakers. On the black-and-white screen was an aerial shot of the robot's claw hovering just inches above the level that had been fastened to the top of the briefcase with strips of duct tape. Sam, one of the bomb technicians, had carefully placed the level on top of the briefcase. Now everyone was out of the house.

Burke manipulated the joystick with his right hand while the fingers of his left depressed a series of keys. On the screen, Johnny Fingers came to life, its claw opening and closing like a vise, a mechanical whine pouring from the computer speakers.

Jack sat against the table behind Burke. Duffy squatted beside him on a milk crate. The interior of the van was filled with the glow coming from the bomb control monitor and from the laptop computer in the front seat. When the wind rushing in through the opened windows died down, Jack could smell the residue of Burke's cigar, coffee, and the sour bite of his own sweat. Raindrops hit the windshield like marbles striking glass.

"The cameras just turned on," Fletcher said. His voice was a monotone, as if he were locked in a trance.

Fletcher sat in the passenger's seat with the laptop computer balanced on his lap. Colored bar graphs and wave frequencies glowed from the tiny screen.

"He's got to be real close," Burke said without turning. "Those wireless cams have a limited range."

"He's not here," Fletcher said.

"How do you know?"

"I tracked down the signal to a black BMW. The car was hot-wired and is still running to keep the laptop computer and cellular phone on the passenger's seat powered."

"You're saying he's dialing into the laptop with another laptop."

"It seems our friend is trying to distance himself from tonight's festivities."

"Where's this car?" Burke said.

"He's wired several blocks of composition C-4 to the car's ignition and alarm system. Touch the car and not only will you blow it up, my guess is that you'll also trigger the bomb you're about to try to move out of the house."

Burke rubbed the back of his head and focused inward on a private thought. Then he said, "You got any ideas about what's going on?"

Fletcher was now staring out the window toward the Beaumont home. It was down at the opposite end of the street, small, like a Monopoly game piece.

"Nothing you would find useful."

A vein of lightning flashed across the sky. News helicopters circled overhead, the thump-thump of their blades barely audible over the wind and thunder, their searchlights sweeping across the street and empty houses. Over the pair of computer speakers, the voice of Sam the bomb tech came on and said, "Bobby, you ready to rock and roll?"

Burke didn't answer him right away. His eyes shifted back and forth as if he were examining several thoughts at once. Raindrops pinged off the roof and front hood.

Burke moved the headset microphone up to his mouth. "Let's do it. Stand by." He looked around the van. "Everyone have their phone and beepers off?"

Everyone nodded except Fletcher.

"Yo, Fletch, you hear what I said?"

Fletcher nodded.

"You're going to have to shut off the laptop too. Once the bomb robot's moving, I can't afford the possibility of electromagnetic interference."

Fletcher moved his fingers over the keys. A moment later the laptop's screen went dark.

Burke leaned back in his chair and pulled the mike back up to his mouth.

"Okay, Sam, how's the lighting inside the house?"

The computer speakers cracked with static; then Sam's voice said, "All the video cameras are positioned along the stairs. Their brights are on, and I put some flashlights down. The lighting inside should be okay."

"As long as you can see the level on the briefcase."

"I can see it." Sam coughed nervously. "Bobby, this is as strange as it gets, man."

"Tell me about it. Fire department ready?"

"At the end of the street and good to go. Same with ambulances. All the cruisers are out of here. How's our man Johnny Fingers doing?"

"He's fine, everything checks out."

"He makes it out of this one, I think Johnny deserves a medal."

"Stand by."

Burke pulled the microphone away from his mouth. "The black-and-white monitor shows the robot. We got cameras hooked up all over Johnny, allowing me to see the briefcase, the track, the bedroom, you name it. Johnny's going to pick up the briefcase and run it down the hallway. Like I said, the real problem is getting it down the stairs. That's where Sam comes in."

Burke hit the power button on a twenty-one-inch computer monitor. A color shot of a camera's lens looking up the stairs into the semi-dark hallway filled the screen. Jack could see his own bloody handprints on the banister railing, saw the red smears across the white walls from where his blood-soaked clothes had touched.

"That's the first section of stairs Johnny has to travel down. All he has to do is make it to the first landing, turn the corner, go down two more sets of stairs, and then we'll move him out of the kitchen onto the porch. The bomb containment vessel is waiting for him in the backyard."

Burke rapped a knuckle against the color monitor. "Video cameras have been set up in positions all over the stairs. Sam will be cycling through the cameras, keeping his eye on the level while I edge Johnny over the stairs. If we can keep the bomb level, it won't go off. Sam's job is to watch it and tell me how to adjust the controls.

"This is real dicey. I've never done anything like this before, but it's the only option we got short of blowing the bomb up. If Semtex is in there and the bomb goes off, I'm not going to lie to you, it's going to get *real* hairy. But I think we got an honest shot at making this work."

Jack looked at Fletcher, who was still staring out the window, his eyes searching.

He's troubled about something, Jack thought. He opened his mouth to ask the question, but Burke had already moved the microphone back up and was speaking.

"Okay, Sam, here we go."

Burke slid the joystick toward him. Jack felt his stomach leap.

On the black-and-white screen the mechanical claw slid down the arm, then slowed as it approached the top of the level. Burke nicked the claw forward a little more, then a little more, right there, got it; then he switched to another camera showing a flat shot of the side of a briefcase. The claw's pinchers were set wide and hovering less than half an inch from the level.

Burke inched the claw forward one more time, until it almost touched the level. Then the two pinchers came together and fastened themselves around the briefcase. With a press of a button, the claw slid all the way back up the arm and then came to a full stop. Next, the arm swiveled in its base, slowly turning the claw and its cargo in a ninety-degree arc, Jack tensely watching as the briefcase slowly made its way above the floor, sailing past the bed, bureau, and then coming to a stop in front of the door. The flashlight mounted on the robot's base was pointed into the hallway, lighting up the track and the bloody handprints on the wall.

Johnny Fingers started to move down the track, the sound of its motor barely audible over the roar of rain pummeling the van. Jack watched the robot move out of the bedroom, down the hall, turn the corner, and come to a complete stop at the head of the stairs. The briefcase now hovered in the air above the steps.

Jack swallowed hard, noticing how dry and tight his throat felt. Divots of sweat were running down his back and under his arms. The knot in his stomach momentarily loosened, then tightened again when Burke switched to the camera that showed the steep dip of the stairs the robot now had to travel.

Burke moved his hands away from the controls as if they'd suddenly become too hot to touch and rubbed his palms across the thighs of his jeans. He cleared his throat several times.

Sam said, "Switching to camera one."

On the color monitor, large and bright and vivid, was a three-dimensional side shot of the robot. Sam zoomed the video camera in on the level. The bubble of air inside the level filled the entire screen.

"How's that look to you?"

"Good," Burke said, and lifted his hands from his thighs. "Keep your eye on the bubble and tell me what to do."

Burke moved his hands back to the controls. Looking at the view on the black-and-white monitor, Jack felt as if he were sitting in the front car of a roller coaster that was about to dip forward and careen down the track.

Sam said, "Ready whenever you are."

Lines of sweat ran down Burke's face. "Let's do it."

Johnny Fingers inched forward, a tank about to crawl down the side of a mountain. Jack's eyes were welded to the color monitor, watching with growing fear as the air bubble inside the level rocked slowly back and forth in the glowing green-and-yellow liquid, Burke working the controls to keep the air bubble steady and even, knowing that if it dipped too much, the house would blow.

Sam told Burke when to pull back on the arm, nick it just a hair, that's it, you got it, and Jack looked at Burke's monitor, saw the robot inching forward, felt the weight of all of that metal hanging in the air. Jack squeezed the table as the weight of the robot momentarily gave way to gravity, Burke working the robot's arm back, listening to Sam the entire time, that's it, go slow, until the rubber-encased wheels descended on the stairs as gently as a prowler's foot, the base of the robot hugging the descending section of track like a drowning man gripping a life preserver, the briefcase shaking slightly.

Briefcase and robot grew still. The house was still standing.

Jesus Christ, Jack thought. A sour taste rose in his stomach. How the hell did Burke do this stuff day after day without ulcers?

Burke moved the joystick forward just a hair, and on the screen the robot's wheel gently bounced over the series of steps toward the first landing, the mechanical claw solidly holding the briefcase in the air.

"That's it," Burke said under his breath. "That's it, just take your time, Johnny, nice and slow and—"

The beeper inside the briefcase went off.

chapter 41

JACK PUSHED HIMSELF AWAY FROM THE TABLE AND MOVED DIRECTLY BEHIND BURKE'S SHOULDER. On the screen Johnny Fingers was still traveling down the stairs.

Over the speakers, Sam said, "Bob, that came from—"

"Pull out, everyone *pull out now,*" Burke said, the skin on his face pinching tight and washing of color.

The cell phone inside the briefcase started dialing, its sound echoing inside the van.

Jack, his eyes riveted on the still-moving bomb robot, felt slow-motion terror wash through him, ringing inside his head like a fire alarm.

Lightning quick, Fletcher slid behind the wheel. The van was already running. Burke was out of his chair and grabbing the edge of the table with one hand, his other reaching out to hold the passenger's seat headrest; Duffy placed both hands on the edge of the table and pushed himself into the back of the driver's side chair. Jack was searching for something to hold on to when the van lurched forward.

It was as if someone had jerked the rug out from under Jack's feet. He fell backward, his right shoulder and arm hitting the floor; above him objects broke free from the Peg-Board; tool drawers spit open; nails and screws flew into the air, showering down around and on his legs, chest, and face.

He rolled onto his stomach. The casters of Burke's chair went rattling past him and smashed into the slightly opened back doors. The van cut hard left, and Jack was thrown against the side of the van. The back doors kicked open, and the chair went sailing out into the rain-whipped night with a trail of screwdrivers, nails, and rope. A gust of wind rifled through the opened front window, keeping the back doors pushed open.

The chair tumbled across the street. Quickly Jack wedged his palms against the metal divots in the floor, pushing his body back to stay inside the van. Burke yelled something, but Jack couldn't make out the words. The blades of rain slicing in through the windows hit the back of his head, neck, and arms like needles, and he could feel the tires hydroplaning across the street as Fletcher raced the van away from the Beaumont home.

The second van containing the man named Sam had pulled out of a driveway and was now racing toward them, its headlights coming on in a white burst of light that highlighted the silver daggers of rain. At the opposite end of the street, several houses away from the Beaumont home and so far away that Jack could barely see them, a series of flashing red lights came to life. Fire trucks and ambulances, looking like Matchbox cars.

On the speakers now, the cell phone started ringing.

The house in front of the scrambling vehicles exploded.

From far down that end of the street the thunderous sound of wood splitting, glass shattering, and metal tearing all at once filled the air. Vehicles were kicked off the ground like toys caught in a tornado and thrown back onto the street. The vehicles tumbled sideways along the street and up the lawns, snapping trees as if they were mere splinters of wood and ripping through the houses. The van's floor shook from the pressure wave.

Another house exploded, four houses up from the last one, taking the surrounding homes with it.

The force of the blast almost knocked the van off the ground. The tires connected back to the road in a wet squeal while the van racing behind them swerved across the road, almost losing control.

Jack's eyes were welded to the street receding from him. It was happening in such a rush that his mind had shut down and the only thing he could do was lie on the floor with the rain hitting his back and face and stare.

Another house exploded, closer to them, moving *closer,* Burke behind him screaming, *"HE'S BOMBING THE ENTIRE STREET!"*

The Beaumont house exploded next. Ambulances caught in front of the blinding white flash were thrown sideways into the air, Jack's eyes following them as they crashed and tumbled.

Another house went and then another, the explosions racing toward them, deafening, Jack's hearing leaden now, almost completely muted but clinging to Burke's faraway voice screaming, *"PUNCH IT, PUNCH IT!"*

Jack felt the van cut hard right. Instantly he was thrown back into the wall. The back of his head hit something hard and flat. The pursuing van was off the ground and sailing through the air, and Jack watched it hit the ground and tumble past them, hit the curb, and then roll up the lawn and tear through the two columns of a Victorian home. Someplace close, another house exploded, too close he thought, and in that instant he knew he couldn't prepare himself for what was about to happen next, that his life and the lives of everyone else inside this van had been surrendered to chance.

The van was kicked into the air. Jack saw Burke falling backward along with the table, the bomb control unit, and the computer monitor, everything hanging in the air before the van landed on its side with a crash of metal. A jolt screamed through his body, and then he was sliding across the floor and sailing out the back door into the rain and darkness. In that precious moment of time, he saw Amanda leaning over to kiss him good-night; then saw Taylor's body stiffening against his touch.

His shoulder slammed into the ground and then his head, and all thoughts disappeared.

Jack didn't know how long he had been unconscious. Sometime later, his body twitched and his senses came back on, broken and disjointed. The explosions had stopped. His hearing was horribly muted except for the throbbing inside his skull. He was lying on his stomach. His ribs were throbbing. Something sharp had pierced his arm, he was bleeding, and blood was seeping out from the back of his head. Rain poured down on him like drill bits.

It took time for his eyes to focus. Tongues of flame stretched up into the black sky, the orange glow washing over a street that was running with water. The white van that had nearly crashed into them was lying on its roof, its back wheels still spinning in the rain.

He shifted his weight to one hand and turned his body around. Burke's van was lying on its left side, having crashed against the curb. The back doors had been torn off and were resting on the street. Deep inside the van Bill Duffy was crawling out from underneath a table. Across the street Bob Burke lay on his stomach, his arms splayed out as if gratefully hugging the road.

Jack forced himself up onto his knees. Slowly, taking in deep breaths, he stood up, so dizzy he nearly fell down, and staggered through the rain-whipped night.

He bent down and held Burke's wrist, feeling a pulse. A wave of relief spread through him. It disappeared when he saw the screwdriver that had entered through the base of Burke's skull.

Jack didn't know how long he knelt there, staring at Burke. Wet black pants and shoes walked up to him. Jack was finally aware that Fletcher stood above him, his clothes torn, his black eyes staring down.

"We've got to get him to a hospital," Jack said.

Fletcher held Jack's cell phone. Water ran down his hand and sluiced over the phone's keypad and screen, blurring its single, blinking green dot.

"It's for you," Fletcher said.

There was something strange in Fletcher's tone, a stillness that made Jack reach for the phone without question. He looked up at Fletcher's impassive face and thought of Ronnie Tedesco.

Jack pressed the phone against his ear, closed his eyes. Rain pounded against his skull. *Please, God, don't let it be Taylor.*

"Casey."

"Good evening, Jack," Miles Hamilton said. "I hope I'm not catching you at a bad time."

chapter 42

TAYLOR WAS DRESSED IN BOXER SHORTS AND A TANK TOP, HER EYES PUFFY AND WET AND LACED WITH A NERVOUS ENERGY WHEN JACK WALKED INTO THE LIVING ROOM. The fear fluttering inside his chest vanished when he saw her. She bolted upright, relief washing across her face. Then she saw his torn, bloodstained clothing, and her eyes clouded again with fear. It was after 1 A.M.

"I'm fine," he whispered. "Where's Rachel?"

"Upstairs with the dog." She looked him over, glanced over her shoulder at the TV, looked back at him. "Jack . . . Jesus Christ, it was all over the news, I saw it and . . ." Her voice trailed off, her tone tight.

Taylor reached out and hugged him tight. Jack winced. He had spent the last two hours at Newton-Wellesley Hospital. His ribs hadn't rebroken, but they were bruised and hurt like hell. The back of his skull was a stapled, throbbing mess, and he still felt nauseous. The ER doctor had given him a painkiller, which Jack hadn't taken.

"Shhh, it's okay, I'm okay," he whispered. The TV was on, muted, replaying the eleven-o'clock news. News helicopters had captured the entire footage; on the screen, a shaking aerial shot as the first house exploded. Jack watched another house explode and then another, saw the van being kicked off the ground, all the images from just hours ago as raw as a fresh wound. Then his mind flashed to Fletcher handing him the phone, Jack thinking that Taylor had been hurt or killed, and his body went cold.

He closed his eyes and hugged her tight. Thank God. Thank God she was okay.

This time.

He kept squeezing her against his chest, not caring how much his ribs hurt, he just held her close to him, inhaling the clean smell of her hair and skin. All he wanted to do was slide into bed with her, feel her warmth against his skin. Feel her sanity.

Taylor moved away from him and wiped her eyes. "Why didn't you call me?"

"I know, I'm sorry, I should have."

"All I could think . . ."

"Taylor, I'm sorry. It's been a long night." In a flash Jack saw Bob Burke in the ER, the neurologist from Boston working on him. Bob Burke was now a permanent vegetable being kept alive by feeding tubes. The boy, Eric Beaumont, was heavily medicated and locked in a psychological coma.

He stared at Taylor. *She's next.*

"What?" she said. "What is it?"

"It's time we move you and Rachel."

"Jack, I've thought about it, and I don't want to leave."

"Taylor—"

"Rachel and I will stay here in the house."

"No, it's too dangerous here."

"We're safe here—you said so yourself. And with the bodyguards—"

"Not after what happened tonight."

"Jack—"

"Please, Taylor. For me."

Taylor wrapped her arms around her chest. A strong breeze blew in through the windows. She turned, looked out at the balcony for a moment, and then stared at the TV playing silently. The sound of the rain drilling on the balcony floor was deafening.

"Where will we go?"

"Ronnie has arranged for you and Rachel to go someplace where the Sandman can't find you."

"Where?"

"It's best if I don't know."

She looked up at him, her eyes weighted with anger now. "And while we're in hiding, I can't talk to you."

"Not until I catch him."

"Let someone else do it. Let this guy, this profiler you said was in town, let him do it."

"I can't, Taylor."

"Why? Why risk it all, Jack?"

He tried to form the words but couldn't. All he could say was, "I can't just drop this."

"You mean you won't."

"Taylor, I don't want to fight about this."

"And I don't want to be hiding somewhere, not being able to talk to you, forced to watch the news to see if you're dead."

"I'll be fine."

Taylor glanced sideways at the TV. "Right. After tonight, how can you make that kind of guarantee?"

"I have the best people working with me. We've made progress—"

"If something happens to you, where does that leave me? What am I supposed to do? You're my—" Her voice broke.

"I'll catch him, Taylor. I can promise you that."

Tears streamed down her face. "Even if it kills you."

Jack went to hold her, but she had already turned and stormed out of the room. He listened to her angry footsteps move up the stairs.

Taylor's attic had been converted into an office. He shut the door but didn't close it. He wanted to be able to hear if she decided to come up the stairs.

He called the airline first and made a reservation. Then he called the North Carolina State Hospital for the Criminally Insane and talked to Director Daniel Voyles at length.

Jack hung up the phone. He stood up, turned, and jumped. Leaning against the doorway was Mike Abrams, dressed in jeans, a T-shirt, and sneakers.

His face gave it away. He had heard the entire conversation.

There was no point dodging the issue. It was out in the open. Time to deal with it.

Mike came inside the office and shut the door softly behind him. The only source of light came from a banker's lamp on Taylor's desk; the room was full of lengthening shadows.

"He knows the name of the fourth family," Jack said.

"Let me guess: he wants you to come see him, and then he'll hand over the name."

"Something like that."

"And you think you're going to waltz in there after, what, seven years now, and he's going to hand the information over to you? Jesus Christ, Jack, do you hear what you're saying?"

"Hamilton knew the name of the third family, the Beaumonts. He knew that several homes blew up one after another."

"He saw it on the news. The story's already gone national. The Sandman's front-page news."

"Hamilton also knew how this bomb was constructed, and where it was placed. The press couldn't have known that so soon."

"Why not? We both know the Sandman's feeding information to the media."

"He wouldn't give them information on the bomb."

"You don't know that."

"I think the Sandman's been in contact with Hamilton."

"Why?"

"I don't know. But I do know Hamilton knows the name of the fourth family."

"Let's suppose he does. You actually think he's going to give it to you?"

"He will."

"Why?"

"Look, I have to try. I just can't ignore the fact that he—"

"Try this: you go in there and try to mentally outmaneuver him, you'll reopen every goddamn lesion—"

"Give me some credit, Mike."

"You haven't seen him since . . . Memory and imagination aren't selective. You can't filter out what you don't want."

"This time is different. I can—"

"He's using you, Jack."

"Using me for what?"

"How the fuck should I know? They've had shrinks from all across the country go in and interview this guy. Nobody knows what makes him tick, and you're standing here telling me Hamilton won't protect the Sandman. Jack, he's capable of anything. You didn't think he would—" Mike stopped.

"Go ahead. Say it."

"I've been watching you, Jack. The mood swings. The drinking—I've caught it on your breath. The way you're withdrawing from reality, sinking back into that mind-set. How much further are you going to keep pushing yourself?"

"What the fuck do you want me to do, sit back and wait?"

"I'm asking you to be realistic. You can't see him. You can't go in there and face him and you know it."

The words hung in the silence of the attic.

"We'll find him," Mike said. "We've got—"

"What we got right now is shit. You were there that day on the beach. That was one bomb. Tonight he bombed eight houses in a row. There's a part of Newton that looks like a botched NATO raid. Bob Burke's a permanent vegetable, and I barely scraped out alive. What the fuck do you think he's going to do for an encore?"

"Hamilton's not going to give you what you want."

"He has no reason to protect the Sandman."

"Then why is he calling you now? Have you thought of that?"

"I'm going."

"Don't. It's a mistake."

"I've already made up my mind, end of discussion."

"I'm asking you as a friend, Jack. Don't go."

Mike's frustration was gone. Now his tone was pleading. Tight. Jack knew Mike well enough to know when he was holding something back.

Jack moved in closer. Mike's face looked worn and tired in the shadows. Jack stared at him, waiting for him to speak. A moment later, he did.

"Alicia Claybrook. You remember her, don't you?"

His former neighbor, a single mother of a four-year-old son and an emergency-room nurse, had seen Hamilton walk out of the house with a duffel bag and slide behind the wheel of a black BMW he brazenly parked in the driveway.

"She testified at your trial," Mike said. "Her testimony put Hamilton away. Without it, he would have walked."

"I know, you told me."

"What you don't know is that she and her son, Joshua, had to be placed in the Witness Protection Program. And now she's missing."

It was as if the oxygen had been sucked out of the room; Mike's face went temporarily out of focus.

"Missing," Jack repeated.

"It happened two weeks ago. She didn't show up for work and that set a chain of events in motion. Everything in her house is there, but nobody knows where she is."

"What about her son?"

"He's missing too." Mike's voice was steady. "As to how Hamilton suddenly discovered her whereabouts, my guess is that he hired the same services that matched the cell phone number to you. That number and your credit cards, your paycheck—it's still listed under the name John Peters, the name you used in Colorado. Now Hamilton has it. You're not in hiding anymore."

Information on the alias may have been stored inside the box the Sandman had stolen. *The Sandman must have passed it along to Hamilton,* Jack thought. But there was nothing inside the box on Claybrook—at least nothing that Jack could recall. So that didn't explain how Hamilton had discovered where she was hiding. Was there a leak inside Witness Protection?

"How do you know Hamilton's responsible for her disappearance?" Jack said.

"The guy calls you out of the blue on your cell phone that's listed under another name and you're asking me how I know? Jack, the guy has a history of making things disappear. You worked the case. You of all people know what he's about."

"Hamilton's team of lawyers was broken up years ago when the victim's families sued his estate and won. He's bankrupt."

"Not anymore." There was an odd constraint in Mike's words. He looked like a man staring in shock at a grisly accident.

"What is it?"

Mike blinked, took in a deep breath and swallowed. His eyes shifted back up, avoiding Jack's. "I didn't want to tell you this."

"Tell me what?" Jack said, nervous.

"Hamilton's gearing up for a retrial."

Jack went numb. They were both quiet, the attic filled with the sound of the rain pounding the roof.

"He's already handpicked his legal team," Mike said. "With the star witness gone and the questionable fiber evidence, the word is that the judge is going to allow it."

"Unless I testify."

"You're the only thing standing between him and the sun."

In his mind Jack heard doors slam shut and locks bolt home. He tried to force a thought and couldn't. He stood there, his legs weak, and stared out the window at the rain.

What he felt more than anything was cornered. Hamilton knew about the Sandman and where Jack lived. Fuck Hamilton. He wasn't going to hide anymore. Not now. Not with the fourth family waiting in the wings.

"I'm going."

"Hamilton's not going to give you what you want."

"I have to try."

Mike studied Jack's face for a moment. Then his gaze became steely and cold with a hard truth. "Amanda's not going to return from the grave to grant you absolution. Remember that when you look into his eyes."

chapter 43

ALAN LYNCH, HIS FACE RED FROM A SHAVE, WALKED INTO THE LIVING ROOM OF THE FOUR SEASONS SUITE. His heart jumped. Victor Dragos was sitting at the breakfast table hunched over a plate of eggs Benedict, reading Stephen Covey's *The Seven Habits of Highly Effective People.* A silver breakfast cart was next to him.

Dragos looked up. "Morning, Al. While you were in the shower, I ordered us breakfast. Grab a plate and dig in."

"How long have you been here?"

"Twenty minutes. You were in the bathroom a long time. Everything okay?"

"I didn't hear you knock." *And I remember locking the door,* Alan added privately.

"I didn't. By the haggard look on your face, I take it you didn't sleep last night."

"Not really."

"I hope it has nothing to do with me. Do I make you nervous?"

"Of course not."

"So you always sleep with a chair pinned under your door?"

Alan's face tightened.

Dragos laughed. "Sorry. Just making a little joke."

Alan went about stocking his plate with eggs. He wasn't hungry but knew he had to eat.

"You missed quite the pyrotechnics show," Dragos said. "I've never seen anything like it. House after house blowing up—and I was *this* close. Talk about an adrenaline rush." Dragos whistled. "Seventeen dead. . . . I found one guy screaming under a porch. His legs had been blown off and he was watching himself bleed to death." Dragos forked a bit of egg. "Not a good way to go. Needless to say I did the kind thing and ended his suffering."

Alan had watched the entire spectacle on last night's news. "This morning CNN said the San Diego bomber and the Sandman are in fact the same person."

"The local news stations are saying the same thing. A bombing of a federal building, and now bombing an entire neighborhood, of course they're going to make comparisons."

"The Sandman's feeding them the information."

"Maybe."

"No, not *maybe.* That's *exactly* what he's doing. He's got the entire world watching, and he's controlling the media. He'll kill another family soon to keep the interest alive, and after that, he'll expose the program. We're running out of time."

"You don't know that."

"I've been doing this a long time, Victor. I know how it's going to play out. I wouldn't be surprised if he knows we're in town."

Alan felt the knot in his stomach tighten. He sat down, tried to eat. He felt sick.

"You make any progress on this Graves thing?" Dragos asked.

"With what little records we have left, we've taken names of doctors and nurses. They're scattered everywhere. The only name in the East is Roth's, and we know what happened to him."

"What about the bodies. Any luck there?"

"We found a fingerprint on the woman," Alan said, and filled Dragos in. Roughly three hours ago, the Boston pathologist, Wilson, had moved the cadmium-helium laser across the Beaumont woman's face; glowing on her left cheek was a full latent print. AFIS—the Automated Fingerprint Indexing System—was hooked up to the patient database and was searching for a match. When one was found, the results would be transmitted over a secured phone line to the computer sitting on the table next to them.

"We should know something soon," Lynch said. "How about your end? Anything interesting turn up?"

"Several items, actually. Not ten minutes after you left, Casey called a beeper and entered in four-one-one—did it twice that night, actually, the first time about fifteen minutes before we got there. I'm guessing it's a code."

"For what?"

"Don't know. The beeper number belongs to a man by the name of Parker Davis from Freeport, Maine. Name mean anything to you?"

Lynch thought about it. He shook his head.

"We got the guy's address through Cellular One. A post-office box. When we ran his SSN through the computer, it spit back the name of a boy from Chicago who died over thirty years ago." Dragos drummed his fingertips on the table. "Looks like someone's trying to hide their identity."

"After Jack called the number, what happened?"

"I was watching all this through the window of a house with binoculars—and without the use of night vision. A few minutes later, a guy comes out from behind the house, dressed head to toe in black, like someone out of *GQ*. They started talking but for some reason the mike I had aimed on them couldn't pick up their conversation. All I heard was static. Anyway, *GQ* man and Casey get in the back of the van with Burke and the hometown dick, Duffy. This *GQ* guy . . . he doesn't look like local talent."

"Where is he now?"

"MIA at the moment. I tried to follow him but . . . well, he slipped away. I'm sure he'll pop up again."

Alan took a bite from a bagel. Dragos was staring at him, like a man being entertained by a private joke.

"Guess who called Casey after the explosion?"

"I give up."

"Miles Hamilton."

Alan almost dropped his coffee cup. Finally, he swallowed and watched his hands carefully put his shaking coffee cup back on the saucer. Dragos was leaning back in his chair, his hands clasped behind his head, his grin expansive.

"The call came in at nine forty-five last night, on Casey's cell phone," Dragos said. "We traced the number to the North Carolina State Hospital for the Criminally Insane. Turns out Miles Hamilton was supposed to be making a call to his lawyers. Our national nightmare is gearing up for a new trial."

"He's *what?*"

"Seems that Hamilton's legal team has suddenly taken a renewed interest in him. Phone calls, meetings, the whole nine yards. The hospital director doesn't like it, but he's not going to risk getting slapped with a civil liberties lawsuit. Didn't Hamilton try to sue the FBI?"

"For evidence tampering. His lawyers were getting desperate," Alan said, the words coming out slowly. This case was airplane turbulence. There was nothing to hold on to, it all kept moving. All he could do was sit and wait for it all to be over.

"I heard he almost won," Dragos said.

"What he got was national press coverage. We had Justice crawling up our ass with microscopes for six months." *Why would Hamilton call Jack after all these years?*

"You ever meet Hamilton face-to-face?" Dragos asked.

"At the trial."

"I hear that when people are around him, they can actually feel their bowels loosen."

"He's got presence, all right."

"What's it like?"

Blue eyes as cold as a river in wintertime, a smile that reminds you of an animal taking pleasure just before it feeds.

"You ever been to Germany?"

"Several times."

"Go on a tour of Auschwitz?"

Dragos nodded.

"You know that feeling you get while you're standing there, that you're breathing the same air that gave life to evil? That's what it's like when you're near him. I've dealt with dozens of serial killers, and he's the only one who made me feel that way."

"Casey didn't go to the trial, did he?"

"No. We had an eyewitness who saw Hamilton leaving the house—that and the fiber evidence was enough to get a conviction."

"To a hospital for the criminally insane."

"Hamilton's a top-notch performer. He knew how to work the tests. And he had convincing lawyers."

"Why didn't Casey testify? That would have sealed the deal."

"His shrinks wouldn't allow it. Post–traumatic stress disorder." *And other reasons you don't need to know, Victor.*

Dragos sipped his coffee. "He still suffering from it?"

"Given how the families have died, yes, I think he's struggling with it."

"Then why would Casey book a round-trip ticket to North Carolina to see him?"

Alan had to replay the words to make sure he had heard them right.

"His flight leaves Logan at ten–forty this morning," Dragos said. "Hamilton must have told him something juicy to get him to go down there. I don't have to do the arithmetic to figure out what it was about."

"That's . . . What could Hamilton know about the Sandman? About what's going on?"

"Simple. Guess who paid Hamilton a visit roughly a week ago."

A moment of clarity came to Alan, and with it an exciting rush of hope. The turbulence stopped. He leaned forward, almost knocking over his coffee.

"Dr. David Gardner," Alan said.

"Only we both know it wasn't the real Gardner. Why would the Sandman want to visit Hamilton?"

"I don't know. Before Casey gets there, we have to bug his cell."

"Paris is on the phone right now with the hospital director making the arrangements. Whatever we do, it will have to be discreet. I understand Hamilton spooks easily."

On the table next to Alan the computer started beeping. "The fingerprint results." He stood up.

The screen of the computer monitor was divided into two windows. The one on the left contained a blown-up picture of the latent print, the ridges colored red, the print's minutiae, or centers, designated by tiny white boxes. The right window contained all of the print's technical details. The recovered print had found one match with an accuracy rating of 99.9 percent.

Hope, he had hope now, and for the first time in days Alan felt that sickening fog inside his chest begin to lift. *I got you. I got you now, you son of a bitch.*

Dragos leaned forward over Alan's shoulder. Alan could hear him breathing steadily, could smell the coffee on his breath and his soap and cologne.

The fingerprint disappeared and the words TRANSMITTING PICTURE blinked in the center of the screen. A moment later, the words disappeared. A strip of color ran across the top of the screen. Another strip raced underneath it, the process repeating over and over. Less than a minute later a partial picture had formed. The black head of hair was cut short and combed back tight. Dark eyebrows formed.

The strip ran across the screen again and assembled part of the eyes.

Alan felt a faint tug of recognition. He watched the screen intently.

Then the eyes assembled.

"Well, I'll be," Dragos said. "That's Mr. GQ himself."

It was as if Alan's body had been dipped in dry ice. Suddenly he couldn't blink, couldn't move his eyes away from the screen.

"Something wrong, Al? You look pale."

Alan had to clear his throat to get the words out. "Get Abrams on the phone."

chapter 44

TAYLOR HAD HER BACK AGAINST THE PORSCHE. "I don't mind driving you," she said.

"The taxi's fine."

"Then take the car. The dealer's dropping off the Expedition this morning."

"I'm all set."

Rachel squealed behind him. She was standing on the front patch of grass near the stairs. Mr. Ruffles stood beside her, his tail wagging back and forth like a windshield wiper while Rachel washed him down with the hose.

"Remember what we talked about," Jack said.

"I know, stay inside the house, don't answer the door. No mail."

Jack nodded.

"I have to call my sister and tell her what's going on. I can't keep this from her. She has a right to know."

"Once you and Rachel are tucked away, then you can call her. Ronnie knows all about it. He'll have you call over an encrypted line. You'll be able to talk to her tonight. I talked with Ronnie, it's all worked out."

Taylor studied him for a moment. Her hair was pulled back and fastened with a clip; the long blond tendrils that had escaped blew in the hot ocean breeze.

"Will I at least see you before I leave?"

"Maybe. I don't know."

A taxi pulled up.

"So this is good-bye."

Jack went to hug her. She hugged him back, but it was awkward and reserved, as if she were nursing a private injury that prevented her from momentary vulnerability.

"You shouldn't go there alone," she whispered.

"I'll be fine. This will be over soon, I promise." He hugged her tight and kissed her on the cheek.

He backed away but she wouldn't let him go.

"I love you," she said, and kissed him on the mouth. She stepped back, crossing her arms over her chest, and looked away from him, searching for an answer that would somehow heal this moment.

"I'm sorry about this, Taylor."

She nodded but didn't look back at him.

Jack had opened the back door and tossed his briefcase onto the seat when Rachel's scream pierced the air.

"Uncle Jack!"

Rachel ran over to him. Her face was full of alarm and dotted with soap suds. She looked up at him, and all at once Jack saw his unformed daughter suffocating in the womb, saw a life that should have been and wasn't.

"What is it, sweetie?" he said with a forced smile.

"You didn't give *me* a hug good-bye."

"You're right. I'm sorry."

He got down on one knee.

"I love you, Uncle Jack."

Rachel kissed him, and he hugged her, then stood up and got into the back of the taxi. Through the window, he watched as Taylor wrapped her arm around Rachel's waist and picked her up. They both waved, like a mother and daughter saying good-bye to their father, the picture of this moment now indelible.

He waved back and quickly turned his head away, fearful that they would glimpse the sharp and sudden sadness that had already laid claim to his soul.

His seat was cramped and he couldn't get comfortable. His skin . . . it felt as if it were vibrating. It was a distinctly odd sensation. *It's just nerves,* he thought. *A few drinks and you'll be fine.*

He was vaguely aware of a peculiar taste on the back of his throat, a slowly building thirst that he knew wouldn't be satisfied by water or booze.

His cell phone rang. He reached inside his briefcase.

"This is your subconscious calling," Malcolm Fletcher said, and laughed. "Anxious about your reunion?"

"I'm fine."

You seem to be saying that a lot lately, a voice said. *You sure about that? Then why do you feel as if you're climbing out of your skin?*

"Are you sure you don't want an escort? I've had great success in these matters."

"I'm sure, yes," Jack said. "What will you be doing?"

"Investigating real estate."

Real estate? Jack had the question posed on his lips when the stewardess came by and asked him to turn off the phone.

"I have to go," Jack said.

"Rage and desire, pain and joy, they all spawn in the same river. Remember that when you look deep into his eyes." Fletcher hung up.

Jack put the phone away. He stared out the window. He was tired of thinking. Tired of expending energy deciphering the subtext of words and thoughts.

His eyes closed, and just as he drifted off to sleep, he saw a mind that was shaped like an attic, dark and windowless, the rotted wood planks and rafters reeking of mildew and decay. In the silence that filled the hot, dark space, a black heart was beating, throbbing fitfully like a pulse struggling to cling to life, and behind the building sound Jack heard Miles Hamilton laughing.

chapter 45

THE FINAL CORRIDOR WAS LIT UP BY A SINGLE ROW OF FLUORESCENT BULBS; THE ONLY SOURCE OF NATURAL LIGHT CAME FROM THE END OF THE HALLWAY, A TALL WINDOW CAGED BEHIND WHITE STEEL MESH.

Following an orderly named Rick, Jack kept his eyes pinned on the white linoleum floor, struggling to keep his mind clear. He could hear mutters and cries behind the closed doors. His legs felt awkward, as if he were walking for the first time after having been bedridden for months, and his palms were clammy. He could feel the orderly's sideways glances.

"Dr. Voyles said I could see him alone," Jack said, the words coming out hoarse, as if his throat were packed with cotton.

The orderly nodded. Jack's footsteps echoed loudly in the daylight's throbbing silence. Too urgent, he thought. Too loud. He slowed. A casual pace. A casual meeting of the minds. This was business.

"What's he been doing? Dr. Voyles was vague."

"He reads mostly—chemistry and physics, math texts that I can't even pronounce," the orderly said. "He's corresponding with a research group in Tokyo—something to do with a particle accelerator. Most of the time he just sits and . . ." Rick shook his head.

"What?"

"I was just thinking how he always knows something about people. About our life outside the hospital, our families, what the wife and kids do. It's like he's living inside your head all the time, sees what you see. It's creepy. A lot of people avoid him."

Jack looked straight ahead. The door loomed closer.

"Let me give you an example. We had an orderly here, a newly married guy, very quiet, kept to himself. One Friday morning, he brought Hamilton his breakfast, and Hamilton starts asking him about the dude he picked up last night. Hamilton named the gay bar, named the dude, knew where the orderly lived—he knew *everything.* Guy quit that day and moved out of state."

Jack knew Miles would try to bait him into reliving his past—to show him that even after all these years, Miles could still control his life.

During the flight, Jack had reconstructed that cold, unfeeling psyche, the one that would sandbag Hamilton's madness and allow Jack to think strategy. Through the cracks and fissures, he could hear Amanda trying to talk to him, could see the images from the bedroom growing vivid. He wiped it all away by focusing on the fourth family.

"He's given you a lot of thought," Rick said. "One time—and this was years ago—I went in to feed him and saw him staring at your name on a piece of paper. That's it, just your name. He still has it." Rick frowned. "You know, they've had shrinks from all over the country come here and try to crack him. In the end, they come to the same conclusion I do: the guy's head's a swamp. You want to know what he's thinking, put your hand in an unflushed toilet."

The door was in front of them. Rick found the key on the chain, looked at Jack. He was off to the side, away from the window so Hamilton couldn't see him. Rick opened the door.

A balloon of air expanded inside Jack's chest and closed around his windpipe, leaving him light-headed. He took in a deep breath, held it until it burned. Exhaling, he pictured the fourth family and walked into the numbing void of the stark white container of steel and concrete.

The inside lights were dimmed. Miles Hamilton sat at a table behind the bars, writing furiously on a white pad of paper. His left hand was cupped against his forehead, hiding his eyes. Beneath the pad was a thick sheaf of papers. A Styrofoam cup of oatmeal and a plastic spoon were next to Hamilton's elbow. A half dozen math books were stacked on a small shelf bolted into the wall.

Hamilton held up his index finger for silence so he could finish writing out his thought. Jack took a moment to look him over.

Miles Hamilton had not changed much over the years; it was as if he had been preserved with formaldehyde. His short blond hair was parted on the side and combed wet against his head; his smooth skin was as pale as parchment. His body was thin and as tight as a swimmer's, and the prison whites hung awkwardly on his frame. Only one feature had changed: his age.

Miles Hamilton was now twenty-six years old. Seven years ago, Miles had been nineteen.

Nineteen, Jack thought with a spark of anger and ego. *Nineteen, you're still a boy. A boy outwitted me. A boy killed my wife and destroyed my life.*

And he'll outlive you by at least twenty years, a voice added.

A folding chair had been brought in. Jack sat down, rested his briefcase against the chair leg, then placed his arms on his knees in a casual posture that went along with his casual attire: jeans and a white T-shirt.

Appearances were important with Miles. Dress the role of the common man and his arrogance would rise.

The locks bolted home. Minutes passed.

Miles Hamilton stopped writing. He swung around in his chair, crossed his leg, and tapped his pen against the pad, his face as cold as stone, his eyes as vacant as a doll's. Jack thought of a black widow spider trapped in a glass bowl.

"Special Agent Casey—I mean *Detective* Casey."

"Hello, Miles." Jack's voice sounded confident. Strong.

"I barely recognize you. You've undergone a metamorphosis. You look like a new man, but I guess that's the point."

Hamilton's eyes were a cold, disarming blue, as lifeless as marbles, yet constantly measuring.

"I apologize for keeping you waiting. I had a revelation and was writing it down when you came in. It's on neutrinos—neutral particles that are, for practical purposes, invisible. They generally don't interact with matter."

"I'm told you're working with a research group in Tokyo."

"They're using a fifty-thousand-ton ring-imaging water Cerenkov detector to search for neutrinos, proton decay, muons—I won't bore you with the technical details, but they've made remarkable progress."

"Sounds interesting."

"Not really. There's nothing *tasty* in the pursuit of science, nothing to enliven the senses. All that space and time bound by equations and formulas and one-dimensional theories—I've always found it limiting."

"Why did you pick it back up?"

"To keep my mind busy. Isn't that why you moved to Colorado and picked up carpentry?"

"Who told you about Colorado?"

Hamilton grinned. "A mutual friend."

"The same one who gave you my cell phone number."

"Say, whatever happened to your neighbor Alicia Claybrook, the one who *allegedly* saw me running from your house?"

"I don't know."

"My lawyers have some questions for her but can't seem to find her. Any idea where she might be?"

"No."

"Don't keep in touch with anyone from the old neighborhood?"

"No."

Hamilton watched him. Thirsty eyes lapping up emotion like a junkyard dog drinking from a mud puddle.

"A single mother who worked three late shifts in a row at the ER and could barely keep her eyes open—not exactly credible testimony, but she won over the jury. And then the matter of the hair and fiber evidence they found in your bedroom. Not two days before, you were at my father's estate, walking through our wine cellar, sitting on our furniture—you could have tracked them in from there."

Jack didn't say anything, wanting to let Miles chew on the silence.

"No fingerprints in your home, no evidence when the police pulled me over," Hamilton said playfully. "Then there's the matter of the tool used to slit your wife's throat—a scalpel, the defense claimed. It was never recovered, as you know."

"I didn't know that."

"You haven't read the transcripts?"

"No."

Hamilton smiled. "You will."

"Let's talk about our friend."

"This is called foreplay, Jack. The heat that builds before the orgasm. Surely you must have practiced it with your wife. Or was Amanda one of those types who could fuck at the drop of a dime?"

Jack rubbed his hands together, his mind focused on the fourth family, save us, tick-tick-tick. "I recall that when the police pulled you over, they found a suitcase with a fake passport, birth certificate, and a receipt for a bank wire for several million dollars."

"I like to travel in anonymity."

"The jury seemed to believe you were going into hiding."

"A misperception. A man like yourself should be very familiar with such things."

"You called me. You said you wanted to talk about the Sandman. I'm here."

Hamilton laughed. "What an awful name. Appropriate, but awful. I bet the public is eating it up. A shame what happened to the last family, the Beaumonts. What a tragedy. You're lucky to be sitting here in front of me."

"You've been in contact with him?"

"We've become *very* familiar with each other."

"How did you meet?"

"Pen pals. I get a lot of mail, you know. Haven't you seen my Web sites? I have a lot of fans out there."

"Why would he want to contact you?"

"Mutual interests."

"Like what?"

"You swim in the same pool, why don't you tell me?"

Where's he going with this? Jack thought. *Dead end, try something else.*

"Why are you protecting him?"

"That day you came out to the house, how did you know it was me?"

Jack hadn't anticipated the question; it caught him off-guard.

Then Jack caught the look in Hamilton's eyes: that need to know. He had been discovered and imprisoned, and his arrogance *demanded* an explanation. Jack saw his opening and moved ahead with careful precision.

"It doesn't matter," Jack said.

"It does if you want to save the fourth family."

"I doubt the Sandman would have told you their names."

"He told me about Beaumont—and the two before them, Roth and Dolan."

"You could have read that in the papers."

"Do you want to save them?"

"Give me a name."

"They live in Cambridge."

"What else?"

"The man is a psychiatrist."

"I want a name."

"His first name is Brian."

"His last name?"

"I want an answer to my question."

"I think you're lying. I don't think you know anything. Good-bye, Miles." Jack picked up his briefcase and stood up.

"Eric Beaumont is in room three-oh-two at Newton-Wellesley under the name of Joshua McDermont, an eleven-year-old victim of a car accident."

Jack felt a cold, hollow knocking in his chest. Hamilton sensed it. His eyes went wide, a mischievous grin stretching across his mouth.

"Do I have your attention now, Detective Casey?"

"I want a name."

"Sit down and answer my question. *Now.*"

"No."

"They're scheduled to die tonight. You want their deaths on your conscience?"

Jack didn't say anything.

"I didn't think so. Now sit back down and answer my question."

Jack remained standing. "Give me his name."

"Le Claire. Dr. Brian Le Claire. Go ahead and call and check it out if you want. I'll wait."

"A wine cork," Jack said. "I found it under the senator's daughter's bed. It was a vintage. Your father's estate bought several cases per year."

"*Very* thin."

"You knew her . . . intimately."

"Fucking isn't a crime."

"It is when you scatter her body parts over her parents' home."

"If you were so confident it was me, you had probable cause. Why didn't you arrest me?"

"I didn't have a warrant."

"You could have got one. Why did you wait, Detective Casey?"

Hamilton's stare felt like wasps chewing through the pulp of Jack's brain. And the confidence in his tone made Jack feel somehow outmaneuvered. But how? Jack suddenly felt exposed. He could feel sweat break out along his hairline.

"You're sweating, Jack. Is everything all right?"

"It's hot out. Very humid. I walked here."

"For a moment I thought you were going to tell me you were getting nervous about testifying at my retrial."

Hamilton watched Jack's expression carefully. "You don't seem surprised."

"I heard about it."

"That's it? No comment?"

"I'm not interested in the past."

"But the past is all I have, Jack. Thanks to you, the only sunsets I have are stored in my memory. But that will change. It's only a matter of time before I feel the sun again. As for the new trial, I have the strangest feeling you won't live long enough to testify. This madman has it in for you, I think." Hamilton winked.

In his mind Jack could hear Amanda try to speak to him. This time he listened to it, and the weight of his rage from the past seven years came crashing down on him, and Jack was back inside his bedroom, reliving that moment when Miles Hamilton had yanked back Amanda's throat. Miles Hamilton, the boy sitting just a few feet away from him, saying, *Watch closely, Jack. Watch as I destroy your world.*

"You're not going anywhere, Miles."

"Tell me, did it taste better when Charles Yerkies begged and cried for his life? Did it get you *hard?"*

Jack's mind went blank.

Hamilton removed a sheaf of papers from underneath the pad and held it up against the bars.

"Recognize the handwriting?"

It was a copy of Jack's journal.

"I see you too have learned how to transcend the limitations of skin." Hamilton tossed the pages onto the table. "You're one sick son of a bitch. When my lawyers get through with you, you'll be behind these bars. In time, *I'll* be coming here to visit *you.*"

It was like the phone call that comes in the dead of night and hits you with a horrible knowledge that forever alters your life. Jack had been used. Hamilton had used the fourth family as bait to get him here. *But why? Why now?*

A voice that sounded like Mike Abrams's was telling him to leave. But Jack couldn't move. He stood there, his body frozen in place, his skin cold, watching as Hamilton looked at him with that same arrogant confidence Jack had witnessed inside his bedroom.

"You think I don't know Alicia Claybrook and her son were placed in the Witness Protection Program?" Hamilton said. "That you're hiding under the identity of John Peters? I've been aware of you for *years,* Jack."

A strange rush of heat flooded Jack's eyes, parched his throat. Instead of leaving, he dropped the briefcase and walked toward the bars, gripped them near his waist, and leaned his face close to the bars. Hamilton's eyes were wet and sparked with a disturbing light.

"You'll never feel the sun, Miles."

"And you're just moments away from meeting your wife."

Jack's reflexes were lightning quick; he reached through the bars with his right hand and gripped the tuck between Hamilton's pants and shirt. Hamilton acted like a novice; he used both hands to grip the wrist that was pulling him forward. Jack's left hand came up through the bars, cupped the back of Hamilton's small neck, and smashed him facefirst into the bars. Jack released his grip on the pants, reached up through the bars, grabbed hold of Hamilton's throat, and squeezed.

Hamilton was bleeding from both nostrils. His face was red, his eyes were tearing. His throat made wet, smacking sounds.

"It's like tasting God, isn't it, Jack?" he croaked.

But Jack couldn't hear the words. All of his attention was on crushing Hamilton's skull against the bars, watching as Hamilton's blood ran across his hands, feeling its warmth. Hamilton was wiry and strong, but he couldn't move. Jack's strength—his rage—had Hamilton pinned against the bars.

Hamilton cried out, and Jack squeezed harder. He could crush Hamilton's skull—easily.

Hamilton was giggling.

Do it.

"Do you know where Taylor is?" Hamilton wheezed.

It was like being doused in an ice-cold waterfall. Jack's strength, his rage, vanished, and his grip loosened.

Hamilton jerked himself from Jack's grasp and stepped back from the bars. He wiped a hand across his face and flicked the bloody mess across Jack's shirt.

"The Sandman has something special planned for Taylor and her adorable niece." Hamilton licked his lips and spit. "I can't wait to see the pictures."

Jack grabbed his briefcase and pounded on the door.

"Poor Jack Casey. He's about to lose the second chance he had at life."

Jack kept pounding on the door; the orderly was fumbling for his keys. *Hurry up, Jesus fucking Christ, HURRY UP!*

"How much longer, Jack? How much longer can you hold on to this life before you *drown?"*

chapter 46

ALAN LYNCH DODGED HIS WAY THROUGH CONGRESS STREET TOWARD THE LINCOLN TOWN CAR WAITING AROUND THE CORNER. The muggy air of downtown Boston was thick with exhaust and the sour smell of trash.

The driver, Kenny, saw Alan coming. He opened the door.

"Just hand me the phone," Alan said. His head was spinning. All he could see was Fletcher staring back at him. Out here in the unbearable heat, surrounded by all the noise and people and the throb of traffic, he didn't feel smothered by his thoughts.

Kenny handed him the cell phone equipped with the FBI's newest encryption technology. No one could listen in with a scanner.

"It's lunchtime," Kenny said. "I'll go grab us something."

Alan had already filled Dragos in on Fletcher's discovery of Graves and how he had later connected the hospital back to the FBI and eventually, the Behavioral Modification Program.

Dragos picked up the phone after the first ring. Alan quickly filled him in on his conversation with Mike Abrams: how he had retrieved Fletcher's name and social security number off of several old paper case files; feeding them through the computers and coming up with the Maine address; Jack's "interesting" visit.

"You find Fletcher?"

"I'm looking into it," Dragos said.

"Well, look harder. Fletcher's here to run interference on us so Jack can find the Sandman."

"How would Fletcher know about the Sandman? You told me you confiscated all of his records."

"We did."

"Then how would he know?"

"Maybe he met the Sandman, that's how he knows. Look, it doesn't matter why he's here, the point is that he *is* here and we have to find him—*quick.*"

"Odd that after all these years he's decided to crawl out from under his rock. Why do you think he went back to using his real name?"

Alan had thought about it all morning. "Redemption. It's the only thing he has left." Alan desperately wanted to close his eyes and wait for this entire fucking mess to vanish.

"Forget this guy, Al. He'll be out of the picture soon enough."

Dragos's carefree attitude reopened an old wound. Alan made sure he had pushed the anger away before he spoke again; it was important Dragos listened carefully.

"About three years after Fletcher tried to expose us, I tracked one of his aliases down to an apartment in Chicago. I sent two of your peers to go down and take care of the problem. Fletcher mailed one guy's teeth to my house; we never found the body. The other guy is a vegetable. His wife feeds him through a tube and changes his diapers."

"Sounds like they were careless."

"Don't underestimate his abilities. He's very resourceful."

"So's your friend Casey. Listen to this: he sent Patrick Dolan's hand to the FBI lab. Alex Ninan from Special Photo found a name etched in the skin: Gabriel LaRouche. Right now we're running the name through patient database."

"You won't find it there. I'm sure he took the time to erase his identity off the system."

"You guys perform regular backups, right?"

"Yeah, tape backups. We got them stored in a secured location. I'll make the call. I'll take the name and go through the paper records, maybe get a picture, for what it's worth. Where's Jack now?"

"On a flight back from North Carolina. The guys I have tailing him said he ran out of there as if death was chasing him. As to what went down, you'll find out when I do. I think it's time to take him off the board."

"Fine. How you want to play it?"

"I'm entertaining a few ideas. Is Abrams still in his office?"

"Abrams doesn't know anything."

"He discovered Fletcher, didn't he?"

"By lifting his name off an old case file. That's all he knows."

"Casey and Abrams are friends. Casey would pass on the information he got from Fletcher—"

"I can't have you killing off my men."

"I'm giving you the light at the end of the tunnel and suddenly you're turning into a Girl Scout." Dragos laughed. "Al, if your conscience is bothering you, go to confession. Then kiss the ground and be thankful that you're in an organization which employs people like me to erase problems from your conscience."

"Fletcher must be staying close to Jack. He has to be somewhere in Marblehead. Are your people looking there?"

"This guy really tingles your cherries, huh? Put Mr. Strange Eyes out of your mind, Al."

"Victor, listen to me. He's—"

"Sit back and enjoy the sunshine," Dragos said, and hung up.

For a moment all Alan did was watch the cars trying to fight their way through the congested traffic filtering into the Sumner Tunnel entrance. Then for no reason at all, he had the distinct feeling he was being watched. He turned and looked around. Nothing but crowds of professionals out for lunch, teenagers, and college kids.

Alan got into the air-conditioned limo. On the backseat was a green book. He frowned. The book hadn't been there this morning, and Kenny's reading interests were limited to the *Penthouse* forum.

The gold lettering along the spine had flaked away, but he could make out the imprint: *Le Morte d'Arthur.* The Death of King Arthur. Definitely not Kenny's reading speed.

Alan opened the front cover. There, on the aged flyleaf, were neatly printed words written in an elegant hand:

If into others' hands these relics came;
As 'twas humility
To afford to it all that a soul can do,
So, 'tis some bravery,
That since you would save none of me, I bury some
of you.

I'm watching you, Alan.

Malcolm Fletcher

chapter 47

VICTOR DRAGOS TOSSED THE PHONE ON THE BED AND MOVED OVER TO THE LASER MIKE SET UP IN THE CENTER OF THE ROOM, ITS BEAM LOCKED ON THE THIRD-FLOOR WINDOWS OF THE WASHBORNE INN—MALCOLM FLETCHER'S ROOM.

He put on the earphones, pressed the trigger, and did a final sweep across the glass. The only sounds he heard were the ocean breeze whistling though the screen windows, the distant pounding of the waves, and the seagulls cawing nearby.

When Casey had left his girlfriend's home yesterday afternoon, the surveillance team had tailed him to the Washborne Inn, where he had spent over an hour before leaving for Newton with the then unidentified man dressed in black—Mr. Strange Eyes himself, Malcolm Fletcher. The surveillance pictures had been developed early this morning and delivered to the room ten minutes after Alan Lynch had left for his talk with Mike Abrams.

The rest of it had been easy to arrange. The house across the bay that faced Fletcher's room belonged to Laura Brentwood, a widow with bad eyesight and too many cats. When he'd rung her doorbell this morning, she had needed a magnifying glass to examine his FBI credentials. Once she was convinced of their authenticity, she became accommodating—had even fixed him a late breakfast consisting of ham and eggs, OJ and coffee.

Dragos picked up the eight-by-ten surveillance picture and studied Fletcher's face. Unremarkable except for the eyes. Jesus, they were weird. One big retina, he thought. Black and without light. Intimidating even to Al, who hunted monsters for a living.

Which is why he didn't mention Fletcher's location on the phone.

Al Lynch was an administrator whose main function was to champion the successes of his profiling unit to Washington bureaucrats with deep pockets. Bureaucrats didn't possess tactical skills. A successful surgical strike required patience and finesse—skills that men like Lynch clearly lacked.

Dragos put the picture down and dialed the number for the Washborne Inn. The owner answered on the second ring.

"Mr. Jacobs, this is Agent Dragos. I'm told you've already been briefed."

"Yes, sir. Two FBI agents called me this morning. I've stayed here just as they instructed. Mr. Fletcher still hasn't returned."

"I need a key to his room."

"Not a problem. You need anything else, let me know." Jacobs lowered his voice. "Sir, I told the agents this morning, I don't mind helping out—I'm glad to do it, really—but, well, I don't want to upset any of the guests. Marblehead's a small town and the minds here can be just as small, if you get my meaning."

"This will be handled discreetly, Mr. Jacobs. You have nothing to worry about. Nobody will know a thing."

Jacobs sighed. "Thank you."

"I'll be over in ten minutes."

Dragos hung up. On the bed was the silencer and the Glock loaded with a clip of Hydra-Shok ammo. Of course, more satisfying options were available. Find the right nerve endings and apply the right pressure and Fletcher would *sing* what he knew.

In the warm shadows of the room's small study, well away from the windows, Malcolm Fletcher sat with his eyes closed in the brown leather chair. He had been sitting here for hours now, perfectly still, lost in Goya's enigmatic painting *The Sleep of Reason Produces Monsters,* when he saw the bright red dot of a laser beam moving across the white wall in the nearby room.

It didn't surprise him. He had been expecting this moment. The FBI should have employed a higher grade of encryption technology in their phones.

Inside his hand was a small transmitter that allowed him to switch to the bugs he had planted throughout the inn. Over the headphones he heard Jacobs hang up the phone in the foyer three floors below and begin to pace nervously.

Five minutes later, Fletcher heard the door open. Dragos introduced himself.

"I was on my way out, but I can stick around if you want," Jacobs said eagerly.

"That won't be necessary. I may be here for a while. I need to set up some things in the room. Under no circumstances do I want you or anyone else to enter that room. Understand?"

"Not a problem. I'll be back in a couple of hours. If you need anything, my wife will be in the kitchen. You want me to have her keep a lookout for him, call the room if he comes in?"

"I want her and you to stay away. In fact, the less you tell her, the better. There's no need to upset her."

"Fine."

"Thanks again for your assistance. I promise you, nobody will hear a thing."

How true, Fletcher thought with a grin. He already had something special in mind.

He heard the front door open and shut, followed by the sound of shoes climbing up the stairs. Agent Victor Dragos was coming to visit him.

Only Dragos wasn't a federal agent. Fletcher was certain of that.

Safe to move now, safe to make noise now that the traveling laser beam designed to pick up sound had disappeared from the wall. He placed the headphones and the transmitter on a small oak mission table next to him and looked around the room.

The wooden card chair from the bedroom would do just fine. Put that in the whirlpool bath . . . Yes, it would work out perfectly.

The pager on his belt vibrated. Jack Casey was beeping him again, the third time in the past half hour.

Jack would have to wait. A more pressing matter was coming up the last set of stairs.

Heavy footsteps, slow and deliberate, were coming down the hallway now.

Fletcher picked up his Air Taser gun from the table and moved quietly behind the door. With a press of the button, the dual barbs would deliver fifty thousand volts; Dragos would be unconscious before he hit the floor. When he woke up, they would get acquainted.

The key was in the lock now. Dragos was here, and it was time to discover the man's true intentions.

Malcolm Fletcher smiled.

It was beginning.

chapter 48

MIKE ARRANGED THE TRANSPORTATION. When Jack got off the plane at Logan Airport, two federal agents were waiting for him. They got him to Marblehead in under thirty minutes.

Jack had paged Fletcher twice. He tried Mike's cell phone number, and again all Jack got was static. He tried Mike's pager; no luck. And where was Ronnie Tedesco? Why hadn't he returned any of Jack's pages?

He tried Taylor's cell phone for the umpteenth time, listening to it ring and ring and ring. He dialed the house number. Then the office. Ring . . . ring . . . ring.

He hung up, that gnawing faintness swelling inside his stomach.

She's fine, he told himself. *Ronnie and his men are guarding her. If there had been a problem, he would have called. She's fine. There's a simple explanation for all of this. She's fine.*

Unmarked police cars were parked on both sides of the street in front of Taylor's house. Small crowds of curious neighbors, bicyclists, and joggers were mixed among the mob of reporters and TV cameras. *Why are reporters here? Had something happened?* Dread made him nearly blind.

The driver slowed. Jack jumped out and broke into a run before the reporters could catch up to him. He threw open the screen door and ran down the foyer.

Six troopers were standing near the balcony, drinking coffee out of big paper cups. One of them saw him and said something to the others; the conversation stopped cold.

"Where's Mike Abrams?" Jack said, his throat dry, his breath stale.

"In the backyard," one of the troopers said.

Nightmarish images flashed across his mind as he went down the basement stairs, almost falling. *She's fine,* he repeated again, like a mantra. *She's fineshe'sfineSHE'SFINE.*

A crowd of Marblehead cops, plainclothes detectives, troopers, and federal agents were standing in small groups. Mike Abrams stood away from them near the stairs leading down to the beach, talking on his cell phone, his back to the crowd. Jack approached and heard Mike say, "Okay. Thanks." His face looked grave.

Taylor. They've found Taylor and she's dead. Jack's remaining composure left him; he stumbled and nearly fell. The troopers and plainclothesmen were staring at him.

"What is it?"

Mike took in a deep breath before he spoke. "Alicia Claybrook's body just floated. They found her car in a river. Her son was strapped in a seat belt. It looks like an accident, but it's too early to say.

"I talked to Voyles a moment ago. Hamilton's in the ER with a concussion and a SWAT team. What the hell happened?"

"Fuck him. Where's Taylor?"

"The Porsche is here, so my guess is she packed everyone in the Expedition and went out for a drive. Rachel's not here, and neither is the dog."

"I told her to stay here. She knew what was going on. We were going to move her tonight."

"Maybe she just stepped out to grab some stuff."

"She promised me she'd stay here."

"Any idea where she might have gone?"

He had already replayed his conversations with her this morning. "She said she was going to stay here. And she's not answering her cell phone. She always has it with her, always has it turned on."

Jack looked at the house. *You promised me you'd stay here, Taylor. Why didn't you?*

Because the Sandman lured her out, a voice replied.

No. No, that can't be right. She's smarter than that.

Jack looked around the crowd. Ronnie should be here. Ronnie should have called him, and Taylor didn't go anywhere without her cell phone. Something was wrong, terribly and irrevocably wrong, and if he had listened to Mike and stayed here, if he had listened to Tedesco and told Taylor the truth from the beginning, he wouldn't be standing here now thinking of gruesome scenarios with such intensity that he wanted to rip his head off his shoulders and beat it against the ground. *Should have, should have, should have.*

Just like you should have arrested Hamilton years ago. He destroyed you once and now he's managed to do it again, and you stepped right into it.

"Where did all the reporters come from?"

Mike's face gave it away.

"Tell me."

"They got an anonymous tip," Mike said gravely.

Jack knew there was more. "What did they say?"

"It doesn't—"

"What did they say?"

"The caller said the Sandman had just claimed his next victim."

"And gave them Taylor's name and address."

Mike nodded.

Jack opened his mouth to speak but the words wouldn't come. That familiar empty, throbbing hollowness had consumed him. He could have prevented this. He had deliberately chosen to ignore the ample warning signs, so whatever was coming for him was his fault.

Mike grabbed Jack's arm and moved in close. "We'll find her. There's probably a simple explanation."

"Tedesco's not here and neither are his men," Jack said, the words coming out in a pinched wheeze. "Something's wrong. He hasn't called me back."

"Maybe he's tailing Taylor right now. Maybe he's not near his phone or maybe he can't answer it. It's possible he saw the media circus outside and decided to hang back."

Jack looked out at the beach. His vision went in and out of focus. The tide was out, he could see that, and down at the water's edge, he could barely make out a small gathering of people no bigger than action figures. They were staring up at the house.

A child's scream erupted in the hot air and then died.

It came from his right. Jack turned and saw the barely recognizable dot of a small girl backing up from a tumbled blue chair. A man was draped backward over the chair's armrest, his face looking up at the sky, his baseball cap blowing across the sand and into the water. The girl screamed again. A big dog came charging toward her, barking madly.

Rachel.

Jack brushed past Mike, jumped off the wall, and raced across the sand toward her.

"RACHEL! RACHEL!"

But she wouldn't turn to him, wouldn't stop screaming or staring at the man lying on the sand.

Jack scooped Rachel up into his arms. She kicked and screamed furiously. He turned her around to face him, and when her wide, tear-streaked eyes looked into his, she reached out and clutched at his throat. Jack wrapped her tightly between his arms and pressed her head against his cheek.

"It's all right, honey, it's all right," he said into her ear. A black, quarter-sized hole was in Ronnie Tedesco's forehead, near the hairline. His still eyes looked up at the sun while the hot wind blew his thick blond hair across his forehead and tumbled his sunglasses toward the water. Behind Jack the small crowd gasped. With Rachel clutched to his chest, he turned around, showed the gathering of elderly people his badge, and motioned them away.

"That man's not moving," Rachel sobbed against his ear. "I touched him and he fell over."

"You're okay, honey. Everything's okay."

"Where's Auntie?" she sobbed. "I want to see Auntie."

He carried her up the beach to the house, Mr. Ruffles walking next to him, still barking. Jack kept kissing the top of her head and reassuring her that she was safe. Taylor must have left Rachel with the neighbor, Jay Billings, who lived in the house at the end of the private beach. *But why did she leave Rachel?* Jack didn't know. His terror for her escalated.

Please, God. Please let her be all right. I promise I'll—

You'll promise what? the Sandman's voice countered. *I gave you the opportunity to step aside and you didn't. This is all your fault, Jack. As for what's about to happen to Taylor, you have no one to blame but yourself.*

Everyone had gathered on the porch and the beach. Jack stopped at the foot of the stairs leading up to the backyard and motioned them to the shore. He didn't want Rachel to see the policemen. Seeing them would only increase her fear. Only Mike Abrams remained; he stood next to the porch stairs, his pale face with the expression of a man desperately seeking a solution that would alter a horrible event. It was the same look Mike had had the night Amanda died.

"Rach, I need to ask you a question," Jack said, pulling her gently away from his neck. "Honey, do you know where Auntie is?"

She sniffled and rubbed at her nose. "With you."

"Why would she be with me, sweetie?"

"Because she had to go get you."

"Get me from where?"

Rachel's eyes narrowed in thought.

"Was it the airport?" he asked.

"The what?"

"The place where all the big planes come in."

She nodded. "She went there to get you."

"Do you know why she went to get me?"

"Because you called her."

Jack tried to keep his face bright. "You remember when I called her?"

"After you left. After I said good-bye."

"You sure it was me on the phone?"

"Auntie kept saying your name."

Jack looked away for a moment. His legs felt weak, about to give, and the air seemed oppressively hot.

"She dropped me and Mr. Ruffles off at Mr. Billings's house and went to get you."

"How long ago did she drop you off?"

"I dunno."

"Was it an hour?"

"How long is that?"

Down at the beach Jack could see the elderly Jay Billings trotting toward the overturned beach chair. Marblehead police and troopers had already rushed down there. Jack waved Billings over.

"Was she driving the Expedition?"

"The what?"

"The big black car."

"Yeah, Auntie was in that. That's the one Mr. Ruffles likes to drive in."

Jack wiped the tears away from her eyes with his thumb.

Her brow suddenly pinched with a terrible knowledge. "That man wasn't moving. Why wasn't he moving?"

"He's very sick, honey."

"Will you help him?"

"I'll try." Jack looked up at the house. The cops had moved. "Rachel, I have some people in Auntie's house—people who are helping me out with something. I'm going to put you and Mr. Ruffles up in your room—"

"Don't leave me alone, Uncle Jack."

"I'm just going to go downstairs and talk with them. Mr. Billings is coming over, see?" He turned her around. Billings was walking as fast as he could with his arthritic knees. "I'll be inside the house and so will Mr. Billings. Everything will be okay."

He saw hope and comfort spring to life in her face.

"Promise?" she asked.

In his mind Jack saw Amanda standing on the beach: *Will you keep your word this time?*

"I promise." He hugged Rachel before she could see the fear in his eyes.

Jack tucked her into her bed with the dog. He had just turned on her TV when the phone rang.

chapter 49

JACK CASEY RAN INTO THE KITCHEN, RUSHING PAST THE COPS DOWNSTAIRS. He picked up the phone.

"Taylor?"

"Guess again." The Sandman's voice was deep. Husky.

Jack gripped the phone so tightly he thought he was going to crush it.

"What's going on, Jack? You sound like you're about to come apart at the seams."

"Where is she?"

"Tedesco should have done a better job protecting her, don't you think?"

Angry now: "Where is she?"

"I told you what would happen, so you already know the answer."

Icy winds blew through his soul.

She's alive. She has to be alive. That's the only way he can toy with you, so think carefully.

And what if she isn't? This guy's not a serial—doesn't think like one. He wants her out of the way and told you that and now she's dead—

"Taylor has nothing to do with why you're here," Jack said. "If you want me to play your game, then I need to know she's safe and—"

"My game? *I* wanted to keep her out of this from the beginning. *I* called *you* and gave *you* the opportunity to back out without all of this bloodshed, but *you* decided to show me how fucking smart you are by finding the cameras and rescuing that boy. *You,* Jack, have destroyed Taylor because *you* are a sick fuck who can't help himself."

Through the opening that overlooked the balcony and part of the living room, Jack could see a bald man working the controls of the tracing equipment set up on the dining-room table. Mike Abrams stood behind him, holding the pair of headphones against one ear.

"Your friend Mike is not going to be able to trace this call."

Jack froze.

"If I were you, I'd discount everything he says," the Sandman said. "A man who won't leave you alone with his children, who calls ahead to the hospital director and asks him to stand by with medication—they had the Thorazine and straitjacket waiting for you. That's not really a friend now, is it?"

Jack glanced up at the ceiling.

"Don't bother looking," the Sandman said. "You'll never figure out where the cameras are. The boobs you hired should have done a better job sweeping for bugs."

He's been watching Taylor and me the entire time.

Mike's face was deadpan. The bald guy working the tracing controls was shaking his head in frustration.

"That's right, Jack. I know you told Taylor about our conversation, and I know about your plans to move her. Miles killed your wife and now I have your new love. What would you give to touch her again, Jack? What would you give to feel her the way I'm touching her right now?"

"How do I know she's safe?"

"If you could choose only one of them, who would it be? Amanda with the four-month-old fetus cooking in the womb? Or the beauty behind door number two, Taylor Burton and her healing fucks? Who would you pick, Jack? Be honest."

"How do I know she's safe?"

"Answer the question."

"I need to know she's safe," Jack said, his skin cold with sweat.

"How are your hands, Jack? Are they hungry with the memory of Amanda's skin? The texture of her hair? Deep in the night, when you're lying next to Taylor, do you feel patches of your skin throbbing for Amanda? And what about poor Taylor, alone now, clinging to life? Which part of you throbs for her?"

Hang on. He took in a deep breath, held it, then said, "I want to talk to her."

"Beg me. Beg me for her life."

Jack didn't say anything.

"What's wrong, Jack? Having trouble remembering what it's like to beg?"

Someone said, "The TV."

The TV in the living room clicked on. On the screen the video camera moved from Patrick Dolan to Veronica, and then to Alex. The boy, bound to the chair, was crying, his hysterical sobs and those of his mother booming through the house over the surround-sound speakers mounted in the wall and ceiling.

Alex Dolan begging: "Please . . . please don't hurt me. Don't hurt me or my mom." Patrick Dolan twisting in his chair, desperately trying to break free.

Mike screaming, *"Shut that off now."*

Next came the gloved hand holding a scalpel. Veronica Dolan saw it and her screams exploded through the house.

The Sandman said, over the phone and the house speakers, "Bring back memories, Jack?"

A trooper hit the TV's power button. It didn't turn off. Alex Dolan disappeared, and then came recorded images of Taylor playing on the beach with her niece. The trooper went to hit the VCR button, but the VCR wasn't on, there was no tape loaded, the image was being fed into the TV from somewhere else. *Must be the satellite dish.*

The screen changed; now it was playing with sharp clarity that night out on the balcony. Taylor, naked, her legs wrapped around his waist and her back pressed against the balcony, moaned as Jack made love to her.

The Sandman, on the phone and over the TV speakers, said, "What would you give to touch her again, Jack? To touch her the way I am right now?"

Taylor moaned loudly. The trooper hit the volume button. Nothing.

"Look at them all staring at you," the Sandman said. "Should I destroy your life right now, right here in front of everyone? How much Thorazine will your friend Mike have to pump into your system to keep you from drowning in your insanity?"

"Please."

"I'm listening, Jack."

"Please . . . I'll do anything you want, just please . . . let me know she's safe."

"That's the spirit. Would you like to talk to her?"

"Yes."

"Yes what?"

"Yes please."

"Good boy. Now walk inside the living room and kneel down in front of the TV."

Jack didn't question it, didn't even think about it. The packed room of Marblehead patrolmen, the federal agents, and the state troopers moved back as he walked past them. Taylor's moans boomed throughout the room.

Jack knelt down before the TV, still carrying the phone. Taylor seemed to be looking right at the camera. Her eyes stared down at Jack.

"Now I want you to tell Taylor what you really did to Charles Yerkies and the others. Tell her that you can't help it, that you're sorry for killing her."

It was like standing on a patch of ice that was about to break. The

Sandman needed to get Jack out of the way, and the best way to do that was to feed his fear—and Jack knew he was playing right into it. He needed to remember that this time he had leverage. This time, he had a chance at saving her.

Jack took in a deep breath, held it. He wanted his voice steady.

"Can you hear me clearly . . . Gabriel?"

Silence on the phone.

"The FBI is in town, and they're looking for you. They don't know your full name, but I do. I know your connection to these three families, why you're killing them—I even know what they did to you. I know the name of the next family, I know *everything.*"

The room was quiet except for Taylor's moaning.

"Are you listening to me, Gabriel?"

Off the house speakers and back on the phone: "I don't believe you."

"Your next victim is a psychiatrist who lives in Cambridge."

A long pause. *Hamilton was telling the truth.*

"Let me talk to her," Jack said.

"All the Thorazine in the world won't save you from drowning this time. She's already—"

Static blocked out the Sandman's words.

Dead, did he say dead?

"Is she safe?" Jack said. *"Goddamnit, talk to me."*

The phone went dead.

"Jesus Christ," someone behind him said.

The TV screen was dark; clouds of smoke drifted up from the back of the set. The bitter smell of burning plastic and scorched metal filled the room. The kitchen too was filling with smoke.

The phone in Jack's hand leaked smoke from the earpiece. He tossed it on the floor.

Mike's voice: "What the hell . . . ?"

The tracing unit had caught fire; the dining-room table was covered in a black cloud that drifted up to the ceiling. Mike and the bald man backed away from it, waving their hands through the thick smoke, and moved toward the opened balcony door.

Strange voices yelling:

"What the fuck's going on?"

"My beeper's cooked."

"So's mine."

Footsteps sounded in the foyer. The gray smoke hanging in front of the doorway leading into the foyer was too thick for Jack to see.

Out of the smoke came a gray, cylindrical device; it bounced on the floor next to Jack. It was made of metal, crudely constructed, and at the bottom was a pulsating blue light. The device made a small, crackling sound.

Malcolm Fletcher emerged through the cloud and walked into the living room, his movements graceful, slow, confident. Cupped in his right hand was a laptop computer with an antenna—the same one he had used to locate the surveillance cameras.

"Taylor is very much alive," Fletcher said, his voice showing no excitement or fear. "Right now she's driving around Logan Airport. Don't bother trying to call her. Our friend is jamming her cellular phone frequency."

Jack's jaw dropped. "How do you—"

"Global positioning system." Fletcher turned the laptop around to Jack. A tiny red car moved across a blown-up, detailed section of map. "I took the liberty of attaching a tracking unit to her car. I hope you don't mind."

chapter 50

TAYLOR CLICKED HER NAILS ALONG THE STEERING WHEEL OF HER FORD EXPEDITION AND WATCHED THE PEOPLE, MAINLY BUSINESS TYPES, WALK IN AND OUT OF LOGAN AIRPORT'S AMERICAN AIRLINES TERMINAL. She wanted to go inside and wait for Jack, but he had been very specific on the last call—his third. She was to wait in the car for him, not in the terminal. Of course she pressed him about it, but he wouldn't explain, just gave her specific instructions and told her to hang tight. Jack didn't give her his flight number and arrival time. All she could do was wait.

As she sat there, she didn't think about her safety. It all seemed so surreal, and maybe it would frighten her more if there weren't experienced men guarding her, or if Jack hadn't called right after he left and told her not to worry, that he was about to close in on the Sandman. What consumed her thoughts was the national nightmare, the monster Miles Hamilton. Why would Jack visit him? That was the question that had been tumbling through her mind.

This morning, she had tried to get Jack to talk about why he was going, but as usual he didn't want to talk about it. Talking about anything regarding his past life was a big issue with him. Why? Why wouldn't he open up?

Part of it, she was sure, had to do with Ocean Point. If you're forced to watch someone you love die

(Not someone you love, my dear, the woman was his life, his soul mate, she was carrying his baby, a nasty voice said.)

(Shut up.)

right there in front of your eyes—something that she couldn't even *imagine,* let alone comprehend—you would have to deal with the feelings of guilt and loss. Women cried. They screamed, they lashed out, they threw things—they did whatever they needed to do *to get it out.* But not men. Got to keep up the front. Got to deal with it on my own because I have all the answers, there's no reason to talk about it, I'm fine, everything's just *fine.*

So you had to get help, Jack. So what? I don't think any less of you. I don't love you any less. Jesus, don't you know *that?*

Out of nowhere her mind flashed the image of Jack, his face twisted in hatred

(and pleasure?)

as he brought the hammer down on the faceless creature named Charles Yerkies. Was that what he was afraid of? That she wouldn't understand his killing of a monster? It wasn't as if he had gone in there with the intention of killing him.

And what if he did? the nasty voice said.

Jack was not an evil man; she was sure of that. There was a logical explanation, she knew, and what they were printing in the papers wasn't the truth. The media weren't interested in the truth. What they peddled were T-and-A stories hawked by smooth-talking, camera-friendly mannequins who operated under the guise of journalism. Infotainment ruled the nation. It was the only way to get people to watch.

Still, the story was hard to ignore.

Goddamnit, when are you going to let me inside your world?

The cell phone rang.

Jack, if this is you calling me with another change in plans, you can find your own way home. She leaned forward and hit the speakerphone on the cell phone, which was mounted to a floor bracket, allowing her to drive with both hands.

"Hi, Taylor, me again," Jack said, his voice crystal clear. "Where are you?"

"At Logan, waiting in the Expedition, just like you asked. You want me to come in and meet you?"

"There's a slight change in plans."

"Jesus Christ, Jack, not again."

"I know you're frustrated."

"Try pissed."

"Believe me, this is all going to be worth it. There's a surprise right under your seat. Reach under and grab it."

She frowned. What the hell was this about?

"You got it?"

"Hold on." She reached under the seat. It was a brown, padded mailer, and it had been sealed shut. How did that get in here?

"Got it."

"Good. Now what I want you to do is tear it open and reach inside—*but don't look!*" Jack laughed. "A man has only one shot to do this right, so please don't spoil it."

One shot to do this right . . . No, it can't—*he* can't. A well of excitement rose inside her.

She ripped the thread across the lip of the mailer, stuck her hand inside, and felt a variety of things: thick, glossy paper; what felt like an audiocassette; and something soft, like velvet.

"Okay, my hand's in there."

"You feel the velvet box?"

"Yeeesss." In the back of her mind, caught behind her sudden burst of excitement, was that odd feeling that something was off.

"Okay, pull it out."

She removed a small, black velvet box.

"Oh, Jack . . ." An antique diamond ring. "Jack, this is . . . It's so beautiful."

"Put it on, see if it fits."

It did.

But why didn't you give me this in person? And why are you about to propose to me over a cell phone?

"Okay, Taylor, this is the important part. I want you to drive out of Logan and go to Faneuil Hall. You know where the Purple Shamrock is?"

"Yeah. What's the other thing inside the envelope? I felt something—"

"Stay out of there or you'll ruin the surprise. Promise?"

"Okay, I promise. Now, tell me where you are."

"I'm already in Boston, and I'm planning the biggest night of your life, sweetie."

Sweetie? He never called her sweetie. And what was with his tone? It was almost upbeat. Cheery. And why the hell would he propose to her only a few hours after meeting Hamilton? It was odd.

Not a little odd—VERY odd. You want to commit to spending the rest of your life with a man who proposes to you on a cell phone just hours after visiting the psycho who sliced up his wife?

"Are you all right?"

"I'm fine."

"This is . . . It isn't like you, Jack. What's going on?"

"I've just come to realize a few things, and I want you to know what's going on—what's going on with me and how I really feel about you. Now drive out of the parking lot. I'll talk to you on the way."

She pulled into the traffic and for the next five minutes maneuvered her way through a maze of speeding cars.

"There's a cassette inside the envelope. Reach inside and take it out, but don't play it yet."

"Okay." She tucked it in her front shirt pocket.

"Where are you now?"

"Leaving Logan. The traffic's not too bad."

"You're wearing your seat belt, I hope."

"I always do."

"That's my girl. You on the highway yet?"

"Yep."

"Now reach back inside the envelope and pull out the pictures."

The envelope was sitting on the passenger's seat. With her eyes on the road, she reached inside the envelope, fingered what felt like two eight-by-tens, and held them in front of her. The color drained from her face.

The picture on top was an old black-and-white, a naked, pregnant woman lying on an autopsy table, her throat cut.

Her mind seized. She looked back at the road and in a daze watched the stream of cars rushing by. This was . . . it was so unreal.

"Recognize the woman in the photo?" Jack asked.

She couldn't form the words.

"That's my wife, Taylor. That's Amanda."

"This . . . This is . . . " She couldn't speak. *I can't believe this. This is . . .*

It's sick, a voice answered.

"I thought you told me you weren't the squeamish type."

"You give me an engagement ring and then show me a picture of . . . what happened to your wife?" She threw the photographs on the floor without looking at the second picture.

"You wanted to know everything about my past, about who I am, so I figured what better way than with pictures. You are, after all, a photographer of human suffering."

"This is sick, Jack. This is fucking sick and you're—what the hell's wrong with you?"

"I *am* a sick man, Taylor. I should be locked up."

"Locked up? What are you—"

"I *wanted* to kill Yerkies, I went into that barn wanting to kill him, I had thought about it for days, and when I brought that hammer down on his skull again and again, I loved every delicious second of it, and I'll do it again, Taylor, I'll do it again because I can't help myself, I love it too much."

Something wrong, something terribly wrong.

This isn't Jack.

She clicked off the speakerphone. Her eyes momentarily caught the two pictures on the floor. The first photograph, the one she had seen, was turned over and she could make out writing on the back, a poem of some sort; but her eyes were riveted on the second. Same woman, same autopsy table, same wound. Only the face was different.

The face belonged to her.

Taylor drove into the right lane. An exit was coming up. *Call Jack's FBI friend Mike. Abrams was his last name. Mike Abrams. Get the hell out of the car and call him.*

"I'm afraid I can't let you do that," the man-who-sounded-like-Jack said.

The Expedition acted on its own and shifted back into the left lane. Behind her a car horn blared.

No . . . No, that can't be right. She hadn't turned the wheel.

She grabbed the steering wheel with both hands and swung hard right. All the wheel did was turn around and around and around.

The steering wheel was useless. She had no control over the car.

As if acting on its own will, the Expedition moved left again into the speeding lane.

Someone else was steering the car.

That can't be right. How the hell could someone do that?

Taylor braced her hands on the steering wheel and slammed her foot on the brakes. The Expedition didn't stop.

All the doors clicked shut.

Oh, God, no . . .

In the Expedition's rearview mirror, through the wavering ribbons of afternoon heat, she caught flashing blue and white lights. Dozens of them, with what looked like a silver pickup truck leading the way.

The Expedition lurched forward on its own, pushed her back against the seat.

"Hang on, Taylor," the man on the phone said. "This is where the fun begins."

chapter 51

MALCOLM FLETCHER SHOWED NO FEAR, NO SURPRISE—NOTHING. His eyes were steady and calm as they swept the road, as if leading a brigade of troopers and federal agents down a highway at one hundred miles an hour was as easy as breathing.

Occasionally his eyes would shift down to the laptop set up on the divider between the two seats. Another, mounted on the dashboard under the rearview mirror, showed the GPS map. Jack stared at the blinking red car. Taylor was close. He looked up.

Jack pointed. "That's her."

The cars surrounding Taylor were pulling off to the breakdown lanes. But Taylor kept moving ahead with no signs of slowing.

"Pull up next to her," Jack said, and rolled down his window. Wind roared inside the cab, sounding like the flap of canvas sails caught in a hurricane wind.

All he could see was the back of her head. Taylor looked straight ahead with both hands tightly gripping the steering wheel, her arms locked out straight as if bracing for impact.

Frightened, she jerked her head to him. Her eyes were wet and terrified. She began to scream from behind the rolled-up window. She tore her hands away from the steering wheel, grabbed her seat belt, and tried desperately to free herself. Her foot kept pumping the brakes.

Jesus Christ, he's rigged the brakes—and probably the gas pedal.

Fletcher inched his truck toward the Expedition. Jack reached out and grabbed Taylor's door handle. The door wouldn't open.

With the highway's white passing lines rushing beneath him, the sirens exploding against his ears, he kept working the door handle, pulling on it, praying that it was stuck and would give. Taylor pounded her hands on the window, like a drowning woman trapped under a layer of ice. He was sure he could hear her words:

"HELP ME, JACK, I DON'T WANT TO DIE. PLEASE HELP ME, JACK, OH GOD, PLEASE!"

He almost gave into his rising panic. Before it overtook him, a voice spoke out, a voice bursting with hope: *You've got a chance to save her. Her car is racing out of control and you don't have much time so you have to THINK.*

The Sandman had rigged the gas pedal and the brakes; she couldn't get out of her seat belt; she was trapped and racing down the highway toward the tollbooths. Can't slow the car down, had to get her out of there and quick, Christ, he didn't know how.

Jack slid back inside the truck. Taylor's face was a mixture of disbelief and shock, as if he had abandoned her.

"He's rigged the gas pedal and she can't move out of there," Jack yelled.

"Wedged behind your seat is a green backpack." Fletcher's voice showed no fear, no loss of control. "Reach inside and remove what looks like a radar detector."

Jack grabbed the backpack. *Hang on, Taylor, just hang on,* he thought as he sifted through beepers, cell phones, and other electronic gadgets. The radar detector was on the bottom, hooked up to a cigarette-lighter adapter.

"It's a high-energy-radio-frequency device—the same one I used to destroy all the electronic equipment inside the house," Fletcher said. "All she has to do is plug it in and turn it on. The car's computer ignition system will shut down."

"What if he's rigged the car with a bomb?"

"This is the only chance we have."

"I don't think she can roll down the window."

"Use the tire iron behind you."

"She's wedged in her seat belt. She won't be able to plug the device into the cigarette lighter."

The Expedition had pulled slightly ahead of them. The tollbooths leading into the Callahan Tunnel were closing fast. Jack saw his opportunity.

"Pull up next to her," he said, and slid open the cab window that led into the bed of the truck.

Fletcher grabbed his wrist. "The device is too delicate. If you break or drop it, there's nothing I can do to save her. I'll have to hand it to you."

Jack looked deep into Fletcher's fathomless black eyes.

"Don't let me down."

Fletcher smiled. "I'm your guardian angel. Why would I want to disappoint you now?"

Mike Abrams was driving in the right lane, directly behind the silver truck and wondering why Taylor Burton's Expedition wouldn't slow down. *Got to be the brakes. She's lost control of the brakes. But why is she speeding up?*

He glanced down at the Volvo's odometer: 82 mph. Jesus Christ, they were heading fast and furious to the tollbooths. *I hope to God she has control of the steering.*

When he looked up, Jack had already crawled through the truck's cab window; now he was crouched in the bed of the truck directly behind the driver, the guy with the weird eyes—Malcolm Fletcher. Jack gripped the luggage rack on the roof and pulled himself up, hugging his body close to the truck.

"What the fuck are you doing, Jack?" Mike said to himself.

Troopers in their cruisers were scrambling to get behind them. The tollbooths were less than a mile away, and traffic had pulled over, leaving only two clear lanes.

The Expedition seemed to slow. Several troopers rushed past it toward the tunnel that, hopefully, was clear now. Then Mike watched the Expedition sail smoothly past the tollbooth, Fletcher's truck moving in next to it. A blink later, they were swallowed into the mouth of the Callahan Tunnel.

The truck and Expedition raced side by side at 60 mph. There was a six-to-ten-foot gap between them; the truck was slowly closing it. Mike didn't know why at first, but when he saw Jack place one foot up along the truck's edge, the meaning became clear. *He's going to jump off the truck and try to grab hold of the Expedition's luggage rack.*

If he jumped and missed, the avalanche of vehicles behind would crush him to death.

"No . . . Jesus Christ, Jack, don't do it."

But he *was* going to do it. Jack placed his second foot up on the edge of the truck, both hands locked on the rack. The Expedition inched closer . . . closer . . .

Jack let go of the truck's roof rack and jumped.

He seemed to hang in the air just above the roof of the Expedition, then the SUV cut right, slamming into Fletcher's truck and shoving it against the tunnel wall; Jack tumbled backward over the Expedition's driver's side window. *Too late, it's too fucking late!* Mike thought, wincing, his foot already on the brakes.

But Jack had somehow managed to grab the Expedition's luggage rack with his right hand. With his back pressed against the driver's-side window, with Taylor screaming inside the Expedition, Jack hung there in the wind with his feet dangling just inches from the pavement, the Expedition grinding the truck against the wall in a screech of sparks.

Fletcher hit the brakes. Mike swerved around the truck and watched as the Expedition moved into the right lane with Jack still hanging over the side. He was reaching up with his other hand when the Expedition swerved toward the opposite wall, Jack still hanging there, a moment away from being crushed to death.

chapter 52

LATER MIKE WOULD MARVEL AT HOW QUICKLY HIS INSTINCTS TOOK OVER. He propelled his Volvo up the left lane at 95 mph and got next to the Expedition. If the Expedition hadn't hit the truck and slowed, Mike would not have gained the space needed to save Jack's life.

The Expedition headed toward him like a missile. Mike's body braced for impact.

The Expedition slammed into the Volvo with frightening force; even with the seat belt around his chest, Mike was thrown against the driver's side door, the windows exploding in showers of glass while metal tore into his arms and neck. A split second later the side air bags deployed, and then the steering wheel's, pushing his face and body into the seat.

His right hand was still gripping the wheel. His left came up and pushed down the bag so he could see. A trail of sparks danced across the wall, the sound of the grinding metal deafening. Through a spiderweb of cracks snaking across the Volvo's front window, Mike saw Jack's hiking boots gain footing on the Volvo's crumpled hood. Jack, still gripping the Expedition's luggage rack, turned his body around so that he was facing Taylor. He started banging the Expedition's already cracked driver's-side window with his knee, Taylor's arm coming up to protect her face as she tried to move her body away. *Why the hell doesn't she just unbuckle the damn seat belt?* Mike wondered.

Jack's knee went through the window; shards of glass showered Taylor's head and chest. Even through the wail of sirens, Mike could hear her screams.

Jack yelled something to her and pressed his groin against the window. Taylor's hand reached inside Jack's pocket and came back with what looked like a Swiss Army knife. She flicked open the blade, started cutting through the seat belt.

Mike grabbed a ballpoint pen from his breast pocket and stabbed the air bags. As the bags deflated, the Expedition moved away from him and sped ahead. Taylor had moved into the passenger's seat. The last thing Mike saw was Jack sliding his legs inside the driver's-side window of the Expedition.

• • •

Jack got himself settled behind the wheel and turned it to the left, feeling it spin in his hands like a roulette wheel. He tried throwing the gearshift into neutral. The car kept speeding ahead. The odometer read 70.

The Expedition cut again toward the wall. Taylor screamed. Jack jammed his body against the door, his right arm sliding under Taylor's arm and wrapping around her chest, pulling her close to him just as they slammed into the wall.

They jerked sideways from the impact, the Expedition's frame shaking. The Expedition kept moving ahead, scraping against the wall in a spray of sparks that danced across Taylor's feet. A wail of sirens rushed past him and exited the tunnel. Jack saw Mike's crumpled Volvo charging directly behind him. No sign of the truck. Where the hell was Fletcher?

The Expedition pulled into the other lane. At first Jack thought they were going to crash into the opposite wall; instead, the car accelerated and a moment later roared out of the tunnel and hit the ramp that passed over the North End. They were speeding up 93 North, the small fleet of trooper cruisers already ahead of them, having pushed the light traffic off to the sides.

Then the sound of a diesel engine came closer. Jack saw the truck speeding up the right lane toward the passenger's side of the Expedition. The window was cracked but still in one piece, and he couldn't kick it out unless Taylor moved into the backseat. *No time,* he thought. He removed the Beretta from his shoulder holster and clicked off the safety with his thumb.

"Get down!"

Taylor threw her head onto his lap and covered her ears. He pulled the trigger and the glass exploded.

Fletcher moved the truck up next to him and rolled down his window.

"He's going to hand you something," Jack yelled to Taylor. "Put it on the dashboard and don't drop it."

Taylor moved up on the seat. Fletcher had his left hand through the Expedition's window now, his long fingers cupping the HERF device. She grabbed it from his hand and put it under the rearview mirror, its suction cups gripping the dashboard.

Jack flipped the ashtray down, grabbed the unit's cigarette adapter, and plugged it in. On the floor near Taylor's feet he saw the two black-and-white pictures covered with shards of glass. Amanda's dead, glassy eyes stared up at him from the autopsy table; so did Taylor's.

He used Taylor to lure you out. Now he's going to kill you.

The Sandman wouldn't crash the car. That wouldn't guarantee Jack's death. No, he would keep using what gave him control: a remote-controlled bomb, probably planted on the gas tank.

To operate the car and the bomb, the Sandman had to be close by. Jack looked around him. All he could see were state troopers and Fletcher's truck.

The HERF unit only had one switch. He clicked it on. There was no sound, just a slight vibration under his hand.

The odometer hovered just under 75.

Then 76 . . . 77 . . . 78

Tick-tick-tick.

He had to get Taylor out of here.

chapter 53

THE SANDMAN DROVE BEHIND THEM, HIS LEFT HAND ON THE WHEEL, HIS RIGHT WORKING THE KEYS OF THE LAPTOP SITTING ON THE PASSENGER'S SEAT. The inconspicuous fiber-optic camera mounted in the Expedition's rearview mirror was focused on Jack; on the laptop's screen Jack was staring in disbelief at the speedometer. Did he actually think the car was going to slow down? And what was that thing his friend from the truck had passed through the window?

The Sandman moved his hand away from the controls to adjust the brim of his state trooper's hat and slid his mirrored aviator-style glasses back up his nose. State troopers, federal agents, and Jack's friend Abrams, driving the Volvo right *next* to him—they had no idea that the man orchestrating all this chaos, the one they were so desperately trying to find, was in fact masked as one of their own.

It was all so easy, so simple. Before visiting the Dolan home, and well before Jack's enlistment of the piss-poor surveillance expert Tedesco, the Sandman had attached a pager to the ignition wires of the Expedition. One call and the pager melted though the wires. While Jack was scrambling down leads, his girlfriend called the dealership—a call that the Sandman had anticipated. The plans were already in place. He intercepted the call and thirty minutes later pulled up to her house with a stolen tow truck.

He had dropped the "repaired" Expedition off soon after Jack had left this morning. Using Hamilton was the only means to get Jack away. All Miles had asked for in exchange was pictures—preferably something on video that he could watch at a later date. The camera mounted inside the car was capturing it all.

The Expedition's transmission, brakes, and steering—just about every electrical device that was dependent on the vehicle's computer system—had been modified to respond to a small electric box that had enabled him to take control of the car and operate it through remote control. Originally he had planned to use Taylor to lure Jack and his FBI friends to an abandoned house loaded with fifteen blocks of C-4 that would take them out of the way.

It would have been easier to have planted a bomb at Taylor's home—or to send one in the mail. But with her mail stopped and her home being guarded, it was too risky. The only way was using Taylor to lure Jack out—which is precisely what had happened.

He had planned on Jack's resourcefulness, but how did he find Taylor so quickly? *How did you do it, Jack? And who's your friend in the truck?*

Taylor Burton's body leaned out of the Expedition's mangled passenger's-side window, her hand reaching out for the truck, which was racing alongside of her. The man in the truck grabbed her wrist and guided her hand up to the truck's roof rack. Then the man slipped his arm around her waist as if to carry her out of the Expedition. The Sandman was confused for a moment, and then the meaning became clear. Jack was trying to save Taylor's life, and the only way to do that was to get her inside the truck.

The Sandman wished he could have killed them in the tunnel. It was too risky. Here, on the highway, the Sandman could make a quick exit.

Taylor's chest was pressed against the truck; both her hands gripped the truck's roof rack. The shrink, Abrams, was speeding behind both of them.

The Sandman slowed, letting the cruisers pass him. Good, just enough distance. He moved his finger to the END key. The bomb planted inside the Expedition would take out Jack, Abrams, and the man in the truck.

Bye-bye, Jack. Thanks for playing.

He pressed the button.

The Expedition kept racing along. The truck pulled away with Taylor Burton pressed against the truck's door. The Sandman could see Taylor's frightened face, the wind whipping her hair around and puffing out her shirt.

The bomb had malfunctioned.

No anger this time. The Sandman had learned his lesson from the Dolan fiasco. This time he had a backup plan.

He tapped the up arrow, increasing the Expedition's speed to 86. Jack Casey's death was ten minutes up the road. All he had to do now was to keep Jack away from the truck.

There was no way to feed Taylor Burton through the driver's-side window, so Fletcher had helped navigate her into the bed of the truck. After several minutes of fumbling, Taylor was there, crouched down and safe. The Expedition had sped away.

The HERF device should have slowed it down by now.

Unless Gabriel had anticipated such a maneuver. The resourceful boy he had met all those years ago had transformed himself into an electronics expert; it was entirely possible that Gabriel had developed the appropriate countermeasure. He had, after all, fooled Jack's experienced surveillance team.

The laptop computer on the mobile desk next to his knees beeped rapidly. The computer program had locked onto the cellular frequency that was emanating from the Expedition. Gabriel, he knew, was close. It was only a matter of minutes, perhaps seconds, until he discovered the vehicle Gabriel was driving.

A state trooper's car rushed by him; the whine of the frequency pitched.

"Clever boy."

The handheld police scanner mounted on the section of dashboard in front of him crackled and a strange voice said, "Boston SWAT, the subject is still on course. He has several blocks of C-4 attached to an improvised IED and is preparing to detonate upon impact. I repeat, the subject is preparing to detonate on impact."

A crackle, then SWAT answered back, "Understood."

Fletcher sped up the lane toward the trooper. So Gabriel had called in a SWAT team. How resourceful. Fletcher wondered what other surprises Gabby had planned.

Fletcher picked up the walkie-talkie and changed the frequency to match the one displayed on the police scanner.

"Boston SWAT, ignore that order. This is Alan Lynch, head of the FBI's profiling unit. The Sandman, aka Gabriel LaRouche, a thirty-five-year-old white male, is driving a state trooper's vehicle with the license plate alpha betty omega dash five three. The Sandman is heading straight at you. Look for the trooper vehicle next to a silver truck."

"SWAT, ignore that order, I repeat, ignore that order, it's a trap," the Sandman said. "The call is coming from inside the Expedition."

Boston SWAT came on and said, "What the fuck's going on?"

Fletcher smiled. "Boys, I would appreciate it if you didn't kill him. Gabby has such a lovely story to tell, and I want him to be able to share it with the world."

Fletcher heard a gunshot and exploding glass. The barrel of a nine-millimeter was pointing outside the cruiser's shattered passenger's-side window and firing rapid shots, each round tearing through the truck's steel and landing someplace near the engine.

Fletcher swerved left to hit the cruiser, but Gabriel had already pulled away from him and was speeding toward the Expedition.

Fletcher tried to pursue, but puffs of steam rose from underneath the hood of the truck. Engine coolant and transmission fluid burst like blood from a severed artery.

Clever boy.

Boston SWAT had positioned itself on the section of highway directly across from the two Route 128 exits. Commuters were pulled off into the breakdown lanes; more were parked on the grassy median strip. They were watching the barricade of cruisers, and the half dozen SWAT team sharpshooters leaning across the car roofs and hoods who were now turning to their commander, Buyens, confused and looking for answers.

Ted Buyens, the SWAT team leader, worked a Red Man along the back of his cheek. First had come the call from a federal agent named Mike Abrams about a black Ford Expedition loaded with fifteen blocks of C-4 that was being driven by the Sandman. Abrams wanted the Sandman out and told Buyens to position his team along 93 North, the direction in which the Sandman would be fleeing. The Sandman was not to get through. Next had come a call from that guy Lynch from ISU saying not to shoot. What the fuck was this shit?

The sharpshooter next to him, a black man by the name of T. J. Washington, said, "How we playing it?"

Buyens stared down the highway.

He spat and wiped his mouth. "Take the Expedition and the cruiser down. Go for the tires."

"At that speed, they'll go tumbling."

"The feds called us. They're great at creating shit, they can certainly clean it up."

Buyens placed his elbows on the cruiser roof and stared down the scope of his Remington .308. Through the ribbons of heat floating on the horizon, a dot of silver and black appeared in the crosshairs.

"Stand by, people," he said.

chapter 54

THE ODOMETER STARTED TO SLIDE DOWN. Jack could smell the brassy odor of scorched metal and burnt wires coming through the vents. Fletcher's device was working.

A wave of triumph moved through his chest. He tried the brakes—they still didn't work—and then moved the wheel. The Expedition didn't turn; it was still heading straight down the highway. Through the thick cracks across the front window, he saw flashing pinpoints of blue and white lights. He never saw the state trooper come charging up beside him.

Something hit the side of the Expedition. A loud clicking sound made him turn his head to the passenger's-side window and catch the trooper's hand releasing an object that appeared to be stuck right above the Expedition's gas cap. The mirror mounted outside the passenger's-side window had been torn off, so there was no way for him to see what was there. If he was to see it, he'd have to get out from behind the wheel.

The trooper had sped away toward an exit.

The section of highway Jack was traveling was straight. Jack moved to the passenger's seat. He gripped his fingers along the edges of the window, feeling loose shards of glass cut into his skin, and stuck his head outside. Above him, barely audible over the rushing wind, he could hear the thump-thump of helicopter blades; the media were out.

A white container the size of half a brick was right above the gas cap. The knowledge of what he was seeing tore through him well before his eyes registered the black-stamped letters C-4.

A digital clock mounted on top of the brick was pointed at the sunlight. He couldn't see it so he had no idea how much time he had, but it wouldn't be much.

Behind him, the escort of troopers and federal cars was gone, but Fletcher was in the next lane, trailing fifty feet or so behind, his truck enveloped in clouds of steam and leaking engine coolant. Jack saw Taylor standing in the bed of the truck, her hand pointing to something ahead of him.

Less than two miles up the road was a barricade of patrol cars.

Jesus Christ, they've called in a goddamn SWAT team. The question was whether or not they were going to shoot down the Expedition—or him.

He had to get out. If they had their crosshairs aimed on him, it would be like shooting at an animal trapped in a cage. And even if they missed, the bomb would take care of him.

Jack looked back at the truck. Fletcher had gained some distance between them but not much. Mike had moved behind the truck and was now pressed against its bumper, gunning the engine.

Only one way out of it.

The sharpshooter Washington was looking down the scope when he saw a man pulling himself up to the Expedition's roof. He got a good look at the man's face and remembered the picture inside the *Herald*.

"Boss, that guy's Jack Casey—"

"I see him," Buyens snapped back. His voice crackled over everyone's earpiece.

"Let's give the man a running start. Then we're going to stop that car. Stand by for my mark."

Washington's finger slid across the trigger like a lover's caress.

Jack, gripping the luggage rack, looked at the truck. Fletcher was in the passenger's-side lane, maybe fifteen feet away from the Expedition's back bumper. Despite Mike's pushing, the truck was slowing, its engine starting to die, and the gap between the two vehicles was widening.

Jack couldn't believe what he was about to do.

Hurry!

He released his grip on the rack, stood up, and ran toward the back of the roof, catching a final glimpse of the bomb that was still resting against the Expedition's side like a sleeping volcano.

His left foot hit the edge and he pushed himself into the air, saw the highway rushing beneath him, felt hot wind blowing against his back and pushing him like a giant hand toward the truck. He saw Taylor's shocked face and her hand reaching out for him. With a growing confidence he watched his outstretched hands sailing toward the rack on the truck's roof, and a moment later felt his fingers sliding across the sun-baked steel. His chest and stomach slammed into the driver's side window, knocking the breath out of him, all of his muscles tensing in fear, his mind screaming.

The muscles in his shoulders felt as if they had torn; a burning sensation, like acid eating through tissue, was working its way through his arms. Taylor had wrapped both her hands around one wrist and was pulling him toward her; he felt Fletcher's arm wrapped around his waist, his surprising strength welding him against the truck.

Mike slammed on the brakes and skidded into the breakdown lane. The truck came to a jarring halt.

In the blinding sunlight Jack saw the SWAT sharpshooters as big as toy action figures now, draped across their hoods and staring down the scopes of their sniper rifles.

A gunshot echoed in the air, just a tiny crack and pop. Then another and the Expedition's front tire blew. More shots followed but the Expedition was already tumbling.

A deafening explosion transformed the car into a blinding white ball. The last thing Jack saw before he jerked his head away were flaming chunks of metal suspended under the blue sky of a summer day, the image vivid and burning, as if it had been branded onto the skin behind his eyelids.

chapter 55

SHORTLY AFTER 11 P.M. A BANGED-UP VOLVO AND TWO NISSAN PATHFINDERS SLID DOWN A DARK STRETCH OF ROAD IN DRAKE'S ISLAND, MAINE, AND PULLED INTO A TWO-FLOOR CAPE HOUSE ON THE LEFT. The people out at this hour, mostly college-aged lovers looking for privacy and parents who had put their kids to bed and were off for a moonlit stroll, paid little attention to the men entering the front door, then looking through the house with a sense of urgency.

Outside in the pale moonlight, a tall, muscular man stood at the foot of the porch steps, his hands deep in his jeans pockets. The man's face was bruised and cut and haggard even in the moonlight, as if sleep had eluded him for weeks. His eyes were fastened on the woman who stood leaning against the back of a Pathfinder, her expression clearly pained. Held snugly against her chest was a child, a girl. A tired dog slept on the grass by her feet next to the small pile of suitcases.

This was Drake's Island and almost everyone here was on summer vacation. Their concerns were on rinsing away their own worries, not on the problems of strangers.

On the second floor of the small house, Jack walked quietly into the dark bedroom down the hall from Taylor, who had just put Rachel to bed. That heaviness was back again, booming inside his chest. The events of just hours ago were nothing but blurred film clips that seemed disconnected from him. Downstairs he could hear the agents talking with Mike Abrams about how the shifts were to be broken down, the security they were to use. Mike had stepped in and made all the proper arrangements, just as he had years ago.

The door to Taylor's bedroom was open. She was now sitting on the edge of the bed, her head tilted down, studying something in her hands. Her suitcase lay on the bed untouched, and she had placed a small boom box on the nightstand. She had chosen to drive up here with the agents, not with him.

A voice told him to leave her alone. And what could he say? Words had little value when it came to healing and forgiveness. The answers she needed weren't his to give. Best to say nothing.

Ten minutes later, he was standing at the door again. "Mind if I come in?"

She didn't look up at him, didn't answer.

He entered the bedroom. "How are you holding up?"

"Just like you always say, I'm fine," she snapped back.

"Taylor, I'm sorry about this."

She paused. Whatever words had formed, she dismissed them and began unpacking. He couldn't let it go.

"I know it got—"

"Jack, I don't want to talk. I'm going to be just like you, just keep it all inside, keep all my secrets and feelings hidden away from everyone, and for once *you* can stand there in the dark alone, wondering just what the hell is going on with me. That, Jack, is the essence of our relationship. Feels great, doesn't it?"

"I'll leave you alone." He turned to leave.

"Yes, Jack Casey's patented answer for everything. Leave me alone. Look at me, I can handle it all by myself. That's how you do it, right? Keep it all inside, don't let anyone in on what you're thinking or feeling. Except when we're fucking, of course."

Let her have this, he thought. *You at least owe her that.*

Her anger moved somewhere else and her face became hard and serious. "I understand Rachel saw a man on the beach."

In the confusion after today's explosion, he hadn't found the time to tell her. Rachel may have told her, and then Taylor probably cornered Mike or another agent and got the news. *Shit.* Jack had wanted Taylor to hear it from him.

"Is it true he was shot in the head?"

Jack took in a breath.

"Don't lie to me, Jack. Don't you *dare* lie to me now."

"Yes, he was shot in the head."

"And Rachel saw this."

"What she saw was a small hole in the center of his forehead. That's all."

"That's *all?"*

She didn't see the exit wound or the mess on the back of the chair, he added privately. It seemed an important distinction, but he kept it to himself. "Rachel doesn't know what happened to him, just that he wasn't moving. She thought he was sick."

Taylor wiped a hand across her forehead, her face pale. "Who was he?"

"Ronnie Tedesco."

"The man who was supposed to be protecting us."

"Yes. He and his men—"

"You *told* me we were safe. You *told* me I had nothing to worry about. What the *fuck* happened, Jack?"

"I don't know." Which was the truth. He hadn't been told how the security had broken down, and in his shock and relief after rescuing Taylor, he hadn't bothered to ask.

"I understand he was an ex–Secret Service agent, did body detail for Reagan and two other presidents."

There was a confidence in her words. Suddenly Jack felt as though he were standing far from shore on a thin layer of ice. How much had Mike told her? *No, Mike wouldn't tell her. She must have spoken to someone else.*

"Taylor, I know you're upset about—"

"Don't," she warned, almost choking on the word. "Don't stand there and try to tell me how to feel or tell me how sorry you are. You have no idea, Jack, you have not *one fucking clue* to what I'm feeling right now. My niece could have been lying dead on that beach today, Jack. *My* niece, *my* family. This psychotic could have killed her, and where would that have left me, Jack? Don't you realize what could have happened? You of all people?"

"Why didn't you stay at the house like I asked?"

"Because *you* called me. *You* called and asked me to come get you at the airport. *You* told me to drop Rachel off at Billings's and pick you up in the Expedition. *You* told me she would be safe. *You* told me I had nothing to worry about, and it sure as hell *sounded* like you, Jack. It was *your* voice."

The voice-altering device. The Sandman disguised his voice in the phone calls, it makes perfect sense that he could imitate one. Jack should have foreseen it. Just as he should have foreseen Hamilton's trap.

Miles outwitted you again. He killed your wife and destroyed your life, and he just did it again, almost killing Taylor in the process, and you fucking ran right into it.

If only I had listened to Mike . . .

Too late now.

"You have all these people watching me and my niece and kept it a secret from day one. My life was in danger and you couldn't even bring yourself to tell me? What the fuck is wrong with you?"

"If I told you, he would have killed you."

She glared at him. Then she walked over to the nightstand and with her eyes pinned to his face, she pressed the play button on the boom box. The Sandman's voice came on.

"You and I need to make an oath, Jack. It's the only way to keep Taylor safe. Promise me you'll drop this case. Become a full-time carpenter and spend all your time popping Taylor's muffin, I don't care, but you need to take your final bow and exit. We both know you're not up to this. Those mental scars are already tearing."

The conversation had been spliced. The Sandman's next words were:

"I understand you're having a visitor."

"What are you talking about?"

"Taylor's niece, Rachel. I hear she and her dog are flying in from Wisconsin tomorrow. Ever hear a child scream, Jack? Keep up the pace and I'll mail you a tape of Rachel begging for her life."

Jack's face colored. The room went out of focus. "He . . . the Sandman never said that."

Taylor shut the tape off. "The whole conversation is there, and I listened to it from beginning to end on the way up here," she said matter-of-factly.

"So you heard the part where he threatened to kill you and Rachel if I told you."

"No, that's not there."

"Of course not. He conveniently left that out." Then he saw the disbelief in her face. "What, you think I *lied* to you?"

"You were clearly warned to stay away and you didn't. I don't hate you for that, or for not telling me my life was in danger, but I hate you for risking Rachel's life. She's my *whole* life, Jack. *My* life, Jack. *My* life and my *niece's* life, you son of a bitch, how could you stand there and not tell me? *What gives you the fucking right to put everything I love in danger?"*

He tried to form the words.

"Don't bother," she spat. "I wouldn't believe you anyway."

"You were supposed to be protected and something happened. I'm sorry, Taylor. The important thing is that you're fine. We need to focus on that."

"I'm *not* fine, Jack, and neither is my niece. This isn't some goddamn cut or broken bone that will heal—this will be with her forever. Don't you realize that? You of all people." She looked at him as if he were a stranger. "What the hell happened to you? I look at you and . . . it's like I don't even recognize you."

And here it was, the fear he had carried all this time now a living entity between them, wild and loose, irrevocable. In that instant, the heated words still ringing in the air, he looked in Taylor's eyes and behind her hurt, frightened look watched as the image she had held of him mutated into something vile.

Jack looked out the window at the waves breaking. Everything he loved, everything he had come to treasure and needed to move through the days had just vanished. No amount of words or promises could reclaim his past. Over now. Gone.

He looked back. His chest was hollow with desperation and fear, empty now, like a house that had been left to rot.

"I'm sorry, Taylor. That's all I can say."

"It's not good enough. Not for this."

Words never are, a voice added.

Taylor took a FedEx envelope from her suitcase. "This was in my stack of mail. I opened it on the way up here. I believe it belongs to you."

The top had already been torn open. He pulled the lip apart and looked inside. It was a photocopy of his journal.

"Don't worry, I didn't read it. I don't want to know any more. I couldn't stomach it."

She pulled out a diamond ring from her front pocket.

It was Amanda's engagement ring.

"Where did you—"

"It was in an envelope inside the Expedition," she said, her voice desolate. "With the pictures and the cassette tape."

She placed the ring on his hands. Jack touched her arm, but she jerked away, as if he were a leper.

"Don't touch me, don't you *ever* touch me again."

Taylor moved away and headed to the bathroom. He wanted to follow, to turn her around and scream, cry, yell—whatever it took to make it right. But all he did was stand there, silently. Whatever she was thinking and feeling had to run its course.

She turned on the bathroom light, then turned to him. He would never forget the desolate look in her eyes. It made him shudder.

"You don't love me, Jack. Not in that soul-encompassing way you loved your wife. You love the idea of me and the way I can make you forget your past. How did the Sandman put it? 'Taylor interrupted your plans to bleed into nothingness.' "

"That's . . . Taylor, it's not true."

"It is, Jack. I've felt it for quite some time." Her eyes filled with an irrecoverable hurt, and in Jack's mind, he saw all of his time with her, the good times, just float away like a balloon into the sky, never to come back home.

"Ironic that I had to learn the truth from a psychopath who just tried to kill me," she said as she closed the door softly on him and locked it.

Jack stood in the salty coolness of the bedroom, listening to her sobs. The door to a known life, a good life full of promise and reward, had just slammed shut forever.

chapter 56

COFFEE WAS PERCOLATING IN THE KITCHEN. When Jack walked in, an agent gave him a polite nod, and coffee cup in hand, Jack headed into the living room where Mike was talking to another agent.

Jack tossed the FedEx package on the white laminate counter. He felt . . . he didn't know what he felt. There was just that familiar void inside him, the one that had blossomed into a suffocating stillness in the months after Amanda's funeral, the one that had forced him to seek asylum inside the sterilized white walls of Ocean Point.

His mind was working just fine, playing a haunting procession of mental filmstrips: the terrorized look in Taylor's eyes when she'd first turned to him from behind the wheel; Rachel staring at the bullet hole in Ronnie Tedesco's forehead; the picture of Amanda on the autopsy table, Blake's poem "The Sick Rose" on the back; the altered photograph of Taylor. He couldn't turn the images off.

Jack headed out for the beach. He sat on the edge of the shore and watched the waves break. The cool wind blowing off the water had an edge to it; it helped clear his head.

His cell phone rang.

"Congratulations on your wonderful performance today," the Sandman said. "You're lucky to be alive."

Jack said nothing.

"How is Taylor doing? My, what a terrible ride she had today. And I heard the little one saw a dead body on the beach. I don't think she'll ever forget that, do you?"

Jack stood up. He looked up at the stars.

"You can't hide her from me, Jack. I'll find her and Rachel, and when I do, their fate will be far worse than Amanda's. Don't worry, I'll send you a copy of the videotape at Ocean Point. I already called ahead. They have a room and medication waiting for you." The Sandman laughed.

"The game's over, Gabriel. I know all about Graves, the Behavioral Modification Program, Gardner, the San Diego bombing—I know it all."

"And in a few days, so will everyone else on the planet. I'm going to expose Graves, the program—and you. That blurb in the *Herald* on your stay at Ocean Point is just the beginning. Each week I'll mail out a page from your journal, and by the time I'm done, you'll be a household name."

"You won't live long enough to tell your story."

"And you'll spend the rest of your life . . . alone. How are things between you and Taylor? She looking at you differently yet?"

Unconsciously, Jack's eyes shifted up to the house. Taylor's bedroom window was dark.

"I'm coming for you. You can't hide from me."

"Do you know what I'm doing right now, Jack? I'm watching the next family sleep. You should see the eight-year-old girl, Clara, tucked into her bed, holding her Kermit the Frog, sleeping so peacefully. Oh, by the way, this family, they're not connected to Graves or the FBI program. This is just a normal, everyday family—like the one Amanda had cooking in the womb. Only you failed her, Jack. Just like you failed Taylor and her niece, like you failed your friend Mike, you failed everyone who was ever close to you because you're sick. And you'll fail the next family. They'll be dead within twenty-four hours. But don't worry, Jack, I won't kill the husband. I'll let him watch his family die just like you did. That way you'll have a companion in purgatory."

The line went dead. Jack threw the phone out into the water.

Some time later, he didn't know how long, Mike joined him.

"How's she doing?" Mike asked.

"As well as can be expected."

"She survived one hell of a ride. It's going to be a little bumpy for a while, especially for the little one, but they'll be fine. Taylor strikes me as a tough lady."

Jack nodded. His eyes drifted back up to Taylor's room. Still dark. He wrestled with his need to go back up and hold her.

It's over, Jack. Gone.

"The house belongs to a friend of mine who isn't connected to the Bureau," Mike said. "The six guys I have stationed up there, they didn't know where we were going until I pulled up. Taylor and Rachel will be fine. These guys are experienced."

"So was Tedesco."

Mike didn't say anything, just looked out at the water.

"We know what happened to his men?" Jack asked.

"Poisoned would be my guess. We found the surveillance van down the street. All four of them were in the back with a pizza box. It looks like they had all eaten from it. As for Taylor's car, I called the Ford dealership in Danvers. The car was never there. The Sandman must have intercepted the call."

How could the Sandman have intercepted the call? The phone was supposed to be *encrypted*. And why did Ronnie and his men fail to find the surveillance cameras and the bugs in her house? *The Sandman must have planted them and the equipment needed to unscramble the phones just after the Roth bombing.* With the house guarded around the clock (*supposedly,* a voice countered), there was no way the Sandman could have entered without being detected. How? Answer: he must have used that four-week interval between Roth and Dolan to prepare. But why didn't Ronnie and his men find the bugs? Here, standing in the cool night air, Jack demanded an answer.

You'll never know.

"They found the state trooper's vehicle abandoned in Saugus," Mike said. "The trooper's been missing since Monday. You get a look at his face at all?"

"I saw his hand out the window but not his face. He was wearing sunglasses and a trooper's hat. That's all I can tell you."

"The name Hamilton gave you, Dr. Brian Le Claire, we put some people on him. There's no way the Sandman can get to him."

Jack nodded. There was a lull and Jack suddenly didn't want to talk anymore. He didn't care about those details right now, or how the Sandman arranged to have Boston SWAT set up on the highway or how he could have configured the Expedition's computer steering system to respond to remote control. The point—the thing that had been true all along—was that Jack was standing here again going over the details that would get him nowhere while the Sandman was plotting to kill another family.

"Take this," Mike said. "It belongs to you." He was holding the FedEx envelope.

"Go ahead and read it," Jack said. "Hamilton has a copy. Excerpts will probably be published tomorrow."

"Earlier, when I was talking to the hospital director, Voyles, he told me Hamilton had a visitor about two weeks ago, a psychiatrist by the name of Dr. David Gardner."

Mark Graysmith's words came back to Jack in a rush: *Bomb was a laptop computer in ceiling hooked into building's security system, activated by Gardner's access code, C-4, on a timer in Gardner's office.*

"The name mean anything to you?"

Jack was glad he was looking out at the water so Mike couldn't see his face.

"No," Jack lied.

"At the house today, you mentioned a name. Gabriel."

"That was the name written on Dolan's hand."

"So Gabriel and the Sandman are the same person."

"That would be my guess."

"Why the sudden vagueness?"

"Mike, this place, does Alan Lynch know about it?"

"No."

"You're sure?"

"Alan paid me a visit this morning. He told me he showed up the other night with two vans full of equipment and the best lab guys and you turned him down. What's going on?"

This was dangerous ground. Alan Lynch was still Mike's boss. Mike was still a government employee, with a family to support and a lot more at stake. Would Mike lie to Alan? Probably. Mike knew how Alan operated. But if Jack told Mike the truth, he would be in danger.

But he's already in danger, a voice warned. *The Sandman knows Abrams is helping you. Who knows what he has planned for Mike? For his family? And who knows what Alan is up to? We don't know who this guy Dragos is, how he fits into this. The only thing Mike knows about Graves is that it burned down; he doesn't know the real details of what went down there. What if Alan* thinks *Mike knows something about Graves? About the Behavioral Modification Program? Look what he tried to do to Fletcher.*

Jack had to tell Mike something. He couldn't just leave his friend hanging in the wind, exposed.

"Mike, when Alan came by, was there a man with him, a guy named Victor Dragos?"

"No. Why?"

"Because he was with Alan when I saw him and claimed to be a fingerprint expert from the lab. Only he wasn't."

"Then who was he?"

"I don't know." *And that's what bothers me,* he added privately.

"Alan had questions about Malcolm Fletcher: Where did I get his name? What was he doing here?" Mike frowned. "I think I'm correct in assuming that the guy driving the truck was Fletcher."

"Right."

"What's he doing here now?"

"Assisting."

"He pulls a gun on you, forces you to leave your piece and the case file at his place, now he's here to assist?"

"It was a misunderstanding."

"Jack, cut the bullshit and start leveling with me. Why is Fletcher here?"

"I just told you."

"This has something to do with the bombing in San Diego, doesn't it? This research building nobody seems to know anything about."

Jack paused. "Partly."

"What's Fletcher's connection to the Sandman?"

"Mike, stay away from Lynch and this guy Dragos."

Mike's face turned red. "I risked my life for you today, I put my family at risk by helping you with this case, pulled every fucking string I have within the Bureau, and you can't even give me the fucking *courtesy* of an explanation?"

"You're going to have to trust me on this one."

"That's it?"

"I can't get into it. I'm sorry."

Mike took a few steps closer.

"Are my family or I in danger, Jack?"

For a moment there was only the sound of the waves against the shore and then retreating.

"Jack?"

"Did you move them like we talked about?"

"Answer the fucking question. *Now.*"

"Move them, Mike, get out of here, get you and your family away from me and this case."

Mike tossed the FedEx envelope like a Frisbee. The hard edge bounced off Jack's chest.

"So help you God if anything happens to them, Jack. So help you God."

chapter 57

JACK WATCHED MIKE STORM UP THE BEACH. The back screen door slammed behind him like a gunshot. Taylor's bedroom light turned on. Jack saw her silhouetted figure stand up. *She's probably going to check on Rachel,* he thought, and then saw the bedroom light go off.

"You did the right thing," a voice behind him said.

Jack jumped. Malcolm Fletcher emerged from the shadows.

"Jesus Christ, can't you walk up to people like a normal person?"

"Are we still reeling from this afternoon's joyride?"

"I'm not in the mood for your wit."

"Let me guess: the Sandman called you again."

"He's promised to kill another family in the next twenty-four hours—one not connected to Graves or the program."

"As punishment for today."

"Yes."

"The rules of the game have changed dramatically over the past few hours. You remember the tall gentleman next to Alan, the one that looked like Hitler's poster boy for the Aryan Nation?"

"Yeah, Victor Dragos. The fingerprint expert."

"Only we both know that he isn't."

"Who is he?"

Fletcher's eyebrows danced. "Someone skilled in the art of waste removal."

The words hung in Jack's mind, like a stranger knocking behind a door demanding to be let in. *Waste removal,* he thought again, and his heart filled with a cold dread.

Victor was an assassin.

"Victor's a sick little boy," Fletcher said. "You should hear what he wanted to do to your friend Mike . . . and his special plans for Taylor and her niece."

Jack felt weak, as if he had been robbed of blood. He stood there, numb, looking out at the breaking water. He had just spent the day dodging two psychopaths who had joined forces to kill him. In a way, Jack could understand what drove them. Hamilton was pathological, a genetic freak who had been hardwired in the womb. The Sandman was consumed with avenging his tormentors. At least these two monsters acknowledged who and what they were. But Alan, his former boss . . . the man was using an *assassin* to murder a woman and a four-year-old girl and why? Because Alan knew Jack had the knowledge on the secret research program and the atrocities at Graves, and the only way to keep the big fucking mess a secret was to wipe everyone off the board.

The numbness went away, and what Jack felt burning through his veins was rage, and what he wanted to do more than anything was to get Alan and

(do what you did to Yerkies, remember how good it tasted?)

No. What he wanted was for Alan to stand trial—wanted everyone on the planet to know what a fucking scumbag Alan Lynch was, and Jack wanted to be there at that moment, looking deep into Alan's eyes as the man's world came crashing down, his wife and children finally seeing the man for the monster he really was. More than anything, Jack wanted to be the person to make it all happen.

Better yet, I'll put you in a cage with Hamilton. You're no better than the monsters you helped put away.

"You know where Victor is now?"

"Tucked away for future use."

"I want to speak to him."

Fletcher grinned and tilted his head slightly. "Speaking isn't what's on your mind now, is it?"

"Tell me where he is."

"Victor's not up for company." Fletcher laughed.

"Then take me to Alan."

"If you want to save everything you love, and if you want to find the Sandman, then you'll have to play the game my way."

Jack looked back at the house. His relationship with Taylor was over. Rachel was plagued with nightmares. His friendship with Mike was dissolving. In his mind came the next family, and Jack saw them settling into the evening, pictured their pleasant life together, and his rage shifted. What filled the awful void was desperation and fear. Another family was going to die, he had to save them.

"We'll talk on the way back to Marblehead. But first I want you to listen to this." Fletcher moved in close and held up an audiocassette.

"What's on it?"

"My conversation with Victor. It should do wonders for your imagination."

Fletcher's black eyes were as unfathomable and mysterious as the deepest part of the ocean. Darkness within darkness.

"Come with me, Detective. I have worlds to show you."

chapter 58

THE CALL CAME IN A LITTLE AFTER SIX THAT MORNING. One of the guards was coming down the corridor with his coffee and a paper when he saw all the commotion just outside the room. Eric Beaumont was awake.

An hour later Jack and Duffy were standing in an empty room on the third floor of Newton-Wellesley Hospital. A shouting mob of reporters had gathered in front of the main entrance, waving their microphones and tape recorders. They had discovered that the boy was awake and were now waiting for Eric's doctor to appear before them and deliver the news on the boy's condition.

Only the doctor wasn't coming. Duffy had planted the rumor to move the reporters into one centralized location, and it had worked. The media swarming across the front of the hospital had ignored the ambulance that slowly cruised past them and dropped off the two men right at the emergency room entrance.

"It's been like this all week," Duffy said. "The first night, one of the guards was virtually attacked by the press on his way home. Now I got them packing suitcases and spending the night. Can you believe this shit?"

Jack drank from the coffee Duffy had bought him and watched the feeding frenzy below. "I've seen it from both sides of the fence," Jack said. His eyes followed a cameraman with a telephoto lens breaking away from the crowd. *He's probably going around the back to see if they've opened the blinds on the kid's room.*

For the past twenty minutes they had been waiting for Dr. Stan Temple, Eric's therapist. Duffy had told Jack of Eric Beaumont's early years of abuse at the hands of his biological father, Roger Beaumont, an alcoholic who once hit his four-year-old son for spilling his cornflakes. The punch was so hard it landed him a concussion and a one-week stay at the hospital.

The turning point for Eric's mother, Karen, came five years later, when Eric was nine. She was out to dinner with friends when she got paged: there was a car accident. Roger was fine but drunk (no surprise); Eric was in critical condition. Doctors had already removed one kidney.

Karen obtained a restraining order. The divorce was finalized a year later.

So the origins of Eric's psychological coma for the past six days were not a mystery, Jack thought.

What was a mystery, what was only known by Eric Beaumont himself, was why he had tried to reestablish a connection with his now sobered-up father. At Eric's urging, and after several meetings with therapists and lawyers, it was agreed that Eric could spend a trial weekend with his father. It was a success. Another followed. The third had been planned for the night both parents were executed.

"Have you seen Sally Dowling on the news?" Duffy asked. He was freshly shaved and his hair was still wet; the lump above his right eye had faded into a dark black-and-blue.

"No. Who is she?"

"Eric's seventy-six-year-old grandmother—and his only living relative. The first day she came here to be with her grandson, she needed an armed escort to get in. The next day, after the media figured out who she was, a photographer knocked her down and she broke her leg. Osteoporosis. Now the woman's on crutches and pain meds. Would it surprise you to know they took her picture while she was lying on the ground?"

Jack shook his head. His mind grew silent, the way the world does as dusk settles into evening, and what he felt now was a stillness, as if his thoughts and feelings had simply packed up and deserted him; it was as if he were standing inside an abandoned house and was now forced to look for the substance and texture of thought in the lengthening shadows.

He knew what was happening and welcomed it.

"How you doing?" Duffy asked.

"Fine."

There was an awkward pause. Jack kept looking out the window.

"I saw what happened on the news. Your girl okay?"

"She's holding up," Jack said flatly.

"You tuck her someplace safe?"

Jack nodded, and checked his watch. *Where the hell's the shrink?*

"A few days ago, I was reading the papers and there was a story about that kid that escaped Yerkies's barn—Darren Nigro, that was his name." Duffy paused, as if waiting for Jack to pick up the story. When he didn't, Duffy said, "When this kid was in the hospital, you went to talk to him, right?"

"I tried to."

"I read that the mother came home from grocery shopping and found her son hanging by a belt inside the bedroom. He was on medication, he was in therapy."

Jack turned to Duffy. "I'm not sure what you're asking me."

"When the shrink comes in here, I want you to do the talking."

"Why?"

Duffy cleared his throat.

"Because I've been to a shrink myself," Jack said. The words came out harsher than they should have.

"No. No, that's not it at all." Duffy shrugged. "I just don't buy into any of it. Frankly, I think it's all a bunch of bullshit. Words have no value in healing . . . at least in my experience. Given what you went through, I figured—"

"I'll talk to the shrink. It's not a problem."

Duffy nodded and opened his pack of Marlboros. He started to pull out a cigarette and stopped. "You honestly believe this shrink's going to help this kid?"

"It's worth a shot."

"But you don't buy into it, do you?"

Jack sighed. "Either you listen to the demons or you don't. Those are about the only two choices you have."

"What choice did you make?"

"I'm still caught in a gray area."

Duffy laughed bitterly. "Aren't we all."

chapter 59

DR. STAN TEMPLE WAS JUST SHY OF SIX FEET, WITH A SMOOTH FACE AND A THICK MOP OF BLOND HAIR. His dark brown designer suit was cut to showcase a rugged, athletic frame shaped by daily grinds at the gym. The way the shrink looked reminded Jack of a fraternity boy slinging a backpack full of books over his shoulder on his way to his freshman psych class.

"The key component in this scenario is that Eric was both physically *and* mentally abused during his formative years," Temple was saying. He seemed nervous, but he spoke with textbook clarity and precision; Jack wondered if the young doctor had practiced in front of a mirror. "Because of his traumatic past, Eric has conflicting emotions about both parents, especially concerning his father. He knows what it is like to feel angry, to feel frustrated and helpless, and he's in touch with all of those feelings."

"Which is why he suffered a post–traumatic stress reaction when he walked inside the bedroom," Jack said. He was sitting on the bed so he could be eye level with the doctor; Duffy was across from him, leaning against the wall.

"That's exactly it," Temple said. "Eric felt glad that his father, his physical and mental tormentor for all these years, was dead—he'd fantasized about it for years. However, he's feeling *guilty* about what happened. These two conflicting emotions, as well as witnessing the graphic deaths of his parents, hit him all at once. His brain shut down. He's in shock."

Jack knew all this but wanted Temple to keep talking, to have him feel comfortable before he hit the doctor with what he needed.

"The events from that night are locked away. You go in there and start trying to find out where they're buried, he could relapse right back into that psychological coma."

"I understand your situation, Doctor."

"Good, so it won't come as a surprise to you when I say I can't allow you to talk to him."

"What about routine questions?"

"His mind is just too fragile. I'm sorry, Detective Casey. I wish there were another way."

Tactic one: "I've been in Eric's situation before."

Temple kept silent.

"I believe you know what I'm referring to," Jack said, and smiled to take the edge off. "I take it you've read the papers."

"Yes. Yes, I have."

"So you know about Ocean Point."

Temple ignored this. "Detective, the first family that was murdered, the Roths, you walked inside the house, correct?"

Jack knew where the shrink was leading him.

"When you saw Mr. Roth lying there tied to the bed, when you saw what had happened to his family, what was your reaction?"

"I was taken aback."

Temple's expression remained polite. "So you didn't suffer a post–traumatic stress reaction?"

Jack kept his face blank. "It took me by surprise."

"Given your history, I think it did more than that, Detective Casey." Temple regarded Jack for a moment. "You're an adult and you couldn't absorb what you were seeing. Think about it from the perspective of an eleven-year-old boy."

"Does he know what happened to his parents?"

"He's . . . the best way I can put it is that he's vaguely aware. But he hasn't absorbed the reality of it, nor does he know the specifics of how they died. His grandmother is there next to him, he's surrounded by nurses, he's hooked up to an IV, he's been medicated by a psychiatrist, and now his therapist is making a house call to his hospital room. He's a bright kid. He knows something's up. He's frightened to death."

"Does he know he's been out for six days?"

"Absolutely not. Imagine what that knowledge would do to him." Temple shook his head. "I'm sorry, but the answer is no."

Jack could appreciate the doctor's position and need to protect an eleven-year-old boy. But the doctor's well-placed intentions could not protect Eric from the Sandman or Alan Lynch and his team of federal agents. Once Alan learned of the boy's new condition, there would be no polite talk. Alan would steamroll right over Temple and would take what he wanted. Jack thought of Alan's plans for Taylor and Rachel. Eric's future would be no exception.

Jack had already thought of this and had the plan in place. Tactic two:

"You're aware that your patient has seen the face of the man who's killed three families."

"Yes, I'm aware of that. Still, my position is firm."

"So you realize that you've sentenced your patient to death."

Temple looked at Jack, puzzled. "Excuse me?"

"You see that package sitting on the bed behind you? The one with Eric's name on it?"

"What about it?"

"It's a bomb."

The skin on Temple's face drained of color; his eyes shot wide open.

"My guess is C-4," Jack said. "You familiar with explosives, Doctor?"

"No."

"Eric opens that box and they'll be picking everyone in this hospital up with salad tongs. It's a memorable sight. I've seen it twice this summer."

"Well, it's good you caught it," Temple said, his face struggling for composure.

"This time. The Sandman's waiting for this bomb to go off. When it doesn't, he'll mail another one or do something even more clever. He's very sophisticated. Did you read in the papers about the surveillance camera he turned into a bomb using an ordinary pager? That he can detonate a bomb by a phone call? Maybe he'll do something different this time, like dropping the bomb in the lobby. For all I know he's outside the hospital right now with all those reporters. Maybe this room is bugged and he's listening to us right now."

"We'll move Eric."

"Where?"

"I believe that's your area of expertise."

"Then you'll trust me when I say that no matter where I put him, the Sandman will find him and kill him. And you'll be next."

"Me?"

"Eric might have told you something that you passed along to me. Maybe you even mentioned it to your wife. Right now the Sandman could be making plans to visit you and your family. You know what he did to the two families in Marblehead, don't you?" *Although I doubt the killer will be the Sandman,* Jack thought. *He'll probably be someone hired by Alan Lynch, the director of the ISU—yes, you heard me correctly, Doctor, the federal government wants you dead. Got to wipe the slate clean, can't have any loose ends, this whole thing paid for with your tax dollars, can you believe it?* "Is the picture becoming clear to you?"

"What's becoming clear are your scare tactics."

"I'm telling you the truth."

"I know what you're thinking: 'He's too young, he doesn't know what he's doing.' I'll lay down my responsibility and let you traumatize an eleven-year-old boy." Temple stood his ground, but the words came out sounding more frightened than angry. "Given your own history, I thought such manipulation was beneath you."

Time was ticking by. Time to lay it on the line.

"Doctor, I'm trying to catch a psychopath who has killed three families and is planning on killing another family tonight. I'm running out of time. Your patient is the only person who's seen his face and heard his real voice. Right now, he's the only chance I got. I don't want to go in there, Doctor, but I don't have a choice. You, me, your family, Eric, all the employees of this hospital are on the chopping block. You want to be the one to sentence everyone to death?"

Duffy, behind the doctor and leaning against the wall, was signaling Jack to ease up.

"I was the one who ran into that house and pulled him from under the bed. I know what he saw, I know what he went through, and I'm painfully aware of what's facing him. I don't want to go in there, Doctor, but the truth is that I don't have a choice. Eric could be the only person who can save his own life—and yours."

Temple was close to leaving.

"I don't want another family to die. Help me, Doctor. I'm begging you. Please help me."

Temple shifted his attention to the box. *Think about it all you want,* Jack thought. *I'm going in there, with or without your help. Make it easy for me, Doctor.*

"I'll be in the room when you question him," Temple said finally.

"That's fine," Jack said.

"So will the grandmother."

"Bad idea."

"I agree, but Eric won't let go of her. And her presence might keep him stabilized through your questioning."

Jack and Duffy exchanged glances.

"It's not open for discussion," Temple said.

"Fine," Jack said. "Anything else?"

"You can both be in there but only one of you will ask the questions. Because you've been through a similar situation, Detective Casey, I recommend that you talk with him. Open up. Share with him how you feel. Show him that you're more a person than a policeman."

"I'll do that. Thank you, Doctor."

"Make no mistake: if Eric gets agitated in any way, if he shows even the *faintest* sign of it, I'll step in and the questions will stop. We clear on that part, gentlemen?" Temple's tone allowed no argument. "Let me go talk to the grandmother and prepare her for what's about to happen." Abruptly, he left the room.

Duffy pointed to the bed. "What's really in the box?"

"Cards from some of Eric's friends, some action figures. I threw them in and wrote Eric's name on it."

Duffy grinned. "Pretty slick."

But Jack didn't feel smart. What he felt was manipulative. He told himself this was the only way to protect the boy from the Sandman and Alan Lynch. The coating still didn't make the pill easier to swallow.

chapter 60

Eric Beaumont was sitting on his bed, his head tilted down as if he were somehow ashamed. Temple sat on the windowsill to the right of the bed, looking like Eric's older brother, and on the opposite side of the bed was the grandmother.

Jack stood at the foot of the bed, his head full of strange voices, his mind flashing back to that day in Vermont when he had gone inside a similar room to talk to Darren Nigro.

"Hi, Eric." He tried to keep his voice neutral. "My name is Jack Casey."

The boy shifted uncomfortably in his bed. His face was puffy from sleep and medicine and lined with indentations from the pillow. Jack thought: *An eleven-year-old boy who should be playing video games and baseball is sitting inside a hospital pumped full of chemicals, the victim of a violent father and now an orphan struggling with the gruesome death of his parents.*

"Do you recognize my voice?"

No response.

"Did Dr. Temple tell you who I am?"

Eric's eyes shifted up long enough to look at the badge hanging over Jack's belt. "You're a policeman." His voice was as fragile as eggshell.

"Not now I'm not." Jack pried the badge off his belt and tossed it over to Duffy, who was standing at the door behind him. Duffy already had Jack's gun.

Eric looked confused. "What do you mean?"

"I took my badge off. I'm not a policeman right now. Right now, I'm a person just like you, someone who knows how you're feeling." Jack moved closer. Eric slid toward his grandmother. *Careful.* "Not too long ago, I lost my wife. I loved her very much and it hurt me for a long time. I felt really bad about it. Felt guilty."

Jack paused to let the boy digest it. A moment later, Eric said, "How did she die?"

"She was killed."

"How?"

"That's not important. What is important is how I felt was a lot like how you're feeling now: confused, angry, scared. Alone. I talked with men like Dr. Temple and that helped me."

"And you feel better now?"

Tell him the truth, Jack.

"I feel better. It helped to talk about it."

Like you talked about it with Taylor. Why don't you tell him about that?

"You want to talk about my parents," Eric said. "About what happened."

"Yes."

"I—I don't remember much."

"Can we talk about what you do remember?"

Eric looked at his grandmother. "It's okay, honey," she said. "Go ahead and talk to him. I'll be right here."

Jack looked at the old woman and thought, *She won't be here much longer. And then Eric will have to cope with that and he'll be alone and then where will he be?*

Nowhere. Alone. Having to fight for feelings.

It was difficult—no, impossible—to look at Eric without connecting to himself seven years ago. Or remembering Darren Nigro, his small hand with its three missing fingers pulling a sheet over his face.

Jack felt himself surrender to those awful memories. As he stared at Eric's small body and the frightened, blank look on the boy's face, he felt the rage building inside him like a fire.

Temple was staring curiously at Jack.

"If I can't remember, you won't get mad at me?" Eric asked.

"Absolutely not."

Weighing the promises of an adult with the promises of his father.

"Okay then," Eric said.

"You mind if I sit on the bed?"

"Sure."

Eric's body recoiled slightly from the sudden proximity. Both hands clutched the bedsheet.

"Tell me what you do remember," Jack said.

"It's . . . I can't see it all. It's like . . . It's like it's all jumbled. It's hard to see anything."

"Like someone flicking past TV stations real fast."

The confusion and fear in Eric's face took a momentary backseat to his surprise. "Yeah, like that."

"That's normal."

"It is?"

"Absolutely. Why don't we do this: why don't you let me guide you through it. I'll ask the questions and you'll answer them as best you can. That sound okay to you?"

Eric's body seemed to relax.

"Okay, good. Let's start with your dad. I was told you were going to spend the weekend with him."

"Yes."

"When did he come get you?"

"He was supposed to come get me Thursday night, after my basketball game, but he got tied up at work. I'm in a summer league 'cause I'm going to play varsity this year. My mom picked me up and we went through the drive-through at BK like we did every Thursday night, and then we came home and ate in the TV room and watched *The Simpsons.*"

"One of my favorite shows," Jack said.

"My dad *hated* it."

"You like *South Park?*"

"Yeah, that's the best. My mom kinda squirms, 'cause of all the, you know, fart jokes and stuff, but she still lets me watch it."

Eric's face seemed to take on a shine. *He's still talking about her in the present tense,* Jack thought.

"You *really* like that? You're not just saying that?"

"Let me tell you a secret," Jack said with a smile. "When Mr. Hanky came out of the toilet and yelled 'Hidee-ho' to everyone, I came this close to wetting my pants."

"Yeah, even my mom laughed at that one."

Jack felt like a manipulative prick.

"Did your dad pick you up on Friday?"

"Yeah, Friday afternoon. He left work early. We went out to eat at Pizzeria Uno. We were supposed to see a movie afterwards, but . . . it didn't work out."

"What happened?"

"I left my basketball sneakers at home. We just started eating when I told him and he flipped out because I had a playoff game the next morning. He lives in Medford now, and the game was in Nashua—that's in New Hampshire. That meant he had to drive all the way back to Newton. He was really mad at me." A pause and the boy's body stiffened. "*Real* mad."

"You call your mom and tell her you forgot your sneakers?"

"No. We got right into the car and drove to Newton 'cause I got a key to the house. It's normally, like, forty minutes or something, but it was longer 'cause of all the traffic."

"Did you call your mom from the car?"

"No." Eric bowed his head. "He was really upset and he was yelling a lot. He yelled at me the whole time. That I was irresponsible."

Jack let the rhythm slow. "How are you doing?"

A shrug. "Okay." Eric's voice was low. Guarded.

"You're being real helpful and I want you to know how much I appreciate it."

"But we're going to have to talk about it now."

"Yeah. It might be a little rough, but all these people in the room want to help you. If you don't understand something, if you're getting upset or scared or you want to ask me a question, or if you want to stop, just tell me, okay?"

"Okay."

Locked somewhere in Eric's traumatized mind was possibly the key to breaking open the case. To find it, not only would Jack have to choose his words carefully, he would have to skillfully maneuver around the boy's minefield of emotions. He saw Darren Nigro—saw himself in Eric's frightened expression—and hated himself for what he had to do next.

"Friday night when you pulled into your driveway, tell me what happened."

"My dad got out of the car and rang the doorbell. When my mom didn't answer, he came back and told me to get out."

"Because you had a key to the house."

"Yes."

"Did you expect your mom to be home?"

"Her car was there. And she doesn't go out on Friday nights because—" Eric stopped. Again Jack waited for him to move ahead at his own speed. "My mom was kind of worked up about me visiting Dad. She told me that she would be home, right next to the phone in case there was a problem."

"So you unlocked the door and went inside. What happened next?"

"I went to the TV room. My mom watches a lot of TV so I checked there. She wasn't there."

"Did you notice anything odd?"

"Like about the house?"

"Yeah, anything that looked like it didn't belong. Something that maybe gave you a feeling that something might be wrong."

Eric thought about it.

"No." He sighed. "I'm sorry."

"There's no need to apologize. Eric, what was your father doing?"

"Yelling out for her. Then he went upstairs."

"Did you go up with him?"

"No." Eric's face changed.

Careful.

"Why not?"

"He was really mad."

"Because you forgot your sneakers."

Eric shrugged.

"And you were afraid that your mom and dad were going to argue so you stayed downstairs."

"Yes." A small voice.

"Where were you?"

"In the living room. My mom's cell phone was on the dining-room table. I went over and got it and sat down on the couch."

Jack didn't ask why. *He probably wanted it handy in case he had to dial the police.*

"How long was your dad upstairs?"

"Not long."

Eric's eyes grew still, like someone watching a far-off twister that was moving closer.

"What is it, Eric?"

"I heard something hit the floor. Like when a person falls down. That sound."

His father's body hitting the floor. Jack gently clasped his fingers around the boy's foot and squeezed. "You okay?"

Eric's eyes blinked rapidly. He nodded.

"You hear anything else?"

"He was screaming . . . screaming at my mother."

"Your father?"

"No. Someone else."

Jack wanted to end it. *Fuck it. It wasn't worth frightening an innocent child.* But what filled Jack's mind was the image of the eight-year-old girl named

(Sidney)

Clara, sleeping peacefully, the Sandman's hand pressing a chloroform-soaked rag against her nose. Clara consumed Jack's thoughts with a fevered desperation, had talked to him during the night, and was pleading with him now: *I don't want to die. Save me, save my family.*

Jack's own sense of desperation rose, mixing with his fear and rage, all of it outweighing Eric's terror.

"Eric, do you remember anything he said?"

"He was calling her . . . bad names. My mom was crying. Told him that she was sorry."

"Sorry for what?"

"For what she did."

"What did she do?"

"It was about her . . . I . . . I . . . I went to the stairs. . . . He wouldn't stop . . . he just kept hurting her. . . . My mom was crying. My mom was crying and I wanted to help her, but I didn't because I was scared."

Eric fought back the tears. Temple shifted uncomfortably, weighing the need to step in.

Jack moved ahead. "You saw him, didn't you?"

Eric nodded. Rapid breathing.

"What did he look like?"

"I hid in the closet, downstairs," Eric said, his throat working. "I was scared. I kept it open so I could watch him. I saw him . . . I saw his face."

"Tell me what he looked like, Eric."

"His face . . . it was all red. Like someone had splashed paint on it."

Stop it. It's not worth it. What can he possibly know to help you?

Clara, her blond hair in pigtails, tied to a chair in the dark: *Help me. Please help me.*

"What did he look like, Eric?"

Eric opened his mouth to talk but no sound came out. He looked as if he were choking.

"Tell me, Eric."

Temple was up on his feet and moving.

But Eric had already slipped inside that dark envelope. "I want my mom back," he managed to say. "I want to tell her I'm sorry. I wanted to help her and I couldn't because I was afraid, I want . . . I want her back."

Temple gently pushed Jack aside. "It's okay, just relax, no more questions, isn't that right, Detective?"

Eric's body turned rigid, his eyes wide in absolute terror at the nightmare that was advancing on him. Then they rolled back into their sockets as if he had suddenly been jolted by a strong electrical current; his foot came up and knocked over the tray of orange juice and oatmeal onto the floor.

Eric's grandmother screamed, nearly fell out of her chair. Temple pinned Eric's body to the bed while his other hand reached out for the nurse's call button. Jack backed away as if locked in a trance. A sound like wind rushing through a cavern flooded his ears, and in his mind he saw

Darren Nigro at eight, on the bed and screaming at his mother, the inhuman sound roaring past his lips like an animal screeching in pain.

Darren Nigro at fourteen, out of the hospital, on medication and in therapy, slipping his head through a noose, smiling because the voices shredding his sanity are about to be forever silenced, a small step away from achieving peace.

Eric Beaumont about to embark on the same path, forever alone with voices and images and corners of his mind filled with razor-sharp hurt that will always writhe, that can never be erased with medication or therapy or words lifted from textbooks or excised from laws. He is alone, forever alone, and nothing on this earth can save him.

Clara tied to the chair, watching the scalpel move to her throat: Save me and my mom and dad, please, you're running out of time!

A peculiar thirst was gathering in the back of his throat. He was aware of Duffy gripping his arm and ushering him out into the hall, but all Jack could see and hear was a stark white hospital room and the screams of a terrorized boy who no longer belonged to this world.

chapter 61

ALAN WAS IN THE SHOWER WHEN HE HEARD THE FAX MACHINE RING. He didn't shut the water off. It would take several minutes for the file to come through.

After he toweled off and dressed, he fixed himself a Johnnie Walker on the rocks and then picked up the faxed file. It was now sometime after six. Outside, the beautiful Boston skyline was slowly giving way to dusk and a magnificent sunset. Drink in hand, he settled into a chair in front of the window and began with the formative years of the Sandman.

Gabriel LaRouche was eleven years old when he entered the Behavioral Modification Program. His mother, Susanna, a high school dropout, was working as a waitress at a truck stop in New Orleans when she discovered she was pregnant. Her boyfriend was a twenty-six-year-old heroin mule who was facing a ten-year stretch at Angola for shooting down two members of a rival biker gang inside a bar full of witnesses. Susanna was fifteen, living in a trailer she shared with her father.

A week after Gabriel turned eight, he snuck into the bedroom where his grandfather had passed out on the bed. The TV was on and the sound was loud; maybe it was a combination of cocaine and alcohol that had shut down all his senses. In any case, Dale LaRouche did not stir when his grandson slit his throat and fled into the night to find a phone to call his mother. Christmas Eve was two days away, and Gabriel wanted to give his mother her present early this year.

A judge sentenced him to a psychiatric care unit just outside of New Orleans, one that was associated with the BMP. During his stay, Gabriel tried to strangle another child to death with an electrical cord; he put a pencil through the eye of his therapist. That incident led to his transfer to Graves, a facility that had had much more success with such problematic children—and had access to more experimental means of curbing violent tendencies.

There was no mention of the actual clinical testing that Gabriel had undergone at Graves, but Dr. Larry Roth was listed as Gabriel's new psychiatrist.

Alan's mind slid away from the pages and started reviewing the list of atrocities at Graves, all the experiments that had cost lives. Then he thought of Fletcher and his attempts to expose Graves all those years ago. Now it was happening all over again. *I'll find you, Malcolm, and this time you won't get away.*

A color picture of Gabriel at eleven was attached; behind it were several computer-generated pictures of what Gabriel might look like today at age thirty-five.

The phone rang.

"Lynch."

"Alan, it's Scott Miller."

With Paul DeWitt most likely dead, Alan had placed Scott Miller, a thirty-nine-year-old member of the FBI's Computer Response Team, in charge of monitoring the BMP database. Miller had also been the one recovering the patients' names from the tape backups of the system.

"What's going on, Scott?"

"That Trojan-horse program DeWitt found on the system, the one that acts as a back door to allow Gardner to bypass the security? We left it there in case Gardner tried to log back on, and that's exactly what he did. He just got on."

Alan felt the shiver of hope. With the Sandman logged on to the database, the call could be traced back to the computer he was using; that was the reason for Miller's call. *He's traced the signal to its point of origin. He's found the Sandman.*

"Where is he?" Alan asked, grabbing a pad of paper.

"Somewhere in New London, New Hampshire. That's all I can tell you on my end because he's calling on a cellular frequency, not a regular phone line. He's going though several switching stations to prevent us from finding his exact location, but the call's coming from New London. You want his exact location, you'll need a laptop with a directional antenna. Use the technician I have standing by. The closest airport is in Manchester. You have access to the jet?"

"I'll make the call." Alan hung up and with a shaking hand dialed the director, filling him in on the recent turn of events.

"I want Hostage Rescue in on this," Lynch said. "I got a tech standing by who can lock onto the signal. We set up a perimeter and HRT moves in and extracts the Sandman, nice and neat, nobody knows a thing."

"So tell Victor, that's his job."

"I don't know where he is."

"Don't *know?* What the hell do you mean?"

"You placed him in charge of this operation. He doesn't report to me. I've been trying to reach him all day, but he won't answer his cell phone and his men have no idea where he is."

The director paused.

"The Sandman can log off any second. The longer we wait, the stronger the chance that we'll lose him."

"Okay, Alan, I'll make the call. But make no mistake. You fuck this up, you'll be moving your family to Alaska first thing tomorrow morning."

Alan hung up and called downstairs for Kenny, his driver. Operation Recover had just gone to alert status.

chapter 62

HE DIDN'T PLAN ON GETTING DRUNK. Not in that way you methodically go about dulling the bite of memories. In fact, he didn't even plan on drinking at all, but Eric Beaumont and Darren Nigro would not stop screaming.

Jack finished off the Jim Beam and placed the empty glass on the nightstand inside the Dolan bedroom. The air was hot and full of lengthening shadows. He felt strangely empty. Images and voices had come to life in his head. Safe here. Safe to let the madness run wild under the melting sun.

Evening was coming. Night would be here in a matter of hours, and the Sandman would be on his way to kill family number four.

Jack felt his desperation rising. He had come here right from the hospital. He had walked through the house. Had taken up residence in the bedroom, sinking deeper into black, his red-stained vision filled with wild, frightened eyes. Hours had passed and nothing had come to him.

Jack closed his eyes. His mind was black. A breathless darkness.

The madman is moving up the stairs to meet the fourth family.

Think. What was he overlooking? Something here in the bedroom? What?

Clara's room first. She barely stirs as the chloroform-soaked rag is pressed against her face, it's over . . .

Think, Jesus Christ, think.

The players in the theater are arranged. The scalpel is exposed and screams explode through their drug-induced haze, they are twisting and screaming. Please, God, please save me, God, I don't deserve this, please save me.

The Sandman said, *You can't save them, Jack.*

I can. I will.

By the way, nice job at the hospital. You knew the boy didn't know anything. You just went in there and used him to justify what you want to do to me. You did the same thing with Darren Nigro.

That's not true.

You may be able to lie to everyone around you, but down here, we know what you really are.

Back inside the bedroom, Jack reviewed images and dissected them. Tried forcing thought on form.

Nothing.

"Please," he said out loud. "For the love of God, give me something."

Outside, he heard the giggles of neighborhood children. One of God's own is scheduled to die.

You're going about this the wrong way, a voice said.

Jack opened his eyes. Sitting in the chair was the boy, Alex Dolan, wearing his underwear. His throat was cut, his thin body covered in blood.

This is getting you nowhere. Review the mechanics.

"The what?" Jack's tongue felt thick. Sluggish.

The mechanics. Everything the Sandman does is mechanical. You know the Sandman came in here once to set up the cameras. You know that took a good amount of time, that he would have to feel confident that no one would be home. How do you think he knew that? How did he get from point A to point B?

"He followed your family, got to know their habits and routines."

So he did that and then decided to enter the house. The first time, it was probably the middle of the day when I was at school and Dad was at work. Mom was out doing her thing, so our friend came into the house. How do you suppose he did that?

"A window in the back, maybe. A back door left open. Maybe he found a key under the mat or fake rock—the exact method doesn't strike me as important."

You're right, it's not. The important thing is that he entered. *With that in mind, let's review what we know about him. He's confident in himself—very methodical and careful.*

"Right."

So when he entered the first time, he knew *he didn't have to worry about a security system. What would he have done if an alarm went off?*

"You don't have an alarm. Neither did the Roths."

I bet Eric's parents did. Duffy told you what a violent son of a bitch the father was—an unpredictable alcoholic. The mother worried all the time about her son's safety—Eric told you that today. After she took custody, she would change the locks, sure, that's a no-brainer, but I bet she was smart enough to install an alarm system—and not a cheap one. I'm talking about one of those state-of-the-art security systems with infrared, motion detectors, wiring on the screens. How do you think the Sandman bypassed all that?

Fletcher had given Jack a new cell phone to replace the one he had tossed in the ocean. He grabbed it from the nightstand. Duffy was in.

"Did the Beaumonts own an alarm system?"

"I don't know," Duffy said.

"Find out for me. It's important."

"Where are you?"

"Call me back on my cell phone." He gave Duffy the new number.

He hung up and placed the phone on the windowsill. The sound of the clock ticking down inside his head grew louder. He was running out of time. The Sandman was preparing to meet the next family. Jack stared at the phone. *Please, God, give me something . . .*

Five minutes later, the phone rang.

"Hello, Jack."

It was the Sandman; the voice was Jack's.

"How does it feel to be talking to yourself?" the Sandman asked, his voice—Jack's voice—sounding tired and worn. "It's like having a conversation with your conscience, isn't it?"

"What do you want?"

"Your voice, it sounds desperate. Are you okay? Or did I interrupt something *naughty?"*

Jack glanced at the chair. Alex Dolan was gone.

"Your words sound slurred. I hope you're not hitting the bottle. That's what got you in trouble last time."

"What do you want?"

There was a long pause. Outside, the children's giggling grew louder.

"It's not fair," the Sandman said, his tone hurt. Pleading.

Use it. "What isn't fair?"

"You get to hunt down monsters like Charles Yerkies and play the avenger. You murder him in cold blood and love every delicious second of it, and what does the public do? It *applauds.* I hunt down the monsters that destroyed me and I'm labeled a deviant. *I'm* the one who's hunted. Why? Because I don't have a badge. Take away your talisman and you and I are exactly alike."

"Alex Dolan didn't hurt you."

"His worthless mother did. What do you know about her?"

"She was a psychiatric nurse at Graves."

"What else?"

"That's all I know."

"And that's all you'll ever know. What you can't see, what you and your federal friends will never see, is what's stained behind *my* eyes."

"Everyone's been hurt, Gabriel. You don't own a patent on suffering."

"Twice a week Veronica Dolan pumped me full of chemicals. I had seizures. Tremors. I lost control of my bowels. I begged her to stop and she didn't. Larry Roth once strapped me to a bed for six days without any food or water because I stabbed the man who was going to inject me with some new medicine and throw me into a room and monitor the side effects. I was fifteen years old. Ever had electricity shot through your testicles, Jack? Do you know what it's like to go through life without the ability to obtain an erection? You think Taylor would be with you if you had that problem?"

"Take Viagra."

"My current prescription does a better job."

"What you're doing . . . it won't erase the memories."

"But it makes the rage far more manageable. After you killed Yerkies, you wrote in your journal, 'Lies down to pleasant dreams.' There's justice in spilling blood. You looked for the moral outlines in Bryant's 'Thanatopsis' to explain away what you did. You're just like me, Jack. You and me and Miles, we've traveled through both worlds."

"Let me help you expose Graves."

Silence. *He's listening. You've got him listening.*

"Let's meet, just you and me. I give you my word I'll help you."

"You don't want to help me, Jack. You want to rip me apart with your bare hands. For what I did to Alex Dolan. For the broken road Eric Beaumont has to travel . . . alone. Like you."

Jack stared at the bloody chair where Alex Dolan once sat. "That's not true. I want to bring these people to justice."

"And they will be. But it will be *my* version of justice, much like the brand you delivered to Yerkies."

"I didn't want to kill him."

"There's a line in Dante's *Inferno* where he defines hell as that place where you crave what will kill you. That's why you're drawn to people like me. You can't stand to see it staring back at you in the mirror, so you hide your real appetites under the label of redemption."

A soft click and the Sandman was gone.

Jack slid the phone away from his ear. The Sandman's words didn't mean anything. What mattered was the fourth family. Saving them. He had to save them.

Jack stared at the floor, thought about what Alex Dolan had told him. Thought with urgency.

A moment later he saw bloody feet move across the hardwood.

Are you okay? Alex asked gently.

"I'm fine."

It's okay to admit you're not. Amanda told you that, remember?

"Yes." Jack wiped his face. "God, I miss her."

Amanda? Or do you mean Taylor?

Jack didn't respond. Alex sat on the edge of the bed. Blood ran from his feet and dripped onto the floor in small puddles.

If the Beaumonts own an alarm system, the question then becomes how he bypassed it.

"Cut the electricity—no, that would alert the alarm company. They'd do a callback, and if no one picked up, they'd send someone out to investigate."

Right. So that leaves him entering the house. If he forced his way in and the alarm was on, there's a twenty-second delay before it triggers. Not enough time to dismantle it.

"Unless he turned it off."

And how would he do that?

"He could use a device that would somehow disengage it. High-tech burglars use them. They don't come cheap."

But those items aren't foolproof. There's still a chance of detection. Besides, even if he had such a device, he'd still have to be familiar with this particular alarm system before he started. When he enters the house, he's prepared. He's confident. He knows everything about the family.

"So he knew about the alarm. About its specifics, how it was set up."

And how would he find this out without being detected?

"He's very comfortable with computers." The words came out slowly as the thought worked its way through him. "The last two bombs used laptops."

Everything in the world is now electronically stored somewhere—Fletcher found your medical records at Ocean Point. Everyone uses the Internet. Paper hardly exists anymore. Why not dial onto the company's database?

It was like touching an exposed wire; Jack nearly jumped out of his chair.

"He dialed onto the alarm company's system and obtained the alarm code. That way he could enter the house without alerting anyone."

Alex's smile was wide and bright. *A-B-C, problem solved.*

The phone rang again.

"The Beaumonts *did* have an alarm system," Duffy said. "Priority One installed it. It's a national chain. They have an office in Newton." Duffy gave him the address. "You got something good?"

Jack didn't tell him. If he did, Duffy would want to join him, and Jack needed to be alone.

"It turned out to be nothing. Sorry to have bothered you."

"No bother. I'll be around the office for another hour. After that, I'm heading straight home. Call me if you need anything."

"I will. Thanks, Duff."

"You bet."

Jack stood. Alex Dolan still sat on the edge of the bed, staring up.

"I have to go."

Not going by the rule books on this one either, are you?

"This one's different."

They're all different. Alex stared out the window at an image. All Jack could see were the kids playing across the street. Something in Alex's face had changed. He looked afraid.

"What is it?"

Today I was standing in the garden near the church. I tried the church doors but they wouldn't open. When I turned around, the flowers were gravestones. This place . . . it frightens me. I'm alone here. I keep calling out for my parents, but they won't answer me. Where are they?

"I don't know. I'm sorry."

Your daughter, Sidney, you want her to be with her mother, don't you?

"You know I do."

I want to be with my parents. I miss them. I don't want to be by myself here.

Jack didn't say anything. Alex slid off the bed and hugged him.

Make it right. It's the only way our souls can rest.

chapter 63

ON THE LAPTOP'S SCREEN JACK CASEY RAN OUT OF THE DOLAN BEDROOM. Jack's FBI friends had removed the original pinhole surveillance cameras from the house. Knowing Jack's habits, the Sandman had planted new ones.

The Sandman stared at the empty bedroom. He knew where Jack was going. It didn't worry him. He had plenty of time.

The Sandman dropped his headphones on the keyboard of the laptop computer placed next to the voice-altering/scrambling device on the passenger's seat. How did Jack find out his name? Had he shared it with the FBI? Or had the feds discovered his name and passed it on to Jack?

No. Gabriel had erased his name and anything remotely associated with Graves from the patient database. Was there another database? A backup, maybe? No. It had to be paper files. The FBI must have paper files stored in a separate, safe location. They knew about Graves and were now searching through paper records, getting the names of doctors and nurses, warning the families. The FBI would be waiting for him to strike and would then trap him.

But how had they discovered his name?

Gabriel leaned back in the driver's seat and clicked his nails against the steering wheel. People were carrying their coolers, blankets, and bags up from the beach. It seemed to all point back to the man in the truck, the one with the strange-looking eyes. Who was he? What was his connection to Jack? To the FBI? To all of this?

Gabriel thought of Dr. Brian Le Claire of Cambridge, another psychiatrist from Graves who was living in Massachusetts. For the past two nights Gabriel had watched the doctor eating take-out food alone in front of the TV, overweight and bald, the sad remains of a man whose wife had taken up with a younger, more attractive lover. Le Claire, the man responsible for using him and fifteen other children as test subjects for pesticides for a well-known German pharmaceutical company. Ten boys died of cancer. Two others suffered neurological impairments. Like

Gabriel, the remaining three suffered from severe migraines and black pockets of memory loss.

Sixteen lives used, and Le Claire was paid a handsome six-figure sum by the German company. The pesticide formula was modified and went on the market two years later. Today, the pesticide had annual revenues that stretched well into half a billion dollars.

Then there was Dr. Eliot Ashton of Austin, Texas. Eliot had injected him with several experimental concoctions. Eliot staring down at him impassively while his body was racked with seizures. Eliot, the good doctor and father of two, strapping Gabriel the boy down for another session of electroshock therapy. Gabriel could clearly remember Eliot's blank face as he flipped the switch, his apathy at the screaming and begging . . .

A mail bomb was already on its way to Le Claire. That left Eliot.

The FBI knows about Graves. Would Jack pass the information on to the feds? It didn't matter. Chances were that Le Claire was being protected—either by the FBI or by Jack's people. The mail bomb—if it wasn't intercepted—would kill Le Claire, but what to do about Eliot?

Exposing the Behavioral Modification Program and all of its atrocities was his first priority. Eliot and the others from Graves would have to wait. *Don't get too comfortable, Eliot. In time, I'm going to introduce you and your family to a whole new world of pain.*

But first, Casey.

The thing he liked about Jack was his predictability. When he got into trouble, when he needed something, he turned to his friend Mike Abrams. Mike had been smart enough not to talk about the location of the safe house on a cellular phone, but should have taken the time to get rid of the Volvo with a hidden GPS tracking unit. If Mike had dropped it for a rental or a bureau car, Gabriel knew he wouldn't be sitting here.

But luck was turning his way. God had cleared away adversity and had given him opportunity. Through Him, Gabriel could taste true justice, could feel the sweet healing relief of redemption burning through his veins. Through God, Gabriel could heal.

Now it was time to deal with Jack.

Gabriel looked to his left at the house on the corner. Several minutes later, two agents got into a Pathfinder and headed out to pick up the seafood takeout. Obviously, they had learned from Mike Abrams how Ronnie Tedesco's men had been poisoned, so the agents were taking no chances with food. This was good.

Gabriel watched the Pathfinder whisk by. He secured his patrolman's cap and left the police car. The air was hot, but not oppressive, and a pleasant wind blew past him.

Only two agents were left inside the house. Taking care of them would be easy. After the agents were dead, that would leave Taylor Burton and the little girl, Rachel.

Gabriel smiled. He couldn't wait to hear how they screamed.

chapter 64

JOSEPH RUSSELL, THE MANAGER OF THE PRIORITY ONE BRANCH IN NEWTON, HAD BEEN AT A RESTAURANT WITH A FRIEND WHEN THE DISTRICT MANAGER CALLED AND TOLD HIM TO HIGHTAIL IT OVER TO THE OFFICE TO SPEAK TO THE DETECTIVE IN CHARGE OF THE SANDMAN INVESTIGATION.

Russell sank in his chair as he listened. "Detective Casey, are you telling me the Sandman might be one of my *employees?*"

"I said it's a possibility. All I know for certain is that the Sandman gained access to your computer system and obtained the alarm code for the Beaumont home. My guess is that he hacked on to your system to retrieve it."

Russell's voice was disbelieving. "We have very strict security. First, he'd have to be *very* familiar with our system—the firewall we use, all the software and hardware used to prevent a break-in. Even if he did, he would then have to know several long strings of alphanumeric passwords, all of which change weekly—it borders on impossible."

"Let's try another approach. Say I called you and said I forgot my alarm code. Would you give it to me over the phone?"

"If you called technical assistance and provided us with the correct info, yes."

"What information would I need?"

"Your name and address, obviously. Then the standards: the information on your particular alarm system; your social security number, payment history, your credit card. It's like when you call the bank and ask to transfer money. They ask you for your account number first, and then ask you for information only you would know. We do the same thing."

"So if I was impersonating someone and knew his address, social security number, credit cards, all of it, you'd give me the code over the phone."

Russell cleared his throat. "It's not as easy as you're—"

"If I called you pretending to be Joe Smith and correctly answered all of your questions, how would you know I wasn't Joe Smith?"

Russell trembled. "Detective Casey, every security company, every bank—every *business* today operates like this." Then a new fear pinched his skin. "I'm thirty-one, I've been here for seven years, and—I just bought a house for chrissakes."

"Mr. Russell—"

"The DM will fire me. I—I can't believe this is happening."

"Mr. Russell, relax. The DM doesn't know what I just told you. You're not going to get into trouble. You're not going to get fired." *So quit your fucking whining and help me.*

Russell seemed to relax. "I'm sorry. I'm just not good with stress. Heart problems run in my family."

"I need you to help me."

"Okay."

"You mentioned technical assistance."

"Yes. What about it?"

"Does the computer keep a log of those phone calls?"

"Absolutely."

"Do you have access to them?"

"Of course."

"Then pull up the Beaumont account, one-twenty-two Parish Road in Newton. We'll start there."

Russell turned quickly in his chair and started typing.

Less than a minute later, he pointed at the screen.

"There were two calls this year. The computer accidentally billed the credit card the wrong amount this past February. Karen Beaumont called and told us of the problem, and when the same billing error happened in March, she called us again. The problem was resolved in April."

"Anything more recent?"

"That's it. Sorry."

"Is there another number she could have called?"

"For tech support? No, this is the only one."

Jack straightened. The alcohol-laced energy was gone now, leaving him drained and tired, but still fevered with desperation. What was he overlooking?

Outside the window, the day had turned to evening. Headlights ran down the street. *You're running out of time. Think.*

"This is interesting." Russell's index finger was pointing to something on a new computer screen. "On June twenty-second, at five forty-six P.M., a call was placed to our 800 line."

"I'm not following you."

"The 800 number is listed in the Yellow Pages, TV, and newspaper ads. If you want information on our alarm systems, on stuff about our company, you call the toll-free number that hooks you directly into our main office in Dallas. A customer rep comes on and answers your questions."

"Does it say what Beaumont called about?"

"No, but I can pull it up."

Russell dialed into the company's main database.

"There it is, line two, you see?" Russell pointed to the line on the screen.

The rush of excitement that coursed through Jack's veins caused his hair to stand on end.

Roger Beaumont had called the 800 number for technical assistance. There was a notation made by the customer rep, Carol R, that Roger Beaumont had forgotten his code, and since he didn't have the local number handy, he had called the toll-free number from the newspaper and TV ads; the rep provided him with the number of the branch in Newton, that had installed and monitored Karen Beaumont's alarm system.

Only I know it wasn't Roger Beaumont who called. Karen Beaumont installed the alarm because of him.

On the computer screen, in the last column, Jack saw a telephone number. It didn't match the Newton number he had seen on a previous screen. He pointed to the number and said, "How did you get that?"

"When someone calls the 800 line, an automatic caller-ID system displays the phone number of the incoming call, even if it's unlisted. Anytime you call a toll-free number—or use the Internet, for that matter—someone is collecting pieces of you to sell to direct marketers. Same is true with your credit cards. It's all perfectly legal. Phones are the worst. When you use the phone, nothing is private."

The phone number on the screen had a 603 area code; the call had come from New Hampshire.

Duffy had pored through Roger Beaumont's background. He lived in a house in Medford, Massachusetts. It was the only property Roger Beaumont owned.

The Sandman wouldn't know about the alarm company's caller-ID unit.

He called from home because he needed privacy. That way no one could overhear him, no one could watch him work on his computer. At home, he felt confident. Safe.

With the phone number, Jack could get an address.

"Could I get a printout of this?"

"No problem," Russell said. "Anything else?"

"You want to keep your name out of the papers?"

"Oh, Christ, yes."

"Then keep this information between you and me."

chapter 65

THE HOUSE WAS EASY TO FIND. With the Sandman on the BMP database, Scott Miller's technician had locked on to the cellular phone signal with the scanning device and led them here to the Sandman's hideout in New London, New Hampshire. The location was perfect—the only house at the end of the road and without any streetlights. The closest neighbor was half a mile away. The house was a three-story contemporary with sleek, angular windows, an attached three-car garage, and in the back, at least three hundred feet away from a sprawling porch, a dock that led out to a boathouse.

Alan Lynch squatted in a patch of woods high above the house. The night air was completely black, oppressively hot and buggy. He brought up his night-vision binoculars and looked at the front of the house.

All the blinds around the first-floor windows were drawn with the exception of a pair of windows at the front that contained the single and only light in the entire house. One of the blinds was drawn three-quarters, and in the space between the blind and the windowsill Alan could see an armchair, a section of a black coat arm, and next to the chair, the keyboard of a laptop computer resting on an end table.

Alan pulled the night-vision binoculars away from his eyes and wiped his sweating face on the sleeve of his camouflage shirt. The Sandman, the patient named Gabriel LaRouche, was smart to pick a secluded place like this, no neighbors watching him, seeing when he's coming and going. With the size of the house, he could store the large quantity of explosives and computer equipment he'd robbed from the San Diego building. Gardner's money had ensured LaRouche's privacy.

And had ensured the success of this mission, Alan thought. It was dark out, no neighbors around—all HRT had to do was slip in, remove LaRouche, and make their exit. The media wouldn't know that HRT had been called in to extract the Sandman. In just a few moments, the problem would be gone.

Alan felt the pressure from the past weeks start to ease. It was all working out perfectly. Life was about to be restored. In just a matter of time, he would breathe again.

But you still have to find Fletcher.

One problem at a time.

He stood up and jogged up the incline, moving across a dark road toward the side door of the black surveillance van where Frank Brungardt, the leader of the FBI's elite Hostage Rescue Team, was waiting.

Thick black cloth was hung across all the windows to keep the light from the color monitors from leaking outside. Brungardt was sitting hunched forward in front of a color terminal. He was tall and powerfully built, his cool eyes surveying a night-vision image of the front of the house. HRT was set up on both sides of the house, the images from their night-vision binoculars fed directly into the terminal. Brungardt did not look up when Alan took the seat next to him.

"Our boy doing anything different?" Alan asked.

"Negative. He's just sitting there." Brungardt's deep voice had an odd sound to it, like a man trying to speak through water. "We've got a fiber-optic glued outside that front window. He's reclining in a chair, he's watching TV, and all we can see is the back of his head and his black pants and loafers. On the table next to him is his laptop computer and cell phone."

"Has he moved?"

"No. My guess is that he nodded off."

Brungardt and the rest of HRT only knew they were about to take down the Sandman, who was responsible for the bombing of the San Diego building and the death of three families. Brungardt had no idea of LaRouche's connection to the federal research program.

"We've been watching the rest of the house with this," Brungardt said, and flipped a switch. On the console, the front of the house turned black, then was replaced with a picture of a man lying back on a recliner, his entire body glowing with blue, red, and yellow circles of heat—thermal imaging. Brungardt had picked up the Sandman's heat signature.

"We already did a thermal scan of the rest of the house," Brungardt explained. "The house's central AC is on, so it's picking up the heat signature nicely. Our boy is in there alone." He turned to Alan. "Little odd that a guy who bombed our building and is killing families could afford digs like this."

"He's stolen money. Millions."

"Well, it's worked in our favor. House like this and nobody out here to watch us, it's going to go down nice and smooth."

"You going with forced entry?"

"Too risky. The subject's an electronics expert. Out here, alone, he'd be smart to arm the front perimeter with some sort of security. He could have infrared motion detectors behind the doors or windows, maybe even hardwired the window screens to some sort of security system. He gets alerted to our presence, he even thinks that maybe something is slightly off, it gives him time to react. Worse, we have no way to know if he rigged the house to some sort of bomb."

"The house's central air system is on. Place a chemical in the vents, knock him out."

"There's still the matter of reaction time. If he feels fuzzy, maybe he sets up the house alarm, which is rigged to a bomb. This guy's heavily into explosives. He had one bomb designed to be detonated by a phone call. Who knows what he has here."

"This guy isn't suicidal."

"And I'm not taking chances with Semtex or C-4. We'll go stealth."

"Where's the entry point?"

Brungardt flipped another switch and the screen changed to a wide shot of the front of the house. He tapped a section of roof on the left.

"Right here."

"The skylight?"

"That's exactly what it is. You see that thick limb hanging over the roof? I'm going to send two guys down that limb and have them go in through that. They work their way downstairs, we give the guy a wake-up nudge, and suddenly he's looking down the twin barrels of a Heckler and Koch. He makes a move, he's a SPAM dinner."

"I need him alive."

Brungardt gave Alan his full attention. "Let's get one thing clear. If there's any chance that this guy will get off a round, I'm delivering him to the man downstairs. We clear on that?"

"I need him alive. If he's dead, my problem's not solved."

"My men come first. Not someone's political agenda. We clear on that?"

"Take it up with the director."

Brungardt studied him. "You like cigars, Al?"

"As long as they're not cheap."

"This here's a Cohiba." Brungardt handed one to him. "Light it up and suck on it. Don't open your mouth unless I tell you."

chapter 66

Special Agent George Bond had been celebrating his daughter's sixth birthday when the call came through. Now he lay on the moonlit roof and worked a glass-cutter along the remaining section of skylight. Sweat ran down the greasepaint on his face and into his eyes.

A rectangular square, large enough to fit a hand through, was now etched in the skylight. Bond replaced the cutter inside his tactical vest and tapped on the glass with the ball of his gloved fist. His left hand held a string with a suction cup. The glass broke and fell, then stopped and hung suspended. He removed it, placed the glass on the roof, reached inside, and unlocked the latch. He lifted up the skylight. Plenty of room to slip through.

The Sandman used infrared beams on one of his bombs; it was possible he was using them in a security system. Before they'd touched down at Manchester Airport, infrared detectors had been passed out to all members of HRT. Bond had fastened his to the stock of the Heckler and Koch MP-5 with two thin strips of duct tape. He slid the weapon forward and off his shoulder and pointed it inside the skylight. The LED screen on the infrared detector didn't glow once.

His partner, Jay Nelson, lay behind him. Bond gave him the thumbs-up. They were both wearing LASH microphone headsets that allowed them to talk to CP—the command post—in whispers.

"CP, the skylight is clear, over."

In their earpieces, Brungardt's voice said to them, "The subject is in his original position. We'll be tracking your movements. Proceed with caution. We'll inform you of any changes."

"Roger, CP. Over and out."

Bond slid a knife from his vest and cut an X through the screen below the skylight. Then he flipped down his night-vision goggles and the darkness dissolved into a world of lime-green light.

A queen-size bed was placed conveniently under him and the bedroom door was shut. Bond pushed his weapon around his back and slid legs-first through the screen until he was dangling over the bed. He let go and landed on the bedspread with a soft squeak of the springs. In one fluid motion he slid the weapon around and moved quietly off the bed with his finger on the trigger.

It took less than a minute for Nelson to slide through the screen and move behind him.

They'd keep a stack formation until they sighted the subject. Using the MP-5's barrel, Bond slid open the door and moved into the hallway, keeping a close eye on the infrared detector. The hallway veered off to the right; all of the doors were shut. Since the third and second floors were free of people, he did not have to bother checking rooms. With the subject the sole person inside the house, getting downstairs and securing him would be simple.

Bond moved down the carpeted hallway with deliberate care. The hot air smelled musty and stale, like a house that hadn't been lived in for months. As always, the muscles in his back and shoulders were tight, his heartbeat rapid but steady. The infrared detector remained quiet.

He saw stairs. They too were carpeted, and he listened over his earpiece as CP gave them the order to proceed. Bond descended the stairs first, paying careful attention to how his weight sounded on the boards.

Five minutes later, he stepped out onto a limestone floor. The kitchen was as wide and spacious as an apartment, and he scanned it for entrances and saw only one: a swinging door that was held open by a rubber doorstop. A blade of light sliced the section of floor by the door; the rest of the kitchen remained in darkness.

Bond flipped up his NV and moved to the door, noting the opened bottle of wine, half-eaten sandwich, and jar of Skippy peanut butter on the kitchen's island. He stopped just to the left of the door, placed his back on the wall, and slid down.

As element leader, it was his job to suggest the best mode of attack. He used the 180-degree tactical mirror from his vest, changing the angle until the subject came into view. He saw the back of a head and blond hair peeking over the top of the back of a distressed-leather chair. The TV was playing a western. The sound was turned low, but it would be loud enough to cover their footsteps. The front door was only a few feet away from Bond and he used the mirror to examine it.

Perfect. Absolutely perfect.

Over his earpiece, CP said, "Can you drop a stun grenade on him?"

Too risky, Bond thought. Given the position of the chair, the grenade wouldn't inflict the full damage, allowing the subject time to react. Bond shook his head.

From the back of the kitchen, Nelson whispered, "Negative."

Bond motioned to both of them and then pointed to a distraction device on his front jacket.

Nelson whispered, "Recommend using flash-bang and approaching the subject. Over."

"Understood. The subject is to be taken alive."

"Roger that, CP."

"What about infrared?"

Bond had already checked the front door; it looked clean, and the infrared detector hadn't glowed once. He shook his head.

"Negative."

"The rest of Gold Team will be moved into position and will be ready to assist," CP said. "Over and out."

The subject was still reclining in the chair, dividing his attention between the laptop and the TV. *Or maybe he had nodded off,* Bond thought. It was just after eleven-thirty.

Bond slid the mirror back inside his vest and motioned for Nelson to move into position.

It would be a standard stack formation at first. The noise-distraction device was a class-C explosive that would disorient the subject. By the time the device went off, Nelson would be around the chair, his weapon ready. The electricity to the house would be cut, and with the front door clear of infrared, the home security system (if there was one) would be shut off, leaving the remaining two teams to force entry inside.

Crouched low, Bond rolled out into the hallway first, the MP-5 aimed at the back of the chair, Nelson rolling out behind him. Bond's heart was pumping steadily, his mind locked with a razor-sharp focus. He removed the distraction device from his vest.

Nelson looked to him for the final signal.

Here we go, Bond thought. He yanked the pin free with his teeth and tossed the distraction device toward the fireplace. It hit the floor and then exploded.

Nelson moved up around the chair, brought his weapon to the subject's face, and clicked on the tactical light just as the power went out.

"FREEZE, DON'T MOVE!"

The subject's mouth was stretched open, frozen with a scream that was still trapped inside his throat. His eyebrows were arched up high on his forehead, his dark blue eyes staring at them in terror, his mouth a red hole. He was dressed in a black-and-white tux, not a speckle of blood on him or on the silver-wrapped box with the big white bow that rested on his lap. The man's arms were folded across his legs, his hands resting somewhere under the box.

The front door burst open, windows exploded. Agents rushed inside with their weapons drawn, their tactical lights sweeping across the walls and floor.

"What the *fuck* is this shit?" Nelson said.

Bond, his eyes riveted on the box illuminated by the tactical light, brought the handheld mike up. "CP, are you reading this?"

"Negative. We're getting a lot of static interference. What is the subject's status?"

"The subject is . . . Sir, the subject is dead. He's wearing a tuxedo and holding a gift-wrapped box. There's a folded note card on the top. Sir, I can make out part of the writing inside the card." *It looks like crayon,* Bond thought.

"Proceed forward with caution," CP said. "The box could be a bomb."

Bond checked the card for wires. Not seeing any, he picked up the card and opened it.

"CP, the card says, 'Happy anniversary, Alan. Hope you like our gift. Love, the kids at Graves.' "

The box exploded.

Bond was kicked violently backward, the wind rushing out of him. He stumbled over the table and knocked over the laptop, his mind screaming, *Gunpowder, that's all it was, not C-4 or Semtex, thank you, sweet Jesus.*

The earpiece had been knocked from his ear. CP was shouting to him, he knew, but he couldn't hear it. Confetti showered down on the chair. The air smelled of burnt gunpowder, burnt hair and skin. Through the pockets of black smoke Bond could see the man's singed hair and the black soot that covered his face. The package had burst apart; flames were eating their way through the cardboard.

Bond patted down the flames. He saw the man's charred hands and the object gripped between his mangled fingers. He stared at it. So did Nelson.

Bond pointed down his shoulder camera. This was . . . he couldn't believe what he was seeing.

"CP, the subject is holding an object between his legs. Can you see this?"

"Negative. Can you identify the object?"

"Affirmative."

"What is it?"

"It's a dildo, sir."

chapter 67

ALAN STOOD THREE FEET IN FRONT OF THE CHAIR, STARING NUMBLY AT THE TOOTHLESS BODY OF VICTOR DRAGOS. Alan's mind was devoid of any thought or emotion, as if it had simply shut down. He was vaguely aware of the HRT agents walking along the periphery of his vision, the sound of boots crunching over glass, and the droning of the crickets bleeding in through the blasted doors and windows.

The teeth were what gave it away. Over a decade ago, two cleanup men had been sent down to Malcolm Fletcher's last known hiding spot. One was found unconscious by the police but had never fully recovered. The second body remained undiscovered; the man's teeth had been mailed to Alan's home Christmas Eve. Now Victor Dragos was Malcolm Fletcher's latest victim.

Goddamn you, Victor, I told you not to go up against him alone. And how the *fuck* did Fletcher know about Dragos?

The director had informed Victor about the Behavioral Modification Program, the computer break-in on the patient database, and that back-door Trojan-horse program LaRouche had created to bypass the security. When LaRouche tried to enter the patient database again, the call would be traced. Victor must have let all this out during his . . . session with Fletcher.

Now you're back to square one. LaRouche is still free with the evidence to bury you, and you still *have to deal with Fletcher.* Where the fuck was he hiding?

Members of HRT surrounded Alan, waiting for an explanation. A laptop computer lay on the floor, a patient file on its screen. The screen switched to another patient file . . . then another. A disc was in the drive.

Probably a program to type in keystrokes, Alan thought. *With Victor dead, the program would make it look like Victor was actually typing. It kept him on the system all this time and led us straight here, Fletcher, you son of a bitch . . .*

Frank Brungardt came up and stared at Dragos's body.

"If he was dead, how did you get a heat signature?" Alan asked.

Brungardt rolled up a pant leg. Taped against the fine blond hairs on the white, waxy skin of Dragos's leg were several heating packs, the kind skiers and hikers slip into their gloves or boots to keep warm.

"They're all over his body," Brungardt said. "Whoever did this must have done it recently. The heat in those packs is only good for four hours."

Brungardt handed the note card to Alan. It was singed along the edges, but the crayoned words written by a child were clear.

"You want to explain this?"

"I have no idea," Alan said.

"That right? How about the dude in the chair? You know him?"

Paris's fuckup, Alan thought. Paris wanted to have Victor handle it and Victor went ahead and did it after being warned, so *fuck* it.

"Victor Dragos," Alan said. "He's one of us."

"What the fuck is he doing up here?"

"I haven't the foggiest idea."

"You don't keep track of your men?"

"He isn't one of my men."

"Then who is he?"

"A government assassin."

Brungardt stepped back, got in Alan's face. "You trying to pull my crank?"

"You asked the question, I gave you the answer. You don't like it, too fucking bad."

"If I were you, Al, I'd can the attitude when you talk to our boss, especially when you tell him how HRT was called in to recover a dildo." Agents stifled their laughter. Alan's beeper went off.

"I wonder who that could be," Brungardt said. "You want to use the phone in the van? I'd like to sit in on this."

"Why don't you and your boys wrap it up here."

"You sure you don't want us to stick around? There might be a blowup doll that needs CPR."

Alan felt his skin flush with embarrassment. He moved out the front door.

The road leading back to his car was pitch-black. He moved quickly, the beginning of one pisser of a migraine already set inside his temples. All he could see were the stares from the HRT agents and Brungardt's shit-eating grin. By tomorrow, the story of how Alan Lynch had called in Hostage Rescue to retrieve a dildo from a dead man dressed in a tuxedo would be all over Quantico. It had legendary proportions.

Not that he would be around much longer. Paris would use this against him and bump him off ISU, maybe even drop him altogether.

Well, he wasn't going to give that tight-assed prick the chance. After he found LaRouche and the evidence on the program, it would be time for early retirement. He was sick of being Paris's pincushion. Fuck Paris. Fuck *all* this shit. Time to enjoy the good life. He had been doing this shit for far too long.

The stores along the main street of the college town were dark and quiet under the pale yellow glow of the streetlights. He walked into the church parking lot and saw his van, the only vehicle here, sitting dark and quiet under the sprawling branches of a maple tree.

The side door of the van was locked, but the passenger's door was open, and when the interior light popped on, sitting on the driver's seat he saw a phone along with a Post-it note from Kenny that said he had gone off to a filling station for food and coffee.

Alan climbed inside. He was about to reach over for the phone when he thought about Paris. *Fuck you, Harry. Sit there and let it twist in your stomach.*

Outside the window, a blue truck pulled into an Exxon gas station on his left, probably where Kenny was. A college-age kid got out and went inside. To be that young again, Alan thought. To have that freedom and think you held the world by the balls.

The kid started pumping gas. Alan replayed some of the pleasant memories from his college days, thinking that the black line that ran swiftly down his vision was nothing more than his exhaustion. By the time he blinked, the rope was already wrapped around his throat and squeezing him back into the headrest.

It happened lightning quick, and by the time the thought of what was going on had sunk in, his vision had melted away in a watery blur, his strength leaving him like air hissing from a tire. Through the panic, a voice called out to him: *You still got time, do something!*

Alan reached out for the door handle, his face burning with pressure, as if it were going to explode. His fingers brushed against the handle. *Come on . . . come on . . .*

One shot, you got one shot to get out of this or it's over.

He pushed himself forward. He had gripped the handle when the intruder yanked him back into the headrest. His eyes searched frantically for anything that he could use as a weapon.

But it was too late. His strength had left him in a horrifying rush. The world around him was quickly turning black. His body went limp. Powerless now, lights off, good night, folks.

A part of him felt relieved. God, how he just wanted to sleep. A final tug of rope, fuck it, he didn't care anymore, he surrendered to the dark silence with a blessed calm, vaguely aware that he was being yanked backward between the two seats and onto the table where he and Victor had watched the bomb technicians lumber into the Beaumont home. Through the window he saw the truck pulling out of the filling station. *Kenny,* he thought dreamily. *Kenny is coming back. Kenny will save me, thank God, all I have to do is hang on, thank you, Kenny.*

The rope eased up. Alan wanted to touch his neck but his arms wouldn't move. He breathed deeply and winced, as if the air were full of acid. His vision brightened. He could see the roof of the van.

A shadow of a man's face moved across his vision. Alan could feel breath across his face, made out the strange black eyes.

"Hello, *Alan.*"

Words were buried somewhere in Alan's chest. His mouth worked like a fish's.

"You'll have plenty of time for babbling later. Right now I suggest you rest. You're going to need your energy to survive the ride."

Malcolm Fletcher snapped the rope tight. Alan Lynch felt himself tumbling through a starless sky, his body stretched out to the wind, dark waters awaiting below him. The last thing he saw before he blacked out was Malcolm Fletcher staring at the glowing screen of a pager.

chapter 68

EPPING WAS TYPICAL OF MANY NEW HAMPSHIRE TOWNS. Roads had been paved through what had once been nothing more than dense woods of pine trees. Each of the house plots that lined the road were somewhere between three to five acres, but only an acre or so had been cleared for the modest homes themselves.

Shady Hill Road was no exception. A mile long, it contained only six homes, all of them Colonials separated by enough space to give the occupants privacy and the illusion they were living alone in the woods.

Jack pulled the Porsche over to the side of the road, killed the lights and ignition. House number six was white, cedar-shingled, set back from the street and shaded by pines and maples.

Someone was home. Several lights were on and the shades were drawn.

The phone number along with a second number for Internet service had been issued to Martin Tobasky on May 3. The order for the second outlet was canceled, the notation read, because the customer discovered that his local cable company offered a DSL line. That line, the rep from the cable company stated, was installed on May 10; the name on the bill was also Martin Tobasky. Both bills were paid by a Citibank MasterCard.

Jack sat back in his seat. He had just paged Fletcher with the news of the address. Fletcher would call him back at any moment.

But Jack didn't want to wait. Sitting in the car wouldn't

(make things right)

do any good. What if the Sandman moved from the house? How was Jack going to tail him without being spotted? There was no way. Calling in the police was out of the question. Bring the Sandman into custody and the FBI would wipe him out, the only person who had the ability to cripple them.

He's in there, alone. Nobody knows you're here except Fletcher. You know what you have to do.

A voice told him to wait for Fletcher. Jack took his cell phone, making sure it was turned off, and left the car.

Jack stood in front of the screen door. The door behind it was ajar;

there was no home-security-system sticker, which surprised him. The Sandman would take precautions if he was storing a large amount of explosives. *Or maybe he's arrogant enough to believe he's protected out here in the woods.* It had worked for Fletcher, who had been on the run for years and didn't own a security system.

A TV was tuned to a baseball game. Jack could hear the crowd cheer. He reached out for the doorbell

Eric Beaumont lying under the bed covered in his mother's blood.

Eric back in a coma in his hospital bed.

Darren Nigro

(Eric)

fitting the belt securely around his neck, no choice, he didn't ask for the pain, he had no choice because this was the only way to make the pain go away so he jumped.

and instead opened the screen door slowly and slipped inside. A set of stairs was to his immediate right. A foyer ran past the stairs and to a hallway leading to a dimly lit kitchen. From where he was standing, he could see a beer cooler on top of the island counter and windows overlooking part of a deck.

Jack went into the kitchen. On the island table next to the beer cooler was a plate with a serrated butcher's knife.

Go ahead. Grab it. You don't want to use the gun, do you?

"Drive in the run," a voice said from the living room. It was deep and nasal—unlike any of the Sandman's voices Jack had heard. *His real voice?* "You're getting paid eight mil a year, so earn your money for once, you piece of shit."

The Sandman was sitting somewhere behind the wall. Seeing the knife, he would have time to react, maybe to grab a weapon. But if he saw the gun, he'd freeze.

You can always come back for the knife.

Jack removed his Beretta, cocked back the trigger. He moved to the wall that separated the kitchen and the living room. The Sandman was talking to the TV. Bat met ball. The crowd roared.

Wait for Fletcher.

No, do it NOW.

Jack turned the corner and moved into the living room, the gun drawn.

A man with a blond buzz cut was sitting in a chair in front of a narrow table. When he saw Jack, a beer bottle slipped from his fingers.

"Get those hands up!" Jack's voice sounded strangely distant to his own ears.

The man's hands went up quickly, his face turning white with shock.

He wore a pair of blue shorts and a white T-shirt with the words COED NAKED WEIGHTLIFTING on the breast pocket. The upper half of his body was thick with muscle, and his face and arms were bright with a fresh sunburn.

Jack saw no weapon in immediate view—but a weapon could be resting on the man's lap.

Jack moved across the living room to come full face with his tormentor.

A wheelchair. The man was in a wheelchair.

Trap, it could be a trap.

"Take whatever you want, I've never seen your face, I'm not going to call the cops," the man said, his voice breaking.

"You Martin Tobasky?"

"No."

"Where is he?"

"Damned if I know. The guy's traveling. France, I think. This is his house. I'm renting it for the summer. Look, man, I don't know what's going on—"

"You got ID?"

"In my wallet, in my back pocket."

Jack circled the wheelchair. "You move, I'm pressing the trigger."

"It's your script, man. I don't want no problems."

Jack worked the wallet from the man's back pocket and slid all of the plastic cards onto the floor. The man's name was Matt Windham. His New Hampshire driver's license had been issued in March with this house listed as the address. The American Express and Mobil gas cards were also in his name; they had been issued to him four years ago.

Jack didn't place much stock in what he was seeing. Licenses and plastic were simple items to obtain. Using the gun, he pressed the man's head against the table.

"How long have you been paralyzed?"

"Next month will be my one-year anniversary."

"What happened?" Jack reached into his pants pocket for his Swiss Army knife.

"I was on a Jet Ski, collided with my buddy. My head landed on a rock. I got no feeling from the waist down."

"Your license is new."

"I moved up here from Delaware. I grew up around here."

Jack stuck the blade in the man's thigh; Matt Windham didn't register any pain, just kept talking.

"I needed to get away from the accident, to sort my head out, so I came back up here. My folks told me about a guy who was renting out his house for eight months—that's the guy you want to talk to, Marty."

Jack stuck the knife's blade in the calf, moved it. Matt Windham kept on talking, not registering any pain at all. *This can't be right.*

"This guy Marty, he told me he wanted two bills a month for rent and to keep the house clean, and when I heard that, I jumped on it. This was in February. I sent him a check here to this address. At the end of March, I got on a plane and my folks moved me in here. I've never even seen the guy."

Jack put the knife back in his pocket, his heart sinking. *Something's wrong. This guy should be the Sandman.* Has *to be.*

It's a trap.

The Sandman had no way to know about the caller-ID unit. He had called from this house.

But this is the wrong guy.

Jack looked around the room, looked back at Windham. Jack felt light-headed. *What the fuck am I overlooking?*

"Where do you send your rent checks?"

"To a PO box. The address is taped to the refrigerator. My checkbook's in the kitchen too, right next to the toaster, if you want to take a look."

Jack stuck the gun in his belt and backed up.

"I'm sorry."

"You come charging into a guy's house with a gun and that's all you got to say?"

Jack's adrenaline rush had evaporated. His body felt spent, like that of a man who had just finished running a marathon. He took in several deep breaths. Matt Windham had wheeled himself into the center of the living room.

"Has Tobasky been back in the area?" Jack asked.

"If he has, it's news to me."

"How long has he lived here?"

"Couldn't tell you."

"What *can* you tell me?"

"I told you everything already. I'm just the guy renting this place for the summer."

"I don't blame you for being upset, but this is important."

Windham spread out his hands, palms up. "I don't know what else to tell you. You want me to make something up?"

Jack stared at the man. Windham's body . . . it was *vibrating.*

It's just the adrenaline rush. You're exhausted and it's finally catching up with you. Jack wiped sweat away from his eyes, trying to refocus. The outlines of Windham's body started bleeding color.

"What's with you?" Windham asked.

This is some sort of post–traumatic stress reaction. Just relax and keep breathing.

Yes. A rational explanation. Breathe.

Then another voice, alarmed, starting to panic: *No. This isn't right . . .*

Windham's body now seemed to be shaking like a man caught in an earthquake. Jack stumbled, grabbing the couch arm for balance. The room dimmed.

Windham wheeled over to him. "Hey, you're not looking so good. I'll call you an ambulance."

Jack reached for his cell phone in his back pocket and his legs gave out. He tried to bring his arms up to cushion the fall, but they wouldn't respond. His chest and face slammed against the carpet. He couldn't move. He was paralyzed, about to sink into unconsciousness.

No . . . No, not again . . .

His left eye tried to focus on Windham, who had wheeled around. He picked up the phone.

"Hang tight, man, Jesus Christ, don't die on me, Christ."

Jack opened his mouth to speak. Black spots bled across his vision. Sinking now . . .

Fight it! Don't give in to it, fight it!

Sinking . . .

Behind him, coming from inside the kitchen, he heard the sound of approaching footsteps.

"Phil! Jesus, Phil, I'm fucking glad you're here," Windham said. "Help me move this guy up."

The footsteps stopped behind Jack's head.

"This guy's got a gun," the man called Phil said.

"I know. He's looking for Tobasky, not me. Jesus, Phil, help him up."

Jack's gun was pulled from his belt. A sick feeling exploded inside his gut. His eyes slid over to Windham.

"You remember last week when I told you about that new treatment they have for paralysis?" Phil asked.

"What about it?"

A gunshot blew apart the back of Windham's head like a watermelon.

chapter 69

IT WAS LIKE RISING OUT OF OBLIVION. At first there were no sounds, no memories of who he was—just a dull, distant throb somewhere in the blackness, a throb slowly closing in on him and growing in intensity. Then sensations reappeared. The dryness of his throat. His whiskers digging into the skin of his chest. The saliva pooling under his tongue.

Opening his eyes was a major effort. At first they wouldn't respond, and when they finally did, all he could see was darkness. He felt coarseness against his forehead and a tightness around his throat. Something was over his head—a burlap bag, judging by the feel of it.

The chemical haze was starting to dissipate, but fear was still far away, and so was panic. Jack moved his head. A railroad spike of pain slammed into his forehead. He moaned.

"Just relax, take a few breaths, and it will pass," a voice said. "You know the routine."

Phil, yes, that was the name. That was what Matt Windham had called him before . . .

The pain slamming inside his head had been there one other time: when he woke up tied to a chair in his bedroom and saw Miles Hamilton standing next to his terrorized wife.

Now fear moved through him, strong enough to punch its way through the chemical haze.

Calm, stay calm and focused.

"When I went to visit Miles, he gave me the combination to a safe in one of his family's beachfront homes," the Sandman said. "I found a whole lot of surprises there, including that special chemical compound he created just for you in Virginia. I applied a generous amount to the doorknob, and just like we expected, you stuck to the script. Miles told me you were a creature of habit."

The voice was coming from in front of him. *Good,* Jack thought, and traced his fingers along the nylon rope that bound his wrists to his ankles. His fingernails clicked against the heel of his boot. *Thank God.* He was still wearing the boots Fletcher had given him.

"I think it's time we met face-to-face, Jack. But first, the appropriate music to capture the mood of this momentous occasion."

Ravel's *Rapsodie Espagnole* exploded through the room. Amanda had played it often. Miles Hamilton had played it just before he slit her throat.

Miles waves the scalpel to the music like a conductor. With his other gloved hand, he runs his fingers through Amanda's hair the way a lover would, and then moves his hand under her chin. Amanda's sobs are muted by the duct tape over her mouth, her nostrils wide as she sucks in air, the absolute terror in her eyes as sharp as a dagger.

He moves the scalpel closer to her throat. Jack's gaze shifts up. Hamilton's icy blue eyes are glazed over, distant—a man enraptured by a distant ecstasy.

"How does it feel to be standing on the edge of destruction, to be helpless, so alone, your life, your emotions, everything *you love and are—your* destiny *in the hands of a nineteen-year-old* boy?"

Jack struggles against his constraints like a rabid animal caught in a trap. All he can see is Amanda, all he can see in his mind is the baby, their baby, JESUS CHRIST PLEASE COME HELP ME.

You're reliving it again, a voice from far away says. *You have to stop—*

"Ever hear a soul drown?" Hamilton asks. "I have. It's wonderful. Here. Have a listen." He peels back the tape from Amanda's mouth. Her trapped scream explodes against his ear.

"Please," Amanda begs. "I'm pregnant. My baby, please don't hurt my baby."

"Take me," Jack says, the words trapped behind the tape. He wants to bargain with Hamilton, to trade information and knowledge for Amanda's life, but he can't because of the FUCKING TAPE.

"Don't worry, Jack, I have no plans to kill you," Hamilton says. "I want you to drift through your remaining days and always think of this moment. You'll never be able to escape it. Every second of your life will be a struggle to keep yourself from drowning."

*(*CONCENTRATE. *You've got the* BOOT.*)*

Amanda screams, her body shaking. Jack can't look at her.

She begs one last time.

"Your baby isn't going to be a part of this world," Hamilton whispers to her. He places his other hand on her round belly, and with a smile winks at Jack like a friend sharing a dark secret. "After I slit her throat, the baby will slowly suffocate, Jack. Think about that. Think about that as your wife and child lie at your feet, dying.

"Watch closely, Jack. Watch as I destroy your world."

The bag was ripped off his head. Jack was face-to-face with Gabriel LaRouche.

The Sandman looked like the kind of clown who would inhabit a child's nightmare. His gaunt face, wide, bare chest that was bulging with muscles and cords of veins, and his massive shoulders were all painted black. His short hair was dyed black and spiked up high on his head, and his jeans and boots were also black. He stood six feet away from the chair with his arms outstretched and palms up in a wave of approval, like a stage performer basking in the glow of his performance. Behind him, set up on tables next to the rotted walls, were dozens of candles.

The Sandman smiled. His teeth were red. Ghoulish.

"What do you think?"

Jack didn't answer. He blinked several times and tried breaking free, fighting off the images in his head that seemed to be alive in the room and advancing. Then the room came into a sharper focus. He was tied to a swivel desk chair. His shirt had been removed. *Why?* he thought, alarmed. A ceiling fan spun above him. To his left was a table holding the stereo, the open windows beyond it dark. *Where the hell am I?* He doubted he was anywhere near the house in Epping, New Hampshire. *How did he know I was coming to the house?*

Another trap and you walked right into it.

"It's a little theatrical, I know." The Sandman leaned his face forward, less than a foot from Jack's. "It's like looking at yourself in the mirror, isn't it?"

Don't feed into the fear, that's what he wants.

"The only thing I see is a man who's seriously disturbed."

The Sandman laughed. "You frequently travel into the heart of darkness and each time you come away claiming to be nothing more than a transitory visitor. I love it, Jack, I *love it.*"

The Sandman dropped to his knees on the floor and placed his folded hands on Jack's lap, like a man kneeling before an altar waiting to receive Communion. Black contacts covered his natural eye color. Jack felt as if he were staring down into a pair of dark tunnels.

"Pretend all you want, but I can hear the hunger in your voice, Jack. It's singing inside your blood right now. If I untied you, we both know what you would try to do to me."

The rope around Jack's wrists was tight. With his eyes on the Sandman, Jack turned his hands around, the rope tearing into his skin. He felt around the soles of his boots, felt what he was looking for. *Thank God, oh thank God he didn't find it.* The relief was as life-giving as water across a parched throat. All Jack had to do was to keep the Sandman's attention occupied.

The Sandman moved in and cupped one hand on Jack's chest. "You and I, our hearts beat with the same purpose. After you killed Yerkies, didn't you sleep like a baby?"

Behind the Sandman was an opened door that led to a hallway. Flames from the candlelight in the room lit up part of the hallway stairs.

"Look at me, Jack."

He did, but his eyes focused inward. *All you have to do is slide the knife from the heel of your boot and cut through the rope and your hands will be free. The Sandman doesn't have a weapon in his hands. This close, you can cut his throat.* Jack kept replaying the image, that peculiar thirst on the back of his throat building.

"It's a siren song the way it calls you, unrelenting and maddening in its desire. It's almost hypnotic, isn't it?"

Say something. Keep him off-balance and his attention away from your hands.

"We know who you are." Jack moved his fingers into the groove on the boot's heel. "We know where you live and what you look like. We know everything about you, and in a few minutes, this place is going to be swarming with agents."

The Sandman smiled. "Jack, Jack, Jack. You and I both know you're here alone. And even if what you're saying is true, we're miles away from Epping. It's time for you to embrace the truth, Jack. It's the only way you can save yourself."

The Sandman stood up and went to reach behind the chair. *Shit.* Quickly, Jack let go of his boot. The Sandman turned Jack's chair away from the hallway slightly to the right.

A TV with a VCR was set up on a desk. Jack felt the Sandman place his chin on Jack's shoulder, the breath steady against his ear. Denim brushed against his fingers, near the boot. *I've got to get him out from behind the chair.*

The screen clicked on. Ravel played in the background.

"Watch this," the Sandman whispered.

The footage had been taken earlier that day. Jack saw himself sitting in Dolan's chair, drinking Jim Beam. Saw himself staring at the bloody chairs at the foot of the bed and talking to the invisible presence that stood behind them.

"I took the liberty of replacing the cameras you removed," the Sandman said. "As you can see, the picture quality is remarkable. So's the sound. So good in fact that when you called Duffy and asked for the name of the Beaumonts' home-security company, I could almost hear him say Priority One."

For a moment all Jack could hear was music and the sound of his voice from the TV. Getting angry that the Sandman had outwitted him again was useless. What mattered now was getting him out from behind the chair. *Stay calm and stay focused and you'll get out of this.*

"Always getting so close. Discovering the house alarm and then figuring out how I found the code—ingenious. So *you.*" A small laugh. "The day I was at Matt Windham's house and made that call to the alarm company, I honestly wouldn't have even known about the ID unit that logged my call unless I heard you talking about it. But that's the beauty of technology. Someone's always watching you."

Jack tried to lean forward, away from the Sandman's heavy breath and the oily fingers digging into his skin. The Sandman eased him back into the chair.

"Don't be ashamed, Jack. Not only do I understand your deviant ways, I applaud them. But the public's reaction? I don't think they have the stamina to stomach such a sight being played on the evening news. The public doesn't understand the appetites of men like ourselves. You think the Hamilton affair made you a celebrity, wait until they see this. There won't be a hole on the planet where you can hide your face. But I'm more worried about Taylor's reaction."

Jack kept his face blank. All he needed was a minute, maybe more, and then he could even the playing field. But he couldn't do that with the Sandman behind him.

"No reaction?" the Sandman asked.

"This doesn't change anything."

"Maybe this will get your heart racing."

Again the Sandman turned the chair to the right.

Jack was now staring at the bound figure of Taylor Burton.

chapter 70

TAYLOR'S HANDS WERE PINNED BEHIND AN ORANGE SWIVEL CHAIR AND BOUND TO HER ANKLES WITH DUCT TAPE. Black electrician's tape had been fitted around her mouth and head. She was staring at Jack, her eyes

(Amanda's eyes)

frightened and shocked, confused and hurt. Dark pockets of sweat had gathered under the arms of her gray T-shirt.

The Sandman moved behind, pried the tape from her mouth, and pulled it down on her chin. She sucked in air while he draped his black-painted arms over her shoulders. Taylor stiffened, her lips pursed together tightly to imprison the frightened sounds trying to escape.

Jack lurched forward. The casters bounced back on the floor.

"That's the spirit," the Sandman said. He knelt down on one knee behind her. He turned back to Taylor, ran his tongue up her cheek and forehead, his eyes pinned on Jack the entire time.

"You can taste the fear. Imagine how it will taste when I kill her."

Taylor's thin composure broke. Sobs rocked through her body, the sound caged behind her tightly pressed lips.

"I know how upsetting this must be," the Sandman said in a soothing voice. "To discover that the man you love, the man you *fuck,* is a mental deviant is bad enough, but to find out that he placed you right here in my arms, well, we both know what that means, don't we?" He gave her a consoling kiss on the cheek and whispered, "He can't help it, Taylor. It's who he is."

Jack pushed his fear back and concentrated on his boot. He found the groove in the sole and pulled the knife free. *Careful, that's it, don't drop it . . .* With his left hand he gripped the rope around his ankles and maneuvered the knife around to start cutting. The blade was sharp; two sawing motions and the pressure around his ankles started to ease.

The Sandman cupped Taylor's breasts with both hands and squeezed.

"To give this up all for a chance at redemption in the blood trade. You're a sick man, Jack Casey. Sick *and* disturbed."

Keep his attention on your face and look afraid. And be careful of the rope. If a strand falls to the floor and he sees it, he'll kill Taylor first.

"Maybe I should sample the goods myself." The Sandman gave Taylor's breasts another squeeze. "I'm in a lot of pain, Taylor. Maybe you can heal me the way you healed Jack. We'll fuck and I'll let Jack watch so he can give me some pointers."

"Please," she begged. "Please . . . stop."

"Oh, come on. It shouldn't bother you. I've watched you two go at it that time out on the balcony. I *know* you're not shy.

"You and I know Jack was only fucking you. In his mind, he was making love to his dead wife. How does it feel to be used?"

Taylor looked at Jack with Amanda's expression: the hope and belief that he possessed the solution that would rescue her. *Only this time I can,* he thought. *This time I stacked the odds in my favor.* He continued to cut.

"Jack, please." The words were wet, clogged. Tears ran down her cheeks. "Please . . . Do something."

That's it, Taylor. Keep crying. That's what he wants. Let him think he's in control.

Another strip of rope broke free. He could feel the blood returning to his ankles and feet.

"You're awfully quiet, Jack," the Sandman said.

"What do you want me to say?"

"How about a little begging? Surely you begged for Amanda's life. Or isn't Taylor worth it?"

Jack had to stall for time. The only way to do it was to gamble. "I'm not going to beg."

"You want her to die?"

"You're going to kill her anyway."

"Tell her how sorry you are for doing this. That it's your fault."

"No."

"Don't you want her to carry your apologies into the ground?"

"I'm not going to play your game."

"Jack had the opportunity to arrest Miles Hamilton," the Sandman told Taylor. "Do you know why he didn't? Because your boyfriend wanted time to create the perfect setting in which he could indulge his deviant appetites. What he should have been concerned with was taking the proper legal course of action. If he had, his wife would be alive today. So would you, Taylor. You wouldn't be moments away from a horrible, violent death."

Taylor bucked against her chair, almost falling down. The Sandman grabbed her, pushed her back against his chest with a laugh. Jack started to saw through the rope wrapped around his wrists. He gripped the severed pieces in his hands to keep them from falling.

The Sandman stood up and stared at him curiously.

Shit. Jack's body stiffened.

Keep him away. If he finds out—

Tell him something, quick.

"Let her go and I'll give you the evidence on Graves and the Behavioral Modification Program." Jack's hands were sweating. The knife felt loose in his fingers.

"All the evidence I need is right down the hall."

The Sandman brought up his right hand. He held a scalpel. "Recognize this, Jack?"

Jack's breath left him like a gunshot, his blood running still as he stared at the black spots and lines on the blade. It was dried blood—*Amanda's* blood.

Jack felt the knife slide between his sweaty fingers. He gripped it and his attention snapped back to the Sandman, who was standing behind Taylor, the scalpel hidden from her view.

"That's right. It's the same one Miles used to kill Amanda and your baby. He told me where to find it. Say, did you ever find out if the baby was a boy or a girl?"

Taylor tried to look behind her, couldn't. She looked at Jack. Memories circled him like sharks, looming closer. *Hurry!* he thought. *You have to HURRY, he's going to kill her NOW.* He worked the blade quicker and felt the tip tear deep into his skin. His face pinched slightly from the pain.

The Sandman yanked Taylor back against his stomach by her hair. He moved the scalpel to her throat. "Beg for your life."

A memory lunged at him, sank its teeth deep into his heart: the scalpel on Amanda's throat. Amanda begging. *Please, Jack. Please make him stop.* Hamilton laughing.

Jack blinked it away, frantically working the knife. Control was starting to slip away from him. How much rope was left? *I don't know, but you better cut through all of it right now because he's going to kill her, you only have a few seconds left. Hurry, Jack, for the love of Christ, YOU NEED TO HURRY!*

Panic was chewing through his composure. He felt as if someone was pulling him underwater.

"Beg," the Sandman said again.

"Taylor, don't say anything," Jack said.

"Beg or I'll cut your tongue out," the Sandman said. "Then I'll cauterize it with a blowtorch. You want a blowtorch in your mouth, Taylor?"

Taylor clamped her mouth shut, her body rocking from her sobs. Jack cut through more rope; he could feel the pressure around his wrists start to lessen.

The Sandman swiped the scalpel across her cheek. Taylor let out a cry of pain. The line remained white for a moment, then started to bleed. The Sandman ran three fingers up the wound and then licked them.

"Doesn't quite have that sweet taste the other families did. I don't think the reality of your situation has set in yet. Eric Beaumont's mother suffered from the same problem." The Sandman snapped his fingers. "Wait, I have just the right ingredient."

The Sandman disappeared out the door behind Taylor. Jack heard footsteps fade.

"Taylor," Jack whispered.

She had her head tilted down on her chest, sobbing.

"Taylor, look at me."

Her head tilted up. Her eyes were puffy and wet, her hair pasted to her sweaty face. But it was the desolate look in her eyes that made him want to scream.

"I'll get you out of this, I promise."

"Please," she whimpered. "Please, Jack."

"Just hang on."

But she had retreated into her fear. "I don't want to die like this . . . please . . . please, Jack, do something . . ."

Jack, his heart pounding high in his chest, was still sawing through the rope and duct tape.

Then he heard the squeaky sound of chair wheels moving across carpet. The Sandman reappeared in the doorway behind Taylor and pushed another chair into the room.

It was Rachel.

Jesus, no . . .

NOW, GET IT DONE NOW.

Rachel's body was absolutely still, her eyes vacant and focused on a safe place miles way from the horror surrounding her. Then she saw her aunt. The strip of duct tape across Rachel's mouth stifled her cry, but it was loud enough to cause Taylor to look up.

Her mouth dropped open in shock, and for a brief moment she looked puzzled at Rachel's presence. Then the truth of what she was seeing hit her, and she began to wail, a gut-wrenching sound roaring past her lips.

"No, not her, not her!" Taylor thrashed against the tape binding her to the chair, her face turning a dark red. *"Not her not her please not her PLEASE!"*

"Now *that's* more like it," the Sandman said. He pushed Rachel's chair until it faced Jack and he felt her feet touch his knees.

The Sandman, smiling, stood behind Rachel. Jack stared into the black holes, and like a freight train passing by, he saw the past weeks in fast-forward frames: the explosion of the Roth home; pulling Eric Beaumont from under the bed, jumping in the pool; Eric's mind held captive by real nightmares—Rachel awaiting the same fate now, unable to help her, the damage done. His mind slowed when it showed Taylor pounding on the windshield of the Expedition. The pictures of her dead on the autopsy table. Taylor holding Amanda's diamond ring and a copy of his journal, Taylor shutting the bathroom door on him, shutting the door on their life together, all of it gone now, irrecoverable, because of the man with the black eyes and wide smile standing in front of him.

Jack cut even faster, feeling the knife digging into his skin, not caring. His blood was making the knife slippery. *Don't drop it, you only got one shot at this, don't—*

Tick, tick, tick.

The Sandman knelt down next to Rachel. He peeled away the strip of duct tape from her mouth, his eyes fastened on Jack the entire time. Taylor's screams rattled through Jack's skull like an earthquake.

"Please, God . . . God, no," Taylor pleaded.

"God doesn't exist in this room," the Sandman said. "But I do."

"Please . . . Uncle Jack." Rachel's words came in forced bursts of air. Her eyes were watering. The corner of her mouth twitched. "Please . . . don't let the bad man hurt me, Uncle Jack."

The sound of her voice was like shards of glass tearing through his soul. His vision filled with a wet light. He tried to force it back and couldn't. Their lives were hanging by a thread and he had to hurry, it was up to him again to save them both. Jesus Christ, hang on, just a few seconds more.

"Want a taste, Jack? You haven't lived until you've tasted the fear of a child."

You have to get him close to you.

"I'll do whatever you want, just stop," Jack said.

"Somehow I doubt your sincerity."

"I'm begging you."

Behind the Sandman, a shadow moved along the ceiling.

"You have no one to blame but yourself for what's about to happen next," the Sandman said. "I want you to remember that when you're standing over their graves." He pulled a remote control from his waist pocket and pointed it at the stereo. "Sorry, honey, I'm all out of *Barney.*" He winked at Jack. When the Sandman turned his head, he was looking into the muzzle of a Glock.

Malcolm Fletcher cocked back the trigger.

"My, my, Gabriel. What a sick little shit you've become."

chapter 71

"WHY, IT'S JACK'S GUARDIAN ANGEL." the Sandman's tone was smooth, radiating a confidence that alarmed Jack. "How did you find us?"

"A tracking unit in Jack's boot. You're not the only one with toys. Now be a good boy and get away from the girl."

The Sandman dropped the scalpel.

Jack cut through the remaining section of rope. His hands were free. He could move now. In his mind he saw himself leaping off the chair and grabbing the Sandman by the throat. But the Sandman's smile, the way he was holding the stereo's remote control, gave Jack pause. *Why is he acting so confident?*

The Sandman's thumb pressed a button.

"Oh, no. I accidentally initiated the bomb."

Fletcher grabbed the Sandman's wrist.

"I wouldn't do that," the Sandman said. "My thumb's already on the button. Just a slight press and I'll blow us all to the moon."

Jack looked at Fletcher and let his stare linger before he spoke. "Do it."

Fletcher's eyes narrowed. A moment's hesitation as he considered a thought, and then he slowly moved the gun away. Jack gripped the blade's handle firmly between his sweaty, bloody fingers. He watched as the Sandman's eyes tracked Fletcher, who was still standing behind the Sandman.

Keep looking at Fletcher, that's it . . . good.

"Now ease back the trigger and place it right here on little Rachel's lap," the Sandman said.

Fletcher leaned over the Sandman and gently placed the Glock on Rachel's lap. Jack caught sight of another gun, a Beretta, tucked in the back of Fletcher's black pants.

"Good boy," the Sandman said. "Now go stand by Miss Burton. It's time to get back to the business at hand."

Fletcher backed away; his face showed no emotion. Jack looked at the gun on Rachel's lap, just inches away. He could grab it, but wouldn't be able to fire a round before the Sandman blew the bomb—if there really was one.

It's too risky. Wait. You can still pull this off.

The Sandman picked up the Glock and inched toward the opened door leading into the hallway. *Come on. Put the remote away.*

He punched several buttons on the remote control, the Glock aimed at Fletcher, who stared impassively at him. Even with a gun pointed at him, Fletcher had presence. Jack sensed that the Sandman was intimidated.

"I know you from somewhere," the Sandman said, his eyes transfixed on Fletcher.

"We've traveled similar paths."

The knife was throbbing in Jack's hands. *Come on, put the remote away . . .*

The Sandman tucked the remote in his back pocket, cocked back the trigger, his eyes still on Fletcher.

Do it.

Jack came up with the knife. The Sandman caught the sudden movement and his gun moved quickly to Taylor. Fletcher had already moved; he was pushing Taylor to the floor, his back covering her body like a shield, before a round blew out a section of plaster behind her head. Jack sank the knife in the skin under the Sandman's armpit and drove it deep, pushing him toward the far wall, away from Rachel, who was screaming.

Jack slammed the Sandman's wrist against the corner of the wall, the knife tearing through skin and muscle as if it were paper. The Sandman's roar drowned out Rachel's screams. Jack dove the blade in deeper and twisted, feeling the strength in the Sandman's muscles give way to the pain. With his grip on the Sandman's wrist, Jack kept slamming the gun against the wall until it fell.

But the Sandman's strength was surprising and swift. His head came crashing down and Jack felt his nose crack. Then an elbow came up and swiped him across the jaw, and before Jack could react, he felt the weight of a knee slam into his scrotum.

A blinding white pain exploded in his skull. He stumbled backward, that nauseating pressure swelling inside his groin. The Sandman ran. Through his watery eyes Jack saw the Glock lying on the floor next to him.

Fletcher fired, two tight rounds that drowned out Rachel's and Taylor's screams. Holes the size of basketballs exploded in the plaster. Jack forced himself up, nauseated, his vision settling, the pain in his groin almost causing him to stumble. He saw Rachel first. She was screaming but in one piece. No cuts or bruises. And Taylor, thank God, Taylor was fine. The two of them were safe. They were both *safe.*

Fletcher was about to run out into the hallway when Jack grabbed him by his arm.

"I'll go," Jack told Fletcher. "Untie them and get them out of here."

Jack rushed into the hallway, the Glock in his hand. Downstairs was a maze of rotted wood. He navigated through the hot darkness reeking of mold and decay. In the blades of moonlight bleeding through the broken windows, he saw a rickety screen door. Outside a car started, but there was no squeal of rubber. Jack pushed open the door. A van was in the middle of the dark street, the driver's-side door open, its tires slashed, its headlights pointed at the woods. Branches snapped back. The Sandman was running.

chapter 72

THE SCALPEL WAS SHARP. When Fletcher finished freeing Taylor, he held a handkerchief against the cut on her cheek.

"The bleeding will stop," he said pleasantly. "The cut isn't deep and won't scar."

"Thank you." Like so many victims, her face showed a competing storm of emotions. They both moved to Rachel and set her free.

"Look." The girl pointed.

A door slammed shut, then another. Fletcher heard locks bolting home.

Interesting, he thought, not at all surprised. *Now stay true to form, Gabriel, and show me the timer.*

Taylor Burton said, "The TV."

Glowing white in the center of the bright blue screen were the numbers 9:57.

9:56.

"It's a countdown," Taylor said.

"Obviously." *Apparently you weren't bluffing, Gabriel.* Fletcher looked at the windows, the obvious exit. Mounted on each corner was an infrared device. *What a clever boy you are.*

Fletcher took a candle from the floor and moved behind the TV. He didn't have to look far. Through the vents, he saw the C-4.

Gabriel was clever in his precautions but his designs were predictable.

"Taylor, can you see the scalpel on the floor?"

"Yes."

"Be a dear and hand it to me. And please stay away from the window and the stereo."

He slid the desk out, mindful of the TV cord. He didn't want to unplug it. Gabriel had no doubt built in a safeguard that would detonate the bomb if the plug was removed. Taylor handed him the knife, and Fletcher asked her to hold the candle.

The screws in the TV's casing were standard Phillips head, and the scalpel's blade fit into them neatly. A few quick turns and they popped out onto the floor. Fletcher worked quickly, humming along to Ravel's magnificent *Daphnis et Chloë*.

The screws removed, he grabbed each end of the casing and pried it away. "Could you move the light in closer?" he asked. "That's it. Right there. Wonderful."

Six to eight blocks of C-4—maybe more, he couldn't tell from this angle and the lighting—were fastened together with a coat hanger. The bomb's actual circuitry and wiring were well concealed. Attempting to move it out for a closer inspection would no doubt result in detonation. Snipping the wires was out of the question.

Fletcher looked around the room. The doors were made of wood, he noted. He couldn't shoot through them with the spare gun wedged in his back waistband, but he *could* blow through them.

"What's wrong?" Taylor asked.

The pager was still attached to his belt. He cupped it in his hand so the back faced out and smashed it open until the plastic molding cracked in half. The wires he needed were in full view.

"Time please."

"Seven and a half minutes," Taylor said.

"Wonderful." With the scalpel Fletcher cut away a strip of C-4.

"I need both of you to move the chairs to the wall right behind the TV. Then get on the floor and put the chairs over you."

Taylor moved away, and Fletcher went to the door he had entered earlier. It was free of infrared, which wasn't surprising. With the doors locked, Gabriel assumed his captors would use the windows.

Fletcher molded the plastique in a strip along the three dead-bolt locks and the crack between the door and doorjamb, then pressed the pager into the plastique. He backed away.

"Close your eyes and cover your ears, ladies." Fletcher winked. "One big bang and this unpleasant mess will forever be behind you."

He dialed his pager number and hit the SEND key.

The pager beeped. The door exploded.

He looked at the TV.

5:53.

Taylor headed out first and then Rachel. Fletcher led them down the stairs to the door.

"Run up the street," Fletcher said. "Help is on the way."

Taylor, clutching the girl against her chest, bolted out the door toward the dark street. Fletcher looked back up the stairs. The explosion had knocked the candles on the floor; a fire had started.

All the evidence I need is right down the hall, Gabriel had told Jack. The key to exposing the FBI's classified Behavioral Modification Program was waiting for him in one of the upstairs rooms, but where?

The clock counting down inside his mind was clear.

Five minutes before the bomb blew.

Plenty of time.

chapter 73

THE MOON HAD RISEN FROM BEHIND A LAYER OF THICK, BLACK CLOUDS. A hundred feet or so in front of Jack the Sandman was scurrying over mazes of downed tree trunks and limbs. The ground was still soaked from last night's rain, and the humid air was completely still.

Jack ran behind the Sandman, his left hand protecting his eyes from the branches. There was no way to get a clean shot. The gap between them was closing, but it was impossible to sight the moving figure.

Have to wait for a clearing. And it would have to be soon. At this rate Jack might lose him.

Minutes later, the woods opened up into a wide trail. The Sandman saw where he was and paused, unsure of where to go. In that moment of indecision Jack brought up the Glock and fired. Footsteps rushed through branches and twigs that snapped back like firecrackers.

Shit. Jack ran up the path in pursuit. *He can't run much farther,* he thought. The Sandman's wound had to be bleeding steadily. Soon, he would slow from the blood loss. Then Jack could find him.

And make things right.

The moon went back behind the clouds and the Sandman disappeared. Jack stayed on the trail and jogged around to a clearing, listening. He heard the sound of rushing water. *Where is he? What is he doing?*

After what seemed like a lifetime later, the moon reappeared and the woods once again lit up in silver light. The trail ahead snaked around to the left. Jack couldn't hear anything except the water. *Where was he? He had to be—*

Then Jack heard the sound behind him of twigs snapping, and in one motion he turned around, bringing up the Glock. But the Sandman was swinging a tree limb; Jack felt its thickness slam into his fingers just as the shot went off, the Glock flying from his hands and tumbling onto the trail.

The limb came swinging back down and caught him in the stomach. Jack felt his ribs crack, felt air rush out of him in a terrible, nauseating burst as his vision shut down. He fell sideways into a mud puddle.

The Sandman tossed aside the limb and with one blow to the face sent Jack flying backward. Angry, powerful hands with thick fingers were around Jack's throat and with a terrifying force shoved his head deep into the mud and water. He couldn't move or breathe.

This is how it ends. Deep in the woods and drowning in a puddle.

There was an explosion. The ground shook and an invisible brick wall slammed into them, sending both men tumbling down the embankment of the river.

The coldness of the river water revived Jack. Up on his knees, sucking in air, in front of him a boulder, and beyond that the black skin of the rapids. The ground beneath him was loaded with rock, and the water he was kneeling in was less than two feet deep.

Burning debris fell around him. The Sandman's hands grabbed the back of Jack's head and shoved him back under the water, and in the struggle he managed to move onto his back. But he couldn't pry away the hands squeezing his throat. The Sandman had him pinned on the bed of the river. Jack tried to squirm and felt something sharp tear along his waist. Jack pulled it out from the bed, felt its long, spiked edge. *One chance,* he thought. *One chance to do this right or it's over.*

Jack relaxed, as if he had finally succumbed to oxygen loss. His body went limp. He couldn't hold it much longer. The Sandman moved closer . . . closer . . .

Jack brought the rock out of the water and felt it hit home. The hands left his throat. The Sandman backed away with a howl, his hands reaching for his face. Jack broke from the water, gasping for air. The Sandman stumbled backward toward the boulder, his quivering hands clutching his face. The rock's end had speared through the skin and bone along the temple; his right eye had been pierced and oozed blood.

It should have ended right there.

Primal rage is rare; few men ever experience it. Jack had felt it when children screamed in dog crates and a madman's drill bit deep into bone. When the Roths and Dolans, dressed in their bloody clothing, stood in his mind and told him to move ahead, Jack did. Other voices tried to reel him back in, but Jack saw the cut along Taylor's face and Rachel tied to the chair, saw Eric Beaumont lying alone in that hospital room, and a heated rush of red and black color, like ink twisting in blood, flooded his mind. He gripped the rock.

The Sandman was trying to move around the boulder. Jack grabbed his hair and yanked him back. He brought the rock up and with all of his strength, with all of his rage, brought it down across the Sandman's forehead.

The Sandman howled and tried to squirm away. With one hand Jack gripped the Sandman's throat and pushed him back against the boulder. The howling stopped, replaced now with a gurgling sound. In the moonlight the Sandman's crystal blue eyes looked up at him in terror. The fire from somewhere behind him made the water look as black as oil.

"P-pleeeease. Stop."

But Jack couldn't

(didn't want to)

stop. He could barely hear the words. He hit the Sandman again, feeling bone and skull crush against his hand.

Jack brought the rock up again. He had prepared to bring it down when he saw before him the face of a terrorized twelve-year-old boy being strapped down to a bed for electroshock therapy, a boy whose body had been pumped full of experimental chemicals.

Please, the boy pleads. *Please, don't hurt me.*

Jack froze. The boy starts crying.

I'm sorry, please don't do this.

In Jack's mind the jury box of victims is dark. Alex Dolan is in the front. He stands up, the others standing with him, their faces and limbs decomposed, missing eyes, everyone is there. Sidney stands next to Alex, and they all stare at Jack.

Look at what he did to me and my family, Alex says, crying. *It's not fair.*

Miles Hamilton killed me, Daddy, Sidney says. *He's still sitting in a comfortable cell with all of his warm thoughts and I'm stuck down here. It's not fair.*

In Jack's hands the boy is crying. *Please don't hurt me.*

Alex slams his fists down and screams, *You PROMISED! IT'S NOT FAIR!*

The Sandman had used Miles Hamilton to try to kill Jack and Taylor—had stolen a box full of memories and used it to destroy Jack's relationship with Taylor, the new life he had built in Marblehead, the dead families, it was all gone, no way to go back and reclaim it, gone. But now he had the Sandman, alone—had the chance to make things right and fair, just as he did with Yerkies.

I don't want to stay here, Daddy, Sidney says. *I want to be with Mommy. Don't you want me to be with Mommy?*

The rage was hypnotic. Jack wanted to give in to it, to feel that blessed, healing release it guaranteed. He gripped the rock. But all he could see was a boy at Graves. Frightened. Pumped full of chemicals. Tortured. Alone with his pain, alone as he cried out for help and love that was never given, alone with his hollow soul. A boy manufactured into a monster.

Don't leave me down here, Daddy. Please.

Jack tossed the rock aside. The Sandman's body slid into the water. He tried to stand up and couldn't. Jack grabbed the monster under the arm and carried him to the embankment.

chapter 74

FIRE TRUCKS AND AMBULANCES HAD ALREADY ARRIVED BY THE TIME JACK NAVIGATED BACK THROUGH THE WOODS. The night air was bursting with orange flames and the pulses of blue, white, and red rescue lights.

He found an ambulance and brought the Sandman over. The EMTs scrambled quickly. A New Hampshire state trooper came over, saw Jack, looked at the bloody figure being strapped down to the gurney.

"Is that—"

"Yeah," Jack said. "That's him."

He walked out from behind the ambulance and saw them; the wave of relief hit him so hard and fast his knees buckled. Taylor was cradling Rachel, who would not let go of her neck, while an EMT finished dressing the wound on Taylor's cheek. Jack moved back behind the ambulance. He didn't want them to see him splattered with blood.

Mike Abrams emerged from the strobe of lights. He saw Jack and smiled, looking relieved.

Jack was surprised to see him. Mike answered the question.

"Fletcher called me. Told me that you were in trouble and then gave me the address and here I am. Are you all right?"

"My ribs might be broken. Otherwise, I'm fine."

Mike looked at Jack's wet jeans and bare chest, the specks of blood along Jack's face and arms. They were several feet away from Taylor and Rachel—well out of hearing distance.

Mike moved in closer. "What happened to him?" he asked in a whisper.

Jack tapped the ambulance. "He's in here. He's banged up but alive. Where's Fletcher?"

Mike glanced out at the blaze and looked back at Jack with a heavy expression. "There was a bomb inside the house. He brought Rachel and Taylor downstairs and went back in."

"Why?"

"I don't know. But he isn't here. When the feds come around with their questions, tell them he died in the fire."

There was a new tone in Mike's voice. The question was formed on Jack's lips. Again Mike answered it for him.

"I know about the program. Fletcher told me everything about it . . . about what Lynch was going to do to you, to me and my family." Mike looked angry and sick. "I have a copy of Fletcher's conversation with Dragos."

Jack turned around. The heat of the raging fire was pressing into his skin, making his eyes water. Dozens of firemen were fighting the blaze.

Malcolm Fletcher wasn't dead, he was sure of it. Men like him never died. They rose from the ashes.

Mike stood next to Jack. They were both silent. The time to glue back the torn fragments of their lives would come later, Jack knew. Now, the only thing he cared about was that they were alive. That was all that mattered when the world around you was burning to the ground.

chapter 75

THE STOLEN 1987, DARK BROWN CADILLAC WAS PARKED ON A BACK TRAIL IN THE SEEMINGLY NEVER-ENDING STRETCH OF WOODS, ABOUT A MILE AWAY FROM THE MAIN ROAD. No one could hear the banging and grunts coming from inside the trunk.

Malcolm Fletcher placed a box containing diskettes, two laptop computers, and thick reams of printouts from the FBI's Behavioral Modification Program on the seat beside him. The two other items he needed were in the backseat. He retrieved them, walked around to the back of the car, placed both items on the bumper, and then popped open the trunk. The solitary bulb threw a diagonal patch of light on the sweating, frightened figure inside.

"Ah, good. You're awake."

Alan Lynch's nostrils sucked in the muggy air, his chest heaving. He lay on his left side, his hands behind his back and handcuffed to his ankles. Duct tape covered his mouth.

Fletcher took a hunting knife from the bumper. The twelve-inch blade was well suited for gutting deer.

"I've been dreaming of this moment for a long time, Alan."

Alan worked his throat but couldn't speak.

It took Fletcher a moment to pin him to the floor. He placed the edge of the blade against his cheek and pressed. Alan moaned.

"If you hold still, you won't feel the blade cut your throat." Fletcher pressed the blade just near Alan's lips. "It's time for you to meet the man downstairs."

Alan's eyes clamped shut. His body trembled. His cries were muffled by the tape.

Fletcher smiled. In one swift motion, he slid the blade through the duct tape and ripped it off Alan's mouth, freeing his trapped scream.

Fletcher took a Polaroid camera from the bumper and watched through the small window.

"Smile."

Alan looked up, his eyes all at once relieved and embarrassed. Fletcher hit the flash.

"The camera loves you. You're a natural."

"Fuck you, Malcolm. By the end of tomorrow, everyone in the country is going to know what a sick, twisted fuck you are."

"I've been roaming the earth for years, Alan. What makes you think you can get rid of me so easily?"

"The CIA has your picture and all the information they need," Alan sneered.

"Ah, yes. Government-sanctioned assassins. Get blood on your conscience, call in a team to clean it up. I'd quote *Hamlet,* but its meaning would be lost on you." Fletcher propped one arm up on the trunk and looked down at Alan. "You've always overestimated your importance. No one knows you're here. When they learn of your disappearance, they'll be glad. Your workers don't hold you in high regard, and frankly, neither do I."

"There won't be a fucking hole on the planet where you'll be able to hide your face."

"For the first time you and I have something in common."

Alan's eyes narrowed, then widened as he tried to follow the thought.

"Gabriel LaRouche, the patient from your top-secret rehabilitation program, told me the location of the files," Fletcher said. "I haven't read through them all, but I've discovered enough on Graves and the Behavioral Modification Program to insure the burial of our *former* employer."

Alan's menacing grin was pathetic. "Better men than you have tried to bring me down, and they're all buried in the same place. But don't worry, Malcolm. You'll be meeting with them soon enough."

Fletcher tapped the Polaroid picture against his chin. "Perhaps you're right. I've seen those dimwits at the Justice Department in action. Still, your career—your life, I'm afraid—is over."

"You think a bunch of papers will bury me?" Alan laughed. "They won't even hold up in court."

"What about a live demonstration of your computer system?"

The smile slipped off of Alan's face like a burst balloon.

"Victor gave me all of the access codes needed to log on to the Behavioral Modification's patient database," Fletcher said. "I know the codes haven't changed, since I used them to lure you and Hostage Rescue to the house in New London. I think I'll call in a group of reporters for a private viewing."

Fletcher moved the picture so Alan could see it. "When this makes the covers of *Time* and *Newsweek,* do you think they'll give me a photo credit?"

Alan bit down on his words. His face was a competing storm of fear and rage.

"I think I'll drop you off in the woods, let you sit there and ruminate on your defense. I just hope your survival skills are up to par. I wouldn't want you to starve to death." Fletcher paused, leaned inside the trunk. "Or be eaten."

"You're a dead man. You hear me, you fucking freak, *you're a fucking dead man!*"

Fletcher refastened the strip of tape back across Alan's mouth and shut the trunk.

Vivaldi's *Four Seasons* was in the tape deck; he turned up the volume and lost himself in the music as he drove. He didn't have far to travel.

The road ahead was lit with endless possibilities.

THANKSGIVING

WITHOUT WARNING, THE SEASON'S FIRST SNOWSTORM RIPPED THROUGH NORTHERN NEW HAMPSHIRE AND BY 8 A.M. HAD DEPOSITED NEARLY TEN INCHES OF WHITE POWDER. It was now shortly after eleven on Wednesday, the day before Thanksgiving, and the downtown streets of North Conway were buzzing with people.

The bar at the restaurant was full of mostly college kids home on break. Jack sat in a small booth next to a window and watched the people outside. The sky was blue and free of clouds, the sun reflecting off the blankets of snow so brightly it pierced the eyes. The perfect day to let your worries go.

"Jack."

Standing next to the table was Taylor. She was dressed in a pair of dark blue jeans, Timberland hiking boots, and a charcoal gray sweater. Her face was still tan, but he noticed she had cut her hair since August, the last time he had seen or talked with her. Seeing her like this for the first time, new, different . . . it was as exhilarating as it was painful.

"Hi, Taylor."

She stood there, clearly uncomfortable. What he wanted to do was touch her. The thought of it was so strong that he felt his body respond. Then he remembered the last time he had seen her she was being whisked off along with Rachel in the back of an ambulance. Shortly after, with the media frenzy swarming in Marblehead, she had headed back to LA, staying with friends. No returned phone calls, no idea where she was, what she was doing. And she had not once called him.

Taylor Burton had moved on without him.

"You look great," he said, and took in a deep breath. The scalpel cut along her cheek was no more than a tiny white line.

"I can't stay long," she said gently, and sat down. "We're going to be hitting the outlets soon. Packing up the kids and all that."

Taylor's sister, Tara, owned a place in North Conway, and each Thanksgiving the whole family got together. Jack had spent two of them with Taylor. Wonderful times now too painful to revisit.

"Is Rachel with you?"

"Yes."

"How's she doing?"

"The first month was rough. Lots of nightmares. Now she's better. Mr. Ruffles has something to do with it, I'm sure, and the therapist she's seeing . . ." Taylor's words drifted off.

"Tell her I miss her."

Taylor glanced at the door as if contemplating an exit. Her hands were folded on the table, inches from his. Everything he wanted was less than a foot away from him. He summoned the words but what came to him was that feeling of just drifting, a man haunted with sores of memories, a mind crippled by the torturous examination of a life that could have been and wasn't.

"She liked your cards," was all Taylor would say. Or could.

Jack looked around the bar, caught the stares of college kids looking at her. He had rehearsed this moment dozens of times in his head, figuring out what he would say, how she would respond, and how he would counter. Every possible answer had been analyzed. But sitting here now, his thoughts seemed to have abandoned him.

"How are you?" he asked after a small hesitation.

"Fine." The smile was reserved.

"You sleeping okay?"

"Not really. Every time . . . every time I close my eyes it's there. And after it was over, and when you came around and wanted to talk . . . "

"I reminded you of what had happened."

Taylor nodded. "I keep wanting to crawl inside my head with a scrub brush and clean it all away. I've tried, but it keeps coming . . . it just won't go away."

Fletcher was right. Memory was one of God's many acts of cruelty.

"I'm sorry I didn't visit you or return your calls," she said. "Or respond to your letters. I needed to get away. The media, they were relentless."

"Did they find you in LA?"

"Fortunately, no. It's . . . it's all so unbelievable. Have you been following it on the news?"

He had.

Thomas Preston from the *New York Times* was the first to break the story and seemed to have the inside line. Every day for the past nine weeks he had revealed another detail on the Sandman's connection to Graves and the FBI-sponsored Behavioral Modification Program.

The latest twist had come earlier this week. A security guard had been patrolling the parking lot at the FBI Academy in Quantico when he heard moaning from inside the trunk of a dark brown Cadillac. When the fire department pried the trunk open, they found Alan Lynch bound and gagged, dressed only in a pair of soiled black bikini briefs. Lynch had been missing for two months and was feared dead.

A sign was draped across his neck. Written in red crayon in a child's hand were the words I CONFESS.

The audiotape found inside the trunk contained conversations with an unidentified male who asked specific questions regarding the program and the atrocities at Graves—including the framing and botched assassination attempt on a former FBI profiler who was about to expose Graves and the program. The tape had been mailed to Preston in advance. Now it was in the hands of other news outlets.

The FBI responded to the kidnapping, attributing it to Malcolm Fletcher, a former profiler and renegade assassin responsible for the murder of three federal agents, the most recent one named Victor Dragos.

"Have you talked to Fletcher?" Taylor asked.

"Talked to him? No. He sent me a package containing the things the Sandman stole from my attic." Although it was free of his journal and Amanda's death certificate. Fletcher had included a note: *Brave new worlds.*

"You think they'll find him?"

"No. He's much too smart."

"The FBI harassing you?"

"I told them Fletcher died in the explosion. Now they know he didn't so they'll be coming around. Right now they have their hands full."

"And the Sandman?"

"Still awaiting trial." *Although the Sandman probably won't live long enough to testify,* he wanted to add and didn't. He didn't care. All of that—it was behind him and he wanted to forget it. He didn't want to talk about the FBI or Fletcher—that was not why he was here.

Beats of awkward silence. He took in a deep breath and plunged.

"I see you're selling the house. You moving back to LA?"

"Yes," Taylor said quickly.

A stab of pain stole his voice. He had to clear his throat, swallow.

"When?"

"Next week."

Her tone, it was as if she were talking to a stranger. As if there had been nothing between them. All of her feelings cataloged and packed up and ready to move to the West Coast to embark on a new life. Without him.

"Were you planning on telling me?" he asked.

"Once I got settled."

Jack's eyes dropped to her hands. He remembered the way they had touched him, had held him against her and made him feel whole again. Now they were clasped over each other, a tight ball, as if they were on guard, and what he felt was an exposure so painfully sharp it brought all of his vulnerability and aloneness to the surface. The hope he had carried to this table was drowning.

"I turned my badge in."

She didn't look surprised. "What are you doing for work?"

"Some carpentry."

"In Marblehead?"

"For the moment."

A pause, then, "And you're satisfied with that?"

"Yes."

"You did that in Colorado and got bored. That's why you took the detective's job in Marblehead."

"I've quit. For good."

"You'll never stop being a cop, Jack. It's who you are. It's *what* you are."

"What I am is a man who's spent almost half his life living in the past. You're the single best thing that's happened to me. I wake up every morning and think of you. I miss you terribly. It's like I can't breathe."

Her eyes shifted down to the table. "I'm not Amanda. I'll never replace her."

"You're right. You never will. Amanda's dead. I can't go back and change that. I'd like to but I can't and have to live with that. But it doesn't change the fact that I love you. Not the idea of you, not how you make me feel, just *you*. Who and what *you* are."

She leaned back in her seat, dropped her hands on her lap, and studied them, her eyes darting back and forth as if searching for a response that had abandoned her. He couldn't tell if she was fighting her feelings or searching for the right combination of words to get her out of here, out the door to her life with her family, and then moving on to her new life in LA. *Don't move on without me,* he thought desperately.

Taylor looked up at him. Jack saw a tenderness in her stare. Something was there, a faint connection, he could *feel* it. *Don't let it go.*

"I'm not sure what you're asking me, Jack."

"I want to spend the rest of my life with you. I want to share it with you. Everything."

Taylor's eyes were round and still. He had no idea what she was thinking. Then her eyes pinched with a painful thought and she looked down at her watch. "I have to get going."

"I won't love you any less."

"What?"

"That night on the balcony, you told me, 'I won't love you any less. No matter how bad it was, no matter how bad it gets.' Do you remember saying that?"

"Yes."

"Did you mean it?"

Taylor didn't say anything. Then she opened her mouth, and for one brief moment Jack felt a surge of hope, some gluing of words that would mend that distance between them.

"You mind walking me to my car? I have some of your things."

Have some of your things . . . And just like that it was gone. Suddenly he felt like a man standing at the end of a pier, realizing there was no way to move forward. Only back.

No. He didn't want her to leave. He wanted to talk it out—wanted to fight or make love—to do whatever it took to get her back. He'd make a scene in the restaurant, he didn't care, she couldn't leave him.

But when she stood up and looked down at him, the feelings vanished. It wasn't going to work that way. He couldn't push her to share her hurt, just as she couldn't get him to do it. It was too late.

"Sure," he said, hollow.

They walked in silence while the world around them moved on with smiles and laughter as bright as the winter sun. Several minutes later, with words still unspoken, Taylor stopped walking.

"This is where I'm parked."

"So," he said, almost choking on the word. "This is it."

Taylor was quiet.

It couldn't end like this, he thought. His life, everything he loved, was standing a foot in front of him, a moment away from leaving him forever.

She hadn't moved.

Jack reached out and grabbed her hand. It felt limp. Awkward. A stranger's hand.

"I love you, Taylor."

She looked away when she said, "I know you do, Jack."

"Taylor . . . Taylor, I . . ." But the words wouldn't come.

She went to walk away but he wouldn't let her go.

Gently, Jack pulled her to him. At first she resisted. Then she squeezed his hand hard and looked up at him and their eyes met, and he felt that connection again, that healing relief that filled the hollow pockets of his soul.

Jack hugged her close to him and didn't let go. His eyes closed. He could feel the winter sun on his face, her cold cheek pressed against his, the strength in her hands as she pressed him against her.

"Jack . . . Oh, Jack . . ."

So this is how you're redeemed, he thought. One moment you're drifting through black days, standing on the edge of despair, a man riddled with wounds and crippled by memories, and still she pulls you to her, holds you against her heart, and as you enter the magic of her world, for a moment you feel whole again. Inside that world that exists between skin and skin, that indescribable connection that binds us all, you close your eyes and say hello to heaven.

About the Author

CHRIS MOONEY lives north of Boston, where he is currently at work on his second novel.